WHEN SHE FALLS

A DARK MAFIA ROMANCE

GABRIELLE SANDS

THE FALLEN SERIES

When She Unravels

The story of Valentina & Damiano

Available Now

When She Tempts

The story of Martina & Giorgio

Available Now

When She Loves

Coming Fall 2023

To all the girls who go weak in the knees when he says, "You're doing such a good job, baby."

CHAPTER 1

GEMMA

I TAP my fingertips against the limo's armrest as we glide around a bend in the coastal road that leads to my sister's house. Glimpses of the Mediterranean peek out from between the greenery lining the road, and when the trees suddenly recede, I get treated to an open view of the sea below. A vast expanse of azure stretches all the way toward the horizon, shimmering with the afternoon sun.

My breath catches.

Cleo leans over me to get a closer look, practically pressing her nose against the window.

"You've got to be shitting me," she mutters, her voice dropping into the well-practiced whisper we use when we don't want our parents to hear our conversations. They're sitting just across from us, but we've perfected keeping our communication private over the years. "Gem, is this place for real? Look at that water. Just look at it."

"I'm looking."

"I've never seen water that shade of blue. I mean, in pictures, sure, but I just assumed it was the filter."

A smile tugs at my lips. This is the first time Cleo's been outside of the States, and her excitement is palpable.

She huffs a breath, making condensation appear on the glass. "I could drown in it. In fact, I think I'd rather do that than go back to New York in a week."

And just like that, the smile melts off my face.

My younger sister has always been dramatic. I'm used to it, but we're about to spend a week around people who aren't, and I can already imagine the repercussions of her saying the wrong thing to the wrong person.

But Cleo doesn't care about that.

"Consequences be damned" may as well be her life mantra.

She really outdid herself back in January, though. She was caught in bed with a baby-faced pizza delivery boy from Brooklyn who clearly had no idea who our family is.

That mistake probably cost him his life, although Papà's neither confirmed nor denied it.

It was a real scandal. The eighteen-year-old daughter of a New York City don disgraced. Her maidenhead taken by a literal nobody. Papà had frothed at the mouth, his anger so palpable that even his soldiers left for a long smoke break outside. Mamma whisked Cleo away after Papà was done screaming at her. I stayed behind in Papà's office, and when he leveled his heavy gaze on me, I knew that my fate was sealed.

The responsibility to save our family was now all mine.

His last eligible daughter.

I smooth my palms over my linen pants. "How many times do I need to ask you not to joke about things like that?"

Cleo gives her head a shake. "Who says I'm joking? But here's a less morbid thought. Let's run away like Vale. We can live on the beach like a pair of bums."

I glance at our parents to make sure they're still oblivious. We only have two guards with us on this trip, but the moment Papà hears any talk about running away, he'll fly in a dozen more. It's a sensitive topic after our older sister, Vale, did exactly that. The azure sea on the other side of the window beckons me. The thought of staying here doesn't seem half bad, but I know better than to encourage Cleo.

"How will we eat?" I inquire.

A curly coppery strand slips from behind Cleo's ear and falls across her cheek. "Dumpster diving. Have you heard of it?"

"You've never even taken out the garbage back home, and now you want to dig around someone else's trash?"

Cleo presses her fingertips to the glass, her gaze still fixated on the water. "You're such a buzzkill. Don't act like you want to go home any more than I do. You know, if our places were switched, and I was the one engaged to Rafaele Messero, I'd be opening this door and rolling out of the car right now."

At the mention of my fiancé, my throat tightens.

Rafaele became the newest don in New York when his father died from cancer last year. Papà was gleeful. He'd been trying to set me up with Rafaele even before the Messero patriarch fell ill, and now the marriage would prove even more advantageous since I'd be marrying a don.

I didn't think Rafaele was interested in me based on the few in-person interactions we had, but somehow, Papà made it happen.

And he made one thing very clear to me.

This is an alliance the Garzolos desperately need.

"You've seen what happens when we go to war with another clan. We may have won against the Riccis, but we paid a high price for that victory."

Three cousins, two uncles, and a half-dozen soldiers had died.

I attended every funeral. Held crying mothers and wives in my arms. Gave gifts to confused children, some of them so young they couldn't understand what had happened to their papas and brothers.

"Our enemies know we've been weakened. You're our last hope to regain our footing in the city."

I clasp my hands on my lap. My family is in trouble. And according to Papà, their future rests in my hands.

"You hardly know Rafaele," I say to Cleo. In truth, neither do I. I can count on one hand the number of times I've spoken to my fiancé.

Cleo wrinkles her nose. "Thanks, but no thanks. Cracking my skull open on the asphalt would be better than getting married to that stony-faced fucker."

Cold dread trickles down my back. Cleo is never one to hold anything back, but sometimes, I wish she would.

A second passes before Cleo realizes what she said, and she shoots me an apologetic look. "Sorry."

"It's fine." That's a lie.

Nothing's been fine for a long time. But this week is supposed to be a reprieve before I have to face the music and plan my wedding to a man who is a stranger to me.

A stranger who became a murderer at thirteen.

I stop picking at my cuticles when I accidentally make myself bleed.

Enough.

I promised myself I wouldn't think about all that while we're in Ibiza. After all, we're here to celebrate. One week, two weddings.

The final wedding of the week is between Vale and Damiano De Rossi, the new don of the Casalesi. Two days before them, Martina De Rossi, Damiano's sister, and Giorgio "Napoletano" Girardi, Damiano's advisor, are getting married as well.

I don't know the De Rossis well, but my sister says Damiano is her perfect match.

I'm happy for her. I really am.

They actually want to be married.

Must be nice to do what you want.

Cleo opens the window, letting warm, humid air invade the inside of the limo, and takes a deep inhale. "Do you smell that? That's the smell of freedom."

"Close the window," Mamma snaps, her thin hands sliding over her hair to keep down the frizz. She spent an hour on the plane getting herself ready for our big arrival at Vale and Damiano's house, and even though she'd never admit that she's nervous, an angry kind of anxiety is emanating off her.

It's the first time our whole family will be together since Vale ran away from New York. I don't blame my sister for doing what she did—her ex-husband was a monster who made her torture people. She did what she had to in order to survive. But while she was starting a new life on this side of the world, I had to watch our friends and family struggle like they've never struggled before.

There's a disconnect between us now. One that makes itself apparent in our phone calls. Whenever I mention the names of the family members who died, Vale clams up and changes the subject.

I know she's hurting, and that's how she copes. But in my head, the names play on repeat.

Carlo. Enzo. Renato. Bruno. Tito.

Cleo blows out a breath and presses the button to roll up the window.

"We need to have a word before we arrive," Mamma says, her hands still patting her hair. "There are some rules."

"When are there ever not?" Cleo mutters.

Papà rolls his shoulders back and casts Cleo and me a serious look. "Damiano De Rossi is about to marry your sister, and thus join our family, but given the circumstances of this arrangement, it does not mean we are immediately going to trust him or his people."

The circumstances being that Vale chose her husband this time around.

"Technically, they're already married," Cleo pipes in.

I press my lips together. The elopement is a sensitive topic since Papà and Mamma weren't invited to it. I was the only one who was allowed to come. When I returned home, I wasn't asked a single question about it. Our parents are resolved to pretend it never happened.

"They're married when I say they're married," Papà barks out. "Keep your wits about you. Don't speak to the men unless it's absolutely necessary. Don't wander off the property. Under no circumstances should you entertain any questions about our family's business."

"Like we know much about it," Cleo grumbles.

"You know more than you think," Papà snaps. "No blabbering, Cleo. Your antics are tiresome enough while we're in New York, but they won't be tolerated here at all."

My sister narrows her eyes, shooting daggers at our father. They barely speak with each other anymore. When they do, it usually ends in an explosive argument.

Papà smooths his wrinkled hand down his tie. "Most importantly, remember that we are the Garzolos. Our name means something even when we're away from New York. Do not give anyone an excuse to treat us with less respect than is owed to us."

Respect.

I've grown to hate that word over the last year, because I've seen the lengths Papà will go to ensure he still has it. From his capos, his allies, his enemies.

He fears that one day he'll walk into a room and people won't bow their heads to him in deference. But he's never made an attempt to earn respect from us, his family. For him, our respect is a given. He takes it for granted, assuming we worship the ground he walks on. For a long time, I did, but not after how he handled the situation with Vale. Instead of admitting it was a mistake to give Vale to a man who should have been institutionalized, he blamed anyone but himself. His main concern was his reputation.

"What do you think they're all saying about me? They're saying I can't control my daughters. If I can't control three stupid little girls, how can I control the clan?"

So I can't help it. At his mention of respect, I roll my eyes.

Papà's gaze flashes with anger. He's used to this kind of insolence from Cleo, but it's unacceptable coming from me—the obedient daughter. He doesn't like that. He doesn't like that at all.

An apology rushes out of my mouth, but I already know it's too late. My palms turn clammy. His blazing eyes stay trained on me until the limo turns onto the driveway that leads to a familiar Spanish villa.

"There's Vale," Cleo says excitedly, tugging on the door handle before we even come to a stop. As soon as we do, she hops out and rushes to our sister. Mamma is quick to follow, leaving Papà and I in the car.

"Shut the door," he growls.

My shirt sticks to my back. I know what's coming, but that doesn't make it any easier.

Papà raises his arm and backhands me across the face.

I yelp, and my teeth clank together. Pain blooms across my cheek. For a moment, time slows, and all I can hear is a familiar ringing in my ears.

"Don't you roll your eyes at me," he hisses, his spittle landing on my face.

I bring my shaking fingertips to my stinging skin and force myself to look at Papà.

He crosses his arms over his chest, his jaw a hard line. "You understand how you must behave here, don't you?"

My head lowers in a slow nod.

"Rafaele has options. Don't do anything to make him consider them."

Another nod.

"I don't want anyone else in the family to die. Ernesto was one of my closest friends. And Tito..." Papà sniffs and looks down at his lap.

He knows just the right things to say to make me feel the weight of my decisions.

If I can save more Garzolos from dying, what kind of a piece of shit would I be to not do it?

"Neither do I," I whisper. My throat is bone-dry.

"Good." Papà straightens his tie. "Let's go."

He slips out of the car, but I stay seated, anxiety engulfing me like a flame.

No one but Mamma knows Papà hits me.

No one can know.

I don't know why I became Papà's scapegoat, but it started a long time ago. At first, it was a ruler smacked across the back of my hands when I made him upset. Then a belt. In the last few years, he started slapping me across the face. Never too frequent or too hard, but enough to shock me into obedience.

One night, I overheard Papà telling one of his capos that I looked just like his ma.

Papà hated his ma.

Sometimes, his eyes get all weird just before he hits me, and I think maybe he sees her instead of me. He usually apologizes the next day. I accept the apologies every time, even though they don't mean anything since I know he won't stop.

It's better that he hits me instead of Cleo. If he ever raised a hand to her, she'd fight back. Who knows how badly he'd hurt her then? At least I've learned how to manage Papà. It's best to shut up and go along with whatever he says when he's mad. It's the quickest way to calm him down.

I dig inside my purse for my phone. I don't have a mirror, so I have to check my reflection in the camera to make sure there isn't an obvious mark on my face before anyone sees me.

The image flicks on.

Relief rushes through me. It seems okay.

Then the door is opened and I throw my phone back in my purse just as Vale's face appears. "Gem!"

I paste on a smile and tumble out of the car straight into her arms. She laughs, clutching me around the waist and pressing kisses against my cheek.

"I can't believe you're here," she exclaims.

Her familiar scent nearly undoes me. "I know. God, how I've missed you, Vale."

I tighten my grip on her, some part of me still worried about what she might find if she examines my face too closely. Sliding my chin on her shoulder, I cast a glance at where the men are standing.

Papà is greeting Damiano. They're wearing close-lipped smiles, and I'm pretty sure that handshake is meant to crush a few bones.

My sister's husband is the Don of the Casalesi, a powerful clan in the Camorra. He's tall and intimidating even when he's somewhat dressed down in only a dress shirt and a pair of dark slacks.

A dry chuckle leaves Papà's mouth. "Damiano De Rossi. You're a handsome guy, huh? I can see now why my daughter is so partial to you. You know women, they're drawn to pretty things."

Damiano's smile is a sharp, crooked line. "I wonder what drew your wife to you then, Garzolo."

Papà barks a laugh, but it's forced. Back in New York, this is how made men talk to each other—all jokes and under-handed barbs. It's all fun and games until you press the wrong button and guns are pulled out.

"Let me look at you," Vale says, nudging me away. "Has your hair gotten longer?"

I take a step back and let my shoulder-length hair fall over my face as if I'm showing her my haircut. "A little. My bladder is about to explode. Can I run inside?"

"Oh, sure. You know where the bathroom is."

Brushing past her, I jog inside the house and shut the door behind me.

It's cool inside, the AC on full blast. It feels nice against my burning cheek and my overheated body.

I rush through the airy, light-filled rooms toward the powder room I remember from my last visit.

A relieved sigh leaves my lungs as soon I peer into the round mirror hanging over the vanity. There's just a slight pink mark above my right cheek bone. I already have a half dozen excuses ready in case anyone asks. It'll bruise though. I bruise so damn easily, like a peach.

At least I brought my best full coverage concealer. I pull it out and dab some onto the mark. Cleo said it would be too heavy for this climate, but I packed it anyway. Actually, I can't recall the last time I didn't have it with me, just in case.

The backs of my eyes begin to prickle...and fuck, fuck, fuck. I can't cry.

I can't cry because my eyes will get all red, and everyone will know.

Everyone will know that I'm not okay.

Why did Papà have to do it now? Why couldn't he at least wait until after we got to the guesthouse?

Cleo and I are sharing a room here. I'll have to wear my sleep mask when we go to bed so that she won't see the bruise.

Frustration rises inside of me. I should hate Papà the way Cleo and Vale do, but even though I'm the only one he hits, I still love him.

Despite his many flaws, he's my father. The man who taught me how to read and always let me sit on his knee when I cried at church, terrified by the sermon. If he was all violence and anger, it would be easy to despise him, but he's not. Sometimes, he'll look at me, and softness will creep into his gaze. *"You've always been so clever, Gem. My little girl. You're the one daughter I can count on."*

When he says things like that to me, I melt. I can't help it. His approval feels like a warm hug. It makes me feel safe, and loved, and wanted. It makes me feel like everything that's broken can be fixed.

I finish applying the makeup and wash my hands at the sink. There's a ball in my throat that won't ease.

That won't do.

I have to keep it together this week, no matter what.

So I brace my palms on the sink and start counting my breaths, forcing my thoughts away from Papà.

One Mississippi.

Two Mississippi.

Three—

The door to the bathroom springs open.

My first thought is that it's Mamma, coming to see what's taking me so long.

But it's not.

It's worse.

My eyes narrow on the intruder and the muscular bulk he's managed to pour into a pair of slacks and a gray button-up shirt. His beard's freshly trimmed, his hair's pulled back and tied at the nape, and his small silver earring glints in the light.

A cold shiver runs down my spine. I remember staring at that earring and thinking I was about to die.

I straighten and remind myself that despite the grin on his face, this is a dangerous man.

A bad man.

And I might be the only one here that knows it.

"Do you ever knock, Ras?"

CHAPTER 2

RAS

MY MA RAISED me to be a gentleman, but I've always thought that I'm the perfect example of nature winning over nurture. No matter how hard she tried to stomp out my wild streak, she never quite managed to do it.

When I was a kid, I made her want to pull her hair out. She'd say go left, and so I'd go right. At school, I was always getting into trouble. She'd punish me, but the calls from the principal never stopped. And I absolutely hated wearing the neat little suits she'd force me into for every special occasion. I always got them filthy. Ma would drag me away by my ear and demand to know why I looked like I'd rolled in the mud.

I've gotten better at tolerating suits since then, but that urge to introduce a bit of chaos into something orderly has never quite left. When I became older, I learned that manufactured chaos is a powerful tool, especially in my current position as underboss of the Casalesi. It's saved my ass, and Dem's, more than a few times.

When thrown into chaos, people do things they never would under normal circumstances. The animal brain takes over. The filters come off. People reveal their true desires, and sometimes those desires have a lot to do with seeing Dem or me dead.

The way Gemma Garzolo is looking at me right now... I'd put her squarely into that category.

Narrowed gray eyes.

Pursed lips.

An angry pink blush across her cheeks that might be my new favorite color.

"Do you ever knock, Ras?" She places her fists on her hips and spears me with an irritated gaze. I've become deeply acquainted with that gaze from our two previous encounters.

The first was when I was tasked with finding her in New York so that I could give her a burner phone to talk to her sister. What should have been a straightforward task had turned into a whole Thing because Gemma had assumed I was waiting for her in the changing room of her Pilates studio to kill her.

She saw me and opened her mouth to scream. I lunged at her, stuffed her into a closet, and held my palm against her mouth just long enough to explain that I was here on Valentina's orders. When she went still, I thought we were past our misunderstanding, but I was terribly wrong.

As soon as I removed my hand, she sank her surprisingly sharp teeth into my forearm. I remember staring into those stormy-gray eyes as she drew blood and thinking, *"Fuck, this woman is beautiful."*

A scuffle followed. I may have been rougher with her than I intended because I really hadn't been expecting this sort of resistance, and I was jet-lagged. Nothing makes me feel more like a zombie than hopping through half a dozen time zones.

Long story short, I wasn't feeling myself.

Yet even after we straightened everything out, and Gemma calmed down enough to speak to Vale over the phone that I brought to her, her opinion of me didn't seem to change.

This woman deeply dislikes me.

It feels a bit unfair, to be frank.

But it's for the best.

After all, Gemma's engaged to marry an American *stronzo*, who also happens to be our new business partner, and if our relationship ever progressed past highly acerbic banter into something more civil, I might actually get upset over the fact that she's taken.

No, I've been burned before. Third degree. And I've spent nearly a decade getting really fucking good at keeping women, no matter how alluring, at arm's length.

I drag my palm over my chin. "I do, actually. Didn't realize I needed to when there's a perfectly good lock, though."

"There are a dozen bathrooms in this house. You just happened to pick this one to barge in on?"

Okay, I may have seen her go inside this one while I was going through my messages in the kitchen. I just couldn't resist catching her off guard.

I paste on a grin I know will irritate her. "You know what they say about great minds."

She heaves a long sigh. "Move out of my way, you utter imbecile."

Instead of doing that, I brace my palms on either side of the doorframe and lean into her space. Her eyes widen, and she shuffles backwards, a hint of alarm flashing across her expression.

"I have to say, I thought you'd skip this one."

"Skip what? This trip? My sister's getting married. Even your annoying presence isn't enough to keep me away."

The grin widens. "I've missed you too, Gem."

"Don't call me Gem. And I've missed you as much as someone misses a used condom."

I snort. Her anger looks good on her. Then again, what doesn't?

Chocolate hair, plum rosy lips, and a round, tight ass I've studied so thoroughly whenever she wasn't looking that its shape is practically ingrained in my memory.

The second time I saw her was at the elopement, and while she did her best to ignore my existence the entire time she was here, I did the very opposite.

It's another reminder how far I am from being a gentleman.

Gentlemen don't look at engaged women the way I look at Gemma Garzolo.

That sobering thought forces the next question out of my mouth. "So when's your fiancé coming?"

A shadow passes over her eyes. "The day before Vale's wedding. Don't pretend you don't know that as well as I do." She brushes a strand of hair behind her ear, and my attention snaps onto that enormous ring on her finger. A bright-green emerald surrounded by a bunch of sparkling diamonds.

I reach out, grasp her wrist, and pull her hand toward me so that I can get a closer look.

She sucks in a harsh breath. "What are you—"

"A Messero family heirloom?" I venture a guess, the last name of her stupid fiancé tasting bitter on my tongue.

She jerks her hand away. "Yes."

"A bit gaudy."

"No one asked for your opinion."

"What's he like, Gem?"

"Guess you'll find out soon enough."

I study her face for any hint of what she thinks of this guy, but she gives away nothing.

Rafaele Messero is supposed to be the youngest don amongst the five New York families, which isn't saying much given the other four are ancient. The wedding is a great excuse to get him out here to talk business, and as part of the normal preparation process, Napoletano and I have dug up everything we could on the guy.

By American standards, he seems like a force to be reckoned with.

But to us Casalesi, he's a kid still riding a bike with training wheels. I'm looking forward to having him here and watching Damiano knock him down a notch.

"What were you doing in here anyway?" I ask, remembering her clutching the sink like it was a lifeline when I first swung the door open.

"Taking a piss, what else could I be doing?"

"Tsk." I glance over my shoulder toward the front door. "Is that how you talk around your father?"

"You're not my father."

"No, but I've been called daddy on occasion."

I'd thought she was looking at me like she wanted to murder me earlier, but that had nothing on how she's looking at me now.

She makes a gagging sound. "Seriously, is this some sort of torture method you're testing? Holding unsuspecting women hostage in bathrooms while you share details about your sex life?"

Laughter spills out of me as I drop my arms back to my sides and step to the side to let her pass.

She brushes past me, leaving the scent of cinnamon lingering in the air.

My eyes track her until she disappears from sight. I've always liked feisty women. A weakness you could say. And to find a woman like that living in our world? It's rare.

I drag my palm over my lips and chuckle to myself. Yeah, Gemma might be off-limits, but I'm still going to enjoy pressing her buttons over the next few days.

~

Our first lunch with the Garzolos happens a few hours later on the back terrace that overlooks the sea. While we wait for the food to be brought out, the sisters ooh and ahh at the view with Vale. The Garzolo matriarch, Pietra, stands to the side with Martina, examining some flowers.

The men take their seats. Dem's at the head of the table, Napoletano is two seats to his left, and I'm at his right. Stefano Garzolo is offered the chair directly across from me.

Dem's good at playing the politician, but there's no love lost between him and Garzolo. Their history is complicated, to say the least. But since Garzolo helped us in the early days of Dem making his bid to become the Don of the Casalesi, we're allies now. And Garzolo's determined to milk that for all it's worth.

We've already started supplying him with Italian made luxury counterfeits, the kind of stuff that fetches a pretty penny in a status-obsessed market like New York.

If you ask me, Garzolo should be worshiping the ground Vale walks on. His daughter upgraded from the sick fuck he married her to, to a man with significantly more power and money. A man who loves her more than life itself. Garzolo's not grateful though. In fact, I overheard him giving a stiff-tongued apology to her just a few minutes earlier in Damiano's office. She accepted it equally as stiffly. Who can blame her? Her dad's kind of a piece of shit.

"I'm eager to discuss a few things about our current arrangement," the piece of shit says, leaning back into his chair. "But I think most of it should wait until Rafaele arrives.

Given his role in all of this, it wouldn't be respectful to talk business without him."

I resist the urge to snort. Respectful? Jesus, Garzolo is really sucking the guy's dick.

"He had a swift rise after his father passed away," Dem says.

"Even before the old man died, Rafaele was already running much of the organization. His father's health had been declining for a while," Garzolo says.

"And the two of you are obviously getting on well."

"With Rafaele and Gemma marrying, we plan to only expand our business relationship going forward. The counterfeits deal between the three of us has been a testing ground, and it has exceeded even our most optimistic expectations. We're both invested in this partnership."

"As are we," Dem says. "We're always looking to diversify our business geographically. We like having partners we can trust in New York."

Garzolo's lips tighten into a thin smile. "Likewise. It's good to be doing business with *paisans*. Men who understand honor and the importance of *omertà*. New York's changed since I first took control of the clan, and I'm disappointed to say the changes haven't all been good."

"Anything to be concerned about?" Dem asks.

Stefano makes a dismissive wave. "No, simple annoyances, nothing more."

Dem nods. "So what happened with the Riccis? Has that threat been neutralized?"

Garzolo's expression darkens at the mention of the New York clan he plunged into war with after his plan to steal their business was exposed. "They're done. Rafaele and I have beaten them down to practically nothing. With us taking the counterfeits business from them, they've been left scrambling. Last thing I heard, they were fighting for scraps in the Bronx."

"I heard you suffered significant casualties," Napoletano says.

"So have they."

"We're sorry for your losses," Damiano says.

Stefano waves a dismissing hand. "Let's talk about more pleasant things, huh? Two weddings to celebrate, and another on the way."

Napoletano and I look at each other. Garzolo sure as hell doesn't want to talk about what happened with the Riccis. I wonder if he's trying to minimize how badly he was hit.

Based on what I know, Garzolo kind of asked for it. The whole feud started because the Riccis got tipped off that Garzolo was planning on stealing their counterfeits business from them.

Garzolo succeeded. But it seems like his family paid a price.

I glance over my shoulder to where Gemma is standing. Whenever she's around, I feel an inexplicable need to know exactly what she's doing.

I wonder how she feels about her upcoming marriage. Vale mentioned to me that she wants to feel the whole thing out while Gemma is here, to make sure her sister isn't being forced into something she has no interest in. The truth is, even if Gemma is being forced into something, there isn't much any of us can do without blowing up our relationship with the Garzolos. They're not our most important allies, but they've become a key part in Dem's plan to expand the Casalesi influence across the globe.

The servers appear with trays of antipasti and bread, and the women take it as their signal to join us at the table.

The men are outnumbered. There are the three Garzolo sisters and their mother, plus Mari, Damiano's younger sister. She takes a seat to Napoletano's left and places a kiss on her fiancé's cheek. Honestly, I still can't quite believe those two are a pair. Age gap notwithstanding, Napoletano's always been so reserved, while Mari is as easygoing as one gets. Guess she melted his ice with her sunshine.

When Mari realizes I'm watching her, she grins and sticks out her tongue at me. I huff a chuckle. That girl's always been like a sister to me, and she definitely acts like one.

A server comes around to serve us bread, and I ask for two big chunks. I fucking love bread. It's one of life's greatest pleasures.

When he gets to Gemma, she eyes the basket. She's changed out of her travel clothes into a light-blue dress that makes her eyes stand out even more than usual.

Fuck, she's pretty. Would look even prettier with my cock inside her mouth.

Her gaze flicks to my face, and I wink.

She turns pink, looks away, and points at one of the bread rolls.

"You shouldn't eat that, Gemma," her mother says. "Not if you want to fit into the dress we've chosen for your wedding."

It takes me a moment to process what I just heard.

The fuck?

That's a pretty fucking rude thing to say. Anyone with eyes can see Gemma's already quite thin. Her mom's either projecting or just a bitch.

I run my tongue over my teeth, eager to see Gemma bite back.

But she doesn't. Instead, I watch as she slightly deflates and drops her hand back in her lap. "You're right."

Indignation floods through me.

"Pass the tomato salad," Damiano says, and I do it in a mild trance. Something's seriously not computing, because if I'd said something as rude as that, Gemma would have bitten my head off. But with her mom, she just rolls over and takes it?

"So how are the wedding preparations going?" Mari asks Gemma, oblivious to the interaction I witnessed a few seconds earlier. I don't think anyone but me noticed, because no one else has developed a habit of studying Gemma like me.

Maybe that's a sign you should stop.

Gemma gives Mari an unconvincing smile. "They're going. I have a lot to do when we return to New York."

"Will it be a big wedding?"

"Nearly five hundred people."

Mari's eyes pop wide. "Oh my God. I'm sure I don't even know that many people."

"We both have very big extended families. It seems Rafaele is set on inviting just about everyone on his side."

"Messero is a traditionalist," Garzolo says, tuning into the conversation. "I like that about him. So many Italians have dropped the traditions we held dear before we came to America, but not them."

"What kind of traditions are those?" I ask, already disliking where this is going. In the Casalesi clan, but even more broadly in the Camorra, women have always had far more opportunities than in the Cosa Nostra. If a person can prove they can run a territory and make good money doing it, few give a fuck about what they have going on between their legs.

Garzolo finally deems me worthy of a look. It's amazing how a man with an ego as big as his can be in this business for so long. Usually, it's a ticket to an early death.

"The women aren't allowed to go anywhere unaccompanied. For their safety, of course. Gemma will have at least two guards with her at all times."

Okay, that's not so unreasonable. As the wife of a don, she needs to be protected at all times.

"They don't like having their women drive, so she'll also have a driver."

The other conversations have quieted, and everyone is listening to Garzolo now.

"And the wedding night linens will be displayed the day after the wedding." He chuckles. "That one is a bit silly if you ask me, but one has to admire their dedication."

Gemma turns a light shade of green, but the fire inside of her, the one I was so sure was inextinguishable, is nowhere to be seen.

Valentina's eyes flare with anger. "That's sick."

"It's their family's tradition."

"That doesn't mean it's not despicable. What else? Have they demanded a doctor verify Gemma is a virgin?"

"Vale," Gemma pleads, but her father pays her no mind.

He sneers, his teeth flashing at his eldest daughter. "I assured him that won't be necessary. Unlike Cleo, Gemma's reputation isn't in question."

Vale's gaze narrows. "But he asked?"

"Your sister's marriage is none of your damn business."

I can tell Dem's getting pissed off. "Watch your tone around my wife," he warns Garzolo.

"What about Gemma's terms?" Vale demands. "Does she have a say in this?"

Garzolo gives Vale a blank stare and then laughs. "Have you really forgotten how these things are done? Unlike her sisters, Gemma still remembers her duty to th—"

"Can we please talk about something else?" Gemma exclaims, cutting off her father. "There are two weddings happening before my own. Surely there's plenty of other topics to discuss."

"I agree," Damiano says, his eyes flicking between Garzolo and his fuming wife. For a few seconds, an awkward silence blankets the table, but then Mari says something to Pietra, and the tension eases.

The rest of the lunch proceeds without incident.

Gemma barely eats.

Barely speaks.

And I begin to wonder if I've seriously misread her.

CHAPTER 3

GEMMA

After lunch, Cleo heads straight to the pool, while Mamma, Papà, and I return to the guesthouse. As soon as the front door closes behind us, Papà takes me by the hand and drags me up the stairs to his and Mamma's bedroom.

Mamma watches us wordlessly, her expression tense. That's the way she is. Silent. Controlled. I can never tell if she defers to Papà because of fear or because she agrees with his methods.

I'm not sure it really matters at this point. The end result is the same.

This time when Papà backhands me, he uses far more force.

"Never *ever* interrupt me again."

The hit sends me falling, and my right hip takes the brunt of it against the hard tile floor. I swallow down a yelp and count in my head until the pain radiating through my leg begins to fade. My gaze follows a small ant running along the grout between the tiles until Papà roughly lifts me to my feet.

I'd known there would be consequences for interrupting him at lunch, but I couldn't let him and Vale get into a fight that would result in us going home early. I don't want to be responsible for leaving a dark stain on my sister's wedding. A distinct metallic taste floods my mouth as I will myself not to cry.

Papà glares at me, his nostrils flaring with harsh breaths. "Do you understand?"

"Yes." I breathe out, glancing at the door at his back.

"Do you think I like doing this?"

My gaze drops to the ground. "No."

"I'm doing this for your own damn good, Gemma. Do you think Rafaele will want a wife who can't keep her mouth shut long enough for him to finish a sentence?"

I shake my head.

"You have to be perfect. I don't want you getting in trouble with him, you hear?" He lifts my chin with his fingers, forcing me to meet his gaze. It's filled with righteous anger. "Your marriage will not be a clusterfuck like Vale's. I learned from that experience. I made mistakes with your sister. I should have gotten more involved earlier when things started going off course. With you, everything will be different, because I'm going to make sure you understand exactly what'll be expected of you by a man like Rafaele."

"And what kind of a man is that?" I ask, even though I'm not sure I'm ready to hear the answer.

Papà drops his hand away and straightens his back. "In our business, he's demanding but fair. I imagine he'll be the same in your marriage. We've had a chance to talk about his philosophy on family life, and it closely aligns with my own. You are to be at his service. Always. Your purpose in life will be to make his life as easy and as pleasing as possible. Learn what that means, and he will treat you with all the respect you're due."

I'm marrying a younger version of my father.

It takes everything I have to not let my expression crumble. "Okay."

He pats me on both shoulders. "You will have a chance to speak to him more this week. I have no doubt you will grow to appreciate him and love him in due time."

That's ambitious. I'll be happy if all I manage to do is survive.

I slip out of the room and head directly to a bathroom to tidy myself up.

The thing is, I was raised for this. All of the girls in our family were. Arranged marriages have been the norm in our family for many generations, and they've generally worked out. Divorces are practically unheard of. The only two I can think of off the top of my head were actually love marriages. Two distant aunts on Mamma's side left the family to marry men they'd fallen in love with, only to return a few years later begging to be taken back in. Their stories have always been told as cautionary tales. It wasn't until Vale that I entertained the possibility of a love marriage working out.

I suppose it's too early to tell in her case.

Vale and Damiano are obviously infatuated with each other, but will their love last? Will it survive the challenges that come with marrying a don without a family supporting her? Even Mamma's had to rely on Nona and our aunts and uncles to get through some rough patches with Papà.

Vale doesn't have that anymore.

She's here all alone.

A shiver of discomfort runs through me. I get why Vale ran, but for the life of me, I can't understand how she did it.

She was always the perfect sister. Growing up, Mamma made Vale the ideal that I had to measure up against. I was never as good. Never as beautiful. I was in competition with her, but it was one-sided, and maybe that's why it never managed to create a rift between us.

It just made me hungry for every crumb of approval I could get.

My reflection stares back at me. This concealer deserves an award. It's barely smudged. No point in worrying what I'll discover when I wash it off tonight.

"Gemma?"

My head turns toward the door. It's Vale. I should have known she wouldn't let Papà's comments about my future husband slide without a follow-up interrogation.

She's sitting on the edge of the bed when I come out, and I can tell she's fired up. I know what's coming, so I decide to take the lead.

"Look, I know it's weird."

"Weird? Gem, it sounds awful. They'll display the sheets? I mean, God. It's humiliating."

"I'll be fine." That lunch we just had was far more humiliating, if you asked me. I could do without Papà announcing all the intimate details of my upcoming marriage in front of everyone.

Especially Ras.

I purse my lips. That smug asshole was probably delighted to see me squirm. He seems to enjoy making me uncomfortable.

"No—"

"Vale, why is the tradition humiliating to me?" I demand as I plop down beside her. "If anything, it's more humiliating to the people insisting on seeing the damn thing, don't you think?"

My words make her pause for a second. "Of course it is. But I'm sure it won't be a pleasant thing for you to go through."

"It's pretty low on my list of concerns."

"What are your concerns? Have you voiced any of them to our father? Has he listened? Things have changed, Gem. You know that, right? After what happened with me, you should have a say in who you marry."

"You really have forgotten how things work in our family."

Her eyes flare. "Don't you understand I have leverage now? Damiano can—"

"Damiano can't do anything. He's a don on the opposite side of the world."

"Him and Papà have this deal—"

This time, the scoff slips out. "You really think your new husband will risk an important deal for my sake?" She's delusional if she believes that. Damiano wouldn't have become a don if he made his decisions based on anyone's emotional whims, Vale included.

"Can you stop interrupting me and just listen? Let me handle Damiano. If you just tell me what you want, I can help you."

Vale doesn't get it. She doesn't know what's at stake.

Calling off the engagement would throw everyone under the bus. If the alliance between Papà and Rafaele falls apart, the Garzolos will become a target.

For all I know, Rafaele might decide to destroy us himself.

No, there is no way out of this.

"What I want is to marry him. It will be good for the family."

A shadow passes over Vale's expression. "My marriage was good for the family too. At least that's what Papà said. Look how that turned out."

"That was different," I say. "Speaking of family, they miss you, you know. Nona wanted to be here, but the flight would have been too difficult for her. And our aunts ask about you every time I see them. You should call them."

My suggestion is innocent, but I can see she's taken aback. She crosses her arms over her chest and looks toward the window. "I wouldn't know what to say."

"It doesn't matter. They just want to hear your voice."

She shakes her head, her gaze fixed on the glittering sea outside.

"Are you angry with them?" I venture.

"I was in the beginning." She stands, walks toward the window, and pushes the sheer curtain aside. "But not anymore. Now, I don't know what I feel."

"They had no idea what Lazaro was making you do. None of us did."

Vale links her palms behind her back. "Unfortunately, emotions are rarely logical. But like I said, I'm not angry at them. If anything, I'm ashamed."

I get up and move toward her. "Why?"

"I should have called a long time ago to offer my condolences after what happened with the Riccis, but I just couldn't do it. The questions they'd ask about me and Lazaro... I didn't want to have those conversations. I still don't. It's selfish of me to want a clean break from my life in New York, but that's what I want."

Something cracks inside my chest.

I get it. I do.

But I'm part of that old life.

Does she want a clean break from me too?

My fingertips brush against her shoulder. She looks at me. "I wish Papà would call off your engagement and let you and Cleo move in with me."

There's a flash of hope, like a single match being lit inside a dark room.

And then it's gone.

"You know he'd never let that happen."

Vale's smile is sad. "I know. I just don't want what happened to me to happen to either of you. I don't think I could live with myself if it did."

"It won't." I clasp her hands. "Look, I appreciate you trying to help, but you don't need to worry about me. I've always known I'd marry someone of Papà's choosing. I'm ready for this. My concerns are nothing I won't be able to work out once I'm back home. Now, I didn't come to your wedding to spend the entire time talking about mine. Let's talk about this week, please."

The line of her shoulders softens, but there's a look in her eyes that tells me this won't be the last conversation we have on this subject. "All right, let's talk about this week."

She walks me through the schedule. It's packed. A family-only cocktail reception tomorrow night, then Martina and Giorgio's wedding the next day. Two days later, it's Vale and Dem's turn. The more Vale talks, the more excited she gets. There's a glow about her that's new. She didn't glow like this back when she lived with us in New York.

"You seem happy," I tell her when she finishes describing all the events.

She glances at her hand, the one that's sporting a massive engagement ring and the wedding band from her elopement. "I am. I know we're already married, but it still feels special to do it with all these people as witnesses. Even Vince is coming. I haven't seen him in years."

Our older brother Vince has lived in Switzerland for nearly five years. He rarely comes to New York, and when he does, he doesn't stay long.

I smile. "It will be good to see him. How many guests are coming?"

"For Mari and Giorgio, there will be around one hundred people in attendance. For ours, there will be a few more."

Including my fiancé and his consigliere. They're coming the day before Vale's wedding.

"Do you need any help with anything?"

"Not really. The planner's on top of it. But you need to try on your dress to make sure it fits. It's in my room back at the main house." She stands up and offers me a hand. "Let's do it now before we forget. The tailor needs time to make adjustments."

I follow her out of the bedroom and down the stairs. When we pass by the kitchen, a tempting smell makes my steps slow.

"God, that's heavenly. Did someone make bread?"

Vale sniffs. "Smells like it."

I drop her hand and take a few steps to peer through the arched entryway.

On the counter is a basket filled with those delicious-looking buns Mamma wouldn't let me eat.

"You coming?" Vale calls out.

"Yeah." After a moment's hesitation, I snatch one, break off a piece, and shove it in my mouth.

It's still warm. It's so damn good I barely feel any guilt over breaking my pre-wedding diet. Whichever staff member decided to drop these off is officially my favorite person.

We leave the guest house and make our way over to the main villa. The air is warm and humid, and the slight breeze carries the scent of the waves that crash over the big rocks at the edge of the property. The heat penetrates my skin. My hip still aches from when I fell, but I do my best not to show it.

As we walk along the stone path between the houses, I spy a few red hummingbirds buzzing close to the branches of a nearby tree. One of them spots a flower and dips its long beak inside.

It's lovely here. I wish we could stay for longer than a week.

I'm about to voice that thought as we step through the side door that leads directly into the living room, but my words dry up when I see the man spread out on the couch.

Ras. He's horizontal, one tanned arm folded beneath his head, the other holding his phone. He's typing something, a slight line between his brows.

My gaze skates over his flexed biceps. He was wearing a dress shirt at lunch, but he's changed into a fitted black T-shirt with a small logo stitched in the corner.

"I thought you were going to Revolvr?" Vale asks. Revolvr is one of Damiano's clubs on the island.

Ras looks up, his gaze immediately locking on me. "Yeah, I'm about to go. Just had to take care of some things. What are you two doing?"

"Gemma needs to try on her dress to see if it fits."

He sits up, still staring at me. "If you want my opinion, I'm available." A smirk plays on his lips, but there's something

38

darker than usual behind it. A challenge. Like he's waiting for me to figure something out.

I look away.

Whatever it is, I don't care.

And he can shove his opinions up his ass. I've got enough of those to deal with as is. "I think we'll survive," I retort, keeping my gaze away from him as I move toward the stairs.

"Is Ras going to be around all week?" I ask once we're inside Vale and Dem's bedroom.

"Probably," she says, disappearing inside the walk-in closet.

"Great," I mutter to myself.

She comes out a few moments later with a white garment bag and hands it to me. "Why do you dislike him so much? I get you met him in less-than-ideal circumstances, but I thought you would have moved past that by now."

Less than ideal circumstances? Ras accosted me in an empty change room and manhandled me with far more force than he should have used. He scared the shit out of me. I literally thought I was about to die. And he's never even apologized for it.

He treats it like a funny joke.

I take the dress into the bathroom, not wanting to risk Vale seeing the bruise that's most likely forming on my hip. "I don't trust him."

"He's never been anything but loyal to Damiano," Vale calls out.

Hanging the bag on a hook, I tug on the zipper. He might be loyal to Damiano, but what does that have to do with me?

The scene I witnessed the last time I was here flashes inside my mind, the memory of it as fresh as if it happened yesterday. I overheard Damiano and Ras talking in the office. Well, more like Damiano was listening to Ras run his mouth about me and my family. He joked I had a few screws loose, which didn't wound me, but what he said next has stayed with me ever since.

"You don't need to keep your word on that counterfeits deal, Dem. Garzolo is an asshole. Once we've gotten what we wanted from him, we should cut him off. It'll be fun to watch him scramble."

That told me everything I needed to know about him. Ras is a snake. His word means nothing. It's a good thing my brother-in-law is different. I heard him rebuff his underboss and say he'd given his word.

To which Ras scoffed.

Even now, the memory makes me angry. He was ready to throw my family under the bus just to have a laugh.

I want nothing to do with him.

Quickly, I slip the dress on and come back out. "He's rude."

Vale arches a brow. "Rude? When has he ever been rude to you?"

"Constantly. He always has this mocking smile on his face when he speaks to me."

Vale comes up behind me and starts buttoning up the dozen or so buttons at the back. "I think you're reading too much into it. Ras can be rough around the edges, but he means well."

I straighten the dress, examining it in the mirror.

It fits perfectly.

Should I tell Vale what I heard Ras say?

No, there's no point. She probably wouldn't even care. It's clear she's focused on her new life here and not our family.

She said she wanted a clean break from New York.

But me? I'm never getting out.

CHAPTER 4

GEMMA

THE NEXT DAY, cocktail hour begins at four. We're out behind the house on the meticulously landscaped lawn that overlooks the water. The breeze carries the smell of sea and salt. A waiter passes by me with a tray of canapés, and I steal a little piece of bread with prosciutto on top.

I'm starving.

At breakfast this morning, all Mamma allowed me to eat was a bowl of fruit. She picked out my wedding dress knowing full well it was a size too small, so now she's managing my weight. She's pulled this kind of thing on me before—my high school prom comes to mind—and it never gets any less tiring.

"Is there a naked man on that jet ski?"

My chews slow. "What?"

Cleo takes a sip of champagne and points toward the water. "Right there. I think it's that guy Ras."

The force of my turn nearly makes my red wine slosh out of the glass. He wouldn't.

I squint against the sunlight, suddenly wishing it wasn't so damn bright so that I could see better. Then the jet ski turns, and I see that indeed he would.

"Oh my God."

Ras slices through the rippling water, strands of his long hair escaping his usual man-bun. He's too far to really make anything out, but it's clear he's not wearing any clothes.

The initial shock is followed by a strange heat that blankets my skin.

"It looks fun." Cleo bites down on something that makes a loud crunch. "We should try it while we're here."

Our parents would have a meltdown if I stripped down to nothing in front of everyone. It's the kind of indecency that would put my reputation in question and make all those promises to Rafaele about my virginity irrelevant.

A little bit of bile rises up.

The thrill of a naked jet ski ride is definitely not worth some old geezer poking around my vagina to verify I'm as pure as I claim to be.

Vale appears before us. She's wearing a flattering green dress, a light dusting of makeup, and a sparkling diamond necklace that's no doubt an extravagant gift from Damiano.

"There you are. Have you seen Vince? The guards told me he arrived while I was getting ready."

"We saw him for a second before Papà whisked him away." Cleo reaches out and drags a finger over the necklace. She has a thing for sparkly things. "Nice."

"Thanks. I wonder when they'll be done."

I'm only half listening, my gaze inexplicably being pulled to the sea where a certain someone is frolicking in his birthday suit.

Vale notices and turns to look. She scoffs. "Typical."

"Is that an Ibizan thing or just Ras?"

"A bit of both. One thing I learned about Ibiza early on is that people here aren't shy about taking off their clothes. Let me tell you about the time Damiano took me up to Dalt Vila..."

The jet ski comes closer and turns, and I do something I immediately regret. I check out his ass. It's right there.

And it's...quite nice.

Toned and firm, if my visual assessment can be trusted.

I bite down on my bottom lip.

Here's what I truly loath to admit, even to myself in the privacy of my own thoughts. Ras gives the impression of being the kind of guy who could seduce any woman when given enough time. There's something fiercely attractive about him. The set of his brows, the permanent quirk in the left side of his mouth, the confident way he carries his brawny body. It's obvious he's physically strong, but he doesn't have the ideal proportions men aspire to and put in long hours in the gym to get. He looks like someone who got that body out of necessity. By doing the things that had to be done.

I hate this about him. I despise the fact that if he'd never opened his mouth or displayed his poor character, I may have seen him walking on the street and thought he's beautiful.

I'd rather be strangled and tossed into the sea than ever admit this to him.

When he turns once more, I avert my eyes. I sip on my cocktail and nod along to my sister's story.

Some time passes before I bring myself to look back to the sea, and when I do, the jet ski is gone.

A presence appears at my back. Don't ask me how I know it's him. I just do. Of course, I pretend like he isn't here, and when he joins the conversation, I only give him one quick glance. He's gotten dressed in a hurry—his shirt buttons are half done, revealing a swath of muscular chest, and his hair is dripping water down his back. He seems utterly unbothered by the fact that he just mooned the entire party.

His nonchalance irritates me. "You put on quite the show," I say during a lull in the conversation when Vale pulls out her phone to show Cleo something.

"Did you enjoy it?" he answers without missing a beat.

"I lost my appetite."

He snickers. "I'm ravenous. Being on the water always makes me hungry."

The way he says hungry makes heat rise to my cheeks.

As if to emphasize his point, he snatches a goat-cheese crostini off a passing tray. "You should try it. There's still time left."

"You could try being more subtle about wanting to get me naked."

His eyes spark. "I never said you needed to take off your clothes. But I do tend to have that effect on women."

I roll my eyes so hard I'm afraid they might get stuck facing the back of my head. "The only effect you have on me is indigestion."

His deep laughter is not entirely unpleasant, and it sends something buzzing inside my lower belly.

I give my head a slight shake. The heat, the alcohol, and my nearly empty stomach are clearly mixing some brain signals, because there's no way I find anything about Ras pleasant. Deciding it's time to make an exit, I move to brush past him, but he stops me by grabbing my forearm.

"Tell me, why does your tongue get so sharp around me, but you seem to swallow it around your parents?"

A thrill runs up my spine. Why is he touching me? He shouldn't be touching me. I shoot a nervous glance in Vale and Cleo's direction, but they've moved away to say hello to Vince, who's finally arrived. Mamma and Papà are farther away engaged in conversation with Damiano.

My gaze finds Ras's. His dark-hazel eyes have flecks of bronze in them, I realize. "Why do you care?"

His grip on me tightens, and he tugs me closer. I can't tell if it's to intimidate me or to simply make sure no one overhears our conversation, but I suspect it's the former.

His touch burns along my arm. "You let people push you around, and they'll keep doing it, Gem."

Anger flares inside my belly. I tug my elbow, but his hold on me doesn't let up. "Didn't anyone teach you it's rude to give unsolicited advice?"

"I must have missed that lesson." He arches a thick brow. "So what? Your ma has you on some kind of diet so that you'll be nice and weak when it comes time to walk down the aisle? She making sure you won't have the strength to run away?"

"Why would I run away?" I snarl at him. "For all you know, I can't wait to marry Rafaele."

He laughs at me. "Oh yeah. He sounds like a real catch. Are you going to be all meek and obedient for him? Yesterday at lunch, you put on a convincing performance."

"Get your hand off me before Papà sees it," I grind out, trying to mask the slow simmer of panic inside me. I can't keep getting slapped around. Even my extra-coverage concealer has its limits.

Ras lets go of me, and his expression turns probing. I don't like it at all.

"Here's what I'm trying to figure out," he says in a low voice. "Which version of you is the real Gemma?"

My body grows still and hollow, his question rattling inside the cavity of my chest like a snake. I purse my lips, willing the unsettling feeling away. "I don't know what you mean, but this conversation is far past its expiration date."

His reaction is not what I expect. Something flares to life in his eyes, and he points one thick finger at me. "That, right there. Is that fire real? Or are you just pretending to be someone you're not?"

My teeth clench. "Goodbye." I spin around and march across the lawn, desperate to get away from him and his damned questions.

Because the truth is, he nailed something on the head.

I don't know if the fire is real.

All I know is that it only really started to come out after I met him.

I float around the party, nicking canapés and pondering why I tend to not hold anything back around Ras.

I think it's because he's the first person I've been around whose opinion of me is of no consequence.

He can hate me. He can think I'm a bitch. Or that I have "a few screws loose."

I don't care. My opinion of him is far worse.

I've always had to be careful about what I say to people back in New York. I realized a long time ago that anything I say to anyone in the family has a high likelihood of making its way back to my parents.

But Ras? He's not going to go and tell Papà how I've been speaking to him, that's for sure.

So yeah. It's liberating to be able to say whatever's on my mind.

What's not liberating is him calling me out on it.

I sit down on a stone bench facing the water and pop a shrimp skewer into my mouth.

"Gem."

I turn around at the sound of a familiar male voice.

It's Vince.

My brother looks mildly annoyed as he takes a seat beside me, a glass of whiskey in his hand. I catch a whiff of some expensive cologne. He always smells nice.

"Um, hi? Don't I even get a hug?" I haven't seen him in months.

"You didn't come to say hello," he says coolly.

I sigh. "I'm sorry, your majesty." My brother has what some might call a difficult personality.

When he lived back home, he terrorized our staff. My brother is a perfectionist and a bit of a... Well, let's just say I overheard even our sweet housekeeper, Lydia, call him an asshole.

I wrap an arm around his waist and peck his cheek. After a moment, he hugs me back.

"You look pretty," he says begrudgingly.

I grin. Affection's never come naturally to Vince, but he tries with his sisters. "Thanks. You're looking sharp yourself."

The setting sun glints off the sleek clip he's got on his tie. I study his flawless profile—he's chiseled, with bone structure to die for. His brows are drawn. He's worn that severe expression since he was a kid, but now that he's a full-grown man, the severity is underscored with something more deadly.

I wonder if he's had to get his hands dirty in Switzerland, or if he's still feeding his superiority complex by limiting his illegal activities to pushing money around.

Vince is capable of violence just like any man in our family, but he's never liked the mess that comes with it.

It's one of the reasons he left New York.

Papà wanted him to work his way up the organization by starting as an enforcer—a position Vince immediately deemed to be below him.

So my brother concocted a different career plan. He got into one of Papà's bank accounts and started investing the Garzolo fortune by pretending to be our father. He traded over five million dollars before he got caught.

He's lucky his schemes turned a profit. Papà was furious, but when he saw the new balances, he simmered down.

That's how Vince ended up getting permission to go and keep growing our investments abroad.

He drags his thumb over the face of his watch. "It's good to see everyone together. Vale looks happy."

"Of course she's happy. She's in love."

"She picked a good man to fall in love with. One powerful enough to keep Papà from dragging her back home."

"You make it sound like it was some calculated move on her part."

He shrugs. "Who says it wasn't?"

"You can't be serious."

"Listen, she's smart for doing what she had to do to make a better life for herself."

"Ah. Of course. That's what you did." Vince was twenty when he left, and that was five years ago. He built his own kingdom an ocean away. I wonder who he'll hand it off to when it's time for him to take over the family business in New York.

Papà isn't getting any younger, and Vince is his successor. Eventually, even his finance skills won't be enough of an excuse to keep him away.

The day Vince returns and takes over the family is going to be a good day. If my brother had been in charge, I believe the war with the Riccis may have played out very differently. Papà is a tough guy. He lacks subtlety and restraint.

Vince is the opposite. He's a schemer and an out-of-the-box thinker. Violence is always the last resort with him.

He shrugs again. "Haven't regretted it for a single second. I could never live with Papà breathing down my neck."

"Some of us don't have the luxury of just disappearing for a few years."

Now his attention is on me. "He's lucky to have you, Gem. Very lucky. He raised three selfish kids, and one selfless daughter."

"Vale isn't selfish. She did what she was told in the beginning."

"And now you're doing the same," he says, his gaze dropping to my ring.

"I don't have to explain it to you. You know how bad things could get."

Vince came back for the funerals. He stood by Papà's side with that grim expression on his face. Tito, our cousin who died, was his close friend. They grew up together.

"You've always taken it upon yourself to fix things."

"Have I?"

"Have you forgotten how you'd call me every Saturday morning for years after I left to ask when I'd be back?"

"I was just checking in," I grumble.

"You were doing what Papà was too proud to do. Did he ask you to do that? I've always wondered."

"No."

Vince's lips curve into a knowing smirk. "You did it just for a chance to earn his praise. He would have heaped it on you if you'd managed to convince me to come home."

My cheeks heat. It's embarrassing because it's true. Back then, I'd have done anything to earn Papà's approval.

But I've grown up. At least, I like to think I have.

I'm not marrying Rafaele for Papà to tell me what a good daughter I am. This is so much bigger than that.

I'm doing this for my family.

I tuck a strand behind my ear. "Whatever."

He snickers. "Anyway, tell me about your future husband. Vale seems to already hate him."

"Don't tell me you're also going to try to convince me I don't have to marry him."

"I'm not going to convince you of anything. I don't agree with Vale. You should marry Rafaele."

"How well do you know him?"

"We had a few meetings after he began working with Papà. Despite his reputation, I don't think he's the kind of guy who would mistreat his wife. I asked around. He's had women around him, and there haven't been any complaints."

"You looked into him for my sake?"

"Do you think I'd leave my sister on her own? Yeah, I looked into him."

Something warm burst inside my chest. It's nice of him to look out for me.

Vince leans back on his palms. "I told Vale to let it go. I'm not sure I got through to her. She's all about love marriages now."

"How do you feel about them?"

"I wouldn't bank on one. Love fades. It's too unpredictable. Papà fucked up with Vale's ex-husband, but you can't dismiss the entire system of arranged marriages based on one bad incident."

"What about you? Have you started looking for a wife?"

He makes a dismissive wave. "There's no rush."

"I don't know about that. Given the long list of requirements I assume you're going to have, you might want to start early."

"Smartass. My list isn't that long. Just a few obvious things."

"Like what?"

"Since she'd be around a lot, I'd want someone nice to look at," he says. "Someone without baggage who wouldn't try to turn me into their therapist."

"Charming."

"She'd have to put the relationship first. Complete loyalty. Complete trust. Without it, it wouldn't work. I have enough people who want to stab me in the back. My wife can't be one of them."

It didn't sound too unreasonable, actually. "So you'd be faithful to her?"

He gives me a blank look. "What?"

"You'd want her to be loyal to you and trust you. Would you be loyal to her? Would you sleep around the way Papà does?"

"Sleeping around has nothing to do with real loyalty. Of course my wife would know I'd have women on the side. She'd accept it and move on."

I roll my eyes. "That's the kind of stuff that makes women want to stab their husbands."

"Nothing a pair of diamond earrings and a trip to the Maldives can't fix." Vince tosses back the last of his whiskey and stands. "Dinner's about to start." He eyes my empty wine glass. "How many of those have you had?"

"Not enough."

When I rise, the horizon before me wobbles. Okay, maybe I should have stopped one glass ago.

"C'mon." Vince offers me his arm. "So you're expecting Rafaele to be faithful?"

I frown. I haven't thought about it. The idea is distasteful in principle, but the thought of my future husband with another woman...

I wait for some emotion to surface.

There's nothing.

"I haven't thought that far," I say to Vince. "I just hope we'll get along."

"If you can get along with our parents for as long as you have, you can get along with anyone."

I roll my eyes. That isn't true. Prime example—Ras.

There is no situation, no possible scenario in which I'd get along with him.

CHAPTER 5

RAS

"HOW ARE WE DOING?" I ask the two guards stationed at the gate of Dem's property. We're about an hour from Mari's wedding ceremony, and I'm doing one last round to make sure everyone's keeping their eyes peeled.

We're still being careful these days. Dem's claim as our new leader has been accepted by anyone who's worth a damn, but the only time a don has no enemies is when he's dead. It's my job to make sure nothing ruins these two weddings, and I'm taking that seriously. We expanded the perimeter a few days ago, added more cameras, and put more men on the security detail.

"All good," the older guard says while he peels an apple with his pocketknife. "Enjoy the party, boss."

"Send a message if anything comes up." I pop my head into the security booth and do a quick scan of the cameras, just in case.

Mari deserves to enjoy this. The poor kid's been through a lot recently.

As have the rest of us.

It took a lot to get to the top of the clan, but now that we're here, the view's damn nice, even if I'm still getting used to it.

Dem and I operated in exile on Ibiza for over a decade under the old don—that motherfucker Sal. If I'd gone to his funeral, I would have spit on his grave. He fucked with us for a long time, but he got what he deserved.

Now Dem is in his rightful place.

Dem and I go way, way back. When his and Mari's parents died, they came to live with my family. He's always been around, but we only became close friends a few years after we graduated high school.

If I had to describe my life to someone in one word, it would be "unexpected." I was born into a high-ranking Casalesi family, my father an area capo who often had the don's ear. Everyone told me I'd take my father's position one day. Their expectations were like a living, breathing thing growing up, sucking all the air out of a room.

No wonder meeting that asshole Nunzio in high school did a number on me. Try believing you're destined for leadership when every week you get your ass kicked by a kid who's twice your size and has a vendetta.

My gaze drops to the scar on my arm. Even all these years later, there's an annoying twinge in my chest at the memory of how I got it and who gave it to me.

I tug my shirtsleeve over it and start walking back to the house.

Whatever I have now, I owe to Dem.

He dragged me out of a dark fucking place after what happened with Nunzio and Sara. Nothing quite like having the woman you love dump you for the guy who made your life hell for years.

If Dem hadn't hounded me to help him, I don't know where I would have ended up. But he refused to give up on me. He gave me something to live for.

Now, I'll do anything for him.

The wedding ceremony's sweet and simple. Mari glows with happiness, and Napoletano actually cracks a smile. It looks weird on him.

When they kiss, everyone cheers, and some kind of daytime fireworks explode, making colorful patterns in the sky. We watch as they disappear against the backdrop of the setting sun, and everything feels just right.

It's only when everyone gets up from their seats that I finally spot Gemma.

My breath catches.

She's a vision in a blue silk dress. The way the fabric falls over her body reminds me of those flawless Roman statues. The ones you want to look at for hours from every angle.

She's walking with Cleo toward the bar, that perfect ass swaying with every step.

Fucking mesmerizing.

I shake my head to make myself snap out of it and run my hand over my hair.

I don't even know what I want from her.

Nothing. She's engaged.

No, that's not true. I want *something*.

She's a puzzle I need to figure out.

Then I'll leave her alone.

My feet carry me across the lawn to where they're standing. Gemma notices me approach, and her eyes widen momentarily. Is she tugging on Cleo's elbow? The predator in me smirks. She's not getting away that easily.

"Why are you pulling on me?" I hear Cleo ask just before I cast my shadow over them.

"Going somewhere?"

Gemma's gaze flits over my body before leveling on my face. "Yes, we were just leaving to find some shade. Excuse us."

I block her way and tug on my tie. "Hot, isn't it?"

Her cheeks tinge pink. "Can you—"

"There he is!" a familiar voice calls out behind me.

Cazzo.

I turn around just in time for my ma to pull me into her arms. She presses kisses to both of my cheeks. "Where were you before the start of the ceremony?"

"Working."

She tsks. "You work too much. And who's this?"

"Gemma and Cleo Garzolo," I say. "Valentina's sisters."

"I'm Avena Sorrentino," Ma says. "Cassio's mom."

59

Merda. Ma ignores the glare I send her. Every time I see her, I have to remind her no one calls me that anymore.

You'd think she'd get used to it after a decade.

Gemma's brows scrunch together. "I'm sorry, I don't think I've met him."

Ma laughs. "I think you have." She points at me.

Gemma's eyes widen for a moment as she makes the connection. "You're Ras's mom?"

She says it like the idea of me having a mother is impossible to comprehend. She probably thinks I was forged in the depths of hell.

"When you have children, make sure they don't get attached to stupid nicknames," Ma advises. "Cassio is such a beautiful name, and he's all but abandoned it. And Ras isn't even a real name, it's just what we call—"

"Ma."

She shoots me a look. It's one I've seen countless times before, and it all but screams that I've tossed aside all the things she wanted for me. She used to say that to me out loud, but not anymore. Not since I became the underboss to our don. It's a position many made men would kill for. A position that demands respect. But it's still not what my parents wanted for me. They wanted me to work with my dad, take over managing our family's businesses, and make it into something great.

Instead, the only businesses I've ever given a fuck about are Dem's.

It's easier to help someone else achieve their goals than to meditate too much on my own.

Vale appears and whisks Gemma and Cleo away, while Ma patters on to me about some drama with our cousins until I find an excuse to step away.

I get to the main dinner table before everyone else and scan the names on the place cards.

Gemma and I are on opposite ends.

Fuck that. How am I supposed to figure her out if she's all the way over there?

I swipe her card and swap it with the one that's right across from me.

She arrives a few minutes later with the rest of the guests and looks for her seat. When she realizes how close we are to each other, her gaze volleys to me, and something exasperated passes over her expression.

I grin. This is going to be a fun dinner.

The server comes around offering wine, and Gemma does her best to ignore me.

I'm okay with that. Just looking at her is a thrill, especially when she looks like *that*.

A sparkling pendant glimmers against her skin, as if it's there to draw my attention to where it's nestled between her breasts. The neck of her dress dips low enough to show off a tantalizing bit of cleavage. She's a walking distraction. That dress should have come with a warning.

I pull on my wine. She does the same. My gaze is drawn to the way her fingers are curled around the stem of the glass, and a visual of those fingers wrapped around something else makes my neck feel hot beneath my collar.

"Will you stop staring?" she hisses.

I blink, like I have no idea what she's talking about.

"I was just zoning out," I say.

"Zone out on someone else."

"You're sitting directly across from me. Don't take it personally. It's just convenient." I smirk, hoping to piss her off enough to make those cheeks turn red.

It works, because when does it not? I don't need to work very hard to make Gemma angry. My mere presence seems enough to do it.

She shakes her head. "What's with the name?"

"Hmm?"

"Ras. Why is that what people call you when your name is Cassio?"

It's a question I'm not expecting.

My blood chills. Memories press in from the darkened corners where I keep them.

You're an idiot, Cassio. Nunzio will kill you for what you did.

I smooth my palm over my tie. "Never mind."

She doesn't drop it. "What does it mean?"

Why did Ma have to mention it?

Ras is a term in the Camorra system for someone who answers to a higher boss.

You're not Cassio anymore. You're ras. My ras. And you're going to do whatever I tell you to from now on.

I can still see Nunzio's face as he said those words. He was so angry, so determined to make me pay.

His family wasn't like my own. They lived in the neighborhood, and his father worked as a low-level manager in one of Pa's factories.

Honest people doing honest work.

They used their savings to buy Nunzio a motorcycle as a gift for his sixteenth birthday, and when he showed up one day at school riding it, everyone was awed.

And me?

My first thought was to steal it. Just as a joke. Just to prove I could.

What I didn't realize was that it wouldn't be funny to Nunzio.

He'd been twice my size and freakishly strong for a sixteen-year-old.

When he found out I was the one who took the motorcycle and crashed it, he told my friends I'd pay for what I did thrice over.

Pff.

I made an enemy for life.

He made it his mission to show me just how fucking weak and worthless I was. He knew that I was too proud to run to my family for help. I thought it would end when we graduated, but he never seemed to get his fill when it came to breaking me.

At least not until he managed to steal the woman I loved.

"It's an old nickname," I say, standing. I don't want to fucking talk about this.

Gemma's gaze trails up my body, confusion in her eyes.

I reach for my glass and polish off my wine. I don't like it. It's too sweet. I'll get a bottle of my favorite red from Damiano's cellar.

It's a stupid excuse to leave, but fuck it.

I head toward the house, acutely aware of Gemma's gaze on my back.

CHAPTER 6

RAS

A LONG BREATH escapes me as soon as I shut the side door of the house behind me.

If there's a part of my life I prefer to never think about, it's my high school years. I'm thirty years old. I should be over all of it by now, but the memories still bother me.

When I get to the wine cellar, I take off my jacket. Never liked the damn things. Whenever I'm suited up like this, I feel constricted, but what can you do? The occasion calls for it.

I spend at least ten minutes reading the labels, not registering a single word. It's cool here, the temperature optimized for preserving the wine. Eventually, I settle on a random bottle and make my way back up to the kitchen.

Voices reach me as soon as I step through the door.

"Look, all I'm trying to tell you is that you have a choice."

"Vale, enough." Gemma's voice is strained.

I place the bottle on the counter, careful not to make a sound, and try to figure out where they are. Probably just down the hall.

"You're only making it worse by constantly bringing it up. I'm marrying Rafaele. It's settled, and I'm fine with it."

"But you don't even know him."

"So what? This is what I've expected my whole life."

"That doesn't make it right or normal."

"We aren't normal. We sacrificed normal to be powerful."

"We didn't do anything. Our father did."

"You say that like you're making some kind of a point. We're a family. A fucked-up, messed-up family, but a family none-theless. Papà's made it clear that my marriage is important for our family's survival."

That's interesting.

I thought the marriage was a cherry on top of Garzolo's love affair with Rafaele, nothing more. They're already in business together.

Unless Garzolo's been lying. If things in New York aren't nearly as stable as he made them seem, then this alliance might be more about survival than expansion.

Valentina huffs. "I don't understand. I thought that after you found out what they did to me by marrying me to Lazaro, you'd stop being so blindly loyal."

"What they did to you was a horrible mistake. They both acknowledge it now. You know that, right?"

"Father only acknowledges it because Damiano forced him to. His apology to me was said through gritted teeth."

"He's proud, but deep down, he knows what he did was wrong. And Mamma cries in her bedroom at night. One time, I went to her, and she told me she'll never forgive herself for putting you in that situation."

"I don't believe her. She suspected what was happening, at least in broad strokes. She knew Lazaro wasn't right in the head. When I tried to give her the details, she wouldn't listen."

"You know she's never gone against Papà. She didn't know how to change anything."

"God, Gem! I'm not ever going to forgive them, all right? I feel sorry for Mamma, I do, but not enough for me to excuse her for her role in all of this."

"Fine. I won't try to change your mind. Now do me the same courtesy about my upcoming marriage."

Valentina sighs. "There was a time when you wouldn't have been okay with marrying a Messero."

"Maybe I've grown up since then. I was there when Tito died. You weren't. They brought our cousin to our house while he was bleeding out, and I held his hand as he took his last few breaths. I've seen what perceived weakness can do to our family, how it makes our enemies foam at the mouth. My marriage to Rafaele will ensure things like that won't happen again. So just stop it, okay? I'm fine with my decision. I don't need you to try to make me feel bad about it."

I frown. So Gemma thinks she's saving the family. From what? Did Garzolo make up some imaginary threat to pressure her into this marriage? Or is he in actual trouble?

Either way, Garzolo's lying to one of us.

"That's not what I'm trying to do," Vale says.

"It's what it feels like. Now can we please get back to dinner? Your husband will worry about you."

"Will yours?"

There's a long silence and then the sound of footsteps. I press my back against the fridge and wait for them to pass, but a moment later, Gemma enters the dark kitchen.

She stops by the island and presses her palms against the counter as if to steady herself. Her shoulders and head slump.

A door opens somewhere in the distance. Must be Vale going back outside.

It's just the two of us now.

Given we're working with Garzolo, I can't just ignore this. If he's been lying about everything being stable in New York and Gemma knows something, I've got to get it out of her.

I step out of the shadows.

She hears the rustle of my clothes and whirls around. When she sees it's me, her expression morphs from resignation to fury. "Were you eavesdropping?"

I walk toward the kitchen island and take a peach from the basket. "Didn't think you were such a hero, Gem."

She watches me take a bite. "I don't know what you're talking about."

I wipe a drop of juice off my chin with the back of my hand. "I thought your father got rid of all his enemies. Who is he afraid of now?"

"Oh yes, let me just spill all of my family's business to you."

I study her. Her body language doesn't match her haughty tone. Her eyes flit back and forth, like she can't look at me head-on.

She doesn't know shit.

"Let me get this straight." I move around the island. "You don't even know if there's a real threat or if your papa's just being paranoid?"

Perceived weakness. Why would anyone in New York think Garzolo is weak after he sent the Riccis packing? The casualty numbers might have been higher than we thought... Possible, given how weird Garzolo got when we brought it up.

But if he's really so weak, why is Messero getting into bed with him?

A lot of questions and no answers.

Gemma mirrors my movements to prevent me from getting closer to her. "Do you really think my father shares every detail about his business with me? Why do you care anyway?"

"Did you even bother to ask?"

Her expression flashes with uncertainty.

Cazzo.

Irritation inches along my skin. Seeing her being such an obedient little princess pisses me the fuck off. She's willing to marry Rafaele on blind faith in her Papà?

We're still moving around the island like two hands of a clock. I take the last bite of my peach and place the pit on the granite surface.

Gemma glances at it.

Before she realizes what's happening, I anchor my hands on the counter and haul myself over the island.

I land directly in front of her.

"What are—"

"I think I get it now."

She tries to move to the side, but I bracket her in with my arms.

When she realizes I'm not going to let her escape, her angry gaze moves to my face. "Get what?"

Just being this close to her sends blood rushing to my dick.

My irritation morphs into a simmering kind of frustration. "You're angry and miserable. You're sacrificing your future, and you don't even know what you're sacrificing it for."

A shadow passes over her eyes, but she raises her chin in defiance. "You don't know anything."

"You can't show anyone how you really feel, can you? You're too busy pretending to be perfect for your papa's sake. So you suppress all that rage, and then you take it out on me."

She grips each of my wrists and tries to push my hands off the counter. "You really think it's not possible that I just genuinely dislike you?"

The venom in her voice is convincing, but I haven't done enough to earn it.

She knows I'm right.

I twist my wrists, effortlessly shaking her off.

Her hands fall back to her sides.

They're trembling.

"Look at your hands," I command.

She does. When she sees what I'm seeing, she sucks in a breath and makes two fists.

"That won't do it." I'm so close I can pick up on the floral scent of her perfume. I wrap my palms around her delicate wrists and force her fists against my abdomen.

"Let go of me."

"I'll be your punching bag. Hit me."

She presses farther away from me, probably wishing she could move through the counter. Her full lips part. Waver. "I-I'm not going to do that."

"Why not? I've been that for you ever since we met."

I let my gaze drop down her body. She's breathing hard, making the swell of her breasts rise and fall. The outline of her nipples are visible through that silky dress, and my cock swells against the zipper of my slacks.

She's so fucking beautiful it hurts.

I take a small step back to give her some space, but I keep her fists pressed to my abdomen. "C'mon, Gem. You said you don't like me. Or did you lie?"

Apparently, she really doesn't want me thinking that, because she jerks her right wrist out of my hold and punches me.

A thrill runs up my spine. I don't like that fake, perfect version of her. I like this one. The one that keeps me on my toes.

I chuckle. "That's all you've got?"

She glares at me, teeth clenched, jaw tight.

"Your technique could use some— *Oof*."

She cuts me off with another punch, this time noticeably harder.

"Still not quite—"

She goes for two more, and I tense my abs to absorb the hits. When she feels the difference, her eyes go momentarily wide. She makes a frustrated sound and then really hits me.

"There." I grab her hand and hold it in place. Then I lift it between us.

It's steady.

"You see? Sometimes, you should just let it out. It feels good to do what you want. You should try it more often."

"Fuck you," she hisses.

Anger. So much anger for me.

But I bet for Messero, she'll turn docile and sweet.

A knot of disgust twists inside my gut, and that's when I do something I shouldn't.

I follow my own advice about just doing what I want.

The space between us disappears. My thighs press to hers, and I force her back against the counter.

Her eyes widen. "Ras—"

I grab her jaw with my palm and tilt her face up. "Since you seem so fucking good at bending to your parents' will, let's see how well you bend to mine."

She gasps, her pink mouth falling open.

I lean in and kiss her.

She's always been so sharp around me, so for a moment, I'm taken aback by the softness of her lips. They mold perfectly to mine. I curl my other hand around her nape and pull her closer, holding her in place so that she won't break the kiss until I get my fill.

My tongue lashes out, forcing past her lips and into the heat of her mouth. She makes a sound. A strangled moan. Perhaps, a muffled protest.

Fuck, I really shouldn't be doing this. But after all the buildup, all the tension, this is a heady release. I lick inside her mouth, gorging on her taste. It's laced with remnants of that sweet wine, but now the flavor is perfect. Exquisite.

We fit together. Her smaller body is snug against mine, her breasts pressing against my chest, their nipples hard enough to—

"Fuck!"

I stagger backwards, black spots bursting across my vision and pain shooting up my groin.

She kneed me in the balls.

I grin through the pain. Yeah, I fucking earned that.

"Have you lost your damn mind?"

Her question wipes the smile off my face.

Actually, it's her tone.

Panicked. Afraid.

I glance up at her from my bent-over position. She's all the way on the other side of the kitchen now.

Even in the dim light, I can see her eyes glistening, her chin trembling.

Cazzo.

Despite the pulsating pain, I force myself to straighten up. There's an unpleasant falling sensation in my gut, a delayed realization that maybe I took it too far.

"Who the hell do you think you are?" Gemma wipes her lips slowly, making a show of her disgust.

My stomach bottoms out. She's upset.

Her nostrils flare. "Do you know what would happen to me if my father saw what you just did?" She gives her head an indignant shake. "I should have known. I should have left this kitchen as soon as you appeared."

It's a game between us, isn't it? I kissed her. She kneed me. We're even. Only she doesn't seem to think so. "Gemm—"

She slams her fist against the counter, her eyes blazing with fury. "This is the hardest time of my life. I'm barely managing as is. And you've come along and decided to make me into your entertainment. Don't you think I have enough problems to deal with as is? Or do you think this is fun for me? Hearing people talk about how crazy the family that I'm marrying into is? It's a joke for them, but there's nothing funny about it. It's my fucking life. My life they're laughing at. Me."

I feel my blood seep out of my face.

Fuck. I hurt her.

Now I'm the one panicking. "No one is laughing at you."

She snarls. "You are. You don't even bother trying to disguise it. You're either mocking me or you're trying to dissect me like I'm some lab animal. Leave me alone. I'm not doing this for myself. I'm doing this for my family. Out of loyalty. Do you even know what loyalty means?"

"Of course I—"

"You're loyal to Damiano. If he told you something was important, that it was critical for you to do it, would you?"

I would. It's my job to follow his orders. But I'd ask questions. I'd want an explanation.

And if he refused to give it?

Ice slips inside my veins. Did I criticize Gemma for doing the same thing I would?

She's waiting for my answer, her fist still clenched against the granite counter.

I force it past my dry throat. "Yes."

"That's right," she snaps. "You'd do anything for him. Well, I'm doing this for my family." She drops her hand to her side and stares at me, unblinking. "You should thank God that your loyalty will never require you to sell your body to another. That Damiano will never ask you to let a stranger take you home and spend years pumping you full of his children."

Acid floods my mouth. This is how it is for women born into this life, but for some reason, hearing Gemma say it shocks me.

It's repulsive. The thought of her being forced into starting a family with someone she doesn't want. Doesn't love. Her body not belonging to her, not fully.

The scales were never balanced, but the unfairness of it all has never felt this stark.

"That's what we're ultimately here for, you know? To breed. In our world, my crowning achievement will be birthing the next generation of made men. That's what I have waiting for me. So in my last few weeks of freedom, the last thing I need is you rubbing in my face just how pathetic you think I am." Her voice breaks. "Let me enjoy my time here, damn it. You don't need to rob the last few bits of happiness from me."

My fists clench. I watch a single tear slip out of her eye, and it's crushing.

I'm an asshole. A real fucking jerk.

I fight against the urge to cross the distance between us and embrace her. She doesn't want my comfort. The least I can do is respect that.

She must see how thoroughly she's flattened me. How she's made me into mud at the bottom of her shoe.

If she was afraid of me before, she isn't now. She walks around the island and points her finger at my chest.

"You may have fooled my sister, Ras, but you've never fooled me. I see you for who you are."

"Who's that?"

The tip of her finger presses against my shirt, right between my pecs. "A brute with no honor. You might be loyal to Damiano, but everyone else is fair game. You're the kind of asshole who'd ruin someone's life just for a bit of amusement."

Nunzio's voice flits through my head. *You think this is funny? Do you know how hard my parents worked for that?*

I shake the memory off.

She backs away. "You won't touch me again. Do you understand?"

And then, before I can even think about how to answer, she whirls around and stalks out of the kitchen.

CHAPTER 7

GEMMA

WHEN I WAKE up the next morning, I can still feel the rough press of Ras's lips, the thrust of his tongue, and the weight of his hips against my own as he slammed me into that counter.

I was so mad just before he did it. So damn annoyed with all the probing questions he was asking that I couldn't answer.

But something strange happened when he kissed me.

All of my fear and fury morphed into something else. It turned hot and decadent, sliding over my skin and settling between my legs for a brief moment before I came to my senses and kneed him where it hurt.

I pull the bedcover over my head and groan into a pillow.

There is a reasonable explanation.

That asshole is just the first guy to kiss me who actually knows what he's doing.

I've only kissed two other people before. They were boys, not men. My age. Clueless and sweet. Our brief make-out sessions had been as exciting as waiting in line at the DMV.

No wonder what happened with Ras was more...jolting.

Open your eyes, you idiot. Time to snap back to reality.

I drag the bedcover down and immediately regret it.

It's so, so bright.

After the fiasco in the kitchen, I all but ran back to dinner and decided to drown all my problems in wine.

Delicious, fruity Spanish wine. The waiter understood his job quickly and made sure my glass was never empty. With Mamma and Papà seated at a different table, no one paid enough attention to stop me.

Too bad no matter how good the wine is, your mouth still tastes like acid the next morning.

I sit up and cradle my pounding head in my palms.

Ras returned to the table sometime after me, but by that point, the dance floor had opened up, and I was out of there before his butt touched down in his seat.

Honestly, he should be glad I didn't stick around. With all that alcohol sloshing inside of me, there was a lot more I could have said to him.

I hate him.

The man might be a decent kisser, but there's something seriously wrong with him.

I don't even want to imagine what would have happened if someone had walked in on us.

If my parents got word of me kissing another man? Kissing Ras?

I shudder. It wouldn't even matter that he forced it on me. Papà wouldn't wait for an explanation before he punished me. He'd probably take us all back home, tell Rafaele not to come here, hold this over Damiano's head—

I dig the heels of my palms into my eye sockets. It would be so easy to spiral right now, but I won't. I won't let Ras ruin this week for me more than he already has.

Cleo's still snoring across the room, but I force myself out of bed, eager to get that sour taste out of my mouth.

My hangover sends my thoughts down annoying little detours.

While I rinse my mouth and brush my teeth, I recall what Ras's body felt like. Hard muscle everywhere. Radiating heat like a furnace. His abs may as well have been a stack of bricks. I think I hurt my hand more than I hurt him when I punched him. He barely even huffed in response.

I step into the shower.

I wonder what Ras would have done if instead of hitting him, I'd slipped my hand inside his shirt, raked my nails over those abs, and dipped my fingers behind his belt.

God, it would have been worth it just to see the look on his stupid face. How annoying is it that he thinks he's got me all figured out? He barely knows me.

And apparently, I know him even less than I thought I did.

Cassio. Why does he prefer Ras over his real name? I feel like I should dig up some stuff on him. Knowledge is power. For someone who likes asking me so many questions, he definitely doesn't seem too eager to answer even one of mine.

Cold water hits my skin. I shiver against it, but I don't turn up the heat. I need to get rid of this hangover, so I let the cold drench me, let it seep into my hair and hope it clears my head.

It does.

When I step out onto the heated floor, only one thought remains. The only one that matters.

Ras is a scourge, and I'm going to do everything I can to avoid him for the rest of my time here. Easy enough for him to speak of doing whatever he wants. He hasn't lived my life. He's been here in this paradise for a long time, with a friend for a boss, and a culture that allows him to ride naked on a jet ski across endless clear water, for fuck's sake.

He's found something to toy with—me. But this isn't a game. Did a part of me enjoy our verbal sparring? Sure. But I can't after he's shown me what a loose cannon he is.

My bruised reflection is another reminder of why I can't afford to have Ras mess with me. I will not give Papà more reasons to hit me. I spend a good ten minutes covering up the ugly brown-green splotch on my cheek, pressing the sponge so hard into my skin that I make myself wince.

When I come out of the bathroom, Cleo's bed is empty.

I frown at the mess of sheets. Cleo's bed always looks like the aftermath of a racoon fight.

She drank less than me last night, but enough to get a little rowdy on the dance floor. Papà and Mamma left dinner early, instructing Vince to keep an eye on us. He'd done no such thing and had instead spent his evening smoking cigars with the older male guests.

I chug a bottle of water from the nightstand and check my phone. Nothing from Cleo, but there's a text from Nona.

> You haven't sent me pictures like you promised, cara mia.

I send her a few photos, put on a white linen button-up shirt and a pair of jeans, and venture outside. It's never a good sign when Cleo just disappears.

The sun warms my skin as soon as I step through the front door. Two guards greet me in Spanish, and when I ask them about Cleo, one of them explains in broken English that they saw her walking around the property.

I find her standing at the edge of the cliff that protrudes over the small private beach currently hidden by high tide. She's in an oversized T-shirt with IBIZA spelled out across it— when did she manage to get that?—and a pair of booty shorts. One of her Chanel purses is slung over her shoulder, looking very at odds with the rest of her outfit. She hasn't bothered to brush her hair, so it's billowing around her head like a black halo.

Typical Cleo.

I stop by her side. "This is a nice spot."

She sniffs. "It is. Great cliff."

A seagull soars over our heads.

"I'm thinking of throwing myself off it."

My gaze jumps to her profile. "What the hell, Cleo?"

Her jaw tightens, her hands squeezing into fists. "She won't leave me alone."

"Mamma? I thought her and Papà were still asleep?"

"She's driving me crazy on this whole trip. It feels like I can't do anything without her offering an opinion. She's constantly hovering. Every time I take out my phone, she wants to see what I'm doing. Did you see the dress she made me wear last night?" She extends her arm to show me some light-red marks on her forearm. "I was itchy everywhere."

The dress did have a lot of itchy looking lace. "I'm sorry, Cleo."

She sighs. "Now that Vale and you are matched up, she's focusing all her attention on me. Gem, I can't handle it. I don't even know what she wants from me. It's like she just can't deal with not having me in her sight, but she can't stand being around me."

I bite down on my lips. Mamma's anxiety has gotten worse and worse. The ordeal with Vale is Mamma's biggest failure, at least in her eyes. It destabilized her. Made her hyper vigilant, especially where Cleo is concerned.

"This is a difficult time for her."

"Don't." Cleo's voice hardens. "Don't make excuses for her."

"I'm trying to be sympathetic. It's been a difficult year for all of us."

Cleo makes a dismissive sound and peers over the cliff.

My heart rate spikes.

I reach out instinctively, grabbing her elbow. I don't let go even when she takes a small step back.

"I don't know how much longer I can go on like this, Gem. Sometimes, I feel almost a perverse kind of jealousy." She turns her head sideways, looking at me. "Soon you'll be moving out of our prison of a house and moving in with your husband. And me? I have no escape. No end in sight. I know Rafaele sucks, but I'm pretty sure he won't fucking hover like Mamma. He'll have better things to do."

"One can hope," I say warily. "So what, you want to get married now? For the longest time, you said you wouldn't marry anyone they chose for you."

Her expression crumples. "I don't know what I want. Hence the idea with the cliff."

Gently, I pull her farther away from the edge. She glances down at where I'm holding her biceps and lets out a humorless laugh. "Relax. I'm joking. Kind of. But I might turn serious if I don't get a break from her." She looks up at the sky. "I really need a break," she mutters to the birds. "Can you cover for me?"

Hesitation sweeps through me. I swear, if I had a penny every time I heard those five words from my sister, I'd be richer than Papà. "Cover for you how?"

"I'm going to go for a walk. I've circled this property a dozen times since we arrived. I need a change of scenery." She turns and gives me an expectant look.

"Cleo, we're in a foreign country. This isn't safe."

"It's an island. It's not like I can go very far," she says, pulling her arm out of my grip.

I don't even get a chance to argue before she's walking away.

"Cleo!" Panic rises inside of me. I jog to catch up to her. "Hold on. I never agreed."

"You will though, won't you?" she begs, her eyes wide and pleading. "Gem, I'm serious."

The image of her standing on the edge of that cliff flashes in front of my eyes.

I sigh and scan her skimpy outfit. "Do you even have your phone on you?

She shows me her purse. "In here. If anything comes up, I'll call."

"Where are our guards?" They're literally here to prevent this sort of thing from happening.

"They were dozing off in the kitchen when I left the house."

Papà's going to be furious if he finds out.

"There are Damiano's guards as well," I say.

She snorts. "Please, those guys are nothing. They're watching people coming in, not going out. I'll be back in an hour."

I watch her retreating back and bouncing curls and let out a groan.

Damn it. Will she be all right?

In New York, I'm never too worried about Cleo being able to watch out for herself. She's surprisingly street smart when she needs to be. But we're not in New York, so maybe I should go with her. Although, if anyone comes looking and can't find either of us, they'll sound the alarm.

I better stay.

I drag my fingers through my hair and glance around. What am I supposed to say to Mamma if she asks me where Cleo went? Back home, I have a list of go-to excuses. She's at the sauna. She went to the gym. She forgot something at the mall.

Here, I've got nothing.

They'll be so angry if they find out I let her go. I don't have to wonder about what Papà will do. These days, he doesn't need much of an excuse to raise a hand to me.

I need to stay out of everyone's way until she's back.

I carve a path around the house and head toward a grove of dense bushes. There's a bench there overlooking the water. It's a place I can hide until Cleo gets back.

Sitting down, I drag my sweaty palms over my jean clad thighs. Tiredness weighs down my eyelids.

I had way too much to drink last night. Ras didn't pour the alcohol down my throat, but I blame him for it anyway. It's like he discovered a manual for getting under my skin. I can't seem to get his words out of my head, no matter how hard I try.

"You're sacrificing your future, and you don't even know what you're sacrificing it for."

He doesn't understand. Ras has no idea the kind of trouble my family is in back home.

Do you?

I gnaw on my lip. The other families could choose to move on us at any time. The only reason they haven't is because they know we're joining forces with the Messeros.

After what you did to the Riccis, wouldn't the other families think twice about messing with you? A little voice in my head asks.

That might have been true at one point, but not now. We spent so much on that fight, and we don't have any reserves left. It's why Papà's terrified. He needs this alliance with Rafaele.

God, my head is pounding. I don't want to think about anything right now.

I get myself horizontal on the bench and throw my arm over my eyes. Screw it, I'm taking a nap.

I scramble awake when my phone buzzes in the back pocket of my jeans. It feels like I've only been asleep for five minutes. I glance at the screen and see that it's a text message from Mamma.

> Rafaele is about to arrive, where are you?

I rub at my eyes. The clock on my phone says I've actually napped for nearly an hour.

Shit!

My heart rate spikes as I pull up Cleo's contact.

> Cleo, where are you?

The message sits unread.

One minute passes. Two.

I groan. There isn't any time to wait for her to respond.

So much for my plan to avoid my parents until Cleo gets back.

I quickly text Mamma back to let her know I'll meet them by the front door of the main house. Papà made a big deal of me giving my fiancé a warm welcome.

We get there at the same time. Mamma comes over to smooth some imaginary wrinkles from my shirt.

Papà adjusts his tie. "Where have you been?"

"Just walking around the property."

"Where is your sister?"

"I don't know. I think she might be in the pool," I lie.

Mamma's eyes narrow. Is she onto me?

The gate at the end of the driveway starts to slide open, and a moment later, a black car drives through it.

Mamma's attention moves from me to it, and I let out a breath of relief just as the car stops in front of us. The driver comes around to open the door. The first man to emerge is Nero, Rafaele's consigliere. Rafaele's reputation is closely intertwined with Nero's. The two of them became made around the same time, and Nero plays a supporting role in most of the legends swirling around Rafaele.

This isn't the first time we've met, but every time we do, I have to resist the urge to rub my eyes. Nero's just...massive, built like a linebacker, even taller than Rafaele—who's six-two—and always dressed in black. Nero's nickname couldn't be any more appropriate—Angel of Death. Even his expertly tailored suit can't disguise the sheer muscular force of his body. He gracefully unfurls to his full height, towering over all of us, and gives us a disarming grin.

"Enjoying this sun, Mr. Garzolo?" he says with that wicked smile. "I'm hoping to work on my tan while I'm here."

They shake hands, and Nero cracks a few jokes and says things that are meant to put everyone at ease. Even his charm is intimidating. You never know when he's joking and when he's being serious. He seems like the type who'd try to get you to laugh while he twists your neck.

Then he moves his attention to me, takes my hand, and presses a kiss to it. "Gemma. Looking beautiful as always."

"Thank you."

Rafaele comes out next.

I swallow. My fiancé isn't as physically intimidating as Nero, but he carries an unmistakable air of danger about him. Maybe it's the way he moves, slow and intentional like a panther. Or the way he's able to keep his gaze as cold as ice no matter the circumstances. When that gaze falls on me, I shiver.

Rafaele doesn't greet anyone. Instead, he turns around and reaches back inside the car, apparently having forgotten something.

There's a strange muffled sound.

My jaw drops when I see Cleo's face with silver masking tape over her mouth.

There's a collective gasp.

"We found this stumbling on the side of the road," Rafaele says coldly as he hauls her out by her elbow. Her hands are tied behind her back.

The moment Cleo's feet hit the ground, she tears her arm out of his grip and screams like a banshee against the tape.

Rafaele steadies her by her shoulder, wrapping his big palm around it, and rips the tape off in one fell swoop.

If it hurts, Cleo doesn't show it. Her eyes are blazing. "I was going for a walk, you jerk off. Your thug—" she jerks her head at Nero, "—is the one who pulled me off the road like some caveman."

A gust of wind lifts up the hem of her shirt, revealing a sliver of her belly, and for a moment, I swear Rafaele's gaze drops to it. Then I blink, and his gaze is back on her face. Cold. So damn cold.

Nero chuckles. "We invited you in nicely. It's only when you refused that Rafe asked me to get you."

Rafaele tears his gaze off Cleo and moves it to Papà. "We nearly ran her over."

The direct address seems to snap Papà out of his shocked stupor. His nostrils flare on a breath. "She shouldn't have been off the property."

Cleo bares her teeth at Rafaele. "Get the damn zip tie off my wrists. Right. Now."

I wince. Lovely. My future husband appears to travel with a supply of zip ties and masking tape. Just in case.

Rafaele pulls out a pocketknife and approaches Cleo.

My breath catches inside my lungs. My fiancé is an exceptionally dangerous man, and I can't help but think that having him with a knife close to my sister is a bad idea.

But he doesn't do anything besides quickly snipping the zip tie off.

Cleo rounds on him as soon as she's free and snarls. "You do that again, and you'll regret it."

"Cleo!" I exclaim, more than a little concerned for her life, especially when Rafaele's gaze darkens.

I rush over and tuck her against my side. When I catch a whiff of her, my eyes widen.

She smells like liquor.

The idiot.

She must have hidden a bottle of something inside her purse. It's not even noon, and she decided to get drunk while walking on the side of a road?

Horror floods me. I should have never let her go.

My fearful gaze flits toward Rafaele. Is he going to out Cleo to our parents? There's no way he didn't smell it while they were in the car together.

My fiancé walks over to greet Papà. I barely breathe as I watch them shake hands.

My prayers are answered when they only exchange a few words before Rafaele moves on to say hello to Mamma. She mutters a string of apologies for Cleo's behavior. He just nods and then comes over to me. I push Cleo behind me, trying to get her out of his sight. My sister's insane enough to provoke him even now.

Rafaele studies me in his usual dispassionate way. When he looks at me, I'm never quite sure that he really sees me. For

Rafaele, all I am is a name written on a contract, nothing more.

He doesn't take my hand like Nero did.

Doesn't touch me.

He simply nods in acknowledgement and says, "Hello, Gemma."

CHAPTER 8

RAS

LAST NIGHT WAS A FUCKING SHITSHOW, and that's saying a lot for someone who's lived nearly a decade in Ibiza.

I couldn't get the image of Gemma's tear-stained face out of my head all night. She left her seat as soon as I returned to dinner, like she couldn't stand the sight of me. I oscillated for a while between going after her to say I'm sorry or giving her space. In the end, I chose the latter.

I didn't want to risk ruining the rest of her night.

She'd been trying to enjoy her time here. The thought of her coming here hopeful and excited, only to have everyone shove her engagement in her face made my chest ache.

I left the party early, passed out on a bed in one of Dem's guestrooms with my clothes still on, and dreamt of terrible things.

Now, it's late morning, and Messero's just arrived.

The fact that I think I'd enjoy putting a bullet in his head doesn't bode well for our meeting, but I have to put my feelings aside, because Dem's counting on me.

This deal with Garzolo is important. It's our first time working with Americans. Camorra's influence is widespread throughout Europe, but none of the clans have managed to make inroads in the US in recent years. If Damiano and I can make this partnership work, it will go a long way to cement his position as our leader.

So as much as I hate it, Garzolo and Messero have leverage over us. We want to make this work, but we have to be careful not to come off as too eager.

Let them think they need us more than we need them. It's probably true anyway.

I take a spare suit jacket out of the closet, slip it on, and head downstairs.

Thank fuck Messero and his crew aren't shacking up with us. They're at a five-star hotel fifteen minutes away, and they're only around for two days.

I can handle myself around him for two days.

In the living room, Dem and Garzolo are talking to two other men.

One is the size of a grizzly bear. The other man is tall and slim, with sharp features and a cold gaze that seems to pierce right through me when our eyes meet.

"Ras, this is Rafaele Messero," Damiano says. "And this is his consigliere, Nero De Luca."

We shake hands. Messero's slightly shorter than me, but he carries himself with the confidence of a man who knows he's in charge. No one would mistake him for a foot soldier.

My gun grows heavy in its holster.

Before I do something really fucking stupid, I clench my jaw and step away.

Dem leads us outside for a tour. It's a nice day, perfect for a swim. I glance around, hoping to catch a glimpse of Gemma somewhere by the pool or in the garden, but I don't find her.

Nero falls in step with me, an easygoing grin playing on his lips. "We finally made it to Ibiza, and we won't have any time to go see your boss's clubs. It's a damn shame."

As someone who's used to being the biggest guy in the room, it's somewhat disconcerting to have him peer down his nose at me.

But there are downsides to being that size.

There's a lot of surface area to hit.

"You're welcome to come back anytime," I say to him.

He tips his chin down. "That's very generous. You and De Rossi built this island empire together? You were isolated out here. How did you manage to do it?"

Dem, Garzolo, and Messero are ahead of us, far enough where we can't quite hear their conversation, but I can see that Messero's keeping his mouth mostly shut.

Maybe because he's got nothing clever to say.

I get the feeling Nero talks enough for two of them anyway.

"Slowly. Our clan already owned two clubs when we arrived, but they were being terribly mismanaged. Damiano took over, made them earn, and then used the profits to invest back into the business."

"It's impressive that he came here as a newly minted capo and developed a territory to this extent. Were you made when you arrived?"

"I was not. Back in Napoli, I wasn't exactly on the path for it." I was too busy spending my days and nights drinking in my dark apartment, thinking about Sara, and wishing Nunzio was dead. "It took me a couple years to earn it. In the Casalesi, your bloodline only puts you in the running, but to get made, you have to show that you can be a real asset to the clan and earn. I was twenty-three when Damiano called the meeting."

"Hmm." Nero pulls out a small metal box of cigarettes and offers me one. "We do it differently. For us, becoming made means showing that when you find yourself in a situation with only one way out, you have what it takes to do the hard thing."

The willingness and ability to kill for your family.

We halt for a moment to light up.

"You take your traditions seriously," I tell him over the flame of my lighter. "That's how it used to be done many decades ago for us as well."

"Traditions are important to the Messeros."

I inhale on the cig. "For us, that particular criteria didn't prove to be enough. Our clan wouldn't be what it is today if all we had were fighters. We have enough of those. To be made, you have to show you've also got a mind for business, something that's far more rare than brute force."

The insult isn't buried too deep, but Nero laughs it off and blows out a puff of smoke. "Then I'm even more excited about working with the famed Casalesi. I'm sure Garzolo already told you we're here to talk about expanding our partnership. We're delighted to be attending De Rossi's wedding.

"It might not be taking place in one of Damiano's clubs, but I can guarantee it will be a good party."

"I love a good party. Next time you're in New York, make sure to get in touch. I'll return the favor."

He's laying it on thick, but I'm not fooled by the friendly giant act. This man wouldn't be a consigliere if he wasn't clever as hell.

I have to stay on guard.

"I will. Although, I doubt I'll be there anytime soon. Things are busy here and back in Italy."

"Of course. I remember what it was like when Rafe took over the family after his father's death. There was a lot of work to do in the months that followed."

"Must have been a big adjustment going from a made man to a don. Damiano's been a capo for a decade, so he's had time to earn the respect of our clan. That helps."

We stop at the edge of the cliff to admire the view. Messero's got his hands in his pockets, his expression a neutral mask. I take the opportunity to size him up. His features are sharp. Polished. There's something vulture-like in how he carries himself.

Nero puffs on his cigarette. "Not really. Rafaele's been preparing for this job his whole life. He earned everyone's respect a long time ago. After all, he got made at thirteen."

Fuck, that's young.

I think back to the folder Napoletano shared with us a while back. Inside were all of Messero's known crimes, business deals, alliances, and enemies.

The last section was sparse.

Messero had killed most of them.

An hour later, the six of us spread out across the leather armchairs and sofa in Dem's office. I offer everyone whiskey, and they all accept except Napoletano. He joined us after the tour, and there's a distinct annoyed glimmer in his eyes at having been asked to step away from Mari for this meeting. They haven't emerged from their bedroom all day, and the collar of Napoletano's shirt doesn't quite cover the hickeys peppering his thick neck. Dem noticed them when we first walked in and gave Napoletano a dirty look. He knows better than to say anything though. Mari might be his sister, but now she's Napoletano's wife.

"Should we get down to it then?" Nero throws out once the drinks have been poured. His gaze lands on Dem. "Your second delivery was a fraction of what we agreed on."

Dem props an ankle across his thigh and settles into his chair, looking utterly at ease. "I took control less than four months ago. We're still working out the kinks with the new supply route we established for the counterfeits."

"Have they been worked out?" Nero asks.

Irritation prickles across my nape. That fucking tone. "We don't report to you, so stop talking to us like we're your fucking crew."

Nero lifts his palms up. "I wouldn't dream of it. No disrespect, fellas. We've stumbled onto a good thing here, and it's in both of our interests to get the cash flowing."

"Indeed," Damiano says, his gaze moving to Garzolo. "How much product can you move in the next six months?"

Garzolo takes a swig of his drink and glances at Messero. "That's a question for Rafaele."

I make a note of that. Interesting. So Messero's crew is handling most of the distribution? What's Garzolo's role in all this then? We'd been operating under the assumption that he and Messero were splitting things fifty-fifty back in New York.

Messero is slow to answer. Clearly, he's in no fucking rush. "We have a network of retailers across the East Coast with an eager clientele. The first month you sent us one million worth of merchandise. We could sell five times that."

My eyes widen as I do the math in my head. Given our terms, this operation could bring in two and a half mil per month. Jesus. After expenses, we'd be left with a two million profit each month.

This is a bigger opportunity than we were expecting.

Dem gives me a look that communicates he's thinking along the same lines.

"We can ramp up production next month," he says.

Messero swirls his whiskey. "How much?"

"Three million worth of premium leather goods, that includes shoes, purses, and accessories."

"The quality?"

"Indistinguishable from the real thing. We forge the authenticity certificates too," I say. "Every now and then, we send someone to the boutiques to ask for authenticity checks. They rarely fail. You won't find any replicas better. Even the top-of-the-line Chinese factories don't come close. Some of our factory managers have worked for the actual brands in the past, so they know exactly what to look for."

Nero's brows lift. "Impressive."

"Three million won't be a problem, but to get to five, we'll need to build a new factory," Damiano says. "It's a large investment on our part. We'll want to get more comfortable with the terms and discuss guarantees before we take that step."

"We're about to become family," Nero says with a grin. "What other guarantees do you need?"

Damiano stares at him over the rim of his glass. "We aren't family yet. Perhaps we wait until Rafaele and Gemma are officially wed."

My posture stiffens.

I was doing decently well with putting Gemma out of my mind, but now everything comes flooding back.

The way her lips felt against my own is something I don't think I'll ever forget.

Fuck. I still need to apologize.

Kissing her was a mistake.

The bigger mistake has been allowing myself to get fixated on her.

Yes, she's beautiful. I'm wildly attracted to her. I would have loved to do something about that attraction if circumstances had been different, but that's not the hand I've been dealt.

She's engaged. Spoken for.

She clearly hates my guts.

I need to stop being an ass and leave her alone.

I also need to stop worrying about her like she's my damn problem to solve. It fucking sucks that she has to marry this asshole, but she's an adult.

If she needs help, she's got Vale to turn to. Otherwise, she's responsible for her own life choices.

Rafaele pins me with his gaze, as if some part of him senses I'm thinking about his fiancée.

I scowl. "When is the wedding?"

"Soon," Garzolo answers quickly.

"Is the date set?" Damiano asks.

Rafaele places his tumbler on the coffee table with a soft clink. "March sixth."

That's about five weeks from now. A heavy weight solidifies inside my gut, but I ignore it.

"Then let's settle on three million for now and discuss how we can get comfortable with five after the wedding," Damiano says.

Nero finishes off his drink. "We'll see you there, won't we? I don't imagine your wife will want to miss her sister's nuptials."

"We wouldn't dream of it," Dem says.

My hand tightens around my glass. Great. Just great. That means I'm going too. Seeing Gemma walk down the aisle to this bastard is something I could definitely live without.

"Well, sounds like we've got it all worked out," Nero says. "Is there anything else we should discuss? You've brought us out to paradise, De Rossi. Nothing would make me happier than a few hours to enjoy it."

"What about the other family?" Napoletano asks.

Everyone turns to look at him. He's been even more silent than Messero though all this, standing in the corner and observing us all.

"The one that used to run counterfeits before in New York," he says. "I don't imagine they're happy about you taking over their territory."

"Didn't I already say to all of you a few days ago that the Riccis are done?" Garzolo snaps.

Suspicion licks up my spine. This topic really sets Garzolo off.

He finishes off his drink and slams the glass on the table. "Rabid dogs, that fucking family. They need to be put down. But now that word's gotten around that Rafaele and I are merging forces, they won't try anything stupid."

"We just want to be helpful," I offer. "You'd tell us if you needed any assistance from us, right, Garzolo?"

His eyes narrow on me. "Assistance? Do I look like a man who needs assistance? You want to come to New York and see how I run things down there? You're welcome to come any time."

I glare at him. "I'll be sure to take you up on that."

We end the meeting, exchanging handshakes so as not to end it on that terse note.

Once our guests leave, I turn to Dem. "All right, so what the fuck is going on here? If Garzolo's sole value in this deal is to act as a broker between Messero and us, I don't understand why we don't just cut him out."

"Because he's family now." Damiano drags his palm over his chin. "Maybe this is why he initiated the marriage between Messero and Gemma in the first place."

"Messero isn't stupid," Napoletano says. "If all Garzolo had was his connection to Sal, and now to you, Messero wouldn't have agreed to the marriage. No, Garzolo must have something else. Something Rafaele Messero wants." He walks around the sofa and takes a seat at the end. "I overheard Gemma talking to Vale last night. She made it sound like Garzolo really needs this alliance. Like he's weak without it."

It's an effort to keep my expression neutral since I overhead that conversation too.

Did Napoletano see Gemma and I in the kitchen afterwards?

I catch his eye, but he doesn't react in any way that suggests he did.

"It's possible," Damiano mutters. "Let's review what we know. Garzolo and Messero initially teamed up because the

Riccis were getting too powerful in New York. The Riccis wanted to get their counterfeits supply from my predecessor, Sal, but Garzolo stepped in and tried to convince Sal to make the deal with him. When the Riccis found out, they went on the offensive against Garzolo."

"Probably against Messero too," I add.

"Right. So this alliance was borne out of Messero and Garzolo having a common enemy."

"Who now appears to be neutralized, if Garzolo is to be believed."

"If the marriage between Rafaele and Gemma doesn't happen, the Riccis might decide to attack again," Napoletano says.

"Garzolo said they were all but destroyed. Is he lying about the damage they did?"

I cross my arms over my chest. "It's possible. It would explain why Garzolo is all but sucking Messero's dick right now. But Messero's motives are unclear. Why sign up to protect Garzolo if the guy's nothing but a middleman? He's not pushing any of the product. If I were Messero, I'd call off the marriage, negotiate with Dem to do the deal between just the two of them, and let Ricci and Garzolo fight among themselves. There's a good chance they'll destroy each other, and Messero would come out on top."

"We don't know what's going on in New York. Maybe Messero is having problems in other parts of his business."

"I don't like this," Napoletano says. "I feel like we're missing something. Something big."

Damiano blows out a breath. "Do we need to concern ourselves with this? As long as they pay us on time, I don't give a fuck what happens on their turf."

Napoletano shakes his head. "If there are problems back in New York, this deal might turn to dust. It's in our best interest to make sure things with our partners are stable. If we get to five million per month, our cut will add ten percent to our top line. That's not insignificant."

Damiano drums his fingertips along the armrest. "I hear you. Can you get more information about what's happening on their side?"

"I have some contacts, but it will take time. And even then, I'm not sure if they're close enough to the families to get the details we need."

Dem rises and walks over to the window. "I need to think about how to proceed," he says finally.

I observe my friend. We haven't said it out loud, but we all know that there's another layer to this whole thing. The fate of Vale's sisters are intrinsically linked to that of their father.

And while Vale might be more than willing to turn her back on Stefano, she'll never forgive Dem if her siblings become collateral damage in the process.

CHAPTER 9

GEMMA

RAFAELE'S ARM is steady under my hand as we walk into the buzzing cathedral for Vale's wedding the next day.

I'm technically the maid of honor, but Vale didn't give me any tasks before the ceremony, so Papà arranged for Rafaele to pick me up from the house.

We drove here in uncomfortable silence.

At least it was uncomfortable for me. Rafaele seemed completely unbothered.

I try to keep my nerves at bay by focusing on the elegant decor instead of my fiancé's intimidating presence.

Woven baskets are suspended from the ceiling, with delicate white and purple flowers spilling over their edges. The smell of lavender wafts through the space. A lilac-colored carpet stretches from the entrance of the cathedral all the way to the altar, where a priest stands dressed in a black cassock, a bible in his hands.

Rafaele leads me to the front pew where my parents and Cleo are already seated. Cleo doesn't hide her disdain for my fiancé, her expression morphing into a scowl.

Yesterday, my sister called him every name imaginable. I had to remind her that he could have gotten her into a lot more trouble if he'd told everyone how drunk she was when he picked her up.

I was furious. I dragged her into the shower as soon as we got to our room, and by the time Mamma came up to scream at her, Cleo had washed the smell of Jack Daniels off and managed to sober up. We were told to stay in our room until we were called.

I kept eyeing the door, waiting for Papà to storm in. Turns out he, Damiano, and Rafaele had a meeting, and when he finally returned, he was in a surprisingly good mood.

We got off the hook too easily.

I'm not complaining. It's the only lucky break I've gotten since I arrived here.

We sit down. Rafaele gives Cleo only a cursory glance, which I know must irritate her. She's itching for a confrontation. I give her a warning look. She scrunches her nose and turns toward the altar.

I relax slightly and try to get comfortable in my seat.

Rafaele's platinum cufflink winks against the light streaming through the stained-glass windows. It's engraved with the letters RM.

Those two letters remind me that soon my own initials will change.

Something unpleasant stirs in the pit of my stomach. It's been doing that all morning. I hope it's not the fish I had for lunch. It tasted slightly off.

I turn in my seat and survey the rest of the guests. There's at least a hundred people, most of whom I don't recognize. Vale told me that Damiano invited all of the capos and their immediate families, as well as made men who'd been close to his late parents. Some apparently had a problem with the wedding being in Spain instead of Italy where Vale and Damiano live for most of the year, but Vale explained that the location made the event far more secure. The only person with a private army on the island is Damiano.

A prickling sensation spreads over my neck. Someone's watching me.

I turn in time to see Ras walking down the aisle, his ma by his side.

Our eyes meet, and my breath catches.

He looks damn good.

His suit is a masterpiece, fitted to highlight the broad, powerful lines of his body. A crisp white shirt collar peeks out and contrasts with his skin, making his tan stand out.

But no matter how perfectly his clothes sit on him, there's something disconcerting about him looking so put together. It feels like a disguise meant to make people think he's civilized, when I know he most certainly is not.

A few of the other female guests turn to watch him. Someone whispers his name.

He and his ma turn into the pew across the aisle from us, and he helps her sit down before taking his own seat. She says something to him, but he answers without looking at her.

His gaze unabashedly lingers on me.

My cheeks heat.

We haven't spoken since the kiss, which is exactly what I wanted. Being alone with him isn't something I can risk again, especially not with Rafaele here. Ras's too unpredictable, too likely to get me into trouble.

He stares at me like he knows me far better than he realistically could. Like his gaze can penetrate through the thick layer of makeup on my face and see the fading bruise.

"I think I get it now. You're angry and miserable. You can't show anyone how you really feel, can you?"

"Fucking hot in here, isn't it?" Nero slides into the pew behind us, his sudden arrival making me jump. He grins and unbuttons his suit jacket. The bench is comically small compared to him. He looks like an adult sitting in a kid's playhouse. His knees bump against our backrests. "AC's broken in our hotel too. I'm melting. Tell me the reception is somewhere cool."

I give him a terse smile. My future husband's consigliere has always been friendly to me, but I don't trust him. I get the sense he's constantly trying to disarm people with his charm. Maybe that's how he tricks them into giving him all their secrets.

"It's in one of Damiano's restaurants on the beach," I say. "There might be a breeze if we're lucky. But it'll cool down after seven anyway."

He checks his watch and whistles. "Three more hours. Fuck me." When he lifts his gaze back up, his eyes flash with amusement, and his grin widens. "What's up, Cleo?"

"Absolutely nothing," my sister spits out, making no effort to be civil.

"You planning any more strolls later today?"

She huffs. "If I was, you and your boss would be the very last people I'd tell."

A strange sound comes out of Rafaele. It almost sounds like a stifled chuckle.

I glance at my fiancé. His expression reveals nothing. He's studying the front of the church as if it's the most interesting thing in the world.

But I know I didn't imagine that sound. It wasn't Nero, and my parents are far past the point of being amused by anything Cleo says.

It had to have come from Rafaele.

Weird. I didn't think he had a sense of humor.

"Go, Gemma. They're about to start," Mamma says, nudging me with her elbow.

I get up just as Damiano steps onto the altar. On the other side of him, Ras appears.

Our eyes lock, and heat expands inside my chest.

I must be still angry with him.

The string quartet begins playing. Everyone turns to the back of the church, eager to see the bride.

Vale appears at the end of the aisle wearing a silk-chiffon wedding dress that nips in at her waist before flowing out around her legs. The hem of the skirt is strewn with pearls and white flowers. She looks perfect.

She walks toward Damiano alone, her head held high, and her eyes sparkling as she keeps her gaze on the man she loves. She carries herself with such confident ease. I wonder if any of the other guests note the absence of Papà at her side.

To us, the message is clear. She doesn't need Papà. She's already got everything she needs.

After the ceremony is done, we change into our party dresses, and head to Damiano's restaurant where the reception is taking place. Everyone takes their seats. I'm relieved to find that Ras isn't at my table. Nero and Rafaele are, but they're sitting on the other side of it, far enough that I won't have to make attempts at conversation.

A woman's melodic singing fills the air. Candles flicker in the elaborate centerpieces on the tables. The waiters move around us in deliberate arcs, making sure not a single glass is empty.

Cleo leans closer. "Here's what I've been wondering. How big do you think Nero's dick is?"

My champagne goes down the wrong pipe. Cleo pats me helpfully on the back while I work through my coughing fit. My eyes are watering by the time it passes.

"Come again?"

She lifts her glass of wine to her lips. "I mean, he's got to be like six-six? Six-seven? If his body is proportional, his penis must be—"

"Cleo! He's right there!" I whisper hiss.

She purses her lips at my outrage and casts an unconcerned look to where Nero is sitting across from us.

"He can't hear us," Cleo says. "You probably wouldn't be able to walk after he's done with you."

My cheeks heat. "What's gotten into you? Need I remind you this is the man who tied your wrists with a zip tie and taped your mouth shut a day ago?"

She rolls her eyes. "First of all, my memory is just fine, thanks. And second of all, Nero didn't do that. He just carried me into the car. The rest was your fiancé. Who, by the way, is staring."

I shoot a discrete glance at Rafaele. "Yeah, at you," I hiss. "He probably overheard you."

A smirk unfurls over my sister's lips. "God forbid I bruised his ego by talking about his consigliere's package instead of his. Just look at Rafaele. He's so wooden. Even with that handsome face, something tells me no one's rushing to jump into his bed. He can't exactly glare his way to a woman's orgasm."

I tug on her arm. "Do I really need to remind you that's my future husband you're talking about?" I say, my voice clipped.

Her expression sours. "Right. Sorry." Her gaze drops to my hand and turns admiring. "At least the ring he gave you is beautiful."

"Yeah."

She notes the lack of enthusiasm in my voice and snorts. "You hate it, don't you?"

The ring isn't my style. I like dainty jewelry that I can layer, the kind Mamma always tells me looks cheap. She was thrilled when she saw the enormous emerald.

"I guess we have slightly different tastes," I offer.

My sister studies me carefully. "You don't want him."

A wave of frustration rolls through me. "Just don't, Cleo. You think I haven't heard enough of this from Vale?"

"You keep hearing it because it's true. You don't want to marry Rafaele. It's obvious."

"You're all missing the point. What I want doesn't matter."

Cleo's lips thin with pity. "When did you internalize that, Gem? It's really sad you think that way."

My hands curl into fists on my lap. God, I'm so sick of these conversations. "No, you know what's sad? The way you don't seem to see the big picture. My marriage will strengthen our family. You know, that silly thing you and Vale seem to scoff at. Have you forgotten what we just lived through? Tito's gone. Our uncles...gone. If I have to make a sacrifice to prevent that from happening again, I'll do it."

"God, Gemma. You sound just like Mamma. Always helping clean up Papà's messes for him."

My anger rises to a boil. "This has nothing to do with Papà."

"If he wants to get in bed with Rafaele that badly, maybe he should marry him," Cleo snaps. "Instead, he's getting you to bail him out."

"It's not. About. Him," I growl. "I am not doing this for him. I'm doing this for Nona, who has to worry about her grandsons bleeding out in the street. I'm doing this for Aunt Lia and Aunt Daniela, who've got four sons between them as made men. Don't you care about anyone but yourself?"

Cleo's face turns red. "How noble of you, Gemma. Did it ever occur to you that all those men *chose* to be made? They knew what they were getting themselves into."

I laugh. "Honestly, Cleo, it's time you stop living in fantasy land. We were all born into this life. We can't do anything about it, so why don't you try to accept it?"

"Vale didn't."

"Look where she ended up." I gesture at the restaurant. "She's married to a fucking don. She may have left New York, but she never left our world. Few ever do. So enough, all right?"

Cleo's eyes are shining by the time I'm done. She shoots out of her seat, throws her napkin on the table, and storms away in the direction of the bathroom.

I look at the calm waters of the Mediterranean and let out a long breath. My stomach groans. I think that fish is definitely not sitting well with me.

When Cleo returns, we don't speak. Over the next two hours, there are dozens of courses and as many toasts from Damiano's capos. Their fast-paced Italian quickly becomes background noise since I'm not fluent in the language. I pick at my food but don't get very far with any of it. There's a steady ache inside my belly. The air should have cooled by now, but I'm still feeling too hot.

From time to time, I get the same feeling I had at the church. Like someone's watching me. I don't need to look in Ras's direction to know it's him. For the life of me, I don't know why he keeps staring at me. It makes me feel exposed.

My abdomen is as hard as a rock. I pop a pill from my purse and put on a brave face, because that's the only option I have. This wedding is what we came here for. Mamma would never allow me to leave the dinner early.

I'm sipping on some water when I feel a presence at my back.

"Will you join me for a dance?"

A cold shiver runs down my back at the sound of Rafaele's voice. I force a smile and take his offered hand. "Of course."

My head is aching as we make it to the dance floor where a few couples are already dancing.

Rafaele keeps our right hands linked and places one clinical palm over my waist. Even his touch is cold. Uninterested.

It dawns on me then that I've never really asked why he's marrying me.

Rafaele has something Papà wants, but their agreement has to provide some benefit to both of them, right? What is Rafaele getting out of this?

"May I ask you something?"

My fiancé's heavy gaze brushes over my skin. "Of course."

"Why marry me?"

The rhythm of the song picks up speed, but Rafaele's movements stay slow and steady. This is a man who does everything at his own pace, I realize. Everything and everyone else be damned.

"I need a wife."

"I understand. But why me? Surely, you had plenty of other candidates to choose from."

A single line appears between his brows. Since I can't read my future husband, my first instinct is to assume it's anger, but then his eyes flicker with what can only be confusion.

"Didn't your papa tell you?" he asks, his voice dropping low.

Now it's my turn to be confused. "Tell me what?"

For whatever reason, Rafaele's gaze flicks over to Vince, who's sitting at a table a few feet away. Something dark seeps into his expression. Something that sends a pang of worry through my heart.

"You should ask your father. It's not my place to say."

I blink. My thoughts begin to race, galloping down various paths inside my head. What did Papà promise him? It sounds like something big. "O-Okay."

We turn, and the room spins for what feels like too long. I tighten my grip on Rafaele's hand, using it as an anchor against my dizziness, but he must misread the action for something else. The line between his brows deepens.

"I'll talk to your father. This marriage is a business arrangement, and since you're a part of it, you should know the terms."

I can tell he's attempting to reassure me, but his words have the exact opposite effect. Panic rises inside of me. What did Papà sign me up for?

"May I?" A hard voice slashes through my thoughts.

Rafaele's attention moves to someone behind me. After a moment, he lets go of me without any warning.

I sway, only to feel a new pair of hands settle on me. They're warm and big, and there's nothing clinical in how they wrap around the hollow of my waist.

My eyes lift.

Ras shoots Rafaele a tight smile before moving his darkened gaze to me.

I wait until Rafaele leaves before I glare at Ras. "What are you doing?"

He's removed his tie, and the top two buttons of his shirt are now undone. Dark hair peeks out from within the white triangle of fabric. "I wanted to talk."

"We have nothing to talk about."

"What if I said I want to apologize?"

I slide my hands over his shoulders, trying not to note how hard and muscular they are. It's just to steady myself. My legs feel halfway to jelly.

"I'd assume you were lying since you haven't demonstrated any sign of a conscience," I retort.

His expression hardens. "You know, you're extremely difficult to talk to."

"Which begs the question why you insist on trying."

"Yeah," he says roughly. "I keep wondering the same thing."

I suck in a lungful of air, fighting against the nausea. Jesus, something is wrong with me. "Any hypothesis?"

Ras lowers his voice. "I'm sorry for kissing you."

I notice that he doesn't answer my question. "Apology not accepted."

His shoulders stiffen beneath my palms.

"I'm also sorry for the whole thing in New York."

"Oh, are you? It's been nearly six months."

"Better late than never, right?"

I shake my head. "If you think your two half-assed apologies are enough to smooth things over between us, I'm afraid you're way off mark."

Some color leaks out of Ras's skin. His hands tighten on my waist. "Seriously, what's your problem with me?"

"Problem with you? Didn't you conclude earlier that I'm just redirecting my anger at other people onto you?"

He studies my face. "I'm reexamining that conclusion."

There's a sharp stabbing pain inside my gut that freezes me in place. "Shit." My throat constricts, and a surge of acid comes up.

Ras's gaze flashes with concern. "Hey, are you okay?"

My fingers dig into his shoulders for support. I'm practically hanging off him now. When will this stupid song end? I need to get away from him and sit down, but I'm afraid I'll collapse as soon as I let go.

He brings his palm to the side of my neck and hisses. "*Cazzo.* You're burning up."

"I'm fine."

His eyes narrow. "Like hell, you're fine. Come on."

I'm too weak to argue. He leads me to the closest chair, hands me someone else's glass of water, and gets down on his haunches, his eyes weirdly concerned. "What is it?"

I take a gulp, wince, and put the glass back down. "I'm nauseous. Dizzy."

He stands up and glances around. "Where's Cleo?"

"I don't know." The dance floor is full now. She's probably somewhere in there. "We're not currently on speaking terms."

He slips an arm under my arm and around my back. "I'm taking you home."

I try to push him away and fail miserably. "Don't you dare."

"You need to lie down."

"I can't just skip my sister's wedding party. Mamma will kill me."

"I think your mamma would prefer you not puke in front of a hundred people." He helps me up, effortlessly lifting my entire weight with one arm.

I expect someone to stop us. To demand to know where we're going. But everyone's been drinking for hours now, and no one pays us any attention as we slip out of the restaurant and head toward Ras's car.

He helps me into the passenger side. I drop my head back against the headrest and focus on my breathing. My palms press against the supple leather of the seat. This is a nice car. I'd hate to vomit in it, even if it's Ras's.

The other door opens, and Ras gets in. He reaches over me, his scent blanketing me for a long moment while he clips in my seat belt for me.

"Vanilla. Chocolate. Burnt wood," I mutter, trying to distract myself from wanting to hurl.

He gives me a deeply concerned look. He's close enough for me to count his stupidly long lashes. "Are you hallucinating?"

"Maybe," I rasp. I'm not about to admit to him that I was just cataloging his scent.

Click.

He moves away, his hand gently grazing my waist. "We're just ten minutes away. Hang in there, all right?"

"Uh-huh." My fingers clutch the seat belt, its narrow side digging into my palm.

The car begins to move. "Do you want music?"

I shake my head.

"Do you want to talk?"

"Just drive."

"Okay." His voice is patient. It's weird to have him talk to me like this, without that mocking lilt infusing his tone.

This road is bumpy. I know it is because we went back to the house after the ceremony at the cathedral to get changed before driving to the restaurant. Ras drives carefully, but still, every few minutes the car jumps, and I have to press my palm against my mouth.

"Oh God," I groan.

"I'll pull over."

"No, just get me to the house."

I'm sweating bullets by the time we arrive, and my back is sticking to the leather seat. Ras pulls right up to the guest-house and jumps out of the car before appearing at my side.

"Okay, I've got you," he says, sliding his arm around me once again. I moan pitifully and let him practically carry me inside the house and up to the bedroom I'm sharing with Cleo.

I beeline it to the door that leads to the bathroom.

"What do you need?" he calls out after me.

I slap my palm on the doorjamb and peer at him over my shoulder. "Nothing. You've done enough."

His brows furrow. "You need a doctor."

"No. I need you to leave." The last thing I need right now is Ras watching me puke my guts out.

He gives me a slightly wounded look.

"Goodbye, Ras."

I slip into the bathroom and lock the door.

CHAPTER 10

RAS

GEMMA'S BED makes a soft groan of protest when I sit down on its edge, as if it's also trying to tell me I shouldn't be here.

Too fucking bad. I'm not leaving. There's a good chance she'll pass out on her way from the bathroom to her bed. Gemma can hate me all she wants, but while she's on our turf, her well-being is my responsibility.

I should have realized sooner that she was burning up with a fever. Maybe that's why she wouldn't give me a single damn break while I was trying to apologize.

Wishful thinking.

Here's the thing. That kiss in the kitchen was out of line. It's not every day that I admit to being an asshole, but there's no way around it. I shouldn't have done that.

She's right. If anyone had seen us, there'd have been serious consequences. Dem would've been put in a very uncomfortable situation, and our tepid relationship with Garzolo would have been put at risk.

I should have known better.

But in those minutes in the kitchen, I forgot myself.

Listening to her justify her marriage to Vale had triggered something dark in me.

Just the memory of it sends a crawling sensation over my skin. There was something so wrong with how she talked about her parents.

Does she really still buy into their bullshit even after what they did to Vale?

It makes me sick.

I thought Gemma was clever. Opinionated. Bold.

But as I listened to that conversation play out, none of it added up. She was hardheaded and so insistent on playing her part in Garzolo's theater that I couldn't shake the sense that I'd gotten her wrong.

It's like she wears all these masks and swaps them based on who's around her.

I want to find out who she is beneath them all.

But forcing that kiss on her was wrong.

My chest constricts at the memory of how disgusted she looked afterwards. What the fuck is wrong with me? I've never done that before to a woman. Never even thought to do it until I met Gemma, who I'm starting to realize has some kind of a unique ability to get under my skin.

The sound of her violent retching echoes through the door.

Cazzo. That sounds awful.

I get up and head downstairs to get the first aid kit from the kitchen. If the pills don't help, I'm calling her a doctor. I'm not taking any chances with this. I know taking care of her now won't redeem me in her eyes, but I'm not letting her suffer unnecessarily.

Pills in hand, I pop back into her bedroom. The tap runs in the bathroom while I send a quick message to Dem and Napoletano to let them know I left the party to take Gemma home because she isn't feeling well. After a moment of deliberation, I decide not to mention just how sick she is. Dem and Vale deserve to enjoy their night. Plus, I'm taking care of the situation.

The door opens just as I press send.

Gemma shuffles out in a set of blue pajamas, and when she realizes I'm still here, her tired eyes narrow. "Ras, what are you doing? I told you to leave."

Her skin has a gray undertone, and she's keeping her palm pressed firmly against her abdomen. Something squeezes inside my chest. She looks miserable.

"I'm not leaving you while you're in this state," I say. "Here, take this." I stand and give her the bottle of pills.

She snatches it out of my hand and sinks onto the bed, taking my earlier spot. "Will you leave if I take these?"

"Possibly. Here's some water."

I watch her pop two pink pills and follow them with a small gulp from the water bottle. She makes a grimace, her nose wrinkling adorably. "Even water tastes disgusting right now."

"You must have picked up a bug somewhere."

She hands the bottle back to me and stands back up with a groan. "I guess. I think it might have been some fish from earlier."

"Sit back down. You're practically swaying."

Of course, she doesn't listen to me. Instead, she walks around the bed as if to use it as a barrier between us.

Her stomach makes a loud gurgle. She winces and grabs one of the bedposts. "Honestly, why are you still here? Enjoying watching me suffer?"

Her words cut through me. "I'm really not."

"Let me rest, please."

"Lie down, and I'll leave you."

She shoots me a suspicious look. When I hold her gaze, something like fear flashes across her expression.

My stomach drops. She doesn't trust me. Is that surprising after what I pulled?

"Gemma, the kiss was a mistake," I say in a low voice. "I'm sorry."

"You already apologized."

"I promise I won't do that again."

"I don't believe you."

"Do you really think I'm that much of a liar?"

Her eyes narrow. "Yes."

"Why?" I ask, exasperated. I've never lied to her.

"Ras, I already asked you to leave. You can't be in this room when my parents return, or I'll be in deep shit. I don't want to talk to you. I don't want to see you. Thanks for bringing me here. Now, for the love of God, leave."

Of course. She's worried what it will look like if someone discovers me here with her. I'm a man who isn't a blood relative. It's bad enough we left the party alone. If I'm discovered in her room, her fuckface fiancé won't be happy.

I feel a sudden irrational urge to put that bullet through his head after all. Thankfully, he and Nero are leaving at the crack of dawn.

"Do you want me to call Cleo?"

She shakes her head. "No. Let her enjoy herself. I'll be fine."

I take a step toward the door. "All right. I'll be in the main house. Call using the landline if you need anything."

"Goodbye."

As soon as I shut the door, I let out a heavy breath and press my forehead against the wooden surface.

Well, that's that.

The next morning, I get up before everyone else. And by get up, I mean I unfurl myself off the couch in Dem's living room, wincing at the ache in the center of my spine.

I chose my spot with utmost precision. From here I could watch the guest house through the window. The Garzolos arrived about an hour after I left Gemma in the guesthouse, and it was only after I saw them enter through the front door that I finally allowed myself to get some sleep.

It's a lot of effort for a woman who wants nothing to do with me, but something prevented me from just forgetting about her. Now, that same something sends me out the door to check on the situation in the guesthouse.

I make it as far as their entryway before I'm stopped by Stefano Garzolo. Good, I can ask him for a status update on Gemma's condition.

"How's—"

"Who gave you permission to take my daughter home last night?" he interrupts, his eyes flashing with anger.

"She was about to be sick all over the dance floor. Getting permission to do the obvious thing didn't seem like a priority."

He glowers at me like I've just admitted to fucking Gemma in front of her fiancé.

The fuck is his problem? Has he even checked on her to see how sick she is?

"How is she?" I ask as I follow him into the kitchen.

"Fucking awful." He pulls a cigarette out of his pocket and grabs a lighter off the counter. "We called a doctor thirty minutes ago."

My pulse picks up. "What happened?"

"She's been vomiting all night. Cleo said she thinks she saw some blood in her puke."

My steps freeze.

Garzolo puffs on his cigarette. "We're leaving tomorrow, and there's no way we're delaying our flight."

Is he crazy? Why the fuck is he talking about his flight when his daughter is as sick as a dog?

"Vomiting blood is serious."

Garzolo walks over to the espresso machine and starts making himself one. "Only Cleo saw it, and she has a tendency to exaggerate. It's probably nothing. I have meetings back in the city, so this doctor better give her something to contain this shit show until we touch down."

My fists clench at my sides. "Is someone with her right now?"

"I would have expected some disaster like this from Cleo, but not Gemma. These fucking daughters. Always one thing after the next."

The thought of Gemma being alone right now is unbearable. "Garzolo, is someone with her, or do I need to get Valentina?"

He glances at me, taking note of my sharp tone, and his scowl deepens. "Who the fuck do you think you are?"

Fuck this. I spin on my heel and march out of there, not stopping until I'm knocking on Dem's bedroom door.

To my relief, Vale opens moments later, already dressed. When she sees my expression, her face drops. "What's going on?"

"Gemma's sick. You need to go check on her."

"What? What happened?"

"Last night she started feeling unwell. I took her home. She threw up a bunch, and now they're saying she might be throwing up blood. I just spoke to your father, and I don't know if anyone's taking care of her."

Vale nods, her lips thinning into a determined line. She brushes past me. "I'm going. Tell Dem when he comes out of the shower."

Inside their bedroom are a bunch of suitcases. Fuck, they're leaving for their honeymoon today. I'm supposed to drive them to the airport in—I check my watch—five hours.

I'm pacing their room when Dem comes out.

His brows furrow. "No offense, but you're not the person I hoped to see here. Where's my wife?"

"Checking on Gemma." Quickly, I bring him up to speed. "Her dad's being a real asshole about it," I say. "He's more concerned about his meetings than how Gemma's doing."

Dem's expression hardens. "That's not surprising. Stefano has always been a piece of shit."

"I'm sorry. I know this isn't the ideal start to your day."

"We'll do whatever is needed to take care of Gemma. Vale won't enjoy our trip if she's worried about her sister."

"I'll let you get dressed. See you downstairs."

I go down to the kitchen, make myself an espresso, and sip it while imagining ways I'll rearrange Garzolo's face if he doesn't do what's right by Gemma. Fuck him and his meetings. If he can't be bothered to wait until his daughter feels better, he can fly home on his own.

Sometime later, Vale bursts into the kitchen. She looks pale. A moment later, Dem appears behind her and grips her arm.

"What's going on?" he asks.

Vale turns to him. "Gemma's not doing well. She's burning up, can't even keep water down." She wraps her arms around herself protectively, her worry clear in her eyes.

I slam my empty espresso cup onto the saucer with a sharp crack. "Did they figure out what's wrong?"

"The doctor thinks it's a bad bout of food poisoning. For now, he's giving her an IV to make sure she doesn't get dehydrated, and he gave her some pills to take for her stomach. She needs a lot of rest. The doctor strongly advised she shouldn't travel until her fever goes down. My father's not happy about it."

"Too fucking bad," I grind out.

"That's exactly what I said." Vale walks over to the sink and pours herself a glass of water. "If the doctor says she shouldn't fly, I'm not letting her get on a plane. And there's something else."

Dem comes to stand by my side, placing his hands against the marble counter, his forehead furrowed. "What is it?"

She takes a sip of her drink before she turns to face us. I can't remember the last time she's looked this concerned.

Fuck. I get the feeling I won't like what she says next.

"Gemma fell asleep right as the doctor was leaving. When I wiped yesterday's makeup off her face, I noticed a bruise on her cheek."

There's a slow pounding in my ears. "A bruise? From what?"

"I don't know. I asked Cleo about it, but she said she doesn't know anything. She said maybe Gemma injured herself on a Pilates machine." Vale looks away from us, her gaze settling on the floor. "Cleo said she hadn't noticed it until now."

"How is that possible? They've been sharing a bedroom."

"Maybe Gemma's kept it covered under makeup."

"So she's hiding it..." I take a step closer, trying to keep the sudden rage inside me under control. Red seeps into my vision. "Valentina. Is your father—"

She meets my gaze. "My father has many faults, but he's never been violent toward us. I don't think he would do something like that."

Wouldn't he? Based on what I've seen, Garzolo doesn't exactly have a functioning moral compass as far as his daughters are concerned.

"It could just be nothing," Valentina mutters, but I know she doesn't believe that. "Gemma would have said something to me if it was serious."

Would she? I really fucking doubt it.

Dem apparently agrees with me. He steps around the counter, his face hardened like stone. "You told me she's said she doesn't want you to worry about her. Would she really be honest about something like this?"

Vale grimaces. "I don't know. I feel like I don't know anything anymore."

"We need a plan to get to the bottom of it," I say.

"I have an idea," Vale says, her gaze flicking from Dem to me. "But you probably won't like it."

"Let's hear it," Dem says.

"I told my father that until the doctor clears her for travel, we won't let Gemma leave. We got into an argument. He said that there is no way he's missing his meetings, and that my mother and Cleo have to return to New York since they're expected to meet someone my father wants to set Cleo up with. I told him in that case, they can all leave, and we'll take care of Gemma. I proposed that...Ras keeps an eye on her, and once the doctor says she's better, Ras'll take her back to New York."

The blood in my veins slows. "What?"

"It's not perfect. But..." She trails off, looking between Dem and me with hopeful eyes.

"It puts us in control," Dem mutters, his head already nodding along. "This is good."

I lift my palms up. "Hold on, does Gemma know about this idea?"

"No, not yet. I told her I'd stay behind and take care of her, but she got all stressed out. Said she'd never forgive me if I skipped out on my honeymoon for her sake. If there was any question about her recovery, I'd insist on staying, but the doctor is sure she'll be fine in a few days. I know you'll take good care of her, Ras."

A dry laugh spills past my lips. "Trust me, I have no desire to make you miss out on your honeymoon, but your idea is impossible. Garzolo will never agree to this." Not to mention Gemma. She'd throw a fit if she heard I was being left in charge of her. "He thought I overstepped when I brought her home from the restaurant, for fuck's sake. And it's not like there aren't other options. He has guards he can leave with her."

Vale shakes her head. "Those guards have proven themselves to be useless. Look how easily Cleo was able to evade them. I'm not leaving Gemma under the care of someone incompetent. Or someone who might be hitting her."

Could one of her guards be the culprit? My fists clench.

"I'll make it clear to Garzolo that he doesn't have a choice," Dem says. "You're my underboss, and the fact that I'm assigning you to this shows how seriously I'm taking the matter. It must have been our food that made her sick, right? This is our responsibility. Garzolo has to respect that, especially if he doesn't want to offend us right as we're on the cusp of expanding our deal. I will not have my wife worried on our honeymoon."

I move a step back and take measure of my boss. This is extreme, even given the circumstances. Unless...

Damiano wraps his palm over my shoulder and looks me in the eye. "Once Gemma is feeling better, you take her back to New York, and you stay there for a few weeks."

Fucking hell. I was afraid this was coming. "And what would you have me do while I'm there?"

"You know what. We need to figure out what the hell Garzolo is hiding and why Rafaele is working with him. If our deal blows up, we'll look like fools. This is the perfect opportunity to do some digging and also keep an eye on Gemma."

"How would I keep an eye on her?"

Dem smirks. "Because I'll ask Garzolo to host you. He can't say no. We're cousins, so you're his family now. Distant, but it still counts. It would be extremely fucking rude of him to send you to a hotel after you bring his daughter back to him. I'll tell him we want to get to know our American partners better so that we can get comfortable with expanding our relationship."

Vale appears to think it's a brilliant idea. Her face softens with relief. "I'll feel a lot better if there's someone in New York keeping an eye on her. Maybe that bruise really is from Pilates, but if you go with her to New York, you'll be able to find out what's going on." She glances at her phone. "Cleo just messaged me. I have to go back there. Let me know what you settle on."

She leaves, and I move away from Dem to pace the kitchen.

This is a lot to take in. I have no fucking idea how I'm going to do what Dem wants once I get to New York. I'll be on my own there. Dem and I have pulled off a lot of insane plots together, but he was always the one conducting the show.

"So what do you think?"

Uncertainty inches along my skin. But what am I supposed to say? Whine about how I'm worried I'll fail? I'm a damn underboss now. Refusing isn't an option. Not when Dem's got that determined look in his eyes that says he fully trusts me to do what needs to be done.

I've never disappointed him, and I'm not about to start now.

Dem must see the decision reflected in my expression, because he smirks. "Didn't Garzolo invite you to see how he runs things during one of our meetings?"

I huff a dry laugh. "Yeah, he did." Pretty sure he didn't think we'd be so quick to take him up on the offer.

"He can't very well take back his invitation now."

I rake my fingers through my hair. "I guess you're right."

"Then it's settled," Dem says.

"Fuck. All right. I guess I'm going to New York."

Dem comes around and slaps my back. "Good. Just remember one thing, Ras."

"What?"

"Be careful around Gemma."

I bristle, feeling very defensive all the sudden. Am I that obvious? "What's that supposed to mean?"

Dem's gaze pierces through me. "I've seen how you look at her. Just remember that she's engaged to a don, who also happens to be our business partner. There are plenty of other beautiful women in New York in case you get lonely. I'm counting on you and I don't want you to lose focus."

A heavy weight solidifies inside my gut. The fact that Dem even feels the need to say this is a problem. Of course I'm not going to lose focus.

"I know what I'm doing," I tell Dem.

But I'm not sure if I'm trying to reassure him or myself.

CHAPTER 11

GEMMA

I'M CLUTCHING the sides of the toilet as I violently heave into the white ceramic bowl.

My skin is crawling, and everything aches. I'm somehow blazing hot and ice cold.

Despite my body's efforts, barely anything's coming up. Someone's holding my hair back. I have no idea who it is. Moments ago, I woke up, my stomach clenched, and I flew off the bed in the general direction of the bathroom. There was no time to even register the time of day, let alone anyone in my vicinity.

It's Cleo, probably. If it was Mamma, she wouldn't be this quiet. Every time I've ever been sick, she's made sure to let me know it was my fault.

My knees press painfully against the cold tile floor while my entire body trembles. There's a vague awareness of having been in this position before. It feels like muscle memory.

What day is it?

My sense of time is all out of whack. Vale's wedding could have been a week ago, or it could have been yesterday.

I retch again.

No, it was yesterday. I might not be totally aware of my surroundings, but I recognize the bathroom. I'm still in the guesthouse, which means it isn't time to leave yet.

A wet towel appears in my periphery. I grab it and use it to wipe my mouth, noticing that it smells like cucumbers.

"That's nice," I mutter to Cleo, sitting back on my butt and hanging my head between my knees. "Reminds me of the spa at the Ritz."

"You'll have to take me there while I'm in New York."

My eyes fly open. That's a male's voice. And not just any male.

Ras.

I must be hallucinating. Am I dying? Am I already dead? I must have gone to hell.

That seems fundamentally unfair. It's not like I thought I'd get off scot-free given my family, but I didn't think I'd be judged this harshly.

A sob escapes me. Is this my punishment? Throwing up for eternity while—

"All right, all right. I get it. I'll go there on my own, no big deal." A warm palm lands on the center of my back and starts to move in soothing circles.

I blink at the floor, and a tear falls off my eyelash.

"Is this real life?" I ask tentatively.

"What else would it be?"

My teeth sink into my bottom lip. "Hell." It's hot enough for that to be the case.

There's a long pause and then a low chuckle. "You really think the world of me."

With effort, I lift my forehead off my knees and twist my neck to look over my shoulder.

Ras looks back at me. He's in a low squat, one arm balancing on his left knee while the other is rubbing my back.

I let out a confused groan. "I don't understand."

He drops his hand. "Come on. Let's get you cleaned up and back in bed."

If there's an opening to push him away, I miss it. Even my blinking feels sluggish.

He hooks his forearms under my armpits and hauls me up like a rag doll against his freakishly hard chest.

"Jesus, you're still burning up," he mutters as he leads me back into the room. I resist the urge to put my feet on top of his own so that he can do the walking for me too.

I'm truly pathetic at the moment.

My gaze scans the bedroom. "Where's Cleo?" Her bed isn't made, but the enormous T-shirt with Britney's face that she sleeps in isn't there either. Where's her suitcase?

"Not here."

"Get me Vale."

"She's not here either."

He turns me around and sits me down on the edge of the bed. His touch on me is firm but gentle.

When I meet his gaze, there's a graveness to it that makes a shiver of panic creep up my back. "What happened? Are they okay?"

"Vale and Dem left on their honeymoon."

They were leaving the same day we were supposed to be flying back to New York.

"When?"

"Yesterday."

An outlandish suspicion starts to build. "And my family?"

"They left yesterday too."

"They left me here."

No way.

They wouldn't.

Ras lets out a sigh and lowers to his haunches in front of me. He wraps his palms over my knees in a reassuring hold. "You're with me, Gem."

My chin starts to tremble. I know I should try to keep my emotions in, but my body is so wrung out, I'm incapable of it. "They left me?"

Ras's gaze is soft as he studies me. "Your father had...important meetings he couldn't miss."

"What about Cleo?"

Even if Papà left, she wouldn't just abandon me here.

"Cleo had to meet some guy."

"What guy?"

"A marriage prospect, from what I understand."

I rack my brain for any memory of this. Oh. Ludovico—the stodgy capo Papà promoted recently. He's been sniffing around Cleo for years. She's already threatened him once with disembowelment.

Yes, I vaguely recall Mamma mentioning something on the way over here about meeting with him. But was that meeting really so important that they chose to leave without me?

A sob bubbles up.

"Hey, you'll be okay." Ras's palms tighten on my knees. "I promise, I'll get you all better, all right?" He gets up and comes back a moment later with a tissue. "I'll go get your meds. You need to take them now."

I wait until he's out of the room before I fling myself onto the bed and weep into the pillow.

I'm so weak.

I'm in so much pain.

And my family abandoned me, leaving me with Ras of all people. Ras doesn't even work for Papà. How did Papà allow this?

After a few minutes, my tears stop, and I sit back up, clutching the bedcover in fear. There's no way this was Papà's idea. He would have dragged me on that plane even if I was delirious, which means someone stopped him from doing that.

Vale and Dem.

"Oh God."

Ras picks that moment to reenter the room. He hands me a little white pill and a glass of cool water.

I glance down at the pill. "What is this?"

"Something to get your temperature down."

When I stare at it suspiciously, Ras clicks his tongue. "For fuck's sake, Gemma. What do you think I'd give you?"

"Cyanide."

"Glad to see you're feeling better," he mutters. "If I wanted to kill you, I had plenty of opportunities to do so before you regained consciousness."

He has a point. I swallow the pill and chase it with more water.

"What did you do to make Papà leave me here?"

"Doctor's orders."

"Don't lie to me." Papà would not have let a doctor prevent me from leaving.

Ras's jaw hardens. "We told your father that you were too sick to travel and that we wouldn't allow you off the property until you've been cleared by a medical professional."

"And Papà agreed?"

"It wasn't a negotiation."

I clutch my head with my hands. "No, no, no. I'm screwed. Papà will be furious. There'll be hell to pay when I get back to New York."

God, I can't even imagine the speech I'll get from Mamma. To make myself such an inconvenience for everyone will rank high on her list of my biggest fuckups in life. And Papà won't be happy about me being the cause of Vale and Dem telling him what to do.

Shit, shit, shit!

When Ras doesn't say anything, I tear my gaze off the floor and look at him. He drags his palm over his chin and gives me a look so pregnant with meaning it makes my stomach drop.

"You mean when *we* get back to New York," he finally says in a low voice.

"What?"

"I'm taking you back. And I think I'll stay for a while."

I wake up in the middle of the night, the darkness so thick it makes me question if all light on Earth was permanently extinguished while I slept. My hands pad over the bed. They're sticky with sweat. I don't even know what I'm looking for, but when I don't find it, I start crying.

The bed dips, and there are suddenly arms around me. "Shh, you're okay." Someone's rubbing the small of my back. "Do you need to throw up?"

"No. I'm scared. It's so dark—"

A light comes on. For a moment, its appearance is so shocking that it steals my breath.

We're good. It's all good.

"Breathe, Gemma." Warm palms squeeze my shoulders. "It was just a fever dream." There's an intentional brush over my forehead. "You're still a bit hot. But at least you're not burning up like before."

That deep, pleasant voice. I know that voice.

I... I think I like that voice.

The strange, muddled thoughts inside my head take a back seat as I try to figure out who's helping me.

There's a sense of déjà vu when I find a warm hazel gaze on at me.

"Ras," I breathe.

A wry kind of amusement slips in. "Ah, so she finally recognizes me on the third time."

"Third time? What?"

"This is the third time you've woken up all worked up." He straightens my pajama top and brushes my hair away from my neck. It's all so familiar. He's done that exact thing before.

I suck in a panicked breath.

"Calm down." A glass of water appears in his hand. "Drink this."

He watches me follow his instructions, and I watch him back. This is the first time I've seen him with his hair untied, and it's beautiful. Dark-chocolate tresses hang to just over his shoulders in soft waves. He runs his fingers through it, and I have an urge to do the same, just to find out if it's as soft as it looks.

I glance down at the suddenly empty glass. "I did it?"

His lips curve into a kind smile. The type you give to cute animals and little kids. "Good job."

Confused. I'm so confused. Has he always smiled like that, or is that new? No, it's new. It was never like that when he smiled at me before.

I hiccup. "Oh no."

He brushes more hair out of my face. "What?" he asks softly.

"I hate hiccups."

"Oh." A different kind of smile plays over his lips, one he's trying to hold back. "They are annoying."

"I hate how I c-can't speak properly with them."

"We don't have to speak. Unless there's something you really want to say to me."

The next time he raises his hand to brush my hair back, I clasp it and press his open palm to the side of my face.

Amusement leaves his features, but he doesn't move his hand.

He doesn't move at all as I mirror him and cup his cheek with my own hand.

I don't see him take a single breath as I slide my hand into his hair and run my fingers through it.

My eyes fall shut from the sheer pleasure of it. "So. S-oft."

He shivers.

I tangle my fingers through that hair while he drags his thumb back and forth over my cheekbone. I'm probably giving him a bunch of knots, but he doesn't stop me. He just lets me do whatever I want to his beautiful mane.

"Gem?"

"Hmm?"

One slow swipe over my cheek.

"Who did this to you?"

What is he talking about? I should know... It's on the edge of my consciousness.

I hiccup and take my hand back. A weakness spreads through me, pulling on my eyelids, pulling me down...

"Let's get you back down. You're falling asleep."

Hands appear at my shoulders, a pillow disappears, then reappears, and then I'm being tucked in.

"How did I end up here?" I mumble.

"Beats me." Lips brush against the shell of my ear. "I'm wondering the same damn thing."

CHAPTER 12

GEMMA

I SUCK IN A BREATH, my eyelids popping open. The remnants of my dream ping-pong around my head, disjointed images of fantastical, nonsensical things. Through the window, I see the beginnings of a new day and the glimmer of the sea. I think it's dawn.

A soft snore travels across the room.

I swivel my eyes to Cleo's bed and see a large man lying there, cloaked in shadows.

My skin tightens.

Wait a second.

Oh, those dreams… They weren't… They weren't…

OH MY FUCKING GOD.

I slide up against the headboard.

Ras's ankle slips off the mattress. He's dressed in a pair of pinstriped black slacks and a white undershirt. His jacket and dress shirt are tossed carelessly over a chair by the bed.

Wait, I remember those slacks.

He wore them at Vale's wedding.

An indescribable mixture of horror, apprehension, and embarrassment solidifies right in the pit of my stomach.

I think I might throw up again, because there's no way—*no way*—Ras has been taking care of me since the night of the wedding.

My body breaks out in a sweat. I haul the covers off me, swivel on my butt, and place one unsteady foot on the floor but stop halfway with the other.

What the hell am I wearing?

Definitely not what I was wearing before. I remember the blue pajamas from when Ras straightened them out for me. I thought it was a dream, but at this point, I'm ready to acknowledge that all of my "dreams" are likely part of a nightmarish reality.

Someone changed me out of my clothes, and the only other person in the room is the most likely suspect.

Heat travels in a slow wave up my chest.

Let's add vulnerability to that mess in my gut, shall we?

I pull back the neck of the random pink T-shirt I brought with me from New York and breathe a sigh of relief when I discover that my bralette is still on. An image of Ras handling my body with those big hands, dragging a calloused thumb over the bralette's lacy edge, rudely intrudes inside my head and makes my mouth go dry.

My gaze pings back to my...my...nurse? Guard? Caretaker?

My bare toes dig into the plush carpet.

Ras has been taking care of me this whole time.

On his own.

While my family couldn't even be bothered to stay behind for a few extra days.

My heart constricts.

He doesn't even like me.

He's just doing his job. Which currently appears to be making sure I make it home in one piece.

Everything is slowly coming back to me. When he said he was taking me back to New York and was planning on staying there for a while, I think I momentarily passed out.

That actually may have been the trigger for the rest of the mess in my head.

I rub my eyes. I still don't really understand how any of this happened.

What on earth is Ras going to do in New York?

Is he going on his own? Does he know anyone there besides us? And frankly, doesn't he have better things to do here or back in Italy?

I try to run my fingers through my hair only for them to get stuck on a knot.

Knots. Hair knots.

A fuzzy memory of touching something soft, something that might be Ras's hair, finally gets me on my feet.

I need a shower.

Desperately. And not only because of the multiple layers of sweat that have dried on my body.

I need it so that I can attempt to wash away the thick, humiliating knowledge that I was my most vulnerable, deranged self around my enemy.

My gaze coasts over to the man on the other side of the room.

There are bags under his eyes and he looks like a tired mess, and yet he's still undeniably, irrefutably gorgeous.

If that's your enemy, maybe you should take a second look at your friends.

I smooth my palms over my abdomen, feeling incredibly flummoxed at the thought.

The bathroom is a mere step away when his voice halts me. "Hey."

I fold my lips over my teeth. Here we go. But I'm not a coward, so I turn to face him. "Hi."

Ras yawns and sits up on Cleo's bed. "How are you feeling?"

Confused.

My gaze follows the smooth lines of his biceps as he reaches behind his head to tie his hair.

"Like I was run over by a truck and brought back from the dead."

His eyes sweep over my body before he tips his head in the direction of the side table. "Check your temperature."

I walk over, pick up the ear thermometer, and wait for it to make two beeps before I check the screen. "Ninety-eight."

Ras frowns. "I have no idea what that means. Read the Celsius."

"Thirty-six point eight."

He nods, his profile illuminated by the sun rising on the other side of the window. "Good." He scrubs his palm against his jaw and yawns again, looking unruffled.

Like it's perfectly normal for him to wake up in the same room as me.

I grit my teeth, waiting to see which one of us will be the first to point out the absurdity of this situation.

Instead, Ras asks, "Hungry?"

I blink. Are we doing that thing where we pretend nothing out of the ordinary happened?

Okay, I can get on board with that.

"No. I'm going to shower. Maybe you should do the same."

"You saying I look like I need one?" He arches a brow, a soft grin on his stupidly handsome face.

When I don't answer because words are difficult to come by at the moment, he huffs a quiet laugh. "I probably do. Didn't want to leave you until you were on the other side of it."

Oh God.

I pull on my bottom lip with my teeth and look away. He really has been here the whole time.

Then I remember something. "Did you...take off my clothes?"

"Ah, so you noticed." He stands and grabs his jacket and shirt.

My cheeks prickle. "Ras—"

"You were soaked with sweat," he says, glancing at me from under his brows while he adjusts his hair tie. "I couldn't let you sleep like that. It would have made the nightmares worse."

I don't know what to say, so all that comes out is a strained, "Oh."

He studies me, his hazel eyes shimmering with something guarded. His voice drops lower. "I had to. I was quick."

Rough hands brushing over my bare skin, nudging my shirt over my breasts. When he sees my lacy bralette, his eyes darken.

"Do you like it?" I breathe, delirious.

He sweeps his thumb beneath the strap over my shoulder and then sighs and jerks his hand away. "Put this on."

I blink a few times, my face all hot.

That wasn't a dream either.

Something desperate rises inside of me, and its only intent is to bring us back to safer ground.

Wherever that is, it's not here. Not in this room. Not in these memories.

"Now you want me to believe you're capable of being a gentleman?" I ask.

It's as if the walls suck in a collective breath.

The air stills.

Ras's eyes flash with hurt before he gives me a withering look that fills my chest with bright, hot shame.

This is better, isn't it? The voice in my head is feeble.

"You think I'd take advantage of you while you're sick and unconscious?" His jaw hardens. "You're unbelievable, you know that?"

Is this how you thank him for what he's done for you?

I slump against a bedpost. No, this isn't right. I should apologize.

"The doctor said once your fever's gone, you're in the clear. I'm going to arrange our flight." He crosses the room with jerky steps, irritation emanating off him like a cloud. "Get yourself ready. We'll be leaving today."

"Ras—"

The door slams behind him.

I squeeze my eyes shut.

Okay, I earned that.

That man probably has my vomit somewhere on his shirt, and here I am being an asshole before he's even had a chance to change his clothes.

I'll need to fix that.

Add it to the never-ending list.

But it'll have to wait until after that shower. I move to the bathroom. A strip of light from the skylight above bisects the space. I step into it and turn to the mirror.

A gasp escapes me.

My makeup's gone.

And on my left cheek, there's a fading bruise.

~

Five hours later, I'm showered, dressed in clean jean shorts and a button-up blouse, and my things are all packed up in the trunk of Ras's car.

"We need to make a short detour to my apartment before the airport," he says gruffly as we exit the driveway of the house. Behind us, two guards draw the gate closed and wave goodbye.

I pull down the sun visor and check my reflection in the small mirror. Ras hasn't brought up the bruise he had to have seen, and that makes me nervous. I mean, it was obvious until I meticulously covered it up with makeup a few hours ago. Why hasn't he asked how I got it?

Or did he?

He seems like the type that wouldn't let something like that slide.

Another fuzzy memory surfaces briefly before I lose the thread.

My lips pinch together. It's so frustrating to only have glimpses of what happened over the last few days.

Ras would mention the bruise to Vale. She texted me earlier, checking in on how I was doing, and she made no mention of it.

It's strange.

I shift in my seat. Have they already made up their minds about what happened? That would be bad. Very bad. I need to set everything straight, but if I bring it up, I might just make it seem like a bigger deal.

If Vale finds out Papà hits me, there will be no coming back from it. Our family would be finished. It would be civil war with repercussions I can't even attempt to imagine.

When did everything get so damn complicated? So messy?

I close the sun visor with a loud snap and glance at the man beside me.

"How far is it?"

"Not far. Ten minutes."

He's so angry with me. It's been curt responses and zero eye contact ever since he came to collect me from the bedroom, and it bothers me.

A lot.

"Ras?"

Silence.

"Ras?"

His jaw hardens, but he says nothing,

"Ra—"

"What?"

"Look, I'm sorry."

"For what?"

I open my mouth and shut it, unsure how to phrase it. I settle on, "For what I said. For assuming the worst."

"It's fine, Gemma. You already made it clear what you think of me the night of Mari's wedding."

I wince. "Yes, well, things have changed since then."

"Have they?"

"It's not lost on me that you didn't have to—"

"Oh, but I did. I was just doing my damn job."

"Why didn't you ask someone else to watch over me? One of the staff?"

"I did. And then you woke up crying five minutes after I left. You were inconsolable. The staff called me back. Took me a half hour to get you to calm down."

That renders me speechless.

My bottom lip makes an embarrassing tremble as I attempt to process what he just told me. He had to comfort me for half an hour while I cried? Did I mentally revert to a five-year-old child?

What the fuck is wrong with me?

"You kept saying how you didn't want to be alone."

A bitter taste floods my mouth.

I hate being alone. It terrifies me.

I'm not even sure why. Probably some incident from my childhood that I can't remember. I don't have a lot of clear memories from when I was a kid.

So I'd lived through one of my fears with Ras watching me from a front-row seat.

But he didn't just watch.

He helped me through it, not leaving my side for two whole days, and even though I can't recall everything, I recall enough.

His gentle touch against my skin. His soothing words when I was scared.

His familiar scent.

I cup my hands over my face as a realization cascades through me.

I don't hate this man anymore.

CHAPTER 13

GEMMA

"Gemma?"

I blink, snapping out of my trance. Ras is holding the car door open, his hand outstretched, and his expression questioning. He's probably wondering what's going through my head. If only he knew.

"We're here."

It takes me a moment to process the fact that we're in an underground parking lot.

"Oh."

I give him my hand, and his warm grip swallows it for the second it takes me to hop out of the car. Something zings lightly beneath my skin, and I shiver.

"Come on. This will only take a moment."

I shake out my hand and follow behind him.

As we walk through the lot, we pass by a man with gray hair and a name tag. When he sees Ras, his face breaks into a smile, and he waves. They exchange a few friendly words in Spanish, and Ras laughs at something the man says. The corners of his eyes crinkle, and his whole face lights up.

It's...devastating.

My heart flips inside my chest.

Jesus Christ. What's wrong with me? The fact that Ras is handsome has never been lost on me, but I've always managed to ignore it. I usually filter that part of him out of my awareness.

The last few days must have broken that filter.

"You coming?"

My head snaps up to see Ras arching a brow at me. "Yep."

We get to the elevators, and Ras gestures for me to go in first. He uses a fob, presses on the button labeled A, and comes to stand by my side.

"What does the A stand for?"

"*Ático.*"

"What is that? Penthouse?"

"Yes."

"Fancy. Have a lot of guests?"

"Used to."

The elevator moves at a glacial pace, giving me plenty of time to bask in the awkwardness between us. I might no longer hate him, but Ras seems intent on drawing a clear line between us.

I never thought I'd say this, but I miss the banter. It felt far better than this cool indifference.

Ras's biceps brushes against my arm. His scent fills the tiny space.

Vanilla. Chocolate. Burnt wood.

Something tightens low inside my belly. Why does he have to smell so good?

I roll the hem of my shirt between the tips of my fingers and shoot him a sidelong glance.

He's not looking at me. He's focused on the elevator door, and a thick vein pulses in his neck.

When I let go of my shirt and accidentally brush my arm against his again, his jaw tightens.

Ding.

The door opens, and we both move at the same time.

Our bodies collide.

"Shit—"

"Sorry—"

Those big palms wrap around my shoulders, steadying me. Our eyes meet. His flash with some foreign emotion that he quickly blinks away.

"Go ahead." He nudges me forward with a tap against the small of my back.

I feel lightheaded as we step directly into his place.

My mouth parts. The apartment takes up the entire floor, but it's not the sprawling size that impresses me. It's the view. On the other side of the floor-to-ceiling glass windows lies the Mediterranean, and the peninsula of the island wraps around it like a soft embrace.

I walk across the open-plan living room and stop in front of a window. Directly below is a long promenade with bikers and pedestrians weaving through shops. Open-air restaurants pepper the area, and there's a narrow beach with a few groups of young people drinking beers and soaking up the sun. One guy's taking photos of his girlfriend while she poses like a centerfold model.

I turn around to see Ras washing his hands at the kitchen sink. "You need to eat something before our flight," he says, glancing at me.

"I'm not hungry."

He dries his hands on a checkered kitchen towel before moving to open the fridge and pull out what looks to be a bag full of groceries.

Inside are a bunch of things that he quickly lays out on the counter.

Fruit, granola bars, yogurt, crackers, and a pack of gummy bears. The real ones, not the sugar-free kind Mamma occasionally allows me to buy at the grocery store.

"Pick something."

I walk up to the counter and take the gummy bears. "Thanks."

His eyes narrow. "Gemma."

"What? You said to pick something, and I did."

He plucks the gummy bears out of my hand. "You can have these, but only after you eat something with nutritional value. You lost a lot of nutrients because of your bug."

"Does your job description really stretch this far?"

He runs his tongue over his top lip, shaking his head as he opens a drawer and takes a spoon from it. "Yes, unfortunately, it covers all kinds of unusual scenarios."

He picks up a cup of peach yogurt.

My favorite.

Next thing I know, he's handing the spoon and the yogurt to me. "Eat this."

Our eyes clash together, and I can't stand the way he's looking at me.

Cold and closed off.

There's none of the warmness from before, and the thing is, I've gotten used to it.

I've grown to like it.

And I want it back.

What do I have to do for that to happen? I've already apologized.

Frustration bubbles up inside of me. I fold my arms over my chest and shake my head.

"Do you not like this flavor?"

"I love peaches, but like I said, I'm not hungry."

He observes me with flat-lipped silence before putting the yogurt and the spoon back down on the counter. Then his hands are on my waist, and he lifts me up to sit on it, my bare thighs sliding against the cool quartz.

"Hey!"

"We don't have time for this," he growls. He opens the yogurt and brings a spoon of it right up to my mouth. "Open."

I try to slide sideways from him, but he stops me by placing a heavy palm on my thigh. Warmth spreads over my skin, and my pulse stutters. I wrap my lips over my teeth and shake my head.

Ras glares at me with utter exasperation. "Gemma."

He touches the spoon to my lips, but I jerk my chin up, and the yogurt goes flying. My eyes widen as it lands in a light orange splatter across his shirt. A beat passes, during which darkness seeps into his gaze. I should be worried, but instead, all I feel is a thrill at breaking past the wall of ice.

It doesn't suit him.

Slowly, he puts the spoon on the counter, and flattens his palm against the smooth surface, his thumb accidentally brushing against the side of my bare thigh. He steps closer, forcing me to part my knees to make room for him. My head spins from his proximity, and the few inches between us swirl with electricity.

"If your fiancé knew how feral you are, he'd demand a refund," he growls. His face is so close, I can make out a tiny scar on his right cheek. "He thinks he bought himself an obedient wife, when what he's really getting is a brat."

I suck in a breath, searching for a response that will keep him here for a little longer. "I guess it'll be a nice surprise for him on our wedding night."

I regret it immediately, because his expression turns deadly.

He reaches for something behind me—the yogurt—and says, "If you insist on acting like a wild animal, I'm going to treat you like one." He dips his finger inside the cup, brings it to my lips, and squeezes my jaw with his other hand, forcing my mouth to open.

He slides his finger inside my mouth.

A hard pulse appears in my neck before making a slow slide through my body to settle between my legs. The taste of peaches and something more decadent fizzles over my taste-buds, and before I think twice about it, I close my mouth around Ras's finger and suck.

A slight tremor runs through him, his gaze molten as he watches me. I pull my head back and give the tip of his finger a quick lick as it pops out of my mouth.

He drops his hand to his side and does nothing for a long moment, during which nerves skitter over my spine.

We can only pretend we're not crossing a line if we're both in on it. If he points it out right now, there's a chance I'll combust and die from embarrassment.

My teeth dig into my bottom lip. "I—"

He doesn't let me finish. He moves quickly, as if intent not to let me get the next word out, and puts his peach-flavored finger in my mouth again.

The room spins and darkens as I suck the yogurt off him. His mouth parts on a quick breath, his body visibly tense.

"Stronzo! Stronzo!"

The sudden high-pitched noise makes us break apart. He takes his finger out of my mouth and takes a step back as I slide off the counter.

We stare at each other for a long moment.

Finally, I ask, "What the hell is that?"

"That's Churro," Ras says, turning away from me before... adjusting his pants?

A thrill zings up my spine.

"My parrot," he adds.

My mind struggles to catch up. "Your *what*?"

"My parrot," he says as he makes his way across the kitchen toward where the noise came from.

I follow. "Why do you have a parrot?"

"He's a pet." He glances down and mutters, "I need to get a new shirt."

I watch as Ras grasps the back of his T-shirt with one hand and pulls it over his head, flashing me his tanned, muscular back before he disappears into another room.

I swallow and keep following him.

The room seems to be his bedroom. The blinds are nearly fully drawn, casting the room in shadows.

Ras grabs a shirt out of a drawer and slips it on. "Churro doesn't like it when it's bright, so I keep him here," he explains nodding toward the corner of the room where there's a large bird cage.

I look around, still reeling from the last few minutes. There's a large bed with a modern-looking bed frame, a leather armchair with a stack of books beside it, and a desk.

Ras lifts the blinds a little, and the grays of the room suddenly transform into shades of blue.

I move closer and peer into the bird cage. It's got multiple levels connected with all sorts of ladders, and toys and feeders hang off the bars. Inside, a green and yellow parrot the size of my forearm stares at me with one orange eye.

"Pretty girl! Pretty girl!"

"He says that to every woman," Ras says. "Don't let it get to your head."

I glare at him. "Why do I have a feeling you're lying? I'm going to think I'm special until I see evidence proving otherwise, thank you very much."

Ras's lips quirk up. He taps against one of the bars, and the parrot hops over to peck his finger. Something soft bleeds into his expression. "He's a little Casanova."

"I have so many questions." If I'd had to guess what kind of pet a guy like Ras would have, a parrot wouldn't even make it in the top ten possibilities.

"I'm sure." There's that familiar sarcastic lilt to his voice.

"How long have you had him?"

"About three years. He was supposed to be a gift for Mari, but Dem categorically refused to let him live with them." Ras jingles one of the toys. "I liked the little guy, and I didn't feel like returning him. He's an Amazon parrot. They live for fifty, sixty years, and they're really smart."

The parrot cocks his yellow head. *"Fuck off!"*

"And all you taught him is how to swear and compliment women?"

Ras looks down at me, a grin teasing at his lips. "The most critical skills, don't you think?"

I roll my eyes, but I'm smiling.

Ras checks the watch on his wrist. "I've got to pack. Churro will keep you company. Someone's picking him up in just a few minutes."

He disappears inside a walk-in closet, and I refocus my attention on the parrot, playing with him for a few minutes by tapping on the cage and jingling his toys. He makes happy little squawks. When he hops down to the feeder and starts to peck at it, I let him eat in peace and resume my study of Ras's room.

There's something profoundly intimate about being in a man's space.

Especially his bedroom.

Especially after I just had his fingers inside my mouth.

A shiver runs down my spine. I like being here, and I shouldn't. The only man who's bedroom I should want to be in is my fiancé's.

God, what's happening to me? I'm becoming entirely too interested in Ras.

The room smells like him. I walk over to a set of drawers and study the things scattered over the surface. There's an ornate metal box that I peek inside—cigars—and a leather caddy with some of his jewelry. I put one of his rings on my finger, confirming that Ras's ring size is nearly twice as large as mine.

I'm about to open a thin black notebook when I stop myself.

What am I doing?

I rub my palms over my arms, suddenly feeling awkward, and walk back out into the living room.

When my gaze lands on the half-empty cup of yogurt, my skin heats.

A sound pulls my attention to the front door just in time to see it open and a woman emerge.

I halt. "Hello?"

She notices me. She's dressed in a tiny skirt and a bandeau top that reveals a toned tummy and tanned skin. Her blond hair drapes over her chest in full, luxurious curls, the kind that take ages to style.

I stiffen. *Who is this?*

The woman makes a quick assessment of me, and her red lips curl into a sharp smile. "Hi. Is Ras here? I'm here to pick up Churro."

"Yeah. He's in the bedroom." I gesture at the door behind me.

"Oh, I know where that is. I've been here before."

Irritation crawls up my spine that she felt the need to make sure I knew that. "Sorry, who are you?"

"Isabella," she says, sauntering toward me, her hand outstretched. "And you must be the sick girl he has to take to New York."

Is that how Ras described me? I give her a stiff smile. "That's me."

"You do look a little rough." Her nose wrinkles. "It's not contagious, is it?"

My grip turns crushing. "I guess you'll know soon enough."

She jerks her hand back, gives me a scowl, and disappears into the bedroom.

I hear Ras's voice, deep and rumbling. They exchange greetings, and I try to tune them out, not wanting to intrude on their conversation. But then I hear her laugh, and I can't help but peek around the corner to catch a glimpse of them.

She's standing close to Ras, her hand on his chest, and I feel a pang of something unpleasant.

I tear my gaze away. It's none of my business.

Still, I feel relieved when they appear in the living room only a few moments later, Ras carrying Churro in a smaller cage in one hand and a leather duffel bag in the other.

"*Pretty girl! Pretty girl!*" Churro squawks at Isabella.

My nose wrinkles. Traitor.

Ras looks at me. "Ready, Peaches?"

That nickname is so unexpected, it renders me momentarily mute. I blink at him. "Yes."

"I'll miss you," Isabella croons, running her fingertips over his biceps. "You'll let me know as soon as you're back, right?"

Ras tears his amused gaze away from me and nods at her. "Of course. You know I hate leaving him behind."

Her face falls. Clearly, that wasn't the response she was hoping for, but she picks herself back up in a flash. "I'll take good care of him." She lifts herself on her tippy-toes and leans toward Ras's ear. "And when you're back, I'll take good care of you too," she whispers, loud enough for me to hear every word.

My cheeks burn. Are they hooking up?

He gives Isabella a terse smile and hands her Churro's cage. "Thanks, Bella. Text if anything comes up."

We make an awkward procession as we head toward the elevator together. Isabella switches to Spanish, whispering something to Ras on the ride down, while I wrack my brain for a good reason to be bothered by any of this.

There's none.

I'm the one who's engaged.

The scene in the kitchen suddenly gets colored in a completely different light.

I must be going crazy. What am I doing with him?

He says a quick goodbye to Isabella, and we get into the car.

"Are you okay?" Ras asks as he starts up the engine.

"You never said you have a girlfriend."

"She's just a friend."

I give him a skittish glance and resolve not to probe any further. There's no point. I can reasonably excuse the confusing events of the last seventy-two hours on being horribly ill. Once we're in New York, I'm sure I'll barely even see him.

CHAPTER 14

RAS

DAMIANO'S PLANE lands at an FBO in JFK at midnight.

Gemma's asleep on my shoulder, her dark-brown, nearly black locks splayed over my dress shirt, and her scent in my nose. It usually takes more than that to turn me on, but here I am, sporting a hard-on for the last hour.

What happened in the kitchen might have something to do with it too.

I prop my elbow on the armrest and press my fist to my lips as I recall the memory in excruciating detail.

Fuck me.

Seeing that hot little mouth sucking on my finger was enough to make me forget myself. If it wasn't for Churro, I'm certain we would have ended up with her splayed on the counter, my mouth between her legs, and my tongue buried deep inside her pussy.

Which would have been really fucking stupid.

But unfortunately, I have a history of doing very stupid things.

Especially when those things look like Gemma Garzolo.

A part of me thought that taking care of her while she's sick would work the attraction out of me, but if anything, it's made it stronger.

Those two days with her shook something inside of me. Made me see her in yet another light.

Seeing her so scared and vulnerable made my chest ache. There was no pretense to uphold when she was puking in the toilet, or when she woke up gasping in fear from her dreams. She came to me so easily. All of her hardness melted away, and I wanted nothing more than to take away her pain.

I give my head a slight shake.

It may have been easy to forget she's engaged when we were back in Ibiza, but there will be no escaping that fact in New York.

I can't let whatever the fuck is going on between Gemma and I interfere with the task Damiano gave me, which is figuring out what Garzolo and Messero might be hiding from us. I need to play everything very carefully. Garzolo thinks I'm coming here to get a better sense of their operations. At least that's what Dem told him. He also dangled a carrot by suggesting I'm looking for other opportunities to do business together.

It's a diplomatic mission.

The pilot makes an announcement over the PA to let us know we're taxiing to the customs area, and Gemma stirs.

"Shit," she mutters. "Why didn't you move me?"

Because I fucking like you there.

Instead, I say, "Don't worry about it."

We get off the plane to show our documents to a miserable-looking agent and then make our way to area where they're scanning our baggage.

She looks around, her expression tense. I can't decide if it's because she regrets what happened back in Ibiza, or because of something else.

"Happy to be home?" I ask once we've collected our suitcases.

Her response is a non-committal shrug. Given what I've observed of her parents, I doubt they have a particularly happy home life.

It was pretty shitty of them to leave her back in Ibiza. It might have only been three days, but that girl went through hell and back. Something strangely protective stirs inside of me. That bruise on her face was hard to look at.

And by hard, I mean it made me homicidal.

Who the fuck would raise a hand to her? Vale said it couldn't have been their dad, but who else? Even if Garzolo didn't do it himself, someone may have done it on his orders.

Or maybe there's a made man with a death wish roaming around.

Well, no matter. I'll find out who it was, and I'll make them pay. Now that I'm here, no one's going to touch a hair on her head.

"So where are you going?" she asks me as we walk toward the exit.

Oh, right. She doesn't know I'm staying with them.

I grin at her. "A few rooms over, I suppose."

Her steps slow. "You're staying...in our house?"

"Where else would I stay but with family?"

Her eyes turn wide and worried. "You're not my family."

"I'm Dem's cousin. He's your brother-in-law. We're family, Peaches."

Although what I want to do to her is decidedly not familial in nature.

Her hand shoots out and wraps around my bare wrist. "Papà is letting you stay with us?"

My gaze drops to where she's touching me. She immediately lets go, and a blush spreads over her cheeks. "Sorry. I'm just shocked."

You never have to apologize for touching me. The words are on the tip of my tongue, but I bite them back. "Don't worry. He's expecting me."

Garzolo's driver is waiting for us just outside in a black Suburban. He introduces himself to me as Armando Vitale. Gemma appears to know him, but not well, judging by their curt greeting and the guarded expression on her face. I look for any hint of fear and find none.

Still, I dislike him immediately. No particular reason. Just his vibe.

"Your father wanted me to let you know that I'll be your security detail until your wedding," Armando says. I guess the two guys they brought to Ibiza got sacked for spending more time drinking from Damiano's wine collection than keeping an eye on the girls.

"You've been working for Garzolo for a while?" I ask.

"About a year," he says, patting his pockets for a lighter.

A year? That's nothing. There's no way he's made. If I had to guess, he's someone's useless cousin who's spent the last few decades failing at whatever he was doing, and he's begged to be brought in.

We reach Manhattan, where despite the late hour, throngs of cars are stuck in slow-moving traffic. Everyone's honking at each other as if it'll make things go faster.

I drag my palm over my beard. It's overdue for a trim. "This place is a zoo."

"Have you spent a lot of time here?" Gemma asks.

"No. Just a few short trips."

"So you don't know anyone?"

"I have a few acquaintances." Just one, actually.

I already have a meeting set up with him, courtesy of Kal Parasyris, a Greek that runs his own version of the Cosa Nostra up in a tiny village in Crete. Zoriana? Zoniana? I always get the name of that place wrong. Kal's been one of our weapons suppliers for years, and he's got a cousin, Orrin Petraki, out here in Brooklyn, running what they call "the Greek Crew." Kal made him sound like a small fish in a big pond, but if I know anything about the Greeks, it's that they're hustlers. I'm going to try and get Orrin to help me figure out what the fuck is really going on with Garzolo.

That's as far as I've gotten in terms of having a plan to accomplish the mission Dem gave me. It's not much, but it's better than winging it.

Gemma doesn't ask any more questions. She stares out the window for the rest of the long drive, her skin pale.

"You okay?" I ask when the car stops. We're in New Jersey now, in a neighborhood right on the Hudson River. The streets are lined with dense rows of bare-branched trees and thick pines. Must look nice in the summer.

"Just tired," she says, but it rings false. Her whole demeanor changed when we stepped off the plane. She's smaller somehow, anxiety practically emanating off her.

It gives me pause.

We get out of the car, and *holy fucking shit*. It's freezing cold out.

I pull my jacket tighter around me. Fucking February. This has got to be the worst possible month to be here.

My breaths come out in misty puffs as I take in the red-brick house in front of me. It's enormous—three sprawling stories with an array of arched windows. It's kind of traditional looking. There's a separate garage to the right, big enough for at least six cars, and on the left is a tennis court.

The wind picks up, sending a shiver through me. "Jesus Christ."

"Not used to this?"

I glance at Gemma, who's come to stand by my side. The lamps on the front of the house send light scattering across her rosy cheeks. She seems to be dealing with this temperature far better than me despite only wearing a hoodie.

"Can we go inside?" I ask through chattering teeth.

Amusement flickers in her eyes. "Such a baby."

"More like I want to have babies one day, but I won't if my balls freeze off out here."

This earns me a laugh. "Come on. I've got the key."

As soon as we get inside, I sigh with relief. Much better. I've never been this grateful for central heat.

We're standing in a grand foyer that opens up to a large living room with a crackling fireplace. To the right is a staircase leading to the second floor, and to the left is the kitchen.

Armando comes in behind us and opens a shallow cabinet attached to the wall. Inside is a row of hooks with keys hanging off them. He hooks his car keys on an empty one and closes the cabinet.

We get about four steps in when Gemma's mother emerges from the shadows. She's wrapped in a long house robe and her hair is tied back in a braid. You'd think she'd rush over to give her recently ill daughter a hug, but instead, all she gives Gemma is a critical look.

I hear Gemma's intake of breath. "Mamma."

Pietra examines Gemma for a moment before pressing a chaste kiss to her cheek. "You look terrible."

"It was a long journey."

"Your father wants to speak with you."

Gemma's shoulders tense up. "I'm really tired. Can't it wait until tomorrow?"

Pietra shakes her head. "Go, Gemma. He stayed up waiting for you."

I grind my teeth. Gemma's legs are barely holding her weight, and she's still weak from her illness.

"Mamma, please."

Any normal mother would back off, but I'm starting to realize that Pietra is far from normal. When she opens her fucking mouth to argue, I step in.

"Mrs. Garzolo, the doctor instructed Gemma to take it easy for the next few days. It's past one am. She needs to lie down and get some rest."

Both of the women look at me, one cautiously grateful and the other annoyed.

It doesn't take a mind reader to know what Pietra is thinking. I'm in her house, and I don't make the rules here. But I hold her gaze, challenging her to voice that thought.

I don't give a fuck where we are. Gemma's wellbeing is my priority, and I'm not going to let her mom get away with being a cunt.

There's a long pause before Pietra finally says, "First thing tomorrow. Go to your room Gemma." Her eyes narrow on me. "He'll speak with you right now."

I'm tempted to make a comment about their shitty hospitality—we've been traveling for nearly fifteen hours—but I swallow it down. I knew that I wasn't exactly going to be welcomed with open arms. Garzolo is only hosting me due to obligation.

Gemma locks eyes with me for a brief moment, looking almost apologetic.

I shrug. She has nothing to apologize for.

I don't get a chance to say goodnight before Pietra's gestures for me to follow her and I'm led away.

My eyes fly open, and I don't need to check the clock to know that definitely wasn't the recommended eight hours of sleep.

Fuck jet lag. Why haven't they developed pills for it by now?

I groan as I sit up. The clock on the wall tells me my bed and I have been acquainted with each other for a grand total of three hours.

It's five am.

I thought I was going to fall asleep in Garzolo's office when he kept me there for an hour after we arrived. The conversation was essentially him attempting to figure out why I was really here. I repeated three times the same thing Dem had already told him. That we were just taking a look at his operations and seeing if there's an opportunity to collaborate on more things. He finally accepted that was all he was getting from me and let me leave.

I hop out of bed and take a quick shower before slipping on my warmest clothes, which is a gray Italian wool suit I somehow had the foresight to pack with me. Actually, it's probably the warmest thing I own, period. Living in Ibiza and Southern Italy, I don't exactly need a robust winter wardrobe.

There's no way around it, I'll need to do some shopping soon, or I'll slowly succumb to hypothermia.

Garzolo would probably like that.

I despise shopping, but I'm willing to do it if it'll keep a smile off that fucker's face.

First, I have a more pressing problem to address. I need to figure out how I'm going to keep an eye on Gemma when she's out of the house. I need to be around her. After all, I promised Vale I'd find out the real story behind that bruise.

The most straightforward option would be to somehow convince Garzolo to let me be her bodyguard and driver while I'm here.

Problem is, she already has one of those.

Armando Vitale.

So step one is to get rid of that prick. Step two is to figure out how to convince Garzolo I'm the right man for the job.

I leave my bedroom and wander around the house for a bit, getting familiar with the layout. I do this every time I stay in a new place. The last thing you want is for a bit of trouble to come up and not know where all the exits are.

Once I've cataloged it all away, I pop into the kitchen for an espresso.

While I wait for the coffee machine to grind the beans, I grab a newspaper from the counter. A headline catches my eye. *"US Attorney General Vows to Continue Fight Against Organized Crime."*

A smile pulls at my lips. Whether in Italy or the United States, they always vow this kind of thing. Back home, it rarely amounts to anything. How can it, when we have most of the elected officials in our pocket? We budget each year for that shit.

I grab one of the small cups lined up by the coffee machine and get the espresso going. When it's ready, I take it up to my room to drink.

There's a big arched window in my bedroom. On the other side, it's still so dark, you can see the stars above. I'm hovering by the windowsill, trying to make out the cars Garzolo has parked out front, when the glare of a phone screen catches my eye.

I squint. Did someone just walk out the side door of the house?

It's hard to see who it is, but the shape and height implies it's a man. He's too tall to be Garzolo so...

Shit, that's Vitale.

What's he wearing? No winter coat, that's for sure. Hold on. He's dressed like he's about to go for a run. A subtle rush creeps up my spine. The kind that comes with a good idea.

I wait until I see what direction he goes in, and then I leave my bedroom once more and quietly slip through the house until I get to the foyer.

I open the cabinet I saw Vitale put his keys in last night and take out the one for the Suburban.

Freezing cold air slams into me as soon as I step outside. My jaw snaps shut, and I hurry to the damn car. This weather is a fucking nightmare. How do people survive here?

It doesn't take me long to find Vitale. I grin. He's not even wearing any reflective clothing. Doesn't he know that's the smart thing to do when running while it's dark out?

My foot presses on the gas. I'm worried he'll hear me approach, but the man's oblivious. Listening to music probably.

It all comes together like a symphony.

The car rams into him. He yelps, flies over the windshield, and then his body crashes to the ground with a dull thud.

I get out of the car and go to check on him. He's knocked out, but there's a steady pulse. He might not be able to walk for a while, but he'll be okay. It's not the worst thing I've done by a long shot. I pat his shoulder and then get back inside the car.

A grin plays on my lips.

This trip is off to a good start.

I make it back to Garzolo's a whole hour before the rest of the house wakes up,

CHAPTER 15

GEMMA

THE MORNING after Ras and I return, I wake up feeling tired and groggy.

I'd expected a full interrogation from Mamma last night, but she let me go to bed after only taking my temperature and asking if Ras behaved himself around me.

I assured her that he did. Actually, I lied and said he only had to check in on me a few times, even as I shivered at the memory of his hands on my skin.

I think I'm...developing an attraction to him. It's the only thing that would explain why what happened in his kitchen made my body feel hot all over.

How did I go from hating him to feeling *this*—whatever this is—in the span of a few feverish days?

He's still the same cocky Camorrista who stole a kiss from me at Martina's wedding. I wasn't attracted to him then, was I?

I bite down on my lip. Even then, I felt something when he kissed me.

I swipe my palm over my brow. There's really no point in ruminating on my feelings for Ras. I'm an engaged woman, and he is a temporary guest who'll probably be out of here sooner than later. Plus, my schedule before the wedding is busy. I'll mostly be out of the house, so I'll hardly see him.

Now that I'm back in New York, my imminent future is a shadow looming over me. My gaze drifts to the calendar hanging on the wall and the date that's circled with a red pen. There are five weeks left until I become a married woman.

I go to take a shower and get dressed. Cleo barges into my room while I'm brushing my hair and asks me a million questions about how I'm feeling. I assure her that I'm all better and we head downstairs for breakfast.

As soon as we enter the dining room, I pick up on the weird atmosphere. My parents are already sitting down with Ras. His gaze jumps to me when I walk in, but he quickly slides it back to Papà.

"Are there any cameras in the area?" he asks.

"Not on the streets. We had them taken down years back," Papà grumbles, taking a sip of his coffee. "The idiot was wearing dark clothing while it was pitch black out."

"What are you talking about?" I ask as I take my seat.

"There was a car accident," Mamma says, her expression drawn. "Someone ran over Armando this morning."

My eyes widen. "What? Is he okay?"

"Four broken ribs, one broken leg, and a concussion." Papà sneers.

Ouch. "Who was the driver?"

"It was a hit and run."

I frown. That's strange. Our neighborhood is as safe as it gets.

Mamma shakes her head. "I'd bet anything it was one of the Nelson boys. One of them has supposedly developed a drug problem."

"I'm going to look into it," Papà says, "But in the meantime, Armando is out of commission for at least a few weeks, and the timing couldn't be worse. I have eight of my guys tied up across the border with the Mexicans this month, and you know it's our busy season." He moves his attention to me. "I'm going to have to ask Joe to drive you around."

Cleo groans. "Joe's half blind. Didn't he get his license taken away?"

"He's fine as long as it's light out," Papà says, but Mamma frowns.

"Cleo's right, Stefano. The last accident he got into was in broad daylight. I don't want to risk it."

"You drive Gemma then," Papà snaps.

Mamma's eyes narrow on her husband. "Gemma's schedule conflicts with the things I have going on with Cleo. Her classes are important."

I take a sip of my coffee. Mamma's doing everything she can to make Cleo seem eligible despite the whole lack-of-virginity thing.

"We can cancel the classes until Gemma is wed," Cleo offers helpfully, giving me a meaningful look. "I don't mind."

Mamma breaks the shell on her egg. "Of course you don't mind. Your piano playing is atrocious, Cleo, as are your table manners."

I glance down at my sister's plate. She's gotten flakes of her croissant all over the tablecloth.

"Until you demonstrate at least some semblance of being a lady, you're not missing a single class. Especially not after you completely embarrassed me in front of Ludovico."

I make a note to find out about what happened there when Ras clears his throat. "I can drive Gemma. My schedule is flexible while I'm here."

My eyes snap to him. No way. The last thing I need is to confuse myself more by spending hours alone in a car with him.

I clear my throat. "That's really not—"

"That's a generous offer," Papà interrupts. "But you're our guest. I can't put you to work like that."

"Nonsense," Ras says. "It would only be a few hours a day. Dem and Vale instructed me to do everything I can to ensure Gemma's recovery, and if I'm being honest, I think she's still a bit unwell."

I glare at him, my eyes communicating that I'm perfectly fine.

"She does look a little pale," Cleo says.

My irritation spikes. Does Cleo think she's helping me? Probably. She has no idea what happened between me and

Ras. She smiles and pops a piece of croissant into her mouth.

I try again. "Papà—"

"Are you going to be comfortable driving in the city?" he asks Ras, ignoring me.

Ras nods. "Piece of cake. Trust me, I'll keep her safe."

"It's settled then." Papà gives Ras a close-lipped smile before turning to me. The look on his face tells me his decision is final. "Give your schedule to Ras, Gemma."

Frustration simmers inside me. Is my opinion completely irrelevant? It's me he'll be driving. But I know what'll happen if I start arguing at the dinner table. Papà will shut me down, and I'll still be stuck with Ras as my driver.

I clench my fists under the tablecloth. "Tomorrow, I have a private shopping appointment. It'll probably be super boring and take a long time."

Ras's gaze sparks. "Perfect. I need to stock up on clothes. Didn't pack for an arctic climate."

Hmm. How convenient.

"What time is the appointment?" he asks.

"Noon. Manhattan."

Ras reaches inside a bowl on the table and takes a moment to pick out a cup of yogurt.

When he finally decides on one, heat travels down my chest in a slow wave.

Peach.

He glances at me from beneath his brows as he tears open the cup, his expression pure innocence if it weren't for the flash of wickedness inside his eyes. "We'll leave at eleven to beat the traffic."

The next day, I step through the front door at eleven sharp.

Ras is already waiting inside the car, and when he sees me, he hops out to open the passenger door.

I clench my teeth. A part of me hoped he'd be late so that I could complain to Papà about his punctuality and insist on getting Blind Joe as my driver.

Yes, I'd rather risk an automotive accident than spend the next few weeks in Ras's orbit.

I'm scared. Scared I'll do something stupid around him.

Scared that my attraction might develop into a full-grown crush and make the next five weeks even harder than they are already going to be.

No matter how hard I try to tap into my previous dislike of Ras, I can't seem to do it.

Not after he spent days nursing me back to health.

And not after what happened in his kitchen.

Last night, I had a dream about him. We were on a bed, and I was feverish, my back pressed against his front. He dragged a cool washcloth over my neck and then dipped it down over my chest. It was at that moment in the dream that I realized I wasn't wearing any clothes. The washcloth slid between my breasts, over my abdomen, and down between my legs where everything felt so sensitive that I couldn't help but moan. Lips pressed to the side of my neck, and a familiar voice asked. "Are you wet for me, Peaches?"

I woke up then, aroused and sweaty and in desperate need of a release.

I've never lusted after a man like that before, and there's a flicker of guilt at the back of my mind. After all, I'm engaged to marry someone else in just a few weeks. Even though I don't love Rafaele, it still feels wrong to be having sex dreams about another man.

I swallow and glance over at Ras. His long hair is neatly pulled back at his nape in a loose man-bun, and he's trimmed his beard. His tanned hands flex on the wheel as he takes us out the neighborhood, following the GPS. One of the rings he's wearing is the one I tried on in his bedroom. The realization makes something hum beneath my skin.

"Ras, what are you really doing here?" I ask, unable to keep an exasperated note from slipping into my voice. "Whatever it is can't be that important if you're willing to spend all this time chauffeuring me around."

"Did your papa tell you to ask me that?"

"No." I frown. "Why would he?"

"He didn't seem to believe me when I told him I'm here on a diplomatic mission to get to know our American partners a little better."

"What does that mean?"

"It means that when Damiano commits to doing a deal as big as what we're considering doing with the Messero and

Garzolo clans, we need to be sure the two of them can deliver what they promise."

The line sounds rehearsed, but the gist of it makes sense, I guess. It doesn't sound so unreasonable, although I can see why Papà wouldn't like it.

If that's what Ras is here for, why is he so eager to volunteer to drive me around?

Something is off with all of this.

I have a feeling it has something to do with the bruise on my face. Vale still hasn't brought it up, and I know my sister. She wouldn't let something like that go.

Is Ras here to also keep an eye on me?

I guess I should be grateful if Vale did ask him to do that. Papà isn't stupid enough to hit me while Ras is staying at our house.

I'm safe from him for the time being.

But there is a new threat. The one posed by the man in the driver's seat.

Maybe I need to remind myself of all his flaws so that I can nip this crush in the bud.

He's arrogant and shameless.

He's unable to stand the cold. As in, he's a total baby about it. A smile tugs at my lips at how miserable he looked last night.

I scan him. Even now, he isn't dressed for the weather. He's wearing a wool suit and a crisp gray button-up, but no coat. The heat in the car is on full blast. He really didn't pack for a New York winter, did he?

What other flaws does he have? Have I ever seen him ruffled by anything?

A memory resurfaces. "Tell me how you got your nickname."

By the way his brows furrow, I can tell he wasn't expecting that to come out of my mouth.

"Why?" he asks suspiciously.

"Just curious. Does Ras mean something?"

He switches into the fast lane. "In the system, it means someone with authority who still reports to a higher boss."

That makes sense. After all, he reports to Damiano. "So Dem gave it to you?"

He shifts in his seat. "No, I've been called that since I was sixteen."

"How come?"

There's a subtle shift in the mood inside the car. His profile hardens, and I get the distinct sense that I'm wading into something uncomfortable.

He hesitates for a while before finally answering. "I got it from a kid in my class," he says in a low voice. "We didn't get along. I did something I shouldn't have, and that started a war between us. He gave me that nickname as a way of humiliating me."

Whatever I was expecting, it was not that. My nails dig into the soft flesh of my palms. "What did you do to him?"

"I stole his new motorcycle and crashed it. His parents worked for my father's business, and they had saved up for years to buy it. It was a bad thing to do," he admits, dragging a thumb over his bottom lip. "And Nunzio made sure I paid for it."

"Did he beat you up?"

Ras huffs a humorless laugh, like there's far more to it. "Yeah."

I rake my gaze over his powerful, muscular body. "I have a hard time imagining that."

"I didn't look like this back then. I was a skinny kid. As son of the area capo, I could have told my father about it all and gotten Nunzio taken care of, but that would have been admitting that I couldn't handle the situation on my own. I was too proud for that. So I took his beatings for nearly two years until he finally decided to deal the final blow the night of our graduation."

Ice slips inside my veins at his tone. A foreboding of something terrible. "What did he do?"

He clears his throat. "His friends held me down while he tried to slit my wrists in the playground behind our school. They wanted me to bleed out slowly, so that I'd feel myself go. They almost managed to do it, but then one of the teachers came out to have a smoke and saw them."

Horror wraps around my throat and squeezes as we pull into the parking lot of the department store. I turn to look at Ras. His profile is a mask. There's no hint of what he's thinking or feeling.

Suddenly, I'm at a loss of what to say.

He could have died.

My chest squeezes with the need to comfort him, even if this happened long ago. I can't imagine how traumatic that must have been. To be held down like an animal while someone cut up your veins.

My stomach lurches. "Ras, I'm so sorry."

He doesn't say anything as he parks the car. When he turns off the ignition, I reach over and wrap my palm around his wrist.

He freezes. Stares at where I'm touching his skin.

Gently, I pull his arm toward me. Dark ink seeps out from under his sleeves, and when I push the sleeve up, I see it. There's a thin scar about three inches long right in the center of his wrist. The tattoos wrap around it without crossing over even once. It's like he made a point to make it stand out.

"Why not cover it up?"

"I want to remember it."

I drag my thumb over the scar, and he shivers in response. Slowly, I lift my gaze to meet his. "Tell me you killed him."

A fire burns inside his eyes. He takes his hand back and says, "Not yet."

CHAPTER 16

GEMMA

WE WALK into the department store, Ras's story looping over and over in my head.

My heart clenches at the realization that he trusted me with something deeply personal. When I asked the question about his nickname, I was searching for a flaw. Instead, it feels like I found a strength. Made men don't like to show their vulnerabilities. In fact, they like to pretend they don't exist. But somehow, seeing Ras embrace his, makes him all the more impressive in my eyes.

We get off the escalator, and I realize people are staring at us. Two elderly ladies stop to whisper to each other, their eyes on Ras.

Ras notices and frowns. "Something on my face?"

I bite down on my lip, because how do I explain to him that he's too damn handsome for his own good? He fit in better in Ibiza among all the other tanned Spaniards and Italians, but here, he stands out.

A group of high school girls walk by us, hearts in their eyes, and burst into giggles when Ras gives them a smile.

He stops, looking back at them over his shoulder with a confused expression before turning back to me. "Seriously, is there?"

"No, there's nothing on your face. You just..." I wave a hand in his general direction.

"What?"

I pluck at his vest. "They think you're handsome. And you're all exotic with your tan and long hair and tattoos."

Realization cascades over his features, and then his lips turn up into a self-satisfied smirk. "You know, I'm starting to like New York a lot more."

I roll my eyes and start walking again. "I shouldn't have said anything. Your ego doesn't need another boost."

He quickly catches up to me. "Tell me, what do you think about my looks?"

"Fishing for compliments?" I ask even as my face grows hot. Is he flirting with me?

"You tell me what you think about me, and I'll tell you what I think about you."

We're passing through the lingerie section now. "You go first."

"Ms. Garzolo!"

I halt. *No, not him.* Mamma said Melanie would be helping me today. But a glance to the right is enough to confirm that Benjamin is working.

My stomach drops.

The forty-something-year-old man has always given me the creeps. Two months ago, my gut feeling was confirmed when he walked into the dressing room while I was changing and tried to "help" me with my clothes. I didn't cause a scene because I didn't want Mamma to tell Papà who might have set one of his men on Benjamin. Or more likely Papà would have found some way to blame the incident on me. So I just told Mamma I wanted to work with a new sales associate. Something must have gotten lost in translation.

I pick up on Benjamin's overly strong cologne from a dozen feet away and brace myself when he goes in for a hug. He's about to make contact when Ras steps in between us.

"Can I help you?" Ras asks, his voice as sharp as a knife.

I peek around him.

Benjamin blinks at Ras, looking taken aback. "Oh, hello there." He moves away, putting some more distance between them. Ras towers over Benjamin, his muscular frame intimidating. "I'm Ms. Garzolo's sales associate. Benjamin Scott." After a moment of hesitation, he offers up his hand.

Ras takes it.

Benjamin winces at the grip and goes a little pale.

"I'm Ras. Can I call you Ben?"

"I prefer Benja—"

"Ben, I'm Ms. Garzolo's friend. I'm accompanying her for this appointment."

"I see," Benjamin mutters, extracting his hand. His fingers look smushed together. "Well, let me show you to the private shopping area."

Ras's palm lands on the small of my back, firm and possessive. Something swoops inside my belly. He keeps it there as we walk to our destination.

Benjamin glances at us over his shoulder. "I know there's one particular dress you wanted to try, Ms. Garzolo, so I have that ready for you. I also brought in a few other pieces that I think you'll enjoy."

"Thank you," I say stiffly.

We reach the private dressing rooms. "Just give me one moment to make sure everything's ready. You can wait right here." Benjamin gestures at the sofas in the waiting area and disappears through a door.

Ras frowns in his direction. "You know this guy?"

As I sit down, his hand falls away. The fact that I'm so aware of it makes my face heat. "He's helped me a few times before. But I thought I'd have someone else today."

His hazel eyes move back to me, studying me carefully. "You don't like him."

Am I that easy to read? Ras must be good at picking up on body language. I suppose it's a handy skill to have in his line of work.

"Why not?" he presses, sitting down beside me on the sofa.

I don't want to cause any problems. Benjamin is a creep, and he deserves to be reprimanded by his supervisor, but I don't want to set the literal mob on him.

He didn't kill anyone. He just tried to cop a feel.

I need to get my dress and get out of here.

"It's nothing. I'd just prefer a woman."

Ras shakes his head. "Tell me why."

He's like a dog with a bone, intense and focused. How do I make him drop it? "He just gives me a weird vibe."

Ras throws one arm behind me and turns, his chest brushing against my shoulder. This man has no concept of personal space. His face is inches away from mine as he says, "If you're not going to tell me what happened, I'm just going to assume the worst."

I glance at him from under my lashes. I've never seen him look this serious. Almost stern. Heat spreads through my core. What is wrong with me?

Benjamin reappears. "All right, we're all ready—"

"We need a few more minutes, Ben. Do you mind?"

I nudge Ras with my elbow. What is he doing? We're in a common waiting area, and he's acting like this is our personal meeting room. He just stares at Benjamin until the man slowly backs through the door.

"No problem."

"Ras, this is—"

He leans even closer, forcing my back against the sofa, and cradles my chin between his fingers. "What. Did. He. Do." His minty breath brushes over my cheeks.

I swallow, searching his eyes for any sign that he might still drop this.

He won't. He's going to keep me here until I give him an answer.

"Fine," I grind out, jerking my chin out of his grip. Not because he's hurting me, but because being touched by him makes my body buzz all over. "Last time he walked in on me while I was changing."

Ras's eyes darken. "On purpose?"

"Yes. He grabbed my ass, okay? He tried to play it off like he was just helping me with my dress, but I'm not that gullible."

Ras's jaw clenches. He gives me a terrifying smile and pats my cheek. "That wasn't so hard, was it?"

"Ras, it's not a big de—"

He's already up, prowling toward the door Benjamin disappeared behind.

I jump to my feet. "Ras, don't—"

The door flies open. I catch a flash of Benjamin's panicked face before Ras blocks him from my view.

"Sir?" Benjamin squeaks, sounding appropriately frightened. "What's wrong—"

Ras grabs him by the neck, forces him backward, and slams him against the wall.

"Shit," I mutter, running after them and pulling the door closed. We don't need any witnesses.

"You fucked with the wrong girl, Ben," Ras growls.

He loosens his fingers just enough for Benjamin to squeal, "What did I do? I didn't do anything! This is a misunder—"

"Ms. Garzolo told me you touched her inappropriately the last time she was here."

"I di-didn't!"

"Are you saying Ms. Garzolo is a liar?"

Benjamin's eyes look on the verge of bursting out of his head. "No, of course not."

"She said you walked in on her changing in one of these rooms. Did you, or is she lying?"

"I-I-I—" Benjamin's desperate gaze lands on me. "Ms. Garzolo, I'm sorry!"

Ras punches him in the gut. Once. Twice.

Benjamin bleats in pain. I cover my face with my hands. This is hard to watch, but for some reason, I'm not rushing to stop it. My heart is racing inside my chest.

Ras is standing up for me.

"Please, sir—"

I slide my fingers open and peer through the gap.

Ras heaves him up and slams him against the wall again. "You know, in the old days, we'd cut off your hand for that."

Benjamin is bawling. "Not my hand. Please, not my hand!"

"No problem. I can be a reasonable guy."

Ras knees him in the balls—hard—and throws him to the ground.

Benjamin screams in pain, curling up like a shrimp on the floor.

"If you ever as much as look at her again for a second too long, I won't just cut off your hand. I'll cut off every limb. I'll make you into a stump. Do you understand me?" There's no hint of humor left in Ras's voice. It's hard and cold, meant to leave no doubt about whether he'd deliver on that threat.

Ice spreads through my lungs. It's like I've forgotten that Ras isn't just any man, but the feared underboss of the Casalesi.

He lifts Benjamin's face with the toe of his shoe. "Say it."

"Yes! I understand."

"Enough," I squeeze out.

God, I almost feel bad for Benjamin. Almost. But not quite.

This isn't like me. I don't like violence. Especially not violence on my behalf. So why do I feel strangely thrilled at this display?

I lower myself to the crushed-velvet sofa. I can't remember the last time someone stood up for me this way. Not because of what their disrespect meant to my family, but because of how it affected me.

That's what Ras just did.

Ras crosses his arms and peers down his nose at Benjamin's squirming, sobbing form.

"All right, wrap it up, Ben. We don't have all day." He prods him with his shoe again. "I need some things as well. Winter wardrobe. I trust your taste. I'm six-four, usually size extra-large. My shoe size is forty-seven. I think that's size thirteen over here, but do me a favor and check."

Benjamin manages to peel himself off the floor and mumbles without looking at either of us. "O-of course, sir."

"Thanks. Appreciate it."

My gaze snags on the shimmery yellow dress I picked out online for the party next week. It's Rafaele's aunt's fiftieth birthday, and all of the Garzolos are invited. A dinner at a venue downtown followed by a party in one of Rafaele's clubs, which means I need something that will work for both. When I checked the measurements, they were slightly too big.

I clear my throat. "Ras, he needs to mark the alterations for my dress."

Ras glances at me, and I tip my head in the direction of the coffee table, where there's a tray with measuring tape and a pincushion.

Benjamin halts, one foot already out the door and looking desperate to get out of here.

"Nah, I've got it," Ras says, walking over to where I'm sitting and picking up the pincushion.

I cross my arms and press my fist to my nose as Benjamin bolts through the door.

Ras gives the cushion a toss and meets my gaze.

I sigh. "He's going to need therapy."

Ras shrugs. "Should have thought of that before he laid a finger on you."

Warmth rushes over my skin. "I'm going to go change, and you're going to use that time to Google how to use those pins. I'm not showing up to a party in a lopsided dress."

He gives me an amused look. "Don't worry, it can't be that hard."

I snatch the dress off the rack, walk into the change room, and draw the heavy curtain closed with a loud swish.

As I slip out of my clothes, my heart starts to dance to an awkward rhythm at the thought of Ras standing just outside with only a curtain separating us. I undo my bra and hang it off a hook.

"Yeah, this won't be a problem," Ras calls out, and it sounds like he's right there. "I found a video on YouTube."

A thrill runs up my spine. "Okay, great."

I shimmy into the dress, and when the fabric drags over my curves, everything feels a little more sensitive than normal.

The dress is a smidge too long, and an inch or so of fabric pools on the floor. I bunch it up and decided that with a small heel, the length should do.

The chest area is a problem, though. The neck is a low-cut V, and it's made for someone with bigger boobs. I do up the side zipper and step out of the dressing room, holding up the straps at my shoulders.

I stop in front of the mirror, and Ras looks up from his phone. He does a double take.

I feel a flush rise to my cheeks. "What?"

Sliding his phone into his pocket, he takes a few slow and deliberate steps toward me. I can feel my heart in my throat.

"I never told you what I think of you," he says, dragging his thumb over his bottom lip while he stares at me like I'm something edible.

What is he talking about?

Oh. Right. My mind's so focused on this moment, it's forgotten all the other ones.

He stops right behind me, close enough for me to feel the heat of his body spread across my back. Our reflection makes nerves scatter over my skin. He's so much bigger. Taller. While I was changing, he took off his suit jacket, and that shirt does nothing to hide the muscular lines of his shoulders and arms.

"Want to hear it?" The words rumble inside his chest.

"Sure," I say lightly. I'm expecting I'll get something about how I clean up well or how he likes my haircut.

Instead, his eyes darken. "You're exquisite. The most beautiful woman I've ever seen."

Suddenly, I'm breathless. I press my thighs together, trying to contain the heat that appears between my legs.

In the mirror, I see his gaze dip lower, noting the small movement. The air in the room presses down on me. I'm so thoroughly stunned, I can't formulate an appropriate response, although I'm not sure such a thing even exists given the context.

He must notice how flustered I am, because he shows mercy and gives me an out. "How does the dress fit?"

I swallow. "The straps are too long." My voice is so weak, I sound like I just ran a marathon.

"Let me see."

He lifts his hands to my shoulders and places them on top of where my fingers are holding the straps. I let go and let him take over.

"I think they need to be adjusted by at least an inch."

Ras threads his index fingers under the straps and gently tugs on them.

I suck in a breath as the fabric flattens over my breasts, pressing against my hardened nipples. The heat at my center pulses insistently.

"How's that?" Ras murmurs, his hot breath brushing over my nape like a caress.

"Maybe a little more."

Another tug. I bite down on my lip so that I won't gasp. My nipples tighten even more, and there's no way he can't see them pushing against the delicate fabric of the dress in the reflection.

"That's good," I breathe.

"Hold," Ras says, his voice a rasp. "I need to get the pins."

I take over, our hands brushing in the process.

When he comes back, there's an unmistakable hunger simmering inside his gaze. I watch as he presses his thumb on the strap and pushes the pin through.

I wince when the second pin slips through the fabric and pierces my skin.

He clicks his tongue. "Shit, I'm sorry."

"It's nothing."

But he won't take my word for it. He slides the strap off my shoulder, each one of his fingertips a hot brand across my skin. "You're bleeding."

Someone's filling the air in this room with electricity. It skates over my face, my neck, my chest, and I don't know how to turn it off. "I— It's fine."

"I don't like seeing you hurt."

The words hang suspended in the space around us. All I hear is the loud pounding rhythm in my chest.

Slowly, so slowly that I think I'm imagining it, he lowers his head and presses his lips to my shoulder.

My breathing stops. There's a hot, warm brush of his tongue over my skin, and I feel it in places I shouldn't. My eyes flutter closed. A new kind of need appears inside of me, the kind that buzzes inside my bones. It carries echoes of that stolen kiss in Damiano's darkened kitchen.

This is so wrong. This is exactly the kind of trouble I was afraid of when I told myself I needed to stay away from him. I've never felt this way around another man.

"Ras, we shouldn't be doing this," I murmur, sounding breathless.

His lips move against my skin. "Tell me to stop then."

I intend to pull away, but instead, my body leans into him.

He makes a sound of satisfaction and slides a palm over my waist.

I feel his teeth gently bite into my skin, and my lips part. My chest rises and falls. I'm a hundred degrees. He drags his palm up over the center of my abdomen until the fabric stops and he encounters bare skin above the low cut of the dress.

He moves his mouth to the sensitive place where my neck meets my shoulder and lifts his gaze to meet mine in the reflection. I arch slightly, enough for my ass to press against the front of his thighs, and there I make contact with something I'm sure has earned him more than a few compliments.

He makes a low groan. "Fuck."

His eyes still locked on mine, he slips his hand through the gap in the front of my dress, cups one breast, and gives it a squeeze.

My thoughts scramble as he pinches my nipple with his fingers. I didn't expect him to go this far, but I also didn't expect to feel such a thrill at what's happening.

God, I'm screwed.

There's a knock on the door.

We break apart, and the air in the room ripples with released tension.

Ras sucks in a heavy breath, adjusts his pants, and glances at me.

I straighten out my dress. "Come in."

Benjamin enters, dragging a rack of clothes behind him. Ras finishes with the other pin and calls him over to check that the markings are right.

We get the okay, and I go to take off the dress. I pull the curtain closed and press my forehead to the mirror. I was right earlier. Being around Ras is a terrible idea. But when I open my eyes and glance at the light-pink mark he left on my shoulder, I'm not sure I have what it takes to stay away.

CHAPTER 17

RAS

BREAKING into Garzolo's study isn't something I'd planned on doing, but the perfect occasion presents itself when Gemma's mother texts me to bring Gemma to have a late lunch with Cleo and her after the appointment at the department store.

Pietra is driving them back home, so I'm off the hook for the day.

Gemma and I didn't speak on the ten-minute drive over to the restaurant. What happened in the dressing room seems like something that's better left without commentary, even though I'm dying to know what's going through her head.

I'm used to pushing boundaries and doing ill-advised things, but what I'm not used to is having Gemma, of all people, as a willing accomplice.

All I could think about as I looked at her standing in front of the mirror in that fucking dress was how unfair it is that

Messero will have the privilege of having her for the rest of his life.

That idiot doesn't get it. He doesn't get *her*. I saw it when I watched them together in Ibiza. He was like a robot around her. Barely touched her. Barely even talked to her.

If she was engaged to me, I wouldn't squander a single second. She'd be glued to my side. If she wanted to eat, I'd feed her. If she wanted to sit, it would be on my lap. If she wanted to shower, I'd wash every inch of that perfect skin and then dirty her up again.

I clench my jaw. I'm going fucking crazy.

Pushing the tip of my knife into the lock on the door, I wiggle it around. The lock gives with a soft click.

I slip inside the room and close the door behind me.

It takes me less than five minutes to sweep through the study, and I find absolutely nothing of value. No wonder that lock wouldn't deter even a child from getting in. This place is just for show. Garzolo must do his real business elsewhere, or he's done an excellent job of cleaning everything out before I got here.

I leave the study, stop by the bar in the living room to splash some whiskey into a crystal tumbler, and take it with me as I head upstairs to my bedroom.

"Be careful around Gemma."

Those words are looping on repeat inside my head as I dial Dem's number. I need to give him an update on my progress here and pretend like I don't know what Gemma's skin tastes like or the exact pitch of her little moans.

Out of all the women I could lose my mind around, why the fuck does it have to be one who's already engaged to another man? And not just any man. A don. I can't dispose of that fucker without setting off an avalanche of problems for Dem.

I press the cold tumbler against my forehead. The fact that I'm actually thinking through the potential repercussions of murdering Gemma's fiancé is just fucking great.

Damiano picks up on the third ring. "Ras."

"Sorry to interrupt the honeymoon." They're in the Maldives right now, on a small private island with just them at the hotel.

"It's fine, Vale's taking a nap. How are things?"

"I managed to convince Garzolo to let me be Gemma's minder while I'm here."

"How did you pull that off?"

"Put the other guy out of commission."

He chuckles. "Well done. Has Garzolo brought you around his crew yet?"

"Yeah, I had dinner with them last night. He wasn't too happy the night I arrived, but since then, he's been Mr. Hospitality. Took me to his restaurant, La Trattoria."

"And?"

"They were all clearly instructed to avoid answering any of my questions. I didn't get anything from them besides big talk about how well their business is going."

"Hmm. Maybe it was easy to convince him to let you be Gemma's driver because he doesn't want you sniffing around his business. He thinks he'll keep you occupied that way."

I frown. Damiano has a point. I should have thought of that. "Shit, you might be right."

"It wouldn't surprise me. He was cagey enough in Ibiza. You're going to have to find an outside perspective on the situation in New York. Have you met with Kal's contact?"

"Meeting Orrin tomorrow morning."

"Good. See what you can get from him. Don't be shy about sweetening him up either."

"I'll let you know how it goes."

"All right. Any leads on Gemma's situation?"

"Nothing yet."

"You should ask her about her dad. Napoletano said he overheard her talking about how Garzolo needs this marriage to happen, so she might know something."

I scratch my chin. Yeah, the last time we touched on that topic, it ended in disaster.

I'm about to tell Damiano I think that's a bad idea when I stop myself.

A rush of something unpleasant slides down my spine. Am I compromising my efforts here because I'm afraid of upsetting Gemma?

I owe my boss more than that.

"All right. I'll see if I can get something out of her."

We hang up, and I sip on my drink and come to the conclusion that I need to get a hold of myself. I'm here on Dem's orders. I owe him a clear head. I need to focus on my actual priorities, which don't include playing games with Gemma. If Garzolo catches a whiff of how I've already compromised his daughter, no amount of threats will make him allow me to stay. He's desperate for his clan to link up with Messero, that much is obvious. He won't put up with me if he sees me as a threat to that.

This deal with the Americans is important. It's our first major move with Dem as the head of the Casalesi, and our people will be watching to see how it shakes out. I don't want anyone to have any doubts that Dem is the right leader for us.

I remember the moment I realized he had it in him. That was almost a decade ago. No one, fucking no one, was talking to me after what had happened with Sara. I was a shell of a man. Broken, angry, destructive. Her betrayal ripped my heart out. I didn't leave my apartment for weeks.

Damiano was the one who pulled me back from the abyss. He was the only one who really even tried. He saw that I wouldn't—couldn't—see a future for myself, so he sold me on his vision. I believed in him for years before I started to believe in myself.

I finish off the whiskey and put the glass down on the nightstand with a soft clank.

I have to do better than this and focus on my work instead of contemplating the indentation Gemma's body would make in my mattress. There's a reason why I've kept every single woman after Sara at arm's length. I haven't allowed myself to get distracted from what's important in years, and I'm not about to start now.

⌖

I arrive at Poet's Café, the coffee shop where I'm meeting Orrin Petraki, at eight fifteen. It's closed despite the sign on the door saying it opens at eight.

I let out an annoyed huff, which materializes as a white cloud in front of my face. It's minus ten degrees, or what the app on my phone says is fourteen Fahrenheit. Even in my new black cashmere sweater and wool jacket, my nipples feel like they're about to freeze off.

Fuck this.

My fingertips are numb as I take out my phone and give the Greek a call.

"I'm almost there," he says, static cracking over the line. "Pulling up. You the guy in the long coat?"

"Yes," I bark into the receiver. "I'm fucking freezing over here."

He chuckles. "Oh, I remember when I first got to New York. Took me four winters to adjust."

A black SUV pulls up to the curb, the driver a grinning young man with curly black hair and a prominent nose. He waves his phone at me.

I hang up and stuff my hands into the pockets of my jacket, my shoulders nearly at ear height. I should have bought a hat and a scarf at that department store, but I was somewhat preoccupied with getting rid of my raging hard-on after the incident with Gemma.

I wonder if she'll bring it up when I see her later today.

Orrin hops out the car and comes to shake my hand. "Ras, right?"

I scan him over. He's young but there's an old scar slashed over his cheek and a newer one through his brow. They give him a certain kind of gravity. I can already tell he isn't someone who sits on the sidelines.

"Yeah." I tip my head toward the sign above the door. "You the poet?"

He throws me a lopsided grin. "Depends who you ask. You've got a last name?"

"Sorrentino."

"Oh, I know a Sorrentino around here." He rummages in one of his pockets before pulling out a set of keys. "You've got relatives here?"

I shake my head. "Not in New York. My whole family is still in Napoli."

He unlocks the door and motions for me to go inside. "Never mind then. I've never been to Napoli, but you know I've always wanted to go. Your pizza's supposed to be the best, right?"

I shiver in relief as the heated air of the cafe wraps around me. "That's what they say."

"You know, I met a guy from there a while back." Orrin lets the door slam behind him. "He's with one of Messero's crews. Actually, maybe he wasn't from Napoli. Fuck, there's too many damn Italians here, I always get confused where everyone's from."

I slip my jacket off as he walks over to the coffee machine. This guy talks a lot, but that might be a good thing given what I want from him.

"Want coffee?"

"Yeah."

He pulls out a container of ground coffee beans. "So Kal told me to be my most helpful self as far as you're concerned. Sounds like you and your boss have worked with him for a while."

"Kal's a good guy. He's helped us a lot through the years." Kal Petraki is the reason we've never lacked guns or ammunition in Ibiza.

"Congrats, by the way. Heard De Rossi recently became the top dog."

I relax into the chair and cross my ankle over my knee. "The Casalesi leadership was in desperate need of a change."

"Big promotion for you too, huh?"

"Trust me when I say it's not as glamorous as it seems."

Orrin starts making two espressos. "I've been working my way up since I first got here six years ago. Now, I'm leading a crew of about a dozen guys. We're not big players, but I've got a good thing going, and I think I can keep growing it if I keep up the diplomacy with your country men."

"You've got your own territory?"

"Smack dab on the border between the Messeros and the Riccis. It's been a little tense lately." He glances at me. "Maybe you've heard."

"Thought the matter's been resolved."

"Yeah, the Riccis got fucked with a big Messero-Garzolo branded strap-on. It's going to take them at least a decade to rebuild." He brings over the two espressos and sits down across from me. "So how can I help?"

I take a sip. It's good. Strong and bitter.

"You probably pieced it together by now that due to our families recently merging, Damiano now has a common business interest with Garzolo."

Orrin nods. "I gathered that much from Kal."

"Messero's also involved."

"That's right. He's engaged to that other Garzolo girl, isn't he? What's her name...Gia? I only saw her once in passing, but that's a piece of ass you don't forget, you know what I mean?"

I take a drag of my espresso to chase away the flare of displeasure. "Her name is Gemma. Anyway, I'm here to do our due diligence. We want to be sure our American friends have the capabilities required to move our product."

"Very prudent."

"If there's any reason to doubt that they can, we want to be aware of it."

Orrin's eyes flash. "Are you worried about the Riccis? Like I said, they're in shambles. They've lost too many guys to pose a serious threat, no matter how thirsty they are for revenge."

"I got the sense Garzolo's crew took a big hit as well."

"They did. I think it's why he operates differently these days."

"Differently how?"

"He's…" Orrin shrugs. "Cautious. Some are saying he's getting old. He's pulled back on some of the old routes."

Interesting. "He's scared of something? Or just low on manpower?"

Orrin puts his cup down and crosses his arms. "I don't know the details. It's not really in my purview. My guys don't deal with his very much."

"Can you find out more?"

Outside the cafe, a garbage truck passes. It's snowing now.

"I could ask around. We've got a poker game coming up. Someone there might know more."

"No one can know I'm asking."

Orrin smirks. "I wasn't born yesterday." He leans over the table and meets my eye. "Now, tell me more about these counterfeits you Napoletani are so known for."

A half hour later, I wrap up things with Orrin. The guy clearly wants a deal of his own with us, and I leave him thinking there is a good chance of it and drive back to the Garzolo residence. Gemma's got some appointment at ten that I have to get her to.

After this meeting, I'm optimistic. Orrin seems like he knows his way around this place. He's an outsider to the families, but he's got a smooth tongue that's gotten him into people's good graces.

The fact that his crew earns the Messeros good money doesn't hurt. He told me he pays them a protection fee to ensure no one tries to encroach on his crew's territory.

What he said about Garzolo is interesting. When I had dinner with Stefano's crew, they were all big talk about their business. There wasn't a single hint about their apparently diminishing ambitions. I saw a table full of hungry men.

If Garzolo's really shrinking his operations, his crew can't be happy. They've got to eat. So they're either all excellent actors, or there's a damn good reason behind it.

I need to find out what it is.

I park at the house and type out a vague message to Dem to let him know I've got a lead. It feels good to have something this quickly. I toss my phone onto the center console and let out a relieved breath.

Tap tap.

I glance sideways to see Gemma standing on the other side of the car, her hair pulled back in a ponytail. When I unlock the door, she hops in. She's wearing the puffiest winter coat I've ever seen over a pair of leggings and a sports bra. My gaze drops to her toned stomach and heat rushes straight down to my groin.

Cazzo.

I rack my brain for where we're going as I try to ignore the heady feminine scent that fills the car.

Oh, right. Pilates.

"Ready?"

"Yep."

I flex my hands around the wheel and pull out of the driveway.

Why did I tell her about Nunzio yesterday? It's not a story I've shared with many people, but when she asked me about my name, something compelled me to tell her the truth.

"Tell me you killed him."

My gut tightens. She said it with an undercurrent of fury, like she cared.

Or maybe that's just my mind imagining things. Seeing things it wants to see.

Does she feel this connection between us? It's always been there. Yes, from that very first fucking day when she bit me, and I don't care if she insists otherwise.

In Ibiza, that connection is what allowed her to be so fucking unhinged around me.

You said it yourself. She was just taking her anger out on you.

Maybe at first, but not afterwards. Not in my apartment. Definitely not at that department store.

And not now, when she's looking at me with those beautiful gray eyes like she's trying to figure me out.

I'm trying to figure her out too.

There's a fire that burns inside of her, but I suspect her family has spent her entire life trying to stomp it out.

To make her compliant.

To make her obey.

It's clear they have her under their control. She cowers around her parents in a way she's never cowered around me.

What is she afraid of?

Perhaps it's not fear that motivates her. Perhaps it's a sense of obligation that her parents have spent a lifetime instilling.

"What would happen if you don't marry Messero?" I ask, trying to test out my theory.

Her gaze flickers with apprehension. "Why?"

"Back in Ibiza, you said to Vale it's critical to the survival of your family."

She shifts in her seat. "We already talked about this, didn't we? It's what Papà told me. He said the union with the Messeros will strengthen our reputation after the mess with the Riccis. When everything was going down with them, things got bad for a while."

"How bad?"

"They killed a bunch of our men." She looks out the window before she says the next thing. "Our uncles. Our cousins."

"Vale doesn't talk about it much."

"She wasn't here for it, was she?" Some sharpness slips into her tone. "It accelerated after she ran."

I frown. Did that cause Gemma to internalize a certain lesson about what happens when you go against your family? Is that why she argued so adamantly with Vale when Vale just floated the idea of breaking off the engagement to Messero?

No wonder Garzolo didn't have to say much to convince her this marriage is nonnegotiable. She'd been primed for it.

When rationalizing this marriage, Gemma always talks about other people. What they want. What they need. But what about her own needs? Does she even know what they are? Or has she spent her whole life learning how to repress them?

I swallow past the unpleasant taste inside my mouth. This is fucked up. Garzolo is putting the responsibility of his whole family on Gemma's shoulders. That burden should be Garzolo's to carry, not hers.

We come to a stoplight, and she glances at me. "If my marriage can help ensure that never happens again, it's a bargain, don't you think?"

"You really think it'll be enough? In your father's line of work, peace doesn't last."

A shadow passes over her expression. "I wouldn't be able to live with myself if I knew I could have helped my family, but I chose not to."

My heart lodges itself between my ribs.

She's determined to do this.

It should be a good thing. It should make it easier for me to stay focused on what I came here to do. But it sure as hell doesn't feel great to hear her talk about how ready she is to sacrifice herself. And to Messero of all people. That man will never appreciate the gift he's been handed. Gemma deserves better than this.

Still, there's nothing I can do. Not when she's convinced this is the right thing.

When we reach the Pilates studio, she turns to me, her expression grave. "Ras?"

"Yeah?"

"What happened in the dressing room... It can't happen again."

I should have known it was coming, but hearing her say those words still feels like a punch in the gut. We're walking on different paths. Paths that aren't meant to intertwine. Whatever's been brewing between us needs to end, despite how tempting it is. Because no matter how drawn I am to her, she's not meant for me.

Her eyes burn brightly as she holds my gaze, waiting for me to acknowledge her words.

It's me who eventually looks away. "I'll pick you up in an hour."

CHAPTER 18

GEMMA

I MANAGE to keep myself at home for the next few days, avoiding any more alone time with Ras.

The wedding planner comes to the house, showing Cleo, Mamma, and me linens, options for the centerpieces, and bringing us cake samples. I ask lots of questions, forcing myself to occupy my mind with something other than the man living a few doors down from me. My diligence earns me praise from Mamma and an exasperated glare from Cleo.

"Can you chill?" she asks after the planner leaves on Friday. "You're setting way too high of a standard."

"How's Ludovico? I haven't heard anything about him since I got back."

She smirks. "Me neither. Apparently, he's on the fence about me after our last meeting."

"I never asked you what happened."

"In Mamma's words, I ate like it was the first time I've used cutlery, and when Ludovico commented on it, I told him to leave me alone. He called me uncivilized. I told him he probably has a small dick."

I rub my temple. "Cleo…"

"What? It must be true, because he got really mad after that. Mamma's been trying to smooth things over ever since, but I hope she doesn't. I hate him."

"Is he going to be at La Trattoria tonight?"

"I don't think so."

Tonight, we're having dinner with the Messeros. As far as I know, Ras wasn't invited, which is for the best, since I'm not confident in my ability to play it cool around him anymore.

The sex dreams won't stop tormenting me. When I wake up, my body buzzes with need, and my thighs are slick with wetness. It's gotten so bad, I've tried to fix the situation on my own, but I can't do it. My vibrator's been broken for months, and I haven't found a way to get a new one delivered to the house without Mamma knowing. Since Vale ran, she's been checking all of our packages.

I don't know how to make myself come with my fingers. God knows, I've tried, but it's never worked for me. I get so close only to never cross the edge.

I had to deal with the insistent throb between my legs for the entirety of breakfast. During which Ras sat directly across from me.

It was torture.

It's like his touch somehow got encoded in me at a cellular level, and now my skin is programmed to crave it.

I thought a few days with minimal contact would cool things between me and him, but as far as I'm concerned, it's not working.

I crave his presence. His voice. His smile.

But I know indulging that craving will only make things worse when he inevitably leaves. So I try to cram my feelings into a tiny little box and shove it deep into the recesses of my mind.

"I'm going to go get dressed." Cleo rises off the couch in the living room and smooths her palms over her thighs. "Mamma made a big deal about not being late. Did she seem more high-strung than usual to you?"

"I'm not sure." I haven't been paying close attention to Mamma's moods recently.

Cleo holds out her palm. "Come on. I'll sneak a bottle of wine, and we can get tipsy before dinner."

It's a bad idea, but for once, I agree to it. I need something to take the edge off so that I can paste on a smile and act like a perfect fiancée.

Cleo and I are lightly buzzed by the time we leave the house for La Trattoria. Dalida plays from the car's stereo, and Mamma and Papà speak in hushed Italian about things clearly not meant for our ears. I try to make out what they're saying but get bored after five minutes and pull out my phone.

"Let's do a crossword," Cleo suggests.

"You're terrible at those even when you're sober."

"I'm better when I'm a bit drunk. I get more creative."

A notification pops up on my phone—a text from Ras.

Cleo makes an obnoxious oohing sound. "What's your bodyguard messaging you about? Is he already worried?"

Shushing her, I checked to make sure our parents are still not paying us attention. "Keep your voice down. And he's not my bodyguard."

"Oh yeah? Then how do you explain his behavior around Benjamin?"

I shouldn't have told her about that. She kept pestering me about how shopping went during the lunch we had right afterward, so when Mamma went to the bathroom, I told her about how Ras wiped the floor with Benjamin.

I kept my mouth shut about the rest of what happened. What Ras and I had done is so inappropriate, it rivals some of Cleo's worst misdemeanors.

Cleo leans closer. "Open it."

Turning the screen away from her, I tap on the notification.

> Can you send me your schedule for next week?

Disappointment runs through me, but I push it away. What did I expect? For him to tell me something that makes my pulse race?

No, this is for the best.

"What's that face you're making? You look like you're about to lay an egg," Cleo says, trying to catch another peek at my phone, but I turn it off and slide it back into my purse. "What did he want?"

"My schedule."

She yawns. "Boring."

We arrive at our destination, my buzz still buzzing, and we slide out of the car and step onto a frigid sidewalk in Little Italy. Papà hands the keys to the valet and marches toward the entrance, leading the pack.

As soon as we step inside the toasty restaurant, I take a long, deep inhale. It always smells so good in here, like pasta sauce, freshly baked bread, and their house red wine. The smell of my childhood. We used to come here once a week for dinner, and it was always my favorite night. The whole family would be in attendance, aunts and uncles and their broods, and while they ate, the kids would run wild and crawl under the tables. After each dinner, we were allowed to eat as much tiramisu as we wanted. On more than one occasion, that generous offer ended up with Cleo throwing up.

Tonight, we bypass the busy first-floor dining area and head straight upstairs to the lavish private room. Inside, Rafaele and Nero are already seated. Rafaele's at the head of the table with Nero to his right.

I frown. Rafaele's in Papà's seat, and Papà isn't shy about telling people to move. They rise to greet us, and when we all settle down, Papà simply takes the seat to Rafaele's left. It's strange. I can't remember the last time he didn't sit at the head of the table.

But no one else seems to notice except me.

Cleo reaches for a bottle of wine on the table and fills her glass nearly to the rim. She doesn't offer a drop to anyone else. She's not even supposed to be drinking since she's only eighteen, but no one in La Trattoria enforces those rules when it comes to the family.

My fiancé's gaze narrows on the glass, and his lips thin with displeasure.

I hang my purse off the back of her chair and whisper into her ear, "You're being rude."

She just shrugs and takes a big gulp.

"Gemma, how's the wedding planning going?" Nero asks as the waiters file in with heaping plates of antipasti and salad.

"Very well. This week we settled on the centerpieces and selected the cake."

"Chocolate?"

"White chocolate and raspberry."

Nero grins. "Good choice."

"Have you finalized the guest list on your side?" Mamma spears some salumi with her fork before passing the plate to Nero.

"Cousin Emiliano and his family had to drop out at the last minute, but the rest are all confirmed," Nero says.

"Cousin Emiliano? Didn't we meet him a few months ago at that party at your place, Rafaele?"

The plate of antipasti makes it to my fiancé, who doesn't take anything and passes it to Papà. *Great.* If he doesn't like the food here, there's no hope he'll like my cooking. I can't hold a candle to Chef Caruso.

Rafaele takes a sip of his wine while Nero answers for him. "You did."

"I thought he lived around here. Why aren't they coming?"

Nero shakes his head. "He was in a car accident. Some fucker put him in a coma."

Mamma makes a disapproving click of her tongue. "Drivers these days. Did Stefano tell you about what happened just a few days ago—"

Cleo sticks two fingers into her mouth and whistles. "Hey! More wine please."

Christ. Heat travels over my cheeks. My sister is fully capable of acting like a civilized human being, so she's doing this on purpose. I can understand why she would around Ludovico—she's trying to scare him off—but why now? Is she just trying to embarrass Mamma?

The waiter hurries over with a bottle of red.

"She's had enough."

They're the first words out of my fiancé's mouth since we sat down, and they make the entire table go still.

The waiter swallows and pulls the bottle back. "Of course, Mr. Messero."

"Hey, *stronzo*, why are you listening to him?" Cleo snaps. "I said more wine."

The waiter's expression turns panicked and uncertain, and beads of sweat appear on his forehead.

"Cleo, settle down," Mamma says through gritted teeth while Papà observes my sister with a dark look in his eyes.

I reach over to place a hand on Cleo's arm, but she jerks it away and leans over the table to glare at Rafaele. "Who the hell gave you permission to control how much I drink?"

"You arrived smelling of booze, and you've already downed one overfilled glass since we sat down five minutes ago," Rafaele says, his voice low. "You're embarrassing your family."

"You're embarrassing yourself by having such a stick up your ass."

Nero snorts.

I snatch Cleo's arm and dig my nails in. My sister's fearlessness borders on stupidity.

"That's enough," Papà barks. "We're having this dinner because there's something important for us to discuss. Save your tantrum for afterwards, Cleo."

Cleo opens her mouth to argue, but I hiss, "Stop it."

She huffs, slumps in her seat, and stuffs a piece of bread into her mouth, her furious gaze still fixed on Rafaele.

My fiancé lifts his glass of wine and takes a slow sip. Is he taunting her? It's saying something that Cleo can get under Rafaele's skin.

"What did you want to talk about, Papà?" I ask, trying to dissipate the lingering tension.

Papà wipes his lips with a napkin and sends the waiters out of the room with a single glance.

"What I'm about to say is extremely confidential, and it's not to leave this room," he says once the door shuts.

A trickle of unease slides down my spine.

I glance at Cleo, wondering if she knows what this is about, but she gives me a small shake of her head.

"I am naming Rafaele as my successor. When I retire, he will take over as the head of our clan."

My silverware tumbles out of my hands.

What? I can't believe what I'm hearing. This is coming out of nowhere.

"Is this a joke?" Cleo sputters. "Vince is your successor."

"Vince has made it abundantly clear he has no interest in running the business in New York."

No, that's not true. Everyone knows that when the time comes, Vince will come back. That's a given. He might be enjoying his time in Europe, but it was never meant to be a permanent thing.

He won't let Papà take away his birthright just like that.

The room spins.

"Does Vince know about this?" I force past my dry throat.

Papà straightens his cuffs. "He's aware."

"And what was his reaction?"

Papà's hard gaze lands on me. "Like I already said, he's shown no interest in this job. Your brother has done nothing to prove to me that he can lead our people."

Bullshit. Vince has been working abroad for the clan this whole time. He's managing most of our money. They're stealing his birthright from him.

Cleo points at Rafaele. "He's not even related to us. How can he lead the Garzolos when he's not one himself?"

For once, my sister and I are on the exact same wavelength. She's voicing my thoughts.

Why Rafaele? Why not someone else?

"What about our uncles?" I demand. Even on the off chance that what Papà's saying about Vince is true, one of our uncles would step up. I'm sure some of them are itching for an opportunity like this.

"None of the ones that are left are fit for the job," Papà says. "You know as well as I do that the Riccis thinned our highest ranks."

Cleo slams her fists on the table. "Are you kidding me? So make them fit! Why would you choose him of all people?"

"Rafaele's about to become a part of our family. He's marrying Gemma, and no one will dare call him an outsider once he's my son-in-law. Rafaele's already proven himself to be a capable don. He's become my closest ally in the past six months, and he's the best man for the job," Papà says. "It's as simple as that."

Nothing about this is simple. I sit back in my chair, utterly shocked. I refuse to believe Vince is on board with this. Why didn't he say something to me about this when we spoke in Ibiza?

Papà must have been planning this with Rafaele for far longer than that, so he's pulling the rug from under Vince. That's the only explanation.

What if Vince is already on his way back to New York?

My blood runs cold. Is he in danger?

Rafaele is ruthless when it comes to getting rid of his enemies. Will Vince join the ranks of them if he doesn't fall in line?

Papà reaches across the table and clasps Mamma's hand. It's a rare show of affection meant to convey to Cleo and I that they're a united front on this. "I'm not planning to retire for another few years, so the changes won't go into effect for a while."

"And you expect everyone to be all right with this?" I ask, my shock morphing into prickling anxiety. "Do the rest of the Garzolos know?"

"They will soon."

Cleo shakes her head, still in disbelief. "This makes no sense."

She's right. It doesn't.

Papà is proud.

Territorial.

For him, there's always been an "us" and a "them".

Rafaele will marry me, but he doesn't share any blood with Papà. As far as I know, we've never warred with the Messeros, but we haven't been allied for long either.

Why would Papà put so much trust in him? Why would he give Rafaele the key to his kingdom? The kingdom our great-great-grandfather started when he first immigrated to the United States?

Is Papà this desperate for an ally?

I force myself to breathe slowly and move my attention to my fiancé. "You're charging a steep price to stand behind the Garzolos in case our enemies move against us. That's all we're getting from you in exchange for all of this, isn't it?"

Rafaele gives me a strange look. Beside him, Nero purses his lips as if he's making a conscious effort to keep his mouth shut.

I squeeze the armrests with my fingers as cold foreboding slides down my spine. "What is it?"

The room is quiet until Papà clears his throat. "I understand this is a lot to take in."

I shake my head, my conviction growing. "There's something else. Something you're not telling us."

"Gemma, enough," Mamma snaps. "Your father has said everything he's going to say on the subject."

"I deserve to know," I hiss. "Have you forgotten that you're giving me to this man? Sounds like our marriage is what's giving him the legitimacy he needs to become your successor. I want to know under what terms I was sold," I say, my voice breaking.

My lungs are frozen as I wait for Papà to give me an answer, but it's Rafaele who finally speaks.

"The Feds are building a case against your father," he says in a voice that's steady and impartial. "If he gets arrested, I'm the only one with the ability to get him out."

I blink. There's a whooshing sound inside my ears as things start to slowly, tragically fall into place. "Papà is that true?"

I want to hear confirmation from Papà's mouth.

My father glowers at me, his lips pressed into a thin, tight line. He's angry. Maybe he didn't think Rafaele would tell me the truth.

"They're looking to send me away for life. Rafaele has an in with the DA. If the indictment comes, he will make it go away. I'll remain the don for a maximum of five years before handing the reins over to him."

My vision narrows, and darkness seeps in. Unbelievable. This is *fucking* unbelievable.

This isn't about protecting my family.

It's about protecting *him*.

Papà's using all of us—me, Vince, our family—to save his own skin.

"You told me our family was in danger," I whisper.

"There's always danger. Always someone vying to take what's ours."

"But there is no concrete threat, is there? You made it sound like the other families have been foaming at the mouth to come after us after the Riccis. You lied."

Papà's gaze is hard and unapologetic. "If I'm put behind bars tomorrow, Gemma, this family won't have anyone capable of leading them. This plan ensures that we're not plunged into chaos. It is a good thing. Everything I do, everything I've *done*, has always been in the best interests of our clan."

Liar.

My chest constricts. There's not enough air in this damn room.

I feel like I'm going to burst.

Nero draws everyone's attention by clearing his throat. "Let's all take a breath, shall we? I can see that this is quite a surprise."

"No shit," Cleo spits out.

Nero shoots her a tight smile. "It's good we're talking about it now. This way, there won't be any more surprises after the wedding. We're all invested in making sure this union between the Messeros and the Garzolos is a success, and that's why Rafe and I thought this was a good time for all of us to get on the same page."

My fiancé studies me, his fingers steepled, his expression unreadable.

So this was his idea. Does he expect me to thank him?

Our confusing exchange at Vale's wedding makes more sense now. He thought Papà had told me about what was happening right from the beginning.

Mamma latches onto my arm and squeezes hard enough for me to wince. It's what she does when she wants me to keep my mouth shut.

The rest of the dinner is a blur while I try to control my emotions. I want to cry and scream and throw my plate against the wall.

Dons go to prison all the time. Grandpa did seven years before he died. He had an acting boss carrying out his orders on the outside. Papà could have done the same with Vince.

It would have been the honorable thing to do.

But Papà doesn't have any honor. He only has selfishness and greed.

There's a ball in my throat. I thought I was marrying Rafaele for the sake of my family.

Turns out, I just helped Papà oust Vince. There's not a chance in hell our family would accept Rafaele as their don if we weren't getting married.

I should tell Papà that I won't do it. That I won't marry Rafaele for his benefit.

I'm not a little girl anymore. I don't care about disappointing him.

But what difference would that make? Papà will find a way to force me into the marriage anyway. He's been using carrots up to now. If I resist, he'll use a stick. He'll make my life hell. He'll drag me down the aisle himself if he has to. I know how he is.

I need to talk to Vince. Maybe we can come up with a plan together. He must be just as furious about this as I am. Until then, I need to keep my cool. There isn't anything I can do. Not when there are so many unknowns and consequences I can't predict.

A cord of despair wraps around my throat and squeezes.

My hands shake for the rest of dinner. I don't touch my food. I don't lift my eyes from the table.

It ends rather quickly. Maybe Rafaele and Nero take pity on us. I don't say goodbye to them as we file out of the dining room. Cleo must have chugged an entire bottle of wine when she went to the bathroom because she's barely on her feet.

I deposit her into the back seat, and she passes out on my shoulder, leaving me to spiral on my own the entire drive home. Papà turns up the music. No one speaks.

As soon as I get to my bedroom, I call Vince. There's no answer.

I send a text.

> Call me back. This is urgent.

He must be asleep. It's the middle of the night in Europe.

It feels like there's an atomic bomb inside my chest that's about to burst. I'm tempted to start breaking things. The walls close in on me, and my heart races. I can't stay in here. I need to get some air. I pick up my phone and send a text to Ras.

> You up?

> Yeah, what's up?

> Can you drive me somewhere right now?

Three dots flash at the bottom of the screen. I bite down on my lip.

Please say yes.

> All right.

CHAPTER 19

GEMMA

I CHANGE out of my dinner outfit into a pair of sweats and a T-shirt and creep downstairs to meet Ras by the side door.

He's already there. For a second, I don't recognize him. I've never seen him this dressed down. He's wearing a black zip-up hoodie and joggers, and the loose fit of the clothes make him look even bigger than he does in a suit.

It's been days since we were last alone. My stomach does an inexplicable flip when his gaze lands on me.

I brush past him and put in the code to turn off the alarm.

"What is it, Gemma?"

"Shh. Let's talk outside."

We slip through the door and go around the house.

The light in my parents' bedroom is off, but I wince when the car makes a single beep as Ras unlocks it. If Papà sees us right now, we'll be screwed.

Somehow, that thought doesn't carry its usual weight.

Tonight has lowered my give-a-fuck meter to zero.

We get on the road.

"Where do you want to go?" Ras asks.

"Someplace I can get something to eat." My appetite disappeared at dinner, but now my stomach feels empty, and it's one of the few problems in my life that can be easily fixed.

"I drove past a twenty-four-hour diner the other day," Ras says as he navigates us through the neighborhood.

"Let's go there."

"All right."

I roll down the window and take a deep breath. There's a hint of pine in the crisp winter air.

We pick up speed, and the wind turns cold against my skin. It takes the edge off the unpleasant energy that's coursing through my body, but barely.

I glance over at the man sitting beside me.

Ras must have felt this way before. Helpless, confused, betrayed. He's got nearly a decade on me, and he hasn't lived an easy life. Maybe he can give me some advice.

"Did your old don ever lie to you?"

"Sal?"

"Yeah."

His lips curl into a wry smile. "I used to wonder if he'd ever told us the truth."

239

Us. Him and Damiano. They've always been partners. Always watched each other's backs.

I don't have anyone like that anymore. Not since Vale left.

"Did it ever make you mad that you couldn't do anything about it?"

He adjusts his grip on the wheel, rings flashing on his long, thick fingers. "Sure."

"How did you let that anger go?"

Ras's curious gaze coasts over to me. I can tell he wants to ask about what happened tonight, but I don't think he wants to rush me. "Hit the bag. That usually does the trick. You want to land a few punches?"

"No, I'm good." There are people I want to hit, but none of them are Ras.

"Any physical activity works," he adds as an afterthought.

He probably means running or hiking, but that's not where my mind goes. It goes to skin moving over skin, his hand molding to my breast, his lips pressed to the spot behind my ear.

I drag my palms down my thighs and look out the window.

We get to the diner. The parking lot is empty save for an old truck. Only one half of the sign above the door is lit, but it's enough to make out the name. *Jack's Spot.*

We're greeted by a young waitress with pink streaks in her blond hair. She takes us to a table in the far corner and hands out two laminated menus.

I order a peach milkshake and a burger. If Mamma saw me now, she'd have a heart attack.

Ras gets a burger and fries.

"How old were you when you got made?" I ask when the waitress walks away.

He folds his arms over his chest. "Twenty-three. Dem was my sponsor."

"Did you get a speech about what it meant to join the family?"

"Sure. No way around it.

"What did they say to you?"

He shrugs. "The usual. The clan is my one true family, above my parents, my friends, my future wife and kids. As long as I stay loyal, I'll be taken care of. If there's a problem, I bring it to the don, and he'll fix it for me. And if I die, I die with the peace of knowing that the people I love would be all right." He shakes his head. "I never bought a word of it at the time."

Surprise unfolds inside my chest. "What?"

"They were empty words. Sal was the man who murdered Dem's father, and instead of taking care of Dem, he did everything he could to make him fail. It was Dem's ingenuity, street smarts, and sheer persistence that got him to where he was. Plus, I didn't need Sal to take care of me. Dem had already done that for years. I swore my loyalty to the clan, but to me, the clan was and is Dem. I would raze them all to the ground if he asked."

I blink. "When I got that speech, it made a very different impact."

He arches a brow. "Don't tell me your Papà brought you to an initiation."

"Of course not. I got a version of it from Mamma when I was around ten. She told me that our family should always be my top priority. That if I serve it well, it will serve me. I'll never have to carry my problems on my own shoulders. The family will share the weight and do everything to help me. And the people outside of it would never have my best interests at heart. Going against the family would be going against myself, even if it didn't seem like it at the time."

Ras tilts his head. "What did you think of that?"

"She made me feel like I was born into something very special and rare. Like I was lucky to have the life I was given. She said most people get a far worse deal. They have to navigate the world on their own. Not us. We have a community behind us that will always make sure everyone is all right. And we have Papà. As head of the family, he would move mountains to keep us safe. I thought everything he does is for us."

Emotion swells inside my gut. I drag my palms over my cheeks and wrap them around the sides of my neck. "I bought every word. It's only tonight that I realized what an idiot I've been. After what Papà did to Vale, I started to question his judgment, but I told myself that anyone can make a mistake. Everyone has flaws. But I see it so clearly now. It's all bullshit. The only person Papà cares about is himself."

The waitress comes with our order.

"Want to tell me what happened?" Ras asks in a low voice once she leaves us.

I grab my milkshake and suck on the straw. Papà told us the information is confidential, but for once, I don't feel like I owe him anything.

Ras waits as I slurp my milkshake. The patient look on his face brings me right back to Ibiza, when he took care of me like he did.

Breathe, Gemma.

Screw this. I can't keep all this inside of me. I need to talk to someone about the catastrophe that's masquerading as my life.

I squash a napkin inside my fist.

"Papà's making Rafaele his successor once he retires instead of my brother, Vince."

Ras furrows his brows. "What?" He sounds as taken aback as I'd expect him to.

"I know."

He drags a palm over his mouth and leans over the table. "Your father told you this? Tonight?"

"At dinner."

Ras shakes his head. "He must have a very good reason for doing something like that."

I nod. "He does. Rafaele is his get-out-of-jail-free card. Papà's being investigated by the Feds."

Ras's eyes widen. "Fuck."

"Yeah. Rafaele's going to gain control of our family all so that Papà can stay out of jail. Did you know our grandpa did seven years leading up to his death? Plenty of my uncles have done time too. But Papà isn't interested in all that. He said he'll remain our don for another five years before Rafaele takes over. I imagine he'll have a cushy retirement afterward. He must be happy how everything is working out for him."

I take a bite out of my burger. How did I fail to see the extent of his selfishness? I'm the daughter he beats, and it took me longer than any of my siblings to finally acknowledge the kind of person he is. "I'm such an idiot. This is all my fault."

"How so?" Ras asks carefully.

"You were right when you said I should have asked more questions. Now, I'm complicit in helping Papà force Vince out. It's my fault—"

"Have you always done this?" Ras interrupts.

I glance at him. "Done what?"

"Take on responsibility for problems that you didn't create and that you can't possibly be responsible for solving?"

Something unpleasant runs through me. "I may have contributed to this one. If I hadn't agreed to this marriage as soon as Papà put pressure on me, he'd have had to come up with another plan. Maybe I could have changed his mind."

Ras's gaze fills with pity. "Peaches, have you ever managed to change his mind about anything?"

No.

Papà has never listened to me. At least not when it truly mattered.

Ras sighs. My silence is answer enough. "What do you want to do about all of this?" he asks.

I finish my burger and chase it with the rest of my milk-shake. "I really don't know," I admit sullenly.

Could I call Vale and ask her to get me out? Probably. With Ras here, he might be able to get Cleo and I to Europe and hide us away. But then what? How long could we stay hidden before Papà's men, and probably Rafaele's men came after us? They'd fight over us. Men would likely die.

I refuse to have blood on my hands. No, this isn't a time to act rashly. "I need to talk to my brother," I say. "Papà is lying about Vince being fine with this. I'm sure of it. I'll do whatever I can to support him. For now, I'm still getting married in a few weeks."

Tears well up in my eyes. Everything is so messed up.

Ras slaps a bill on the table and stands up. "Come on."

We leave the diner and get into the car. I'm so tired. I stop trying to hold back the tears and let them flow down my cheeks.

"Take me home," I mumble, letting my body sink into the leather seat.

"No."

I flick my blurry gaze at Ras. All of his attention is on me. "What do you mean 'no'?"

"You don't need to be alone right now." He takes a handkerchief out of his pocket and leans over to gently dab it under my eyes. "I can stay with you."

Something tender and raw squeezes inside my chest. Ras has done a lot for me in the past few weeks. More than anyone else, including my family. Suddenly, I know with absolute certainty that if I asked him to spend all night in this car with me, he'd do it.

A sob rattles my lungs. I've always been scared of being alone, and I hadn't realized just how alone I've been since Vale left. If Cleo were here right now, she'd try to be supportive, but she'd tell me to stop crying because seeing me cry always makes her sad. And I'd do it. I'd bottle up my feelings for her sake.

Ras is different. He's watching me, his presence attentive and steady. He's giving me space to cry and freak out and feel scared.

And I am scared.

But something else is building beneath that fear, something heated by his gaze.

I sniff and wipe my cheeks with the back of my hand. "You were right back in Ibiza. I was angry. Angry that the only way my family can be safe is if I marry Rafaele. But I was also resigned to it. Maybe I'll never be as beautiful as Vale, or as courageous as Cleo, but at least I am selfless. Doing things in service of my family gives me value. It garners me praise. A long time ago, I got into the habit of doing exactly what Papà expects of me."

The diner's sign flickers. Through the tinted window of the car, I watch the lone waitress stroll past the empty tables before disappearing in the back.

When I turn to Ras, our eyes lock.

A slow heat travels through my veins.

My feelings for Ras go against everything I've been taught is right. They're selfish to the very bone.

But they're real. I want him. I've tried to fight it, but the insistent need won't leave. It hums beneath my skin whenever he's around.

Why not listen to it? Why not listen to myself for once? Can I even make out what that little voice inside my head is saying? It's all the way at the back, in the corner, silenced and pushed aside.

I grasp at it, pulling it to the forefront of my mind. "Maybe it's time I stop doing what Papà wants me to do and do what *I* want for a change," I whisper.

His face is shrouded in shadows, and I can't read him, but I think he can sense my intention. His body grows still.

Time moves in slow motion as I lift my palm and press it to Ras's bearded cheek.

He's so damn warm.

My thumb drops to his bottom lip, and I pull on it slightly.

He lets me, his eyes turning coal black. "What *do* you want, Peaches?" he murmurs.

"I want to pretend. I want to be someone else," I whisper.

"Who?"

"Someone who's not engaged."

Ras takes my left hand and slowly pulls off the emerald ring.

He drops it in the middle console with a clank. "Done."

I swallow. "I want to be a normal twenty-year-old."

"What do normal twenty-year-olds do?"

"At midnight, in cars with handsome, dangerous men? I'm not sure."

His lips twitch, and he drags a thumb over my wrist. "I have a few ideas."

My heart pounds against my ribcage. "Show me."

His eyes flash, and he lets go of my wrist and slides his seat back. "Come here." His voice is low and seductive, dragging over the place between my legs.

I reach for him. He wraps his palms around my waist and effortlessly deposits me onto his lap.

My thigh presses against something hard.

I reach behind his head, undo his hair, and watch it tumble down to frame his face. When I push my fingers into his locks, he slides his palms under the hem of my T-shirt and stops just below the underside of my breasts.

His touch leaves me impossibly hot.

"Higher," I urge, tugging on his hair.

He smirks and takes his sweet ass time as he inches his hands to palm my breasts.

My teeth dig into my bottom lip. When he curls his fingers over the top of my bra and tweaks a nipple, I can't help but whine.

I'm aroused, my mind turning hazy, and the words are coming easier now. "After the department store...I started having dreams."

He leans in, pressing his lips to my throat. "Yeah? What happens in them?"

"You kiss my neck, just like that. I love how your beard drags against my skin. It makes me crazy in the dream. You touch me over my clothes, but it's not enough. I wake up all hot and bothered."

He drops one hand, his fingers curling over the waistband of my sweats and brushing against the edge of my underwear. "That must be uncomfortable."

"It is. I...ache. But when I try to get rid of it, I can't."

"Why not?"

"The first time it happened, I spent half an hour trying to... make myself come."

He makes a strangled sound. "Oh fuck."

"But I couldn't do it. I've never done it before without a vibrator. I guess I don't know how."

One hand cups my nape, and Ras sits up straighter, bringing our faces within an inch of each other. His ragged breath hits my cheeks.

"It's okay, baby. I'll show you how."

He kisses me.

This time, I'm not frozen. I don't fight it.

This time, it feels right. Too damn right.

His tongue slips inside my mouth. I wrap my arms around his broad shoulders and plaster myself to his front. His erection presses to the apex of my thighs. The sudden pressure against my clit is enough to make me jump, but he presses me back down onto him and groans.

"Fuck, you even taste like peaches," he mutters between kisses, his big hands roaming over my body.

I start to grind on his erection, the ache between my legs back on full force. He notices, and we're suddenly moving. It takes me a moment to realize he's lowering the back of his seat.

He cups my ass, kneading it for a moment. Then he fists the fabric of my sweats and makes a frustrated huff, like he finds them offensive. "Get these off. Lie down on me."

I do. Somehow, we manage to get my pants off in an impressive display of teamwork.

"What about the thong—"

Ras rips it off me.

"Sit up," he commands and helps me get into an upright position while I'm straddling his waist.

He lifts my shirt over my head and tosses it away before moving to unclasp my bra. He drags the straps down my arms, his gaze flashing with hunger when he sees my bare breasts.

Embarrassment fans through me. I'm completely naked, while he's fully dressed, but when I raise one palm to cover myself, he takes it and pins it to my side.

"No," he rasps. "Let me get my fill. You're so fucking beautiful."

He caresses my skin, memorizing every dip and curve. He slides his rough hands up my bare thighs and then spreads my pussy lips open.

I suck in a harsh breath. There's a steady hum beneath my flesh.

His fingers find my center, and he groans. "Peaches, you're soaked. Let me get a taste."

The heat spreading across my skin ratchets up at that.

"Wh-what?"

His gaze is molten. "Not the time to be shy. Come up here and sit on my face."

While I consider his invitation, he pinches my nipples and rolls his hips, creating delicious friction against my clit. "You want me to beg for that pussy? I want it now, Gemma. Right. Fucking. Now."

I flush all over.

He drops his palms to squeeze my ass and then pushes me up his body, getting me where he wants me in no time.

"Lower," he growls as I hover above him.

My breathing is ragged. "What if you can't breathe?"

"That's the idea." He grips my upper thighs and tugs me down in one fell swoop.

His tongue drags over my slit, and my eyes roll to the back of my head. The pleasure is like nothing I've ever made myself feel before.

He fucks me with his tongue, taking turns between that and sucking on my clit.

Suddenly, that orgasm doesn't seem all that out of reach.

"Shit," I pant.

I slap my palm against the window. "Keep doing that."

He makes a satisfied noise and squeezes my thighs harder.

It doesn't take him long to work me into a state where all rational thoughts are gone.

My fingers are buried in his hair. I'm grinding on his face, forgetting all about my earlier fears of suffocation, and he slaps my ass, encouraging me to keep going.

I moan, my butt cheek stinging deliciously from the impact. Somehow, it only heightens the pleasure.

He slides one hand lower and pushes a thick finger inside of me while he circles my clit with his tongue.

It's that novel intrusion that sends the wave building inside of me crashing.

I gasp through the orgasm, my body undulating above him. "Ras... Oh God."

He keeps lapping at my pussy, gentler now, his eyes trained on me as I shiver and spasm.

When I finally stop moving, he gives me one more long, thorough lick, and then he drags me down his body.

His face lines up with mine, and he pulls me down for a kiss, forcing me to taste myself on his lips.

I feel myself falling deeper into this fantasy. One where there's just me and him, and the rest of the world doesn't matter.

He breaks the kiss, his eyes dark pools of lust as he stares at me.

"What other ideas do you have?" I whisper, sliding my hand between us and cupping him over the fabric of his sweatpants.

He shivers as I drag my hand up and down.

Not that I have any experience, but he seems...large. A shiver runs through me. What would it feel like to have him deep inside of me?

Something shifts in his expression, like he's wondering the very same thing.

"My other ideas—" he swallows thickly, "—would all end with you being thoroughly ruined for your marriage."

My pussy clenches even as reality starts to creep back in.

I'm still engaged to Rafaele. I'm still getting married. Until I talk to Vince, I'm not in any position to make other plans.

I don't know if I should be looking for an exit route. I'm not even sure one exists.

That means Ras and I can't cross that line.

The fantasy comes crashing down.

Ras stiffens as I sit up.

I disentangle myself from him and awkwardly slide back onto my seat. We've made the windows of the car all foggy.

Ras lifts up his seat and wipes the window to his left with his palm while I pull on my clothes.

We sit there in silence for another minute before he gives me a long, searching look and then turns on the car.

CHAPTER 20

RAS

I'M LYING on the bed, staring at the chandelier hanging above my head.

My cock is hard. Weeping. I take it into my fist, close my eyes, and give it a few pumps as my imagination goes back to that car.

Her gasps. The way she clenched her thighs around my ears. Her earthy juices dripping into my mouth and soaking my beard. I can still smell them now.

I wanted to fuck her until she forgot her own name, but I didn't even let her touch me.

Why, you fucking fool?

Because the only thing she wanted from me was a release. A distraction from the bad news she'd received.

And I'm starting to realize I want a hell of a lot more.

I speed up, eager to get it done with and get her out of my head. I don't want to drag this out.

This fucking *need*.

Cazzo. I haven't been this bad over a girl since Sara. Even that feels like nothing in comparison to the fire blazing inside my chest.

I reach inside the pocket of my sweats and pull out a lacy piece of barely there fabric. Her ripped thong. What would she think if she saw me right now? Pressing my nose into her underwear while my balls tighten and my cock gets ready to blow? Would she get on her knees in front of me and beg for a taste?

My eyes squeeze shut, and I come on my stomach. The orgasm wrecks me, just like it always does when I'm thinking of her.

I prowl into the shower, eager to clear my damn head. The news about Garzolo's succession plan was not what I'd been expecting when Gemma texted me to meet her.

I already knew he was a piece of shit, but this takes the cake. Does the man care about anything but his own damn hide?

When Gemma started questioning her marriage, I felt the kind of hope I haven't felt in a long fucking time. I'm not a religious man, but in that moment, I swear I heard angels sing.

But then she walked it right back. And maybe that's a good thing, because I was about to offer to get her out of New York on the next flight out, forgetting that it's not my call to make. It's Dem's.

I send him a text, telling him to call me when he can, and then I drift in and out of sleep for the next few hours.

Dem calls around six am.

"Anything from Orrin?" he asks.

I haul my tired body out of bed and collapse in the wing-back chair by the window. It's snowing again. When will this shit end? The driveway is blanked in white.

"No, but I've got information from somewhere else."

I recount what Gemma told me.

There's a long sigh on the other end of the line. "This just got a lot more interesting."

"Interesting? This is a clusterfuck."

"Both can be true at the same time. Now it's clear what both sides are getting out of this alliance."

"Messero's done pretty damn well for himself," I mutter. A wife, control of another clan, and a long-term deal with us, brokered by Garzolo. "Fuck him. We should call off our deal. This is the kind of information they should have coughed up when we met."

"Sounds like we still have five years left to deal with Garzolo. They would have told us eventually. Probably when the indictment goes out. Any sense of the potential timing on that?"

"No idea. I'll talk to Orrin, see if he's got anything. It might be imminent for all we know."

"The balance of power has shifted. Our deal ensures we have a line to Messero, who's now on track to become the most significant player in New York in five years."

I fucking hate the sound of that. "If Gemma doesn't marry him, his succession might fall through."

There's a drawn-out pause. "Is that what she's thinking? Does she want to call off the wedding?"

I rub my forehead. "No. She's confused, and she doesn't fully understand her brother's position in all of this. I think if Vince told her not to marry Rafaele, she'd try to get herself out of it, but if her brother actually doesn't want the gig, and her father gets put behind bars with no clear successor, her family will fall into chaos. She doesn't know what to do."

And frankly, I don't either. It's like we've lit a spotlight on a corner of a chessboard, and most of the pieces are invisible.

"I'll ask Vale to get in contact with Vince. See what she can find out," Dem says.

"Good idea."

"So Gemma told you all of this?"

"Yeah."

"Why?"

"It was a shock to her and Cleo. Gemma thought she's marrying Rafaele to protect her family from some unknown threat. Garzolo misled her. When she realized he's doing it for his own benefit, she was upset. She needed someone to talk to."

There's another long pause. "And out of everyone, she chose to talk to you?"

Apprehension slips inside my veins at the suspicion in his tone. "She did."

"Ras, did something happen between you two?"

I should tell him the truth.

I want her.

I feel something for her.

She's got a rope wrapped around my heart, and when she tugs on it, I can't do anything but follow.

I can't say any of those things.

The situation has gotten complicated, but one thing is clear. She's still engaged to a man Dem does not want me making into our enemy.

He'll tell me to keep my fucking distance. He's my don, and I'll have to obey him.

So I lie. Fuck, I can't remember the last time I lied to him. "Nothing happened."

"All right," he says, and from the way he says it, I can tell that he believes me. "Good work with all of this. If you hear more rumblings about the FBI and Garzolo, I want you to get out of there. We don't know what timeline we're working with, and there's no need for us to get involved in any mess. It sounds like if Garzolo is taken out of commission, Messero will be capable of holding up their end of the deal, which is all we care about. In fact, I'm not sure if there's any reason for you to stay there any longer."

Ice spreads through my lungs.

No fucking way. I can't leave now. "Let me stay and find out more. What if Messero is implicated in all of this? He might think he has the FBI in his pocket, but it wouldn't be the first time a don has overplayed his hand."

"All right. Let's give it a bit more time," he concedes.

Relief floods me. "I'll call if anything new comes up."

At breakfast, I find out that Pietra is taking Gemma and Cleo with her to their house in the Hamptons for the next two days.

I try to convince myself it's a good thing, because it'll give Gemma time to talk to her brother and process things, but there's a pang of disappointment low inside my gut.

Right before they're due to leave, Gemma finds me in the kitchen. The cook is prepping ingredients, but Gemma gives her a pointed look, and the woman quickly excuses herself to go outside for a cigarette.

I lean against the counter and drag my gaze over her form.

Tight leggings. A T-shirt with a wide neck that falls off one shoulder. A glimpse of a black sports bra beneath.

She's not dressed to impress anyone, and yet she's fucking gorgeous. I wasn't lying when I called her the most beautiful woman I'd ever seen.

I'm going half mad over her, and I don't even know how she feels about me.

Was it me she wanted last night? Or did she just want a willing participant in her fantasy, and I was the most convenient option?

I haven't missed how things have warmed between us since Ibiza, but last night was the first time she took the initiative and came to me. And for all I know, it was a one-time fluke.

If it was, that would be a good thing. I'm supposed to stay away from her. That's what Dem wants me to do, and he's my don. We didn't fuck. She's still probably marrying that cocksucker. She's still entirely out of my reach.

Tell me last night meant nothing. That it was a mistake.

If she says those words to me, I swear I'll leave her alone.

I'll wrap up my business here, go home, and probably spend the rest of my nights thinking of her while staring at my bedroom ceiling, but I'll manage.

Somehow, I'll manage.

She glances at me from beneath her lashes and awkwardly shifts in place. "I wanted to say bye in person." Her voice is husky. Raw.

A shiver runs down my spine.

"That's..." I take a sip of coffee, looking for the right words. "That's nice of you." I sound like a fucking moron.

She bites down on her lip. "Is everything okay?"

"Why wouldn't it be?"

"It's just...last night was..."

I brace myself for what's coming. She's going to say it was a mistake.

"It was incredible. And confusing."

Fireworks explode inside my chest. I file the *incredible* away, and ask, "Confusing... How?"

Pink spreads over her cheeks. "I wish you'd let me touch you. I *wanted* to touch you." She glances away.

Fuck.

"Peaches," I say brokenly. I put my cup down, walk over to her, and lift her chin up with my knuckle, forcing her to look at me. She sucks in a tiny breath, her eyes wide and a little shy.

She's not lying.

And it's not just lust shining in her eyes.

Something tender flashes within them, and it makes my breath catch. We're standing still, but my heart feels like it's soaring.

It's not just me. She feels something too.

She moves first, bringing her hand to my chest.

I back her against the counter, my arms caging her in on both sides. She shoots a look over my shoulder but doesn't tell me to stop.

Her fingertips trace a light path over my abdomen and then drift lower.

I'm already hard. It doesn't take much with her.

She cups my erection.

I swallow down a groan.

Why the fuck is she leaving for two whole days?

And how much trouble would I be in if I crash every single one of Garzolo's cars to keep her here?

"I wanted to make you come," she whispers. "I've never made a man come before."

I press my lips just below her ear. "Trust me, you did."

She shivers when she realizes what I mean. "When?"

"Last night after I got back to my room," I growl, "and every fucking night since I arrived here. Do you know what it's like watching your tight little ass prance around me? Or smelling your scent in the air whenever I leave my room?" I roll my hips against her. "You drive me fucking crazy."

She gasps and slips her hand inside my jeans.

The moment her palm wraps around my cock, I nearly keel over. When she pumps it up and down, I feel like I've made it into heaven.

We're in the kitchen, where anyone can walk in on us, and I'm losing my mind over a hand job.

A door closes loudly in the distance, and we break apart.

Fucking fuck.

This is torture.

She's breathing hard as she watches me adjust myself, her eyes glazed over and hungry. Just knowing that I'd find a whole lot of wet if I reached inside her panties right now makes my pre-cum leak out.

She backs away slowly, her gaze locked with mine. "I don't know what I'm doing. But I don't want to stop."

I must be losing my mind, because although I've just spent all morning convincing myself what a bad idea this is, I still say, "Me neither."

"Gemma!" her mother calls out from a few rooms down. "We're leaving!"

"I have to go," she says. As she moves past me, our fingers twine together for a split second, and then she's gone.

CHAPTER 21

RAS

I KEEP myself busy over the two days by spending some time hanging around Garzolo's crew. They don't say anything to signal they're aware of the trouble brewing with the Feds, but that's not surprising, since they must know better than to talk about anything important around me.

My next meeting with Orrin is far more productive. He managed to confirm what Gemma told me about Garzolo at his poker game. The Feds are preparing a RICO indictment for Garzolo and a few other high-up members of his clan. They're all looking at doing decades or life.

I wonder if his deal with Messero covers getting the rest of the guys out.

Orrin also tells me he's heard rumors about Messero's connection to the DA before, but I ask him to see if he can get anything more concrete so that I can convince Dem I need to stay here a bit longer.

I'm practically counting down the hours until Gemma returns.

It's pathetic.

I'm a made man.

An underboss in the most powerful clan in the Camorra.

And this girl—one engaged to another man nonetheless—has me wrapped around her finger.

Friday afternoon, I'm eating a late lunch in the dining room when I hear her voice.

I stay in my seat, not wanting to seem too eager. But when she comes in and her eyes light up at seeing me, I realize I'm thoroughly fucked.

My heart beats louder inside my chest. My fingers clench as if they're searching for something of hers to grab onto.

"Hi," she breathes. "Were you bored here on your own?"

Bored.

Being bored would be a hell of a lot better than engaging in this dance with insanity.

You can't have her. No matter what happens between the two of you in the days you have left here, you can't fucking have her, you absolute damn idiot.

"I made do," I squeeze out.

Her mother appears behind her. "Ras, how are you?" she asks in an uncharacteristically friendly tone. "You're coming to the Messero party tonight, correct?"

She's in a better mood than I've ever seen her. Their time in the Hamptons must have done her some good, or maybe that's simply the effect of not being around her husband for a few days.

"Wouldn't miss it for the world."

"Good. I don't think Stefano and I will make it to the club, but the girls will go. Gemma needs to be there to support Rafaele. Are you able to accompany them?"

Support him? It's a fucking birthday party for his aunt, not a funeral. I paste on a smile. "No problem."

"Excellent." Pietra turns to Gemma. "You should go shower and start getting ready. Rafaele will expect you to look perfect. Most of his family will be there."

My vision darkens at the edges, and Gemma stiffens as if she can guess the direction of my thoughts.

"Okay," she says, giving me her back. "I'll go do that."

She hurries away to make herself pretty for her asshole fiancé while all I can do is pretend like this isn't fucking killing me.

A few hours later, I'm dressed and ready to go. Garzolo and I are waiting downstairs when Gemma and Cleo appear at the top of the steps.

My gaze latches onto her and doesn't let go.

She's wearing that dress she tried on in the department store, only now it fits her like a glove, highlighting all her soft curves. The memory of that day torments me, spreading heat over my skin. When she moves past me, the backs of our hands brush, and her cheeks redden.

We get on the road, me in one car, and the rest of them in the other. After the club, I'll drive Cleo and Gemma home.

Giulia Messero's birthday party is in downtown Manhattan at a place called the Melody Club. The room is already filled to the brim with Messeros by the time we arrive. On one side is a long bar, and on the other, the food is laid out buffet style. The dress code is formal, but some of the women have taken liberties with their interpretation. One in a tight red minidress with her cleavage practically spilling out passes by me and gives me a coquettish smile.

Gemma appears at my side, her gaze narrowing on the woman.

"How was your trip?" I ask, taking advantage of the fact that her mother isn't hovering around her.

"It was two days, but it felt like a week."

"Tell me about it," I say gruffly.

A small smile pulls at her lips. "I missed you too."

My chest expands, but I manage to keep my expression straight. "Did you talk to Vince?"

Her face falls. "No. I'm so annoyed. I rang him dozens of times and left him a ton of messages. He only responded to one and said we'll talk soon. I don't know what to make of it."

Neither do I. Vale hasn't been able to get in touch with Vince either. It seems like he's ignoring everyone who might be able to help him.

Suspicion tugs at the back of my mind, but I don't voice it to Gemma, because I don't want to risk upsetting her with speculation.

Still, I wonder if Garzolo is telling the truth... What if Vince is happy to have this responsibility taken from him?

Gemma lifts on her toes, trying to see above the crowd. "Anyway, I should go say hi to Nona. I think she's somewhere over there."

"Let's go."

As we weave through the crowd, I spot Rafaele across the room talking to a group of men. One of them, tall and dark haired, turns.

My steps halt.

It can't be.

But then he smirks and waves at someone, and the scar on my wrist prickles.

My blood runs cold with recognition. It's him. I'd recognize that smirk anywhere. I stared at it while I was sure I was about to bleed out.

Nunzio.

I'd heard he left Italy for America shortly after getting married to Sara, but I never would have guessed he'd link up with the mafia here. I always thought part of why he hated me so much was because he despised my family and the power they had over his own.

But it wouldn't be the first time a man pretended to hate something he wanted deep down.

Gemma stops by a table, but I keep moving, as if in a trance.

I told myself that if I ever ran into him again, I'd kill him. My hand reaches for my gun, only for me to remember it was confiscated at the door. The only men allowed to have guns are the guards at the entrance. That's fine. I don't need a gun to kill a man, but this could get messy.

What the fuck is Nunzio doing here? Does he work for Messero?

As if I needed another reason to despise that fucker.

Nunzio starts moving along the edge of the room, and I speed up my steps to intercept him. I need to find out what position he occupies here before I can decide what exactly to do with him.

Our paths collide a few moments later. I stop in front of him, blocking his way. He flicks his gaze to me, his lips curled in an irritated sneer I know all too well. When he realizes who he's looking at, the smirk melts away and blood leaves his face. His hand jerks to his waist, finding air.

Nunzio swallows. I wonder if he's doing the same kind of math I'm doing in my head. We've always been about the same height, and ten years ago, he was far stronger than me, but time hasn't been kind to him. His shoulders are slumped, his gut hangs over his belt, and his lips are dry and thin from what I suspect has been a lifetime smoking habit. At seventeen, he was already smoking a pack a day.

He must realize there's a high probability he'll be dead in under a minute because he takes a step back.

"Sorrentino," he says, not using my nickname for once. "What are you doing here?"

"I could ask the same thing. I always wondered what happened to you after you left Napoli."

His narrowed eyes scan my face. "I heard you're the under-boss of the Casalesi now. Is that true?"

If he's in Messero's inner circle, he would know this with certainty. He must not be that high up.

"I am."

He adjusts his stance, visibly tense. "Congratulations."

"You're with Messero?"

He nods.

"When did you land with his crew?"

"A few years ago."

"Oh yeah? They treating you well?"

"Fine." He sniffs. "So what brings you here?"

"I'm Garzolo's guest. We're family now, haven't you heard?
Damiano, the new don, married one of Garzolo's
daughters."

Some tension leaves Nunzio's shoulders. Is he relieved I
didn't come all the way to New York for him? Maybe he
thinks I'm unlikely to do anything that might jeopardize the
relationship between Garzolo and Messero.

I'll admit, killing him right now wouldn't look good, but that
doesn't mean I'm not tempted.

He swipes his fist under his nose and shoots me an insolent
look. "So you became a ras after all. I have to admit, I
thought as Ras of the Casalesi, you'd have more important
things to do than visit family abroad."

I smirk. He can't keep up his polite act around me for more
than a minute.

Good. Let's cut the shit. "And what do you do for Messero?
Pull things off the back of a truck? Harass small mom-and-
pop stores for protection money? How does it feel, Nunzio,

to do all the same things you used to revile my family for doing?"

Revulsion flashes across his face before he masks it with a cold smirk. "I'll do whatever I have to in order for my family to have a better life here than they did back in Napoli. I know that must be hard for you to understand. You've never cared about anyone as much as you care about yourself. I'm surprised Don De Rossi has put his trust in you. If he knew you like I do, he'd realize it's only a matter of time before you screw him for your own gain."

His words make me bristle with indignation. He's wrong. I may have been selfish when Nunzio knew me, but I've changed. Back then, I was just a fucking kid who felt like he'd already disappointed everyone, so what was the point of trying? But I'm not that kid anymore.

I promised myself I'd never disappoint Dem, and I haven't.

"People change, Nunzio."

Across the room, a flash of yellow catches my gaze.

It's Gemma. I watch her as she walks up to Rafaele. She offers him her hand, and he presses his lips to it. I make the mistake of watching their interaction for a second too long, and Nunzio notices.

He chuckles. "*Cazzo*. You should see your face just now. Subtlety was never your strong suit. That's Messero's fiancé, Gemma Garzolo, right? You're staying with them on your visit. Let me guess, you spent a few days watching her prance around the house, and now you want her."

I keep a flat expression, even as a heavy weight materializes inside my gut. If Dem knew what I've done already with Gemma...

Nunzio smirks. "But you can't have her. My, my, how history repeats itself. Tell me..." He leans in close to my ear. "Have you ever gotten a single thing you've truly wanted? Or do they all slip through your fingers the way Sara did?"

The rage that sweeps through me is so potent I barely realize what I'm doing. I grab him by the scruff of his shirt and swiftly push him through a nearby door that turns out to lead to a small, empty parlor.

He claws at my arm, trying to get my fingers off his neck, but my grip may as well be made of stone.

His face turns red.

His eyes start to bulge.

When his eyelids begin to droop, the distorted voice in my head suddenly becomes clear.

Let go of him.

I snap out of it, throwing him to the floor.

He clutches his throat and wheezes for breath.

Fuck. The pain he inflicted on me still runs deep, as does my need to make him pay, but this isn't the right place or time.

He'll get what's coming to him.

I take a step back just as a woman peeks through the crack in the door.

She makes a loud gasp and rushes into the room.

My heart jumps into my throat when I see who it is.

Sara.

"Nunzio!"

She brushes by me and falls to her knees by the man who's hateful eyes blaze in my direction.

My past slams into me, memories flooding in.

I met her a few months after Nunzio tried to kill me on the playground. She was sitting on her own at a café in the neighborhood, and when I walked by her, she smiled. She had a beautiful smile. Kind eyes that were the same color as the sky. I said an awkward hello and somehow mustered up the courage to ask if I could buy her another espresso. She said yes.

That's how it began.

I fell hard and fast. So did she, or at least that's what I thought. Eventually, I told her about Nunzio and what he'd done to me. It was a stain on my life, a painful past that made me feel weak and ashamed.

She listened. Sympathized.

Then a few months later, she left me for him.

I blink, studying the woman she's become. She's aged, but from what I can see, she's just as beautiful. Thick eyeliner frames her light-blue eyes and wavy dark hair—I used to love that hair—cascades down her back.

What kind of a life did she make with Nunzio? I refuse to believe someone like him could be a decent man to anyone around him.

"What happened?" she asks in a panicked voice, reaching for his arm. He jerks it away from her and starts to hobble back up.

"I'm fine, Sara."

She reaches for him again, and he snarls at her, "I said I'm fine."

Hurt blooms over her expression.

There used to be a time when seeing her hurt would drive me into a fit, but as I look at her now, I feel nothing.

Absolutely nothing.

She twists her head and looks at me. "Who is that?"

Ten years have passed since she last saw me. I look different now.

I *am* different now.

"No one," Nunzio growls, dusting himself off, but she keeps staring at me.

Finally, recognition flashes inside her eyes. "Cassio?"

I don't answer. There's nothing left for us to say to each other, so I turn away and exit through the door.

I'm still trying to pull myself together when Gemma finds me by the bar. I'm about to order a drink I desperately need.

"Hey, where did you go?" She places her hand on my sleeve. "We need to talk."

"I know." I flag the bartender down and order a beer. "I was catching up with an old friend."

"Oh? I didn't know you knew anyone from Messero's crew."

"I didn't know he worked for Messero. It was a...surprise."

She nods. "I need to find Cleo to make sure she eats something before we go to the club. Otherwise she'll be wasted in fifteen minutes."

Out of the corner of my eye, I see Nunzio and Sara step out of the room where I left them. Nunzio's palm is pressed against his neck to hide the marks I left.

His gaze meets mine, furious and vengeful. The next time we meet, I'm not sure there's anything that'll stop us from putting this to rest one way or another.

"Who's that?" Gemma asks.

The bartender hands me a beer, and I tip it against my lips. Nunzio and Sara weave through the crowd until they disappear. "No one."

"What's wrong?"

She gazes at me, looking so fucking lovely and concerned about me that I get a terrible urge to lean down and kiss her.

"Have you ever gotten a single thing you've truly wanted?"

No. Because after Sara, I stopped wanting anything for myself. I didn't want to risk having something I cared about only for someone to take it away from me. Again.

I found my purpose serving Damiano and being his right-hand man, but is that really all I want out of life?

Gemma's brows pinch together as she waits for my answer.

She and I, we're not so different after all. She's been devoted to her family, neglecting her own wants in service of them.

And me... Well, I've devoted myself to Dem and his mission. I've even managed to convince myself I've found happiness doing that.

But I've been lying to myself.

I'm not happy.

Last time I fell hard for a woman, I lost her.

And I think that's going to happen again.

Because I can't have Gemma without blowing everything to pieces and going against my don's will.

CHAPTER 22

GEMMA

WE SIT DOWN FOR DINNER. Something is wrong with Ras tonight, but I can't figure out what. He's been quiet since I found him by the bar, his brows furrowed in thought.

Mamma's last-minute trip to the Hamptons couldn't have happened at a worse time. She said she wanted to give us a chance to process the news we got somewhere calm, but I have a feeling Papà asked her to take us away so that we wouldn't talk about it in the house while Ras is around.

It's way too late for that though. Ras knows what he plans to do to our family.

Mamma made sure to offer us plenty of her usual guidance. *"Remember, you may not understand your father's ways, but everything he does is to protect our family."*

I'm so sick of hearing that. She said it all the time to us growing up.

How did it take me until the age of twenty to realize it's a lie?

I feel trapped. Vince hasn't returned my calls, and I don't know why. My wedding is mere weeks away, and at this point, making any attempt to back out would be like setting off an atomic bomb.

What if Papà's right about Vince not wanting the responsibility? Why didn't I ask him about it at Vale's wedding?

I gnaw on my nail. I don't know what to do. I'm not a political mastermind.

All of this just feels wrong.

Except for what's happening between Ras and I.

Which is crazy, because what we're doing is *objectively* wrong. The Gemma from even a month ago would have never done what I did in that car with him.

I'm cheating on my fiancé. I'm risking us getting caught. I'm being selfish.

And it feels intoxicating.

The scene in the car played on repeat inside my head for the two days we were away.

I couldn't wait to be back around him.

I want more. So much more.

I wish we hadn't stopped.

A waiter snaps me out of my reverie when he comes to refill my water. I glance around the table. Ras is sitting across from me, while Cleo and I are sandwiched between Papà and Mamma. Rafaele, Rafaele's mother, and Nero are here as well.

My fiancé may as well be a ghost. I barely register him. When I first met Rafaele, I was constantly aware of his presence, the way prey is aware of a predator. Now, it's surprisingly easy to pretend he doesn't exist. Why should I save my body for him? This emphasis on my virtue when most of the men in this room possess none is hypocrisy at its finest.

I wish I'd just said screw it and had sex with Ras. The thought of doing it makes my skin buzz with excitement.

I want to feel all of his attention on my body again, but with no restraint this time. I want him to lose himself in me. Those lips on my breasts. His fists in my hair.

He'd be gentle at first. Careful. I'm sure of it. That's how he was with me in the car. But then he'd turn impatient. Demanding. It's that contrast in him that makes me weak in the knees.

Ras cuts into his steak with precision and puts a piece into his mouth. The tendons on his thick neck move, and his jaw flexes as he chews. His big, rough hands make the fork look tiny.

Heat swirls between my legs.

I love those hands.

I love how they feel against my skin.

I love how just before he puts them on me, my body tingles with anticipation and everything comes alive.

He must feel the weight of my attention, because he glances in my direction. The expression on my face makes his eyes darken.

"Ras, when are you heading back to Italy?" Nero asks.

His gaze is still on me, and it flashes with pain. "Soon."

What? My stomach drops. "How soon?" I blurt out, barely hiding my crushing disappointment.

He cuts another piece of steak. "No set date yet, but I'm likely to leave within the week."

It's an effort to maintain control over my features.

What is this? Why is he leaving?

Because you're still getting married to a don. Did you think Ras would stay here forever?

No, but I just want a bit more time.

What for?

My nails dig into the flesh of my palms.

He's somehow become the only good thing in my life. In the midst of all this betrayal, heartbreak, and chaos, he's the only anchor I have left. A light in the darkness.

And it looks like I won't even have that soon.

The dinner wraps up, our parents bid Cleo and I goodbye, and the two of us head out with Ras to Rafaele's club. Once we're there, a bouncer leads us to the private entrance meant for VIPs.

I can count on one hand the number of times I've been allowed to go to places like this. Our cousins took Cleo and I out to Papà's club in the Meatpacking District two times, and there was one birthday party for a girl from my school.

It says something about how close Papà is to Rafaele that he's okay with Cleo and I coming here with just one escort.

"When were you going to mention that you're leaving soon?" I ask Ras under the cover of the blaring music.

His palm finds a spot on my lower back. "I only just talked to Dem about it. I was going to tell you tonight, but Nero asked before I could."

So Dem wants him home. I guess Ras accomplished whatever diplomatic mission he was sent here for, and now he has no reason to stay. I can hardly call my brother-in-law and ask him to lend me his underboss for a little longer because I feel things for him that I have no business feeling.

Maybe Ras's decided I'm not worth the risk. Rafaele would kill him if he knew what we've done. It doesn't matter that Rafaele doesn't feel an ounce of attraction to me—by contract, I'm already his.

That realization is tough to swallow. I'm putting Ras in danger by keeping this thing between us going.

"I'm going to grab a drink," Cleo says, ditching us and heading to the bar.

I'm still trying to collect my thoughts when Nero intercepts us moments after she leaves.

"There you are. This way," he says, gesturing ahead. "Rafaele wants to speak to you, Gemma."

Behind me, Ras stiffens. I shoot him a wary look and slip my hand into the crook of Nero's offered arm.

My fiancé notices us approaching and acknowledges me with a nod. He's in a huge round leather booth with a few of his men around him. They make space for me, Ras, and Nero.

Ras takes a seat on one end, Nero beside him, and I sit by Rafaele. If he notices the inches of space I'm careful to leave between us, he doesn't say anything about it or make an attempt to move closer.

He reaches for a bottle of wine and pours me a glass.

I take a sip. "You wanted to talk to me?"

"You were distressed at our last dinner," he says, pouring a glass for himself. "I wanted to see how you feel about my future role as the head of your family now that you've had some time to think about it."

He wants my opinion. Didn't I make myself clear? "You're stealing something that doesn't belong to you."

His icy gaze drops to me, and fear zips up my spine. Out of the corner of my eye, I see Ras crack his neck. He's watching us but he can't hear our conversation over the noise in the club.

"Stealing? The favor I'll have to call in with the DA is not only worth millions of dollars, but also many lost lives and years of espionage. That favor took a lot of work to get. Giving me control of your family is the only thing your father could have offered me to make it a fair deal. He even managed to get a concession out of me—five more years as don."

I clench my fists. He's explaining all this to me with the confidence of someone who believes they're in the right. It infuriates me.

"How is any of this fair if Papà's using Vince and I as his chess pieces? Papà lied to me about why I had to marry you. He manipulated me."

"And when I realized you didn't know what you were signing up for, I told your father he had to come clean." Rafaele places his glass on the table and rests his elbows on his knees. "He didn't want to tell you the truth, but I made it clear he had to, or I'd walk from our deal. I'm not above lying to my enemies, but if we're to become a family, I don't want us to start on a foundation of lies."

"How do you expect me to believe that when you're still lying to me about Vince?"

Rafaele frowns. "How so?"

"I don't believe for a second that he's okay with this. He's Papà's only son. The position of don is his."

Rafaele stares at me for a long while and then says, "The whole thing was your brother's idea."

I laugh. It's a shock response, a thing to do when I can't formulate words. My pulse gets louder and louder in my ears, and Rafaele just keeps staring, cataloging my reactions.

I want to hit him.

I want to punch him right in the face for being such as a filthy fucking liar. "Bullshit."

"Vince was pulled into our negotiations when Stefano and I couldn't agree on the terms of our deal. Stefano thought his son might have some creative ideas, and he did. He said he didn't want to become don because he wants to continue running his own things abroad. He asked me what I thought about becoming your father's successor. I wasn't sold at first. I thought he wasn't being honest with me. But then I went to visit him in Switzerland and saw what he's built there. It's impressive." Rafaele takes a sip of his drink. "He convinced me he really meant what he said. We had to work out how to get your family to accept me, and that's when it became obvious I'd have to marry my way in. Vince thought you were the best option. I wasn't sure it was going to work out, because you didn't seem too agreeable or interested during our initial meeting. But then the war with the Riccis began, and your papa said you were on board. When I saw you months later, it appeared you'd changed your tune. You seemed committed, just like Vince said you would be. Your brother's not a pawn, Gemma. He orchestrated all of it."

The wineglass in my hand shakes.

I put it on the table and press my spine into the leather seat. I don't want to believe him. My brother wouldn't do that to me.

My brother wouldn't use me like that.

But then I remember the things he said in Ibiza, and I suddenly see them in a different light.

"I could never live with Papà breathing down my neck."

"He's lucky to have you, Gem. Very lucky. He raised three selfish kids, and one selfless daughter."

"I'm not going to convince you of anything. I don't agree with Vale. You should marry Rafaele."

Acid floods my mouth. Back then, I was touched that Vince had looked into Rafaele on my behalf. I thought he was watching out for me. Instead, he'd probably done all that research to make sure his masterplan wouldn't fail. This is why he's been ignoring my calls. He's probably scared of what I have to say.

"Gemma."

I blink. Rafaele looks at me and then glances down at the emerald ring on my hand. "I can't give you love. But I can give you respect and honesty. And I can promise that I'll treat your family the way I treat my own."

I nod numbly.

There is no way out of this marriage. Not when Papà, Vince, and Rafaele are all working together. There's nothing I can do. Nothing anyone can do.

My fate is sealed.

Nero interrupts us. "Rafe, you've got a call. I think you should take it."

Rafaele takes the phone from Nero. "Excuse me." He walks away with his consigliere, and the two of them disappear behind a hidden door off to the side.

Ras is beside me as soon as they're gone, his thigh bumping against mine. "Are you all right?"

I swallow. My throat is bone dry. "No."

"What's going on?"

"Papà didn't lie to me about Vince." It takes effort to get the words out of my mouth. "He really is giving up his position. He doesn't want to be don. He wants it to be Rafaele."

Despair wraps around me. I've always tried to do the right thing, so what did I do to deserve this? A father who lies to me and hits me. A brother who manipulates me and uses me for his own gain. They've laid an elaborate trap and forced me into a corner. There's no way out.

Ras is saying something, but a movement across the dance floor catches my attention. I jump to my feet. "Is that Ludovico?" My eyes widen when the crowd parts. "Oh God, he's all over Cleo."

Ras stands, his eyes narrowing on the scene playing out on the other side of the VIP area. Ludovico is tugging Cleo into him, trying to grind up on her from behind while my sister tries to shove him away. She breaks his hold, whirls around, and shouts something right into his face.

My stomach drops. He's drunk, and I think Cleo's in trouble.

"We have to go," I say urgently. "We need to get him away from her."

Ras and I try to squeeze through the crowd, but it's packed, and we're moving so slowly, I start panicking.

"What do we do?" I shout over the music.

Ras moves ahead of me, parting the crowd by shoving people aside. I suspect he's growling at everyone to get out of his way, and no one's idiotic enough to not listen.

My pulse is loud inside my ears by the time we finally emerge from the crowd, but Cleo and Ludovico aren't in the spot I saw them before.

"Where are they?"

Ras points. "There."

Cleo's standing on a small round balcony that overlooks the dance floor below. Her back is pressed against the rail, and her expression is a grimace. She's angry, but I know her well enough to detect a hint of fear.

Ludovico is crowding her. His hands are on her waist and sliding lower. Cleo yells something and digs her high heel into his foot. He staggers backward, the music swallowing up his shout. Before Cleo has a chance to dart away, he lunges at her, fist raised.

Fear seizes me. He's out of control. What if he knocks her over the balcony? "Cleo!"

Ludovico's fist never makes contact with my sister.

Someone catches his arm from behind.

It's Rafaele.

For the first time since I've met him, there's no mistaking the raw emotion on his face.

Cold, merciless fury.

The crowd quiets, even as music keeps blasting through the club. Everyone is waiting with bated breath to see what Rafaele will do. Everyone but Ludovico, who's still snarling insults at Cleo like a rabid dog.

Rafaele says something I'm too far away to make out, and the effect on Ludovico is immediate. He freezes in place and slowly turns. When he sees who grabbed him, his mouth abruptly slams shut.

Whatever Ludovico sees in my fiancé's eyes makes him visibly cower. He's halfway through uttering what I presume is an apology when it happens.

Something glints in the darkness of the club. A knife in Rafaele's hand.

He jerks Ludovico away from Cleo with such force I think he may dislocate Ludovico's shoulder, and then he lifts his other hand and slashes the knife down.

This time, even the music isn't loud enough to mask Ludovico's shriek.

No one in the VIP area moves.

Rafaele drops Ludovico on the ground like he's a bag of trash and takes a step backward.

A horrified gasp leaves my throat.

The knife is sticking out of Ludovico's eye socket.

Get Cleo.

I'm the first one to move. I run toward her, some primal part of me kicking into action and screaming at me to get her away from here. "Cleo! Come here!"

But she doesn't hear me. When I reach her, she's staring down at Ludovico in horror, her back pressed against the rail. Her skin is milky white with shock.

Rafaele tears his gaze from Ludovico and pins it on her. "You have blood on your shoes." His voice is calm and measured. I suspect if I checked his pulse right now, it would be as steady as a clock.

He just stabbed a man through the eye, and he's acting like nothing happened.

My stomach turns.

Cleo looks down, and when she sees Rafaele's right about the blood, she sags against me.

Rafaele locks eyes with someone behind me. "Get them out."

Ras steps forward. I hadn't even realized he was right beside me this whole time. "Let's go."

He and I grab Cleo under each arm and hurry out of the club.

"Wait here," Ras commands once we step onto the sidewalk. "I'm going to get the car and bring it around."

"Okay." I wrap my arms around Cleo and press my nose into her hair. She's trembling.

"Hey, are you okay?" I squeeze her harder. "Say something."

She shakes her head. I think she's crying.

"Are you hurt anywhere? Do we need to take you to a hospital?"

"No." Her voice is reedy.

When I try to pull away so I can look at her, she clings to me tighter. My chest cracks. I can't remember the last time I've seen her this shaken. When our parents are angry with her, it's like she's Teflon. All of their words slide right off.

"Cleo, I love you," I squeeze past the ball in my throat. "You're okay. You'll be okay."

She produces a wet little whimper. My arms squeeze her tightly, and it still doesn't feel like enough.

"C'mon, Cleo. Talk to me."

She breathes deeply against me for a few moments before lifting her head off my shoulder. Her eyes are red and puffy, and there's a hint of mascara smudged underneath them. "Gem, his blood is on me."

A shiver runs through me. "We'll get you cleaned up."

"I don't want to go home." She clutches my arm. "Can we go to the penthouse? It's not far. I don't want to deal with Mamma or Papà tonight. I just want to go to sleep."

The family has a penthouse that overlooks Central Park. I'm pretty sure it's where Papà takes his whores, but the family uses it from time to time too. It's not a bad idea to spend the night there.

We get into the car, and I give Ras directions.

He nods. "I can call your father and explain everything to him. Do you have a key?"

"I know the code."

Ras dials Papà, and while they talk, I wrap an arm around Cleo and pull her into me.

CHAPTER 23

GEMMA

WE STUMBLE into the penthouse directly from the elevator.

It looks like a museum. Renovated by a famous interior architect that cost Papà a pretty penny, it's all sleek lines, subtle textures, and mood lighting.

It's a status item, not a place meant to be lived in.

Still, it's better we're here than back home where Mamma and Papà would put Cleo and I through an interrogation. I'm not sure I can even stand to look at my father after everything Rafaele told me tonight.

At least this way, that'll have to wait until tomorrow.

I get Cleo cleaned up and set her up in one of the bedrooms. She passes out promptly after taking a sleeping pill. I grab a wet washcloth from the bathroom, wipe the smeared makeup off her face, and tuck her in.

God, she looks so young. Sometimes I forget she's only eighteen. The tip of her nose is pink from crying, and her lips are covered with bite marks. She was gnawing on them the entire ride here, while I clutched her hand and tried to think of something comforting to say.

We've always lived surrounded by violence, but what Rafaele did to Ludovico was more brutal than anything I've ever seen. And Cleo was right there when it happened.

Poor thing.

Did Rafaele jump to her defense because he wanted to help her? Or because he wanted to show me how serious he is about treating Garzolos like his own family?

Papà must have mentioned to Rafaele that Cleo and Ludovico might be getting engaged. With Rafaele being the successor, it's unfathomable that something like that wouldn't come up in their discussions. Ludovico was out of line, but if Papà had been there, he would have gotten Ludovico away from Cleo and reprimanded him. He wouldn't have taken an eye out like Rafaele did.

I sigh. Whatever drove Rafaele to do what he did, it's a reminder that danger lurks just beneath his icy surface.

I press a light kiss to Cleo's forehead and leave.

I stop in the kitchen to get a glass of water. As I fill my glass, my gaze catches on my emerald ring.

I hate the damn thing and what it represents. Now that I'm not around my family or Rafaele, I don't need to have it on, so I slide it off my finger and leave it on the counter.

When I return to the living room, Ras is planted by the floor-to-ceiling window, his hands clasped behind him. The lights are dim. Moonlight spills across the dark hardwood floor.

There's a knot inside my chest that eases at the sight of him.

I don't know if it's because of the sense of safety I feel whenever he's around or because he's beautiful enough to be distracting.

Straight nose, a prominent brow, shoulders that form a hard line. When I first met him, it was his dark, stormy eyes that I first noticed. And that earring. That small flash of silver that taunted me while I went straight into fight-or-flight mode.

And for once, I chose to fight.

But I'm not a fighter. The hits just keep coming, and they're finding their mark. After what I learned about Vince tonight, I feel utterly defeated.

I walk over and halt by Ras's side.

"How is she?" he asks.

"Asleep. I hope she'll feel better tomorrow."

We're forty floors above Central Park—an enormous, open expanse framed by rows of densely packed buildings. In the summer, the lush greenery takes my breath away, but in February, the park is covered in a blanket of snow. I can see the snake-like paths winding through the branches of the trees below, and in the distance, the frozen lake reflects the night sky.

I press my fingertips against the glass. "Do you remember when we stopped at your condo in Ibiza? I never told you how much I liked it there."

"Of course, I remember." He smiles a little and then quietly adds, "I don't think I'm capable of forgetting a single thing as far as you're concerned, Peaches."

I drag my teeth over my bottom lip, letting his words settle over my skin.

"I think I have the same problem," I confess, reaching for his hand.

He laces our fingers together, his hold warm and sure even though everything else about us feels uncertain.

Does he hope he'll forget about me when he returns to Europe?

He'll be gone so soon.

And I'll be walking down the aisle toward another man.

I release a breath. "Vince dreamt up the whole thing. It was his idea to make Rafaele the successor. His idea to get Rafaele into our family by having him marry me. Papà and Vince used me. They traded me away so that the two of them can have the lives they want. I guess no one really cares what kind of life I wanted for myself."

An ambulance moves down 59th Street, its sirens muffled to a barely there whine by the soundproofed windows.

Ras lets go of my hand and steps closer, moving his palm to the small of my back. He looks down at me, his forehead lined with concern. "Peaches, I'm so sorry."

"Rafaele told me everything tonight. I don't think I ever want to speak to my brother again. I wish I didn't have to speak to my father either, but that's unavoidable, isn't it?" A bitter laugh spills past my lips. "You know what's funny? I blame myself for allowing this to happen. I enabled it. When I was younger, I got off on being praised for being such a good daughter. That was my value. If I wasn't good, I had no worth. When I agreed to marry Rafaele, I could tell it made Papà happy, and some part of me sang with pleasure at having that rare light of his shine on me. I never learned how to be a fighter like Cleo or Vale. Honestly, I don't know where they picked it up. Maybe it's just something people are born with, and that particular quality skipped me. I'm paying for it now.

Ras takes my elbow, his grip firm. There's some internal battle playing out inside his eyes, and after a few long seconds, he huffs a heavy breath and says, "Let me help you. I can get you out of here."

Hope flickers for a short second until reality snuffs it out.

There's nothing that can be done against the combined power of the Garzolos and the Messeros. The only way to back out of this marriage would be to run, but my disappearance would make the family implode, and Papà won't allow that to happen. No matter where Ras takes me, eventually they'd find us. Papà would drag me right back to New York kicking and screaming, and I'd end up in the exact same place. Only I'd have put Ras in danger in the process. Dem and Vale too.

If I put myself first, everyone suffers.

Rafaele's offered me honesty and respect. Maybe that's as good as someone like me can get. It's more than what my family has ever given me, isn't it?

I lift my hand to Ras's cheek. If things were different, I could see a life with this man. This beautiful, strong man who's offering me impossible things.

"Do you remember when you asked me why I hated you?"

He nods, his beard scratching against my palm.

"I overheard you talking to Damiano when I came to Ibiza for the elopement. Do you know what I heard?"

"I can make a pretty good guess," he says gruffly.

"I heard you urge Damiano to walk away from the deal with Papà. I remember I got so angry about that. I thought you were horrible for being so flippant about breaking your word, especially when the other party was my family. But now that I know you, I can see I was wrong. Ras, you're one of the best men I've ever met."

Raw, pained emotion flares inside his eyes. "Gemma," he says, covering my hand with his own. "I'll get you out of here. I promise. Say the word, and it's done."

I shake my head. "I'm not leaving. I can't."

He presses his lips to the palm of my hand. "I'll call Damiano right now. We'll make a plan. We'll figure out a way."

"Stop," I plead. "Don't make it harder than it already is."

His eyes flash, and he pulls away from my touch. He's getting frustrated with me now. "Damn it, Gemma. I'm not offering this lightly. Why won't you even consider it? Let me do this for you."

I take in a shaky breath. "There's something you can do."

"Anything. You know I'd do anything."

"Spend tonight with me. I want you to be my first. Not Rafaele. You."

It's my consolation. My last attempt at doing something for myself before I become an empty shell.

When he catches on to what I'm saying, an angry kind of heat flickers behind his gaze. The air around us becomes thick, wraps around my limbs, presses on my lungs.

"So you want me to have you, and then you want me to give you away?" he growls, backing me against the floor-to-ceiling window. "You want me to break you in for him?"

My blood heats. It's the one thing I have left to give to him. "Don't you want to?"

He slams his palms against the glass beside my head. "I don't want to be your first, Peaches. I want to be your last. And I don't want your fucking virginity. I just want *you*."

My heart shatters, but I keep my tears in check because I know if I let even a single one fall, this will be over.

"This is our only chance," I whisper. "In the morning, you'll take Cleo and me home, and we'll never have this again."

He exhales a long breath and slides his palm to cup the side of my neck. "Or I can take you far away. Fuck, I don't know how, but I'll figure it out some way."

"Enough." I hold his gaze, making my conviction shine. "Most of my choices have been stripped away from me. If I mean anything to you, let me make my own choices tonight."

My words manage to get through to him. I can see his resolve start to break beneath the hard layer of his anger. His hand tightens around my neck. "You haven't thought this through."

Oh, but I have. I thought about it plenty at the Hamptons even before tonight happened.

I'm supposed to be a virgin. It's probably written in the contract between Papà and Rafaele. Everyone seems to think it's what's most valuable about me.

The wedding night. The sheets.

Warning bells should be ringing, but like the ambulance, the sound is dulled.

I want to do this for myself.

Whatever price I'll eventually have to pay for this...I'll pay it. By that point, Rafaele and I will already be wed.

"I have thought about it. I know it will create problems for myself." I slide my hand up Ras's warm, broad chest. "I don't care."

His hand leaves my neck, and he pushes his fingers into the hair at my nape, holding it tightly as he tips my head back. I meet his heavy gaze. It's fractured between frustration and desire, and it makes a low buzz appear beneath my skin.

"If you want someone gentle, you picked the wrong man. I'm not in that kind of mood tonight."

My pussy pulses at his words. "I won't break. Treat me like you would anyone else."

"You're not like anyone else," he says gruffly.

A crack appears in my heart.

"Then treat me like we've done this before," I whisper. "Like you've already fucked me dozens of times, and you know I can handle everything you have to give."

He blows out a breath, pressing his hips against mine and letting me feel his growing erection.

Excitement gallops down my spine.

Below us, the city is cold, but here, in the space between us, a fire crackles.

He wants this just as much as I do.

His breath tangles with mine. "You sure you can handle it?"

Nerves skitter up my arms, but the answer comes immediately. "Bring it on."

A shiver goes through him. And then he's pressing his lips to mine.

CHAPTER 24

GEMMA

Flutters explode inside my belly and then drop lower. The moment we make contact feels like a rip in the universe. There's nothing soft about this kiss. Ras's mouth grinds against mine, his tongue snaking its way inside and claiming territory.

He tastes like the whiskey he drank at the club.

He kisses like he wants to conquer me.

Suddenly, we're moving. One hand gripping my hair and one molded to my waist, he walks me backward in the direction of the main bedroom, his mouth never leaving mine.

I'm oxygen. He's a man starved for air.

For a second, I wonder how he knows where to go. Did he map out this place while I was with Cleo? But the thought becomes irrelevant when my back slams against the wall, and he drops to his knees before me.

My breath hitches.

He's still in his suit, but as he stares up at me, he slowly undoes his tie—a frustrated, beautiful beast taking off his leash.

He shucks off the tie and drops it to the floor. "Take off your dress," he directs, his voice a low rasp.

Fingers trembling, I reach for the hem and pull the entire thing over my head. It feels inelegant and awkward, but when the dress hits the floor beside his tie, my embarrassment is forgotten.

Ras's gaze burns a trail up my body. Reverent. Worshipful. Hungry.

I'm wearing a black thong and no bra.

The cloud of frustration he has swirling around him seems to dissipate slightly as he takes me in. His eyes linger on my breasts for a few moments before he closes the distance and presses a kiss to my stomach.

Another to my hipbone.

Another to the little bow at the waistband of my thong.

He said he wouldn't be gentle, but it's as if he can't help himself.

I shut my eyes in response to the sudden ache inside my chest.

His palms land on my ribcage and move skyward until they're wrapped around my breasts. An appreciative breath escapes him.

"Fuck, these feel good," he rasps against my skin, his lips still pressing kisses to my abdomen.

Warm pleasure slips through my veins at what he's doing to me. How he's touching me.

He drops one hand to my thigh, lifts my leg, and slings it over his shoulder.

I grab onto him to try to find my balance, but his hands tighten on my legs, and he lifts his gaze to meet mine. "You're not going anywhere unless I let you, Peaches."

There's a steady drumbeat inside my chest.

Ba-dum. Ba-dum. Ba-dum.

When his lips brush over the thin fabric of my thong, it speeds all the way up.

He hooks two fingers around the fabric, pulls it aside, and presses the flat plane of his tongue against my wet entrance.

"Oh God," I moan as my pussy begins a slow, insistent ache that only grows with each pass of his tongue.

He licks around my opening, slow and unhurried. His fingers delve into my folds, pulling me apart so that he can drag his tongue over every exposed inch. Goosebumps spread over my flesh as he gets closer and closer to my engorged clit.

Need pangs inside of me. "Please."

He understands. The first swipe he makes directly over my clit sends my pussy fluttering. I let my head fall back and shut my eyes, focusing all my attention on the pressure building between my legs.

The waves come slowly and then faster and faster. My nerve endings sing. Ras is making noises, satisfied and unashamed sounds, and they're doing something to my head.

His lips wrap around my swollen clit, and he sucks. Hard.

I sob. My fingers dig into his scalp, pushing the hair tie down until it falls somewhere on the floor.

I'm right at the edge. My hips start moving, fucking his tongue.

"More, just a bit more," I whine, feeling like an animal in heat.

He slips two thick fingers inside of me and curls them forward.

The orgasm crashes through me. A full-on collision. For a few seconds, I can't breathe. All I can do is move my hips to the rhythm of the contractions deep inside my core while he pumps his fingers in and out of me.

When my movements slow, he pulls out of me and sucks my juices off his fingers like it's his favorite dessert.

A shiver runs through me.

Ras nudges my leg off his shoulder, sits back on his heels, and lets go of me. Without him supporting me, my legs won't hold. He watches me slide against the wall. My wetness coats his lips, his beard. When I land on my ass and my legs fall open on their own accord, his gaze latches onto my pussy. I'm trembling, panting, baring myself to him, and he's feasting on the sight like he could stare at me forever. Like he's worked for this, and now he's enjoying the fruits of his labor.

After a minute, he stands up, straightens out his slacks, and pulls down the sleeves of his shirt. It's like he's getting ready to walk out of here and pretend his tongue wasn't just deep inside my cunt. He glances down at me, doesn't offer a hand, and walks to the bed.

I follow every movement through hooded eyes, waiting for him to make his next move.

Ras sits down on the edge of the mattress and starts undoing his cufflinks.

He's quick. Efficient. The cufflinks go on the nightstand. Then he makes quick work of the buttons on his shirt. When he pushes the fabric over his shoulders, it's my turn to gorge on the sight of his bare skin.

Smooth, tanned, muscular back. Rounded biceps. When he moves, tendons dance beneath his flesh. He's got a full-sleeve tattoo on his left arm, and another one nearly finished on the right. There's a smattering of ink over his abs.

I want to get closer, but I realize I'm waiting for instructions. He's in control now. He doesn't need to say it. It's in the air.

Ras tosses the shirt behind him onto the bed and then unfastens his belt, pulling the leather through the loops on the waistband of his slacks. He undoes the button and the zipper.

When he reaches in and takes out his cock, my mouth grows wet. It's jutting out, bigger than I expected, glistening at the tip.

He doesn't finish taking off his pants, just leans back on his palms, spreads his legs, and dips his chin toward his erection. "Get on your hands and knees and crawl to me."

My breath catches. A gush of wetness runs down my thigh.

His eyes are taunting as he waits for me to do it. Maybe he thinks I won't. Maybe he thinks it's already too much for me.

It's not. My body pulses with arousal, ready to do anything he demands from me.

When I start moving, his eyes become burning embers. He watches me move closer, my hands and knees pressing into the low-pile rug.

My cheek bumps against his leg. I drag it against his thigh until I reach his groin. His cock is an inch away from my mouth, hard and veiny, a drop of pre-cum sliding down his shaft.

I wrap my hand around the base and slowly lick above it. I do that a few times before I look up to see if I'm on the right track. A nervous energy swirls inside my gut. I know what to do in theory, but I'm low on practice.

Ras's taking shallow breaths, his eyes glued to me. He drags his thumb along my jaw and pulls on my bottom lip. "*Cazzo*. You look so fucking good kneeling between my legs."

I let his low, rumbly voice wash over me. His praise scratches an itch I didn't realize I had inside me.

Suddenly, I'm determined. I'm going to do this well. I'm going to *crush* this.

His thumb leaves my lip. "Now, put it in your mouth and suck."

I'm ready. I take his thick cock all the way in until the head hits the back of my throat. My gag reflex kicks in. I choke, eyes watering, but I breathe through it until the unpleasant sensation disappears.

Then I do it again.

He groans and curses in Italian. A hand lands on my shoulder and gives me an appreciative squeeze.

It's not good enough. I want to hear the words.

The next time I take him all the way in, I add a swirl of my tongue and suck in my cheeks.

"Fuck, that's it," he groans. "Peaches, you're taking it so well."

There's a burst of satisfaction in my chest followed by a pang between my legs. It shocks me. He just made me come minutes earlier, but when I squeeze my thighs together, I can feel my pussy's getting even more wet.

I think I'm finally getting the hang of it when he pulls my mouth off his cock, his fist in my hair. A wave of disappointment crashes through me. What did I do wrong?

But when I look up, he doesn't seem unimpressed. Not at all. He's panting, trying to catch his breath, his eyes flicking to my lips even as it seems he wants to keep them fixed on the wall behind me.

"Why did you stop me?" I demand.

He lifts me off the floor by the waist and makes me stand between his legs. "Because I was about to come in your mouth, and I'm saving that for when I'm deep inside your tight little cunt."

The lust in his eyes mirrors my own. Rough hands drag over my aching breasts before he drops them to cup my ass. "Straddle my thigh and show me just how badly you want me to fuck you," he says harshly. He moves me again, putting one of my legs on the other side of his own, and then pushing me down.

I gasp when my swollen pussy makes contact with the fabric of his slacks. Everything is still so sensitive, and even the soft wool feels like too much. But when I move to rise, Ras won't let me. He places one palm firmly on my thigh, grips my chin, and forces me to meet his eyes.

"Have you changed your mind?"

"No."

"You want my cock, don't you?"

"Yes."

"Too bad. All you're getting for now is this. So rub that sloppy cunt on me. Show me how you get yourself off."

A gush of liquid trickles out of me, right onto his leg. My cheeks turn hot. "I'm going to make a mess."

He takes my wrists and clasps them with one hand behind my back. My back arches, displaying my breasts to him.

He darts out his tongue and licks a circle around one nipple. "Yeah, you are. I want to be drowning in your juices, Peaches. When I think you've made a big enough mess, then I'll fuck you."

He sucks the other nipple into his mouth and scrapes his teeth over it.

I gasp at the sensation. My hips start moving on their own, my wet pussy rubbing back and forth against his leg.

His grip on my wrists doesn't let up. "That's it. Good fucking girl. Keep going."

His praise sends me soaring. My hair falls into my face. I don't know who I am. I'm not Gemma. I'm a wanton, greedy thing, ready to do anything this man tells me to.

I chase my high, feeling it just out of reach. My breasts bounce as I hump his thigh, and drops of sweat slide down my spine. My legs ache from the effort, but I still keep going.

Ras's gaze never leaves me. "God, I wish there was a mirror here so that you could see yourself," he says. "So fucking desperate for it. Let that wet cunt leak all over me."

My pussy clenches. God, I'm so close.

"You're fucking perfect, Peaches. You're doing such a good job."

A wave of heat cascades over me. "Am I?" I pant, needing more of his praise.

"Of course, you are. Look at you, working so hard. You're making a mess, baby. It's seeping through the fabric. I can't wait to put my cock inside that pussy. You're going to take it so well, aren't you?"

"Oh God," I moan, nearly at the point of no return.

And then it stops. Ras lifts me off him, depriving me of that exquisite pleasure.

It's agony. I let out a sob. "What are you—"

He presses a kiss to my lips and grabs my nape. "Look," he growls, forcing me to look down.

There's a big, wet, milky puddle on his thigh.

I should be embarrassed. Instead, all I can think about is how badly I want that thick cock inside of me.

The arousal in his gaze flickers. "Shit, I don't have a condom."

I barely think about it before I say, "I'll deal with it later." There's no way we're stopping now.

He seems to be of the same opinion because he only gives me a terse nod, and then he's *finally* taking off his pants, grabbing my ass, and helping me straddle him on the bed.

He kisses me, pulling on my bottom lip. "Put my cock in you. Since you did such a good job, I'll let you set the pace."

I wrap my palm around his hard length and position it against my dripping entrance. Maybe I should be nervous right about now, but all I can think about is getting that orgasm he just stole from me.

That's probably what he wanted, I realize. To get me so turned on that any worrying about possible pain would be an afterthought.

I lower myself onto him. Inch by inch, he disappears inside of me until there's some resistance. I halt, breathing deeply as I get adjusted to his size. His hold on my hips is firm. He's tense all over.

Our eyes lock. He's hardly breathing. I think it's taking all of his control to stay still.

"I just have to do it, don't I?"

He kisses me. Licks my bottom lip. "You can handle it."

I grasp his shoulders and impale myself onto him in one fell swoop.

Ras hisses while I gasp. The pain is sharp, but it only lasts a moment. I suck in air, my muscles trembling, and my heart pounding inside my chest.

"Peaches, you all right?"

"Fine," I squeeze out, pressing my face into the crook of his neck.

His hands rub circles over my lower back. "Try to relax. You're clamping around me."

I slow my breathing and concentrate on getting my muscles to soften.

Seconds pass. The pain is nearly gone, flashing only at the edges, so I make a tentative rock with my hips.

Ras moans. "Fuck." He makes a shallow thrust, meeting my next movement. I gasp and find a rhythm that works for me, riding him with more and more confidence.

I'm so full, but it's good. So damn good.

Ras kisses me and then pulls back, looking down between us. "*Cazzo*," he mutters as he watches his cock disappear inside my tight hole. "That's my fucking girl."

He grabs me by the ass, and I have the sense to wrap my legs around him right as he stands up. The move is so smooth, it's like I weigh nothing.

We cross the room. He presses my back against the floor-to-ceiling window and slams into me, not holding back this time. I glance over my shoulder and feel a frisson of fear mix with the frenzied pleasure.

The glass is tinted enough so that no one can see inside, but I can definitely see out.

The city sprawls below me. We're on the sixty-second floor.

Ras's teeth clamp down on the side of my throat. From the way his rhythm is becoming broken, I think he's getting close.

Then he shifts his grip on my hips, hits a new spot just right, and the flame inside me roars.

"I'm close," I whine. "I'm so close." My eyes flutter shut as I hurl toward oblivion.

"That's it," he grunts against my neck. "God, baby, that's it. You're doing so fucking well. Come on my cock."

Everything shatters.

My pussy clamps down on Ras again and again, each spasm making my toes curl and my legs twitch. I'm delirious with pleasure as I grab onto him, my nails carving half moons on his muscular back.

He keeps going for another few pumps before he groans, spills himself into me, and holds me even tighter than before.

My forehead falls against his shoulder. I'm not sure where he ends and I begin.

"Fuck," he pants. "It's a miracle I'm still standing."

I thread my fingers through his hair and press a kiss to his shoulder. There are no words.

Eventually, he pulls back and kisses me.

Takes me into the shower.

Cleans me.

Puts me in bed.

It all blurs in a tender, languid haze.

The last thing I remember before I pass out is him scooping me against his chest and his heart going *ba-dum, ba-dum, ba-dum* against my cheek.

CHAPTER 25

GEMMA

THE BED IS empty when I wake up the next morning.

There are voices coming from the living room. It's Ras and Cleo, but I can't make out what they're saying.

I sit up in bed, noticing the slight ache between my legs, and that's all it takes for last night to come flooding back to me.

Ras and I had sex.

And God, if it wasn't everything I wanted.

I drag my palm over my cheek and wrap it around my throat, remembering how he held me.

I don't regret it. Not a second of it.

Whatever happens now, it was worth it.

Gingerly, I swing my legs over the side of the bed, and my gaze lands on the bedside table.

There's a box on it. *Plan B*. Ras must have gotten up early to buy it this morning.

For a second, I allow myself to wonder what would happen if I didn't take it. If I got pregnant with Ras's baby. There's a perverse kind of pleasure at allowing my mind to wander in that destructive direction, like when you're driving down the highway and you imagine what would happen if you swerve into the incoming lane.

That would be one way to call off the wedding.

What would Rafaele and Papà do then?

They'd probably try to kill Ras.

And they'd probably kill the baby.

I pop the pill out of its packet and swallow it dry.

I pull on the party dress from last night, leave the bedroom, and find Ras and Cleo having espressos in the kitchen.

His hazel eyes lift to mine.

There, I see all the same emotions that are currently tormenting me. Longing, despair, and a stubborn kind of joy at what we did last night.

Despite everything.

Despite having to survive this morning where reality is like a prison around us.

"Coffee?" he asks in a voice so afflicted that even Cleo notices.

She looks between the two of us, her brows pinching together. "Did I get you in trouble, Ras?"

Ras's expression flattens, his mask once again in place.

If only Cleo knew the trouble we're both in now.

She finishes her espresso. "Is Papà mad at you about what happened with Ludovico? I'll tell him there was nothing you could do. You were watching Gemma."

"Don't worry about me," he tells her, going over to make me an espresso even though I never answered his question. "We're all just glad you're okay."

When he hands me the espresso, our fingers brush.

Sparks. Electricity. Goosebumps.

I sip on the bitter drink and look out the window.

It's snowing again.

We get home an hour later. The car ride is tense. I catch Ras looking at me, and there's something wounded in his expression.

I remember how he tried to convince me to leave, and how I shut him down over and over again. I might have hurt him, but it's for the best. I can't risk getting him sucked into this mess.

"Mamma?" I call out as I take off my jacket, surprised she's not here to greet us. She's been blowing up my phone with messages all morning.

The door to Papà's office swings open, and he comes out clutching his cellphone in his hand, looking like he just hung up on someone.

The expression on his face makes my stomach drop.

It's been a while since I've seen him this furious.

"Where's Mamma?"

Cleo takes a step forward. "Have you heard—"

"Pietra left an hour ago to go see Ludovico's mother. Ludovico is dead."

There's a twinge of relief inside my chest. *Good riddance.* It's a horrible thought, but after last night, it's clear he wouldn't have made Cleo a worthy husband.

I wonder if Papà even bothered thinking about what a poor match those two would have made. Probably not, since everything Papà does is in his own best interest.

It's hard to believe that wasn't painfully obvious to me until recently.

Cleo is damaged goods as far as everyone is concerned. Papà knows he can't lie about her being a virgin. Cleo would never go along with that lie. He decided to give her to Ludovico so that the man would keep breaking his back for him.

At least he'd get something out of it.

"Ras, leave us. I need to speak to my daughters." Papà's tone brokers no argument, but Ras doesn't move from his place behind us.

I glance at him over my shoulder and give him a barely there nod. He clenches his jaw, and then he hesitantly walks in the direction of the kitchen.

Cleo and I follow Papà into his office. The air vibrates with tension, and the house is deathly quiet. I wouldn't be surprised to learn Papà has sent the servants away. He's done that before when he was so angry he couldn't stand the thought of seeing anyone in his space.

"Sit down," he barks.

Cleo and I exchange a look. She didn't do anything wrong. Ludovico crossed a line and paid for it. Papà can't blame his death on her.

"We'll stand," Cleo says.

"Suit yourself." Papà plunks an empty glass on his desk and splashes some whiskey in it. He downs it in one go. "Ludovico was one of my top earners. An excellent asset. You knew this, Cleo. It's why I wanted you to marry him."

"Yes, I know. I was to be a reward for good work," she retorts.

I close my eyes. My sister's brave, but she can be so damn stupid. This is not the time to push Papà's buttons.

"Tell me exactly what happened."

"As soon as we got to the club, he wouldn't leave me alone. He was grabbing me, Papà. Trying to pull me on the dance floor and grinding against me. It was disgusting."

"You made a scene?"

"When he tried to kiss me, I punched him and stomped on his foot. That made him mad. He was about to hit me when Rafaele stopped him."

Papà's mouth becomes a thin line. "You provoked him."

"Are you kidding? I didn't provoke anything."

"Don't lie to me!" He jumps out of his seat, the chair scraping loudly against the floor. His eyes are wild with anger. "I know how you are, you ungrateful brat. You made him mad. If you'd just danced with him like he wanted you to, all of this could have been avoided. Instead, you had to humiliate him in front of nearly everyone important in the family. What the fuck am I going to do with you? No one will want to touch you with a ten-foot pole after this fucking mess."

Cleo snarls. "Good. I don't want to marry any of the losers who work for you."

Papà lunges toward Cleo, and I put myself between them. "Papà, Cleo doesn't mean it! She's shaken up from last night. I was there. I saw how drunk Ludovico was. Cleo didn't provoke him."

Cleo sucks in a breath like she's about to say something else, even though anyone in their right mind would know to stay quiet.

He's never hit her. She doesn't know what he's capable of.

I speak before she gets a chance to make things even worse. "Papà, let her go lie down. She watched Rafaele kill somebody. She was right there. It was horrible."

Papà's nostrils flare, but he seems to consider my words.

Somehow, Cleo manages to keep her mouth shut for the few seconds it takes him to give a slight nod. "Fine. Get out of my sight."

My sister flies out of the room, and Papà's gaze slams down on me.

I do my best to keep my voice steady. "Rafaele didn't have to kill him. He pulled that knife out of nowhere and plunged it into Ludovico's eye. You can't blame Cleo for Rafaele's short fuse."

Although it *was* strange. Rafaele doesn't strike me as someone to act on impulse. Did he have a history with Ludovico?

Or was it seeing Cleo getting hurt that made him snap?

He's always been a little off around her, hasn't he?

Papà shakes his head, the tension loosening from the cords in his neck. "I didn't expect that from Rafaele."

"Maybe you don't know him as well as you think you do." The words are out of my mouth before I realize they sound like an accusation.

Papà's eyes narrow. "I know everything I need to know to be confident he'll make a good don. Don't start with me on that again, Gemma. The matter is settled. The Garzolos will be in good hands. You know I always do my best to take care of our family."

I clench my fists, feeling a wave of anger wash over me. The way he lies is outrageous, because he somehow *believes* the lies. He really thinks he's doing what a good don would do.

I'm good at keeping my mouth shut around Papà, but after last night, my nerves are fried. The words are right there on the tip of my tongue.

Fuck you.

I got one night with Ras. One measly night with a man I have real feelings for. And now I have to face a lifetime with Rafaele, a man I do not love, all the while knowing that I'm in this position because my father and my brother care more about themselves than anyone else.

"Are you confident Rafaele will make a good don?" I ask. "Or are you just happy you won't have to pay for your mistakes?

Last night, Rafaele told me how Vince helped you craft this entire plan. The two of you must be very pleased with yourselves."

Surprise flashes inside Papà's eyes before he tampers it down. He places a fist on the desk and gives me a condescending look. "Rafaele has a strange moral compass. His insistence on telling you the full details about our arrangement drove me up the fucking wall. I told him it would only make you upset. But he's apparently fine with that, and also fine with committing murder in front of his future wife."

My nostrils flare on an intake of breath. "You know what? I don't mind. At least with him, I know exactly what I'm getting myself into. What I do mind is how you and Vince shamelessly manipulated me. Why didn't you just tell me everything from the start? If you'd come and asked me to do this for you and Vince, if you'd showed me some respect and explained the situation, I probably would have done it anyway. I would have volunteered myself for a lifetime of unhappiness if you'd just been honest with me. But I know why you weren't."

Papà flexes his jaw. "Watch your tone. You don't know anything."

I take a step back, my internal alarm ringing, but I have to get this off my chest. I just don't have the strength to hold it back anymore. "You weren't honest with me because you're a selfish coward. You're terrified of ending up behind bars, aren't you, Papà? That must be embarrassing to admit, given many better men in our family have served their time. But not you. All you care about is taking good care of yourself. You're a disgraceful don. I'm starting to think you're right. Our family will be in good hands with Rafaele. After all, he can't possibly be any worse than you."

My only warning is the low growl Papà makes.

Pain bursts over my cheek, sharp and deeper than I've ever felt before.

The impact sends me to the floor.

"You think you know better than me?" my father grinds out.

I catch myself at the last second with my hands, and my left wrist screams in pain. A weak sob escapes me.

"You think I made this decision lightly?"

Before I get a chance to catch my breath, a hit comes to my side. A kick. I squeeze my eyes shut.

"You dare to blatantly disrespect me after everything I've done for you?"

Another kick against my ribs. I moan in pain, shrinking into myself, clutching my knees to my chest.

And then I hear something that makes the hairs on my neck stand.

A roar.

The books on the shelves shake. There's a loud crash. A big tome falls a few feet away from me.

I'm trembling, and the pain in my side is spreading and spreading. The shirt I'm wearing sticks to my back with cold sweat. My stomach clenches, and I throw up. There's nothing in my stomach but the coffee I drank this morning.

A few moments later, someone's hauling me up. I recognize who it is by his scent.

"Ras?"

Familiar hands cradle my face. "Are you okay?" he asks, his voice shaking with fury.

I blink at him. "There's something wrong with my side."

I get a single glimpse of his murderous expression before he carefully tucks me behind him and moves toward Papà.

My father's slumped against the bookshelf, a trickle of blood running down his chin. His furious gaze is locked on Ras.

"Get out," Papà says with a sneer. "Get the fuck out before I—"

Ras lunges at him, slams him into the bookcase, and wraps his fingers around his throat.

"You fucking decrepit piece of shit," he spits out, the veins on his forearms growing more prominent as he squeezes and squeezes. Papà's face turns beet red beneath his grip.

"I knew it was you." Ras's voice is clear and deadly and ricochets off the walls. "You've done this to her before."

Papà's eyes bulge. Ras is going to kill him.

I should try to break them up, but I'm frozen as I watch everything play out.

He punched me and kicked me while I was on the ground.

The halting words on the tip of my tongue dry out, but Ras stops short of choking him. Just as Papà starts sputtering, Ras lets go off his throat and lands a hard punch on his face.

Papà's nose explodes with blood.

That visual gets my throat unstuck. "Ras, stop." I reach out, grab his arm, and pull him back. "No, stop. Don't."

His rage is infernal. He throws Papà to the ground. "She's your fucking daughter. You get off on beating women? Does it make you feel tough? You're a sad joke, you goddamn asshole."

My father glares at him from where he's sprawled on the ground panting. His nose gushes blood.

"Who the fuck do you think you are?" Papà snarls, red spittle flying from his mouth. "This is none of your business."

Ras's response is a vicious kick to my father's gut.

Papà groans, spits out blood. "You'll pay for this," he wheezes.

Ras steps on his hand, and a moment later, there's a crunching sound, and Papà's face goes white.

"Ras! Stop," I beg. "Don't do this."

"You're a dead man," Papà hisses through the pain. "You hear me? A dead man."

I dig my fingers into Ras's forearm. "That's enough. Please."

Papà hits the floor with his fist. "Get out. Get out so that I can hunt you down."

Ras lowers on his haunches and grabs Papà's shirt, bringing his face close. "I'm taking Gemma to the hospital. You better not be here when we come back. I don't give a fuck that this is your house. I don't give a fuck that she's your daughter. No one touches her. You hear me? No one. If I'm a dead man, I'm dragging you down to the depths of hell with me."

There's a loud gasp. "Gem!"

I whip my head around to see Cleo standing in the doorway, her hand covering her mouth.

Shit.

She flicks her gaze over the scene, and I can see the realization of what happened slowly dawn on her. Her eyes turn red and watery, and she rushes to my side. "Oh my God, are you okay?"

My body is in so much pain, but I can still feel my heart break. The secret is out. I've spent so long trying to shield Cleo from this.

Ras prowls over to us. "I'm taking you to get checked out."

I hesitate. My mind is sluggish, but even in this state, I know Ras is in trouble.

He just beat the shit out of a don.

Papà will send his men after him.

They can't kill Ras. I can't let that happen. Maybe if I stay behind, I can talk Papà down. "Ras—"

"We're going," he says resolutely. His eyes lock on mine, and something inside of them makes my protest die out.

I swallow. Nod. "Cleo, go up to your room, lock the door, and wait until Mamma comes home."

My sister's crying now, tears running down her face. "Papà did this?"

"Please, Cleo. Just do as I say. Go to your room."

When she doesn't move, Ras takes her arm and lifts her off the floor. "Go, Cleo."

She blinks at me, her lips trembling, and she then turns to him. "Please take care of her."

"I will," Ras says.

"Don't you dare leave," Papà growls at me as Cleo runs out of the room. "You leave with him, and I swear, Gemma, you'll regret it."

Tears spring to my eyes. How could he do this? My own father?

Ras wraps his arm around my trembling shoulders. "Don't listen to him. They're nothing more than the words of a desperate man who's aware his days at the top are numbered."

Papà's face blanches.

And with one final look at my cruel, broken father, I let Ras whisk me outside.

CHAPTER 26

RAS

SNOWFLAKES SLAP against my face as Gemma and I walk out the front door.

I shrug my jacket off and wrap it around her shoulders. She's trembling, her skin white with shock except for the blooming pink mark on one side of her face.

He hit her there. He raised his hand and struck her.

My vision bleeds red. It takes everything for me to keep moving my feet forward instead of turning back around to finish what I started.

No matter how much I want to decimate Garzolo, my priority is Gemma.

I open the car door and help her inside, careful not to touch the side she's clutching. She's taking short, shallow breaths. The vein in her neck pounds fast and hard.

I lean over and clip in her seat belt. "You're okay. I'll make sure the doctor sees you right away."

She nods, her hands finding mine.

"Show me where you're hurt," I ask, pulling a handkerchief from my pocket and pressing it against her bleeding bottom lip. When I pull it away, she seems surprised to see the fabric is stained red.

Garzolo split her lip.

I clench my jaw and swear to the heavens that Garzolo will pay.

"I don't know," she says brokenly. "My ribs, I think."

"Okay, we're going to figure it out." I cup her cheek with my hand. "Gem, you're safe now. I promise."

Fear slips into her gaze. "Ras, you have to flee. Call Damiano. Papà—"

"Don't worry about me." She's the one who's hurt, and she's thinking about me. The back of my throat prickles. *Fuck.* I can't stand this.

I press a soft kiss to her forehead. "Give me your phone. We're going to turn it off so that your father can't track us while we get you taken care of."

She slides it into my hand. "Where are we going?"

"To the closest hospital."

"And afterwards?"

"I don't know. I'll figure it out. But you're never going to be alone with your father again. Ever."

She gives me a wary look, like she thinks that's impossible, but she doesn't argue.

I give her shoulder a squeeze, shut the door, and climb into the driver's seat.

Yes, the next time I see Garzolo, I'm going to kill him. Rage burns beneath my flesh as I imagine all the ways I'd like to disfigure that motherfucker before he takes his last breath.

Watching him kick Gemma while she was curled up on the ground woke something primal inside of me. I heard the commotion from where I was waiting in the living room, and I immediately ran to the office, but I was seconds too late.

And in those seconds, he managed to knock her to the ground and land a few hits.

My hands strangle the wheel.

I should have never let her go into his office without me.

"Peaches, how are you doing?" I ask, trying to keep my voice calm for her sake.

"My side hurts badly when I breathe in." She prods her ribs, wincing as she does it. "I don't think anything's broken though."

My teeth grind against each other. "How often has he done this to you?"

A long while passes before she answers. "Until recently, it was only every few months. Whenever he was in a bad mood and had no one else to take it out on. But after Vale ran, he started doing it more."

"Fucking unbelievable," I growl. How dare he? It's bad enough that he's been hitting her, but the fact that he's been doing that while planning to use her to save his own hide makes it even more perverse. Does he even view her as a human being? Or is she just a fucking object? "And your sisters didn't know?"

"I've always hidden it. In the past, he rarely hit me hard enough to leave a bruise, so it was easy."

"But in Ibiza, he didn't hold back. How did Cleo not see anything?"

Her fingertips lift to her cheek. "I wore an eye mask in bed to make sure she wouldn't notice. She's not big on details anyway."

Yeah, she sure isn't. When Vale asked her about it, she was clueless.

Gemma's been protecting her and Vale all this time by keeping this secret to herself. She's been carrying the burden of her father's anger and violence. There was nothing her sisters could have done when they were younger, but why not say something to Vale in Ibiza? Why not ask for help?

I stop at a red light and glance at her. "Why didn't you say anything to me? Or Vale?"

"If I'd told Vale, she would have done everything she could to get me out of here, and Papà wouldn't give me up easily. That's a fact. I didn't want to be responsible for more violence. Especially with my family on both sides of the fight. Plus, he stopped when you arrived. I thought maybe it was over, but then I fucked up. I told him what I thought of him for the first time. I didn't hold anything back." Her voice wavers. "It was stupid. I provoked him."

The fact that she thinks this is somehow her fault lights a fire inside of me. "Gemma, you did nothing to deserve this."

I take her hand, pulling her attention to me. "Do you hear me?"

Her eyes are filled with tears. It takes all my willpower not to drag her over the center console and press her against my chest.

"Yes," she whispers.

We drive for another ten minutes before we get to the emergency clinic.

Inside, it smells like antiseptic and something medicinal. My arm is wrapped securely around Gemma's waist, and she's holding my handkerchief to her lip as we approach the counter.

"We need to see a doctor right away," I bark at the male receptionist sitting behind the counter.

He slides a clipboard over to us without looking up. "Please fill this out."

I'm about to tell him to fuck off with the damn form when Gemma nudges me. "I need to list my medications and previous health issues, just in case."

I grab a nearby pen and lead her to a chair. It's not too busy. There are just a few other people waiting around. A security guard wanders in, says something to a nurse, and then walks out the front door. I see him light up a smoke.

Once Gemma finishes filling out the form, I bring it back to the receptionist.

"Please wait over there." He tips his head in the direction of the waiting area.

"We're not waiting."

The receptionist looks up. When he registers the murderous look on my face, he swallows. "All of the doctors are busy."

"I just saw a patient walk out of room six."

"That doctor is about to go on his lunch break."

I lean over the counter and snatch him by the neck of his shirt. His pupils widen with fear as he appears to finally realize I'm not someone he wants to argue with.

"Listen to me carefully," I bite out. "Take that fucking chart, get your ass out of that chair, and tell the doctor to get the examination room ready. My girl needs help. She's going to get it. *Right fucking now*. If the doctor as much as utters a protest, ask him what he prefers—to take his lunch a little late or eat it with a few missing teeth." I twist the shirt for good measure and then let go, dropping him back into his seat.

He grabs the form Gemma filled out and jumps out of the chair, putting a few meters between us. "Okay," he squeezes out, rubbing his neck. "I'm going."

"We'll be there in one minute."

Gemma's eyes are closed when I get back to her. The mark on her cheek is brighter now, looking painful and slightly swollen.

I should have trusted my gut when it told me Garzolo was hitting Gemma, then maybe I could have prevented all of this. I failed her.

I reach for her hand, and she blinks her eyes open, focusing her gaze on me. "Ras, you can't go back home with me. Papà will kill you."

"Don't worry about that now. We need to make sure you're okay first."

She adjusts her position and winces a bit. "My ribs are sore, but I think they'd hurt a lot more if he broke one. You should leave. Papà might come here any minute with his men."

"He won't. Not unless he wants his relationship with Dem to go up in flames. Garzolo will have to get approval from him before he does anything to me."

"You're assuming he's thinking rationally at the moment."

"Your father's been in the game for a long time. He's not going to risk everything just to get payback."

Gemma looks skeptical, but our discussion ends when the doctor appears. "Gemma Garzolo?"

"Right here."

I help her up and lead her toward the man. He gives us an uneasy look, noting the split lip. I know what this looks like, especially after I just threatened the receptionist.

"Would you like to come in alone?" the doctor asks.

Gemma glances at me. "Um."

"Go ahead," I tell her, nudging her forward. The last thing we need is the doctor calling the cops because he thinks I was the one who hurt Gemma. "I need to make some calls anyway." I move my attention to the doctor. "Doc, check everything there is to check. Then check it again."

He nods and walks Gemma into the examination room.

I run my fingers through my hair. Fuck, I have to call Damiano and bring him up to speed.

When my phone buzzes, my first thought is that it's him. Maybe Garzolo already called Dem and gave his version of what happened.

But it's Orrin's name on the screen.

I pick up.

"What?"

"You won't believe what just happened," he says, sounding out of breath.

"Don't make me guess."

"I just got a call from my contact at the local police department."

I take a seat. "And?"

"They're moving in on Garzolo right now. He's fucked. They had an informant deep inside his org who gave them everything they needed."

My blood slows inside my veins. It's happening.

"I tried to see if your name came up, but I couldn't find out."

I don't care about that. The chances of the Feds building a case on Dem and I are low. We operate outside of their jurisdiction.

"How much time does he have until they have him?" I ask.

"I don't know. They're already on their way. Why?"

"Trying to figure out if there's enough time for me to go back to his house and take care of him first."

"What happened?"

"He's…" I drag my palm over my mouth. What do I tell him? I might need his help once I figure out what my plan is. "Fuck, never mind. We better talk in person. I might need to swing by the shop in the next hour or so. Will you be around?"

"Are you in trouble?"

"I'm not sure."

"You should probably be on the next flight out."

"It's more complicated than that."

"All right. I'll be at the shop."

"See you then."

The door to the clinic opens, and a few more people come in. I can't talk to Damiano in here.

I send a text to Gemma to let her know I'm just going to be outside in the car and leave the waiting area.

Damiano picks up on the second ring. "Ras? What's going on?"

I check the clock on the dashboard. It's three am in Italy. Judging by his tired voice, I woke him up, so Garzolo hasn't gotten in touch yet. I guess Garzolo's too busy preparing to get handcuffed. "Something happened. We need to talk."

"All right, give me one second." There's a rustling sound. I wonder if he's getting out of bed so that he won't disturb Vale.

Fuck. Vale's going to be devastated when she hears about what happened.

"Tell me," Dem says.

I realize I don't even know where to fucking start.

Nunzio's words ring in my mind. Maybe he was right. Maybe I haven't changed.

Last night, when I saw how upset Gemma was, I wasn't thinking of Dem. I was only thinking of what *I* wanted to do, which was to steal her away from here.

And now, that thought is right there again, in the center of my head.

"Garzolo is about to be arrested," I say before I recap everything that happened in his office. By the time I'm done, my fists are clenched so hard my nails are digging though my skin.

Dem lets out a long breath. "Fuck. All right. Here's what you're going to do. As soon as we get off the phone, you're going to take Gemma to Rafaele. Their wedding is in three weeks. He can take care of her for the time being. I'll get you a flight out in the next two hours. You need to be on it, all right? This is a fucking mess we don't want to get involved in."

It's what I expected him to say, but it sends a wave of dread through me anyway. "Dem, I can't just leave Gemma with Rafaele. She's scared and hurt. She just got beat up by her fucking father."

"She has Cleo and her mother. Rafaele is duty bound to take care of them with Stefano locked up. His succession will be announced before Garzolo's fingerprints are taken, and this will become his problem to solve. As soon as you get Gemma to him, your work there is done."

Panic rises through my lungs. He wants me to leave her. That's fucking impossible. I have to make him understand that Gemma needs me by her side.

"Rafaele is not going to give her the comfort she needs right now," I argue. "And you know how her mother is. She needs someone around her who can support her."

"As soon as it's safe, Vale will go over there. I know she'll want to."

"But when will that be? What happens in the meantime?"

"Damn it, Ras. How many times are you going to make me repeat myself? You have to get out of there. There's nothing you can do."

"That's not true. I can stay here with her."

"And risk getting arrested? Garzolo might give you up to the Feds just to get payback for what you did to him. You've got no support there."

"The Feds don't have anything on me here."

"They'll detain you anyway. We'd get you out, but why risk it?"

"Then let me take Gemma with me back to Italy."

Dem makes a frustrated sound. "What part of she's engaged have you forgotten? To a man who's just become the don of her damn family nonetheless. You cannot take her anywhere but to Rafaele."

"What if she doesn't want to be engaged anymore?"

"Has she said that?"

"No, but I know she doesn't want this! Why would she marry that asshole to save her Papà when her Papà's been fucking beating her? This is bullshit."

"I get it, but it's a fucking inferno over there right now. Everything is blowing up. This isn't the time to throw gasoline on the flames. Come back, and we'll talk it out. We need to let the situation settle before we do anything that could make it worse."

"Damiano, you don't understand—"

"For fuck's sake, Ras. I *do* understand," he says, his tone turning empathic.

Something lodges inside my throat.

"I do fucking understand, but there's nothing you can do. I told you to be careful around her, didn't I? You knew she was off limits."

"I know." My voice is hoarse. "But I couldn't stay away."

There's a drawn-out pause. Damiano is giving me time to process. To come to the conclusion he's been driving at this entire call.

I have to leave. I have to go home.

The door to the clinic opens, and Gemma steps out. A bruise is blooming on her cheek. She looks so strong and fragile at the same time.

The silence stretches until Dem says, "Ras, this isn't a discussion. This is a fucking order."

I press the edge of the phone to my forehead. My head feels like it might split in two.

On one side is logic. Duty.

And on the other is a feeling buried so deep inside my gut that if I ignore it, it might rip through my organs and kill me outright.

My heart pounds inside my throat.

As an underboss, disobeying your don's direct command is as good as handing in your resignation. There won't be any coming back from this. Dem's my brother. I'd die for him. I'd kill for him. I *have* killed for him.

But I can't do this.

I can't leave her.

I just fucking *can't*.

I press the phone back to my ear.

"The answer is still no. I'm not leaving her here."

"Ras—"

"I'm sorry, Dem. I am."

I hang up. There's a whoosh of blood in my ears as I try to pull myself together. There's no time to ruminate on what I've just done. I have to figure out my plan.

I get out of the car and rush to help Gemma.

"You can stop fussing over me," she says. "The doctor said my ribs aren't broken, just bruised. They will heal on their own. And my lip didn't even need a stitch."

Relief floods me, but my hold on her stays firm as I help her into the car. "Good, but you're still in pain. Did he give you anything for that?"

"He prescribed me oxycodone. I don't know if I need it though."

"Give me the script."

She hands me the piece of paper and clasps my hand, making me meet her gaze. Her eyes are tired, but there's so much damn resilience in those gray depths.

I have no fucking clue what we're going to do, but the fact that I'm still here feels like a damn good start. There is no version of this universe where I'd get on a plane while she's hurting.

"Where are we going?" she asks.

"We'll stop by the pharmacy."

"And after that?" Her voice is flinty. "I... I don't want to go back home. Not yet."

I bite on my tongue. She's not going back to that house, that's for fucking sure, but where do I take her? Do I tell her about the impending arrest? Garzolo may have been taken in already. Her sister or her mom might be trying to contact her right now, but her phone is off inside my pocket.

If Gemma gets in contact with them, she might ask me to take her to them.

And I'd have to say no. Because as soon as she leaves my hands, Garzolo's or Messero's men will force me out. I didn't go against Dem's commands only to lose her in the next few hours.

Fuck, this is a mess. Going to Orrin's will buy us a bit of time while I try to figure out what's next.

When I put my hands on the wheel, I realize they're shaking.

"I have an idea," I say gruffly. "We're going to go see a friend."

CHAPTER 27

RAS

WE PICK up Gemma's meds and then head straight to Orrin's. Poet's Cafe is empty when we arrive. The sign says it's closed, and the lights are dimmed. When I open the door, a bell rings above us. There's a lingering smell of coffee and sugar in the air.

"What is this place?" Gemma asks in a hushed tone as she takes a step inside.

"A friend owns it." I follow her in and lock the door behind us.

A moment later, Orrin comes out from the back dressed in a black turtleneck, with an empty gun holster strapped across his chest. "You got here quickly," he says, giving me a nod before moving his gaze to Gemma. His eyes widen.

Gemma presses into my side, and her instinctual reaction to seek safety with me makes warmth spread through my chest. I wrap an arm around her shoulders.

Orin raises a brow. "Who's this?"

"Gemma."

"As in Gemma Garzolo?"

"Yes."

His eyes narrow. "Ras, what the fuck. What happened to her face?"

Gemma tenses beside me.

"Stefano Garzolo happened," I mutter. "Do you have a change of clothes? Something she can wear?" Gemma's still dressed in the yellow party dress from the night before and my suit jacket. I wish I'd remembered to take her winter coat when we left Garzolo's house, but it wasn't the biggest thing on my mind.

Orrin runs his fingers through his hair. "Yeah. Give me a minute. But then you better explain what the fuck is going on."

I nod at Orrin and watch him disappear into the back room. The half-hour drive gave me some time to think, and no matter how I look at it, there's only one move that makes sense.

I have to get Gemma far away from here.

Garzolo might be off the chess board for the next few hours while he deals with his arrest, but by evening time, someone's bound to come looking for Gemma. And if they don't find her by tomorrow morning, it'll be all hands on deck.

We have to be somewhere far away before that happens. Garzolo and Messero have too much reach in New York,

339

maybe even in the entire country, so we need to get off their turf.

If we manage to get to Europe, I have connections I can use, but I'll have to be careful not to go to anyone who'll go straight to Dem. I can't risk him finding out where we are, not after he made his position on Gemma clear.

A heavy weight presses on my shoulders as I think about him. *Cazzo*. I had to do what I did, but the guilt is already creeping in.

Gemma leans against me like she's struggling to hold up her weight. I snake my arm around her waist and use my other hand to pull out a chair. "Sit down. You shouldn't be on your feet."

Gemma sinks into the chair, wincing in pain. Seeing her like this makes my heart clench. I dig inside my pocket for her meds and hand her the pill bottle. "Stop being stubborn and take two of these. You trying to win an award for being tough?"

She laughs weakly and winces again. "Don't make me laugh. It hurts."

I get her a glass of water and watch her swallow the pills.

"Happy?" she asks, giving me a shaky smile.

I squat down in front of her and cup her cheek. She's trying to put on a brave face, but I can tell she's still shaken up, and who can blame her?

That family doesn't fucking deserve her. Thinking about what they've done to her stirs up my simmering rage, so I force myself not to ruminate on it. I need to keep a clear head.

"I'll be happy when I know you're no longer in pain," I say as I brush her hair out of her face.

When I stand up, I see Orrin in the doorway of his back office watching us. He's got a bundle of clothes in his hands and a pair of white sneakers. My body tenses when I see that his holster is no longer empty.

Is he going to give us up to Garzolo or Messero? I'm putting my trust in him mostly because of my history with his cousin, and because my gut tells me that I can, but it's a gamble.

Orrin walks over and hands Gemma the clothes. "It's a uniform. The only thing I have close to your size."

"Thank you," Gemma says quietly.

"Should she get checked out?" Orrin asks. "That bruise looks like it's going to be nasty."

"She already has been checked out. I was getting her medical attention when you called."

Orrin links his hands behind his neck and gives a shake of his head. "Jesus. I'm sorry about what happened to you, Ms. Garzolo. I'm Orrin Petraki. Can I get you anything? Tea? Coffee?"

"I'm all right, thanks," Gemma says.

I wrap my hand over her shoulder. "Get her a tea. And then, you and I will go to your office for a chat while Gemma changes."

"Sure, no problem," he says while giving me a wary look, like he's wondering exactly what the fuck kind of trouble I've brought to his doorstep.

Once Gemma has a steaming cup on the table in front of her, I follow Orrin into his office.

He sits down in the squeaky desk chair and crosses his arms over his chest. "Care to explain what you're doing? The last thing I want is for Messero to get word that his fiancé left her house and somehow ended up in my coffee shop with you."

"I wouldn't have come here if I had other options."

"You think I don't realize that?"

"I need to disappear for a while with Gemma."

He laughs like he thinks I've lost my mind. "What the fuck are you talking about? And who are you to her exactly?"

The guy who's going to do right by her, no matter what it takes or what it costs me. "I'm going to get her out of New York. I'm not giving her to Messero. I'm also not taking her back to the fucking house where her father just beat the shit out of her."

Orrin hooks his thumb around the thick gold chain hanging off his neck and blows out a breath. "This is one of the worst ideas I've ever heard, and you haven't met my cousin Hector, but trust me, that's saying something."

"I'll pay you forty grand."

He taps his index finger against his head. "This thing's worth more than that."

"Name a price, and I'll pay it. No one knows we came here. No one in New York even knows you and I know each other."

"Your boss does. Did he sign off on this genius idea of yours?"

At the mention of Damiano, something unpleasant runs through my veins. "Don't worry about Damiano. He won't fault you for helping a friend."

"A friend?" Orrin cocks a brow. "I thought you were his underboss."

When I don't answer, he groans. "Fuck me. No, honestly, *fuck me*. This is what I get for having this friendly mug, isn't it? If I looked like a mean motherfucker, you wouldn't have come to me with this bullshit."

"We need a way to get out of the country." Orrin is my best bet for making that happen. Gemma doesn't have a passport, and even if she did, Garzolo would be able to use it to track her, so we can't just show up at the airport and catch a flight.

He sighs. *"Ton chtýpise i malakía sto kefáli."*

I have no idea what that means, but I'm guessing it's not particularly flattering. "You bring in your cargo by plane, don't you? Where do those planes land?"

He gets out of his seat and paces the cramped space before kicking a half-empty crate of condensed milk cans. "I'm going to regret this."

"You won't. I'll owe you."

He snorts. "Unless you're the luckiest man in the world, it's highly likely you'll be dead within a week."

"Not if you help us get out."

A few seconds tick by while he stares at me, just shaking his head like he thinks I'm out of my fucking mind.

I probably am.

Courtesy of the woman on the other side of the wall.

At last, Orrin sighs. He grabs a pen and starts writing a string of numbers on a pink Post-it note. "Fine. I want a hundred grand wired to this account in the next forty-eight hours. We use an airfield about an hour out of the city. There's a cargo plane leaving in two hours."

I take the Post-it from him and put it in my pocket. "You can get us on it?"

"It won't be a comfy ride."

"Where is it flying?"

"Crete. I have a house there where you could stay. That'll be another ten grand. *A week.* And I'll have to tell Kal about this eventually. Maybe it'll slip my mind when he and I talk in a week, but after that, I have to tell him, or I'll be in deep shit. So you'll have some time before he knows where to find you."

Which means so will Dem if he thinks to ask. Kal won't go running to Dem on his own with this information—we have enough of a friendship between us for him to keep his mouth shut for as long as he can—but it's not a risk I can take.

"Deal. We'll move somewhere else as soon as Gemma's doing better."

Orrin points his thumb toward the door. "You sure your precious cargo out there will go along with the plan?"

Gemma's going to take some convincing, but I'm getting her out of here. She may not have canceled her engagement yet, but she will. When we're far away from here, I'll make her understand that her place is with me.

That girl is *mine*. She just doesn't know it yet.

"She took two oxycontin for the pain. I'm hoping it will make her more agreeable to what I'm about to tell her."

Orrin laughs dryly. "And what happens once those wear off?"

"I'll figure it out."

"Your funeral." He picks up his phone. "I need to call the pilot and tell him to wait for you. You should go talk to her now."

I stand up. "Thank you. I won't forget this."

He waves me off, and I leave the office, praying Gemma's groggy enough to maybe have taken a nap, but nothing's ever that easy. She's holding her tea mug in her palms, taking tentative sips.

"Where's Orrin?" she asks when she sees me.

"He had to make a call."

My palms are clammy as I pull out the chair beside Gemma and sit down. She's changed into a white T-shirt that says Poet's Café in a cursive green font and a pair of black slacks that are at least two sizes too big for her. At least the shoes seem to fit.

"Cute," I say, bumping her knee.

Her lips twitch, but her eyes stay sad. *Cazzo.* I can't stand seeing her like this. I wish there were a way for me to absorb all her pain so that I could free her from the burden. I've done enough things in my life to deserve that kind of punishment. She hasn't.

"What now?" she asks in a soft voice.

Now, I fight for what I want.

"Your father was arrested after we left."

Her eyes widen. "What?"

"The Feds got him. Rafaele will probably take over as don in the interim until he manages to get your father out."

Color leeches out of her face. "Oh my God. I can't believe it's happening." She swallows. "I think we need to go back," she says quietly, and I can sense her despair.

She doesn't want to do it. She just needs someone to tell her that she doesn't have to.

I reach for her hand. "We're not going back. We're leaving New York."

She blinks at me. "We can't."

"Yes, we fucking can."

"Ras—"

"Do you trust me?"

Her brows pinch together, but she nods anyway. "Yes, but—"

I lean closer, taking her chin between my fingers. "Then here's the honest truth. Those things you said to me after I kissed you at Mari's wedding? You were right about me, Gem. I'm not a man of honor. I don't give a fuck that you're engaged. I want you, and I'm taking you. It's not a question. It's a fucking statement. There's no scenario where I'm taking you back to the assholes that have mistreated and manipulated you. You deserve better than them. Your papa deserves to rot in that fucking jail. Let them scramble. Let them try to sort out this fucking mess. But we're not going to stick around for it. We're leaving. *Now*. Do you understand?"

She's breathing quickly, her eyes frantic as they scan my face. "What about Cleo? I can't just leave her."

"She'll be fine with your mamma. You'll be able to talk to her once we're far away from here."

"Ras, this is crazy."

I shake my head. "You came to me last night. You wanted to be with me. Well, here's our chance. And I'm taking it for both of us, because if I walk away from you right now, I know I'll regret it for the rest of my life."

I've caused a lot of chaos throughout my life, and God knows, I've often paid a price for it. This time, the price might be my life. Once we get on that plane, we'll be on our own. Messero and Garzolo will put a price on my head, and if anything goes wrong, I won't have Damiano there to back me up.

I should be fucking terrified.

But I'm not.

The only thing I'm scared of is hearing Gemma say no.

She's quiet for a few long seconds, during which I tell myself I'll carry her onto that plane against her will if I have to.

But then she takes my hand and presses a light kiss against my lips. "Okay." Her eyes shine with unshed tears. "Let's do it. Let's go."

CHAPTER 28

GEMMA

I'M RUNNING AWAY and breaking off my engagement.

In the past, whenever I had dared to imagine doing something like this, the decision came with immediate, catastrophic consequences. I'd never considered the possibility that those consequences might be delayed, and that for a while, all I'd feel is pure bliss.

It's disorienting. Papà's not flying off the handle, my body isn't being pummeled, and Mamma's not telling me what a disappointment I am.

Instead, I'm tucked against Ras's side, his arm warm and heavy around my shoulders, while the engine of the cargo plane makes a steady hum.

This plane isn't like any I've been on before. It's completely utilitarian, devoid of any windows or seats. Stacked crates of God knows what are securely attached to the locks built directly into the floor.

Ras and I are nestled on a pile of blankets between two such stacks, our backs pressed against the wall of the plane. It should be uncomfortable, but somehow, it's not. In fact, everything feels softer than it should.

The earlier pain I felt in my side has completely faded away. There's no tension in my muscles, and a comfortable warmth has spread through my body. A smile pulls at my lips. The pallets are painted such pretty colors.

"Ras?" I lace my fingers through his. "I feel kind of weird."

He pulls me into his chest and presses a kiss to my temple. "It's the oxy. It'll go away before we land."

Oh. I giggle. How did I not realize I was high? "I should have taken just one. You told me to take two."

"I didn't want you to feel any pain. The pills the doctor prescribed aren't a high dose."

My eyelids drift closed as I snuggle up to him. I don't think I'll ever get over how warm he is. A human radiator with the exact perfect temperature.

I slide my fingers under the bottom on his T-shirt and splay my hand over his abs. "I like these," I mumble, feeling very content.

He chuckles, pulling me closer. "*Cazzo,* you're cute like this."

My nails start tracing circles over his taut stomach, and Ras sucks in a low breath. I'm trying to remember what tattoos he has there. I wish I'd looked at him more the night we slept together.

That was last night.

My brows rise with surprise. It feels like a week has passed given how much has happened since. I think I should be scared right about now, but I'm not. The gravity of what we're doing hasn't hit yet.

It's probably the oxy.

I sigh. When Papà realizes I'm gone, he'll send his men after me and Ras. I don't see why he wouldn't. Although it might be tricker for him to organize all that from jail. I wonder if Rafaele will help him. He might prefer to walk away from this entire mess, but there's a chance he'll try to find me. No one knows I left with Ras of my own will, and it's possible they'll think he forced me.

But Ras has Damiano to try to smooth things over. They must have worked out some kind of plan when Ras talked to him at the hospital.

What will happen with Rafaele's succession? Without us getting married, the Garzolos won't accept him as their don, so the deal must be off.

Unless Rafaele tries to marry Cleo instead of me.

I sit up straighter, a burst of panic flashing through my mind. No, Cleo isn't a virgin, and everybody knows it. She made sure of that. Papà tried to get her to keep her mouth shut, but she told everyone about the pizza-boy fiasco. That cat is out of the bag, so there's no way Rafaele would even consider her as an option.

I settle back down against Ras. Rafaele will just have to walk away from the deal and leave Papà to fend for himself.

"You okay?" Ras asks, peering down at me.

"Hmm?"

Ras brushes a strand of hair off my face. "You got all tense for a second."

Should I tell him? We haven't even landed in Greece, and I'm already worried. "I was just thinking about what's going to happen back in New York."

His expression turns pensive, and he drags his fingers over my face, as if trying to commit the angle of my jaw and the swell of my cheeks to memory.

"Do you remember what you wanted that night after I took you to the diner?" he asks.

I nod, the memory of us in the car fresh in my mind. "I wanted to be with you."

"You wanted to pretend you were someone else."

A normal twenty-year-old. "Yeah."

"Let's pretend again." He drags his thumb over my bottom lip. "We're a couple about to go on a vacation to Greece. No one's going to contact us because we're going to turn off our phones so that we can enjoy our time away."

Another fantasy. I smile. I like how this one sounds.

"So we're dating?" I ask.

One corner of his mouth rises. "Yeah, we're fucking dating."

"Exclusive?"

He arches a brow. "Do I seem like someone who shares?"

"I don't know, you seem like you could get a little wild," I say with a smile.

He dips his head to give me a deep, searching kiss. When we break apart, I'm breathless.

"Yeah, wild about you," he murmurs.

Warmth spreads through my chest. "What are our plans for our vacation?"

"We're lazy travelers. The absolute worst. Most days we won't even bother putting on our clothes."

I laugh. "Do we at least shower?"

"Of course." He places one hand on my tummy and slides his thumb under the hem of my shirt to touch bare skin. "But we're environmentally conscious, so we always use the shower at the same time."

Goosebumps spread over my flesh. "That must save so much water."

He leans down and presses a slow, wet kiss on the side of my neck. "Heaps."

I snuggle up to him and imagine our vacation until his warmth and the low hum of the plane eventually lull me to sleep.

Our landing is bumpy and disorienting since there aren't any windows and we can't see the outside. When the plane touches down, the crates rattle against their restraints.

Ras keeps a firm hold on me until the plane decelerates, one palm snug around my shoulder, and the other wrapped around my knee.

The oxy's almost completely worn off by now, and the ache in my ribs is back, but it's not as bad as it was before.

What hurts more is what the pain reminds me of. The moment I fell to the ground and curled up to protect myself. The shock of Papà's foot connecting with my body.

Until that moment, some part of me still believed he loved me.

But now that part is dead.

"Where exactly are we?" I ask Ras.

"Heraklion airport."

"Won't we have any problems getting off?" I ask as the plane comes to a stop.

"Don't worry," he assures me. "Orrin's got us all set up."

Despite his reassurances, I'm sweating as we disembark the plane and step out into warm sunshine.

I blink against the bright light. I've never been to Greece before. The sea stretches across the horizon ahead of us, so close it feels like it's only a stone's throw away from the landing strip. A cruise ship creeps across the surface of the water against the backdrop of a rocky landscape in the far distance. There's the unmistakable smell of brine in the air.

Ras takes my hand and leads me to a buggy that's waiting for us. The driver greets him and makes no comment about the fact that we just got off a cargo plane and have no luggage.

I glance down at my ill-fitting Poet's Café uniform, and I can't help but laugh at the absurdity of the situation.

Ras arches a questioning brow.

"I'm going to need some clothes."

He does a scan of my ridiculous outfit and smirks. "I'll take you shopping in town."

The buggy takes us around the airport and drops us off at what seems to be the employee parking lot where we transfer to a car.

It's all seamless. No one gives us any trouble. No one asks us any questions, not even the airport officials, or the driver.

How did Ras set all of this up on such a short notice?

"Did Orrin do all of this for us?"

"Yeah."

"Not that I mind being in Greece, but why aren't we going to Damiano and Vale?"

Something flashes in his gaze, but it's gone so quickly I decide I imagined it. "It would have been too obvious. It's better we stay somewhere off the grid until things settle down."

That makes sense. "So where are we going?"

"To one of Orrin's houses."

"Will Dem and Vale come to see us soon?"

Ras coughs. "I'm not sure."

"Will you ask the next time you call Dem?"

There's a slight pause before he says, "I will."

"When can I call Cleo?" I want to know how she's doing. She must be worried about me, although Vale's probably told her I'm with Ras.

"I'll get some burner phones in town when we go shopping tomorrow."

"Okay." I smile at him.

We drive for about fifteen minutes and then turn onto a windy cliff-side road lined with simple houses, so I'm not expecting the stunning villa that appears when we reach the end of a narrow driveway.

"Wow," I breathe. Whitewashed walls, terracotta-tiled roof, and vibrant-blue wood shutters on the windows. The property is tucked behind a dense barrier of trees, so it's completely hidden from the main road.

Ras unlocks the antique-looking wooden door and holds it open for me.

The interior of the villa is just as stunning as the exterior. I manage to take in the high ceilings with wooden beams that run across them and the rustic furniture, but the show-stopper is the view. My jaw falls open. "Holy shit."

The windows face the Mediterranean, and the breathtaking view of the water is framed with two olive trees.

"Do you like it?" Ras asks, appearing at my side.

For a moment, fantasy merges with reality. It's so easy to believe that we've just arrived at a perfect vacation home where we plan to spend the next few weeks wrapped up in each other.

We're here all alone.

Ras and I can do whatever we want without fear of being discovered. Without checking the clock to make sure it isn't time for us to be somewhere else.

The realization sends a tingle down my spine.

It's just him and I in this beautiful house, pretending we're dating.

Dating.

The word feels woefully inadequate to describe what's happening between the two of us right now.

"Of course I like it," I whisper, watching as a flock of birds cross the sky in a V-formation.

I get it then—what Vale meant when she said she wanted a clean break from her life in New York. Our flight couldn't have been more than nine hours, but it feels like we're a world away from that place. The idea of letting go of everything that happened there is seductive, even if only for a few days.

Can I let myself forget? Can I enjoy these moments with Ras and take some time to heal without all that baggage hanging over me?

I'm not sure. But I resolve to try for a few days.

I slip my hand through Ras's. "Let's go explore everything."

He looks down at me with a tender smile and my heart swells in response.

We spend the next half an hour exploring every nook and cranny of the property before finally lying down on a daybed that overlooks the hot tub and the pool. Ras tucks me against his side and wraps his arm around me, careful to avoid the area that's hurt.

"I'm just going to close my eyes for a bit," I mumble.

He presses a kiss to my hair.

And for the first time in forever, I have a dreamless sleep.

CHAPTER 29

RAS

THE NEXT MORNING, I take Gemma into town for clothes and supplies.

On the taxi ride over, I try to figure out when to tell her that Vale has no idea where we are. Gemma seemed so sure that Damiano's aware of what we've done, that I froze and lied to her.

How will she react when she finds out it might be a very long time before she sees either of her sisters again?

Guilt pulses inside my chest at the knowledge that if we want to stay hidden, Gemma will have to wait to talk to them. We can't risk getting in touch with anyone for a while. Even with burners, we could be tracked using cell towers. I don't know about Garzolo's men, but Napoletano could pull something like that off in his sleep. It's best if Gemma waits to call anyone until we're about to leave Crete. Then, even if they manage to track us here, we'll be long gone.

I rake my fingers through my hair and retie the knot at the back. Will Dem make Napoletano his underboss now that I've abandoned my duty? Napoletano and him might not have the same history we do, but he's capable. He'd do the job as well as I ever could.

Damiano will be okay. One day, our paths will cross again, and maybe I'll even convince him to forgive me.

I chase the painful thoughts away by focusing my attention on Gemma. She seems to be feeling better after sleeping for nearly eighteen hours. We ask the taxi to drop us off by a pharmacy because she's self-conscious about the bruise on her face, and she wants to buy some makeup to cover it up.

The fact that she has to do that at all infuriates me. Fuck Garzolo. I hope he's enjoying his cell.

We walk into the pharmacy, and Gemma quickly buys some things before ducking into the bathroom. When she comes up with her bruise covered up and a smile on her face, my anger loses its edge.

I finally have Gemma exactly where I want her—by my fucking side. That's the only thing that matters now. I won't let my anger at her father stop me from enjoying this.

The old town of Heraklion is filled with cafes, tavernas, and shops selling everything from pottery to souvenirs. We pass by Orthodox churches and walk through fountain-filled plazas. Gemma takes in everything with wide eyes, excitedly pointing things out to me on every block. A scruffy but kind of cute street dog starts following us around, and Gemma insists on stopping and giving him a scratch. My thoughts go to Churro who's still back in Ibiza. I'll have to find some way to get the little guy to us eventually.

Gemma leaves the dog alone and comes to me, tucking herself against my side. Warmth spreads through my chest. The longer we spend together, just the two of us, the more certain I am.

I'm going to build a life with her.

It might not be easy, especially not at first, but all the best things take work. I'll spend each day doing whatever needs to be done to make sure she's safe and comfortable and happy.

There's nothing better than seeing her happy. It's contagious. I'm fucking floating as I walk beside her, holding her hand inside my own.

"I love this town," she tells me once we reach the shore.

I can't help but smile at her enthusiasm. "I'm glad you like it, Peaches."

We won't be able to stay on Crete forever, but Greece has a shit ton of islands. I'll find her one she likes even better and buy her a house. I have enough money scattered across my personal accounts to last us a few lifetimes.

No, scratch that. I'll *build* her a house. It'll take longer, but it'll be fucking perfect, just like her, and we'll be so happy, we won't miss any of the things we left behind.

"What would you do if you could do anything?" I ask.

Gemma peers at me. "What do you mean?"

"How would you spend your time if we lived here for a few years?"

She grins. "Are we pretending we're that couple that goes somewhere on vacation and then falls in love with the place and decides to move there?"

Maybe we'll stop pretending sooner than you think. "Right."

She scrunches her lips and moves them to the side. "I'm not sure. I like fitness, so maybe I'd start my own Pilates studio. I'd have to get certified first. When I was younger, I really liked to paint, but it's been years since I tried it. I probably wouldn't be any good."

I stop walking and point at the storefront right in front of us.

Gemma gasps.

It's an art supplies shop.

I insist we go in, and despite hesitating at first, Gemma quickly warms up to the idea. We walk out of there fifteen minutes later with a bag of paint, brushes, and some canvases.

I grin to myself. In our future house, I'll build her an art studio, and we'll decorate the walls with her paintings.

Our next stop is a clothing shop. While Gemma tries on little linen dresses, all I can think about it is getting her out of them. She brings me a few things she thinks would look good on me, and I buy them without even checking the sizes. I'm too eager to get her back to the house.

I feel high. Around her, I'm incapable of thinking straight. I hate shopping, and yet somehow doing it with her feels like this special fucking treat.

We leave the shop with four big bags, and I'm about to start heading to the taxi stand when she stops by another store display.

It's a jewelry store.

She starts walking away, but I pull her back. "What were you looking at?"

"Nothing," she says, waving me off. When she realizes I'm not going to move until she tells me, she sighs and points at a pendant.

"Come on." I tug her inside the store.

The jewelry store is small and quaint, and chimes ring above us as we step inside. Glass cases line the walls ,and the miniature gray-haired shopkeeper comes over to ask if there's anything in particular we'd like to see.

"That black pendant in the display," I tell her.

"The onyx piece." She smiles knowingly. "It's one of my favorites."

Gemma follows her to take a closer look, but not before giving me a light smack on the butt.

A rush travels up my spine. I fucking love how comfortable she's getting with my body.

She talks to the shopkeeper, completely oblivious to how my obsession with her is growing with every hour we spend together. I don't think I realized how much I was restraining myself around her while we were in New York. Everything was forbidden. Every wrong move could've gotten us in trouble. But now, the shackles are off, and I'm not sure she's ready for what's coming next.

The shopkeeper steps away from Gemma, and I quickly take her place, looking at Gemma's reflection in the mirror. "What do you think?"

The pendant is a smooth black stone nestled in an intricate gold frame on a delicate chain. It catches the light just so, and there's wonder in Gemma's eyes as she looks at it.

"It's beautiful. But I don't have any money," she adds sheepishly.

"I do." I hand her my card. One of my accounts is at a secure offshore bank that not even Napoletano can trace.

"Are you sure? You've already bought me a lot of things." She drags her finger over the pendant.

I snake my arms around her waist. "If you knew how much pleasure I get from spending money on you, you'd realize you're doing *me* a favor by getting that necklace."

Her cheeks turn pink. "That sentence just did something to my insides."

I let out a low chuckle and press my lips to her ear. "Wait until tonight, Peaches. There are plenty of other things I can do to your insides."

Her breath hitches, and she gives me a heated look while the shopkeeper carefully wraps the pendant in a small box.

We walk out of the shop, and I can't resist the urge to press her against a wall and kiss her. Her lips are soft and pliant, and she moans into my mouth as I deepen the kiss. People walk past us, probably staring, but I don't give a fuck.

Let them see us.

Let them know she's *mine*.

363

I drop Gemma off at the house and get the taxi to take me to the closest grocery store. Orrin's supposed to have someone drop off a car we can use at the house today, which is going to make shit a lot easier. It'll also give us a way to get out of here quickly if we need to.

I grab stuff off the shelves in a rush, not wanting to leave her on her own for more than fifteen minutes.

She's safe there, I know she is, but I'm still fucking anxious to be away from her. When I get back, I leave the bags on the counter and prowl through the house in search of her.

"Peaches?"

There's no answer. Panic spikes inside my gut, but a moment later, I find her in our bedroom.

She's napping.

A smile pulls at my lips. I halt, placing my hands on the doorjamb above me, and just take her in.

It's warm despite the window being open, and she's tossed off the thin sheet we've been using as a blanket. She's lying on her stomach, wearing only her underwear, and my gaze falls to her ass.

Cazzo.

The scrap of black fabric leaves little to imagination. It's not a thong, but it's barely more than that.

I bite down on my tongue. Fuck, my handprint would look good on that ass. My hands twitch with the urge to prowl over and fondle her smooth, curvy flesh. I'd shuck those panties off, spread her open, and eat her ass and cunt until she turns to jelly beneath me. Then I'd sink my cock into her warm, swollen pussy over and over until she was squirming and begging for another release.

I shudder, acutely aware that I'm already hard inside my jeans.

She turns me on like no one ever has.

She must sense my presence, because after a minute she stirs, flips over, and gives me a few sleepy blinks. My gaze drops to her perky tits. She stretches her arms over her head with this confused expression, like she's completely oblivious of the effect she's having on me.

"Hey. What are you doing over there?"

"Imagining all the ways I'm going to fuck you once your side is feeling better." No matter how badly I want to be inside of her, I'm not going to risk hurting her while she's injured. There's a purple bruise the size of my fist on her ribs.

Her eyes slide down my body. When she notices the bulge inside my jeans, she blushes and bites down on her lip.

My hungry gaze soaks her in. She's so fucking beautiful.

"Come here," she says softly.

I move across the room, unable to resist her. When I sit down on the bed beside her, she wraps her arms around my shoulders and presses a kiss against my neck.

"It doesn't hurt that bad," she murmurs. Her hard nipples brush against my back and send more blood rushing to my groin. "I want you."

A groan rumbles inside my chest. "I want you too. So bad, you have no idea. But I don't want to hurt you."

She takes my earlobe between her teeth and tugs it lightly.

Fuck, it feels *so* good.

"You won't. We can take it slow." Her hand slips inside the front of my pants, and she sucks in a breath. "You're rock hard."

The sensation of her fingers wrapped around my cock makes my thoughts scramble. I turn my head to press my lips to her throat, desperate to taste any part of her. "If you keep touching me like that, I'm not going to be able to stop."

"I don't want you to stop." She climbs onto my lap, giving me access to all that smooth, supple flesh. "I want you to fuck me."

"Fuck, baby." I fill my palms with her ass and pull her closer so that her pussy presses down against my cock. "You know I'm not going to say no to that."

I flip us over, carefully placing her on her back, and hook my fingers around the straps of her underwear. The fabric slides down her creamy thighs, leaving goosebumps behind.

She sucks in a breath when I spread her knees apart to take a look at my favorite view.

Her wet, pink pussy is as perfect as the rest of her.

I slide my hands down her inner thighs, which makes her shiver in the most satisfying way, and then I drag my thumbs over the outer edges of her cunt.

She lets out a helpless little moan.

I press my face into her pussy and slide my tongue into the place where she's wettest. She clutches my hair. "Oh God."

She's so damn sweet. I could live off this. Feeling her shudder and moan from how I'm eating her out is a privilege. A profound pleasure. But I want to taste all of her, so I grab her ass, raise it off the bed, and go lower.

She startles. "Ras."

When she tries to pull away, I tighten my hold on her hips, and glance up. She's breathing hard, her cheeks redder than normal. "What are you..."

"Living out the fantasy that's been playing in my head on repeat while I was watching you sleep."

"You want to..." She swallows.

"Do I want to eat your tight little ass?" I grin. "Yeah. One day, I'll enjoy fucking it too."

Her gaze turns hazy with arousal. "I knew it. I knew you'd be like this in bed."

"Like what?"

"Wild. Ravenous. Overwhelming in the best way possible."

"Don't get overwhelmed too quickly, Peaches." I bring my lips back to her pussy. "We've got all night."

Gemma's shyness appears to be momentary, because it doesn't take her long to start grinding against me while my tongue takes turns between fucking her two holes. I can feel her orgasm building from the way she starts to tense up, her back arching against the bed. She gasps when I take a hard suck of her clit and comes apart, my name on her lips.

I shuck off my jeans and take out a condom, admiring my handiwork. Gemma's chest is rising and falling with heavy breaths, her full breasts on display. I roll the condom on and drape myself over her once again, my mouth latching onto one hard nipple before moving to the next.

"Are you going to take it like a good girl?"

She licks her lips. Nods. Gasps as I push inside her.

Her eyes squeeze shut. "God, you make me feel so full."

I let my forehead fall against the crook of her neck, rendered mute by the sensation of being inside of her.

This is not normal.

This is not how sex is supposed to feel.

It's supposed to feel good. It's not supposed to feel like entering fucking heaven.

A tremor rolls down my spine. Her nails drag down my biceps, and I make a shallow thrust.

Fuck.

The sheer restraint needed not to immediately come makes sweat roll down my back. I suck on her neck, kiss along her jaw, claim her lips in a searing kiss.

When I manage to gather myself, I sit up and throw her legs over my shoulders.

The view is unbelievable.

Her swollen pussy swallows every inch of me, and I'm fucking mesmerized.

Utterly obsessed.

"This is mine," I growl, my pace picking up. "All fucking mine."

She whimpers.

I squeeze her thigh. "Say it."

"It's yours," she gasps.

When I alter the angle, I get treated to seeing her eyes roll to the back of her head. "Oh God. Ras, I'm going to come again."

"Good. Come all over my cock, Peaches. Let me see it."

She fists the sheets, and her small body trembles all over. I reach over to tweak her left nipple. Her face twists into a perfect mask of agony and ecstasy before she makes a sob and squeezes around my cock. Hard.

"That's it," I say through my teeth, feeling her contract around me again and again.

My own release comes like a faraway roar, rising and rising until it's all I can hear. My balls tighten. The pleasure is so intense, I'm gasping for breath.

She reaches for me, taking my hand and holding it tightly, as if she knows she's the only thing anchoring me in place.

Our eyes meet, and I see the universe inside of hers.

Outside, the wind stirs and makes the olive trees sway. The leaves rustle, their whispers streaming through the open window.

You love her, they say.

CHAPTER 30

GEMMA

OUR FIRST FEW days in Heraklion are a kaleidoscope of sunshine, lazy hours by the pool, slow dinners on the patio, and Ras's skin against mine.

We have sex on every surface imaginable. Each time, I think it can't get any better than this, only for him to prove me wrong.

He soaks me up. Learns every minute reaction of my body when he touches me just so. Becomes a master at making me see stars.

And I consume him in equal amounts.

He fascinates me, and that fascination grows with every hour we spend together.

His body is a work of art that I spend countless hours studying. My fingertips trace over every ridge and valley of his muscles. My throat becomes very familiar with his thick cock.

He tells me about his tattoos. Shares the story behind every scar.

A lot are from Nunzio.

My blood runs cold every time I think of that man.

I think he's the first person I genuinely want dead.

We talk about everything. Ras tells me about his parents, and how they spent his teenage years trying to make him into someone he's not. I think he's brave for never caving to that pressure, but he tells me it wasn't so much bravery as stubbornness.

One evening, he makes me a meal that makes my mouth water. Pasta carbonara, braised artichokes with tomato and mint, and a rich tiramisu for dessert.

He laughs when he sees the size of my portion. "Peaches, we've barely eaten all day. Tell me you're having more than that."

An uncomfortable feeling spreads through my chest. I put more food on my plate, but he notices something off in my expression.

"What's wrong? You don't like it?"

"Are you kidding? This looks amazing."

"What is it then?"

I lick the sauce off my bottom lip. "I would never be allowed to eat more than a tiny bit of this back home."

"What do you mean?"

"Mamma has this thing with food. She's always been concerned about my weight. I was a little chubby in my early teens, and it drove her crazy. She wanted me to be thin."

He leans back in his chair, his eyes narrowed. "She controlled your eating a lot?"

"It came in waves, depending on her mood. She could go months without saying anything, but then we'd go shopping or out for lunch with her friends, and something would just switch on. She'd monitor everything I ate for a while afterward. Then the cycle would repeat. At some point, I just learned to monitor myself, I guess. It was easier than anxiously waiting for her to snap at me."

Ras's brows furrow. "I remember how she talked to you when you were in Ibiza. As soon as lunch ended, I went to the kitchen, got those rolls you wanted, and dropped them off at the guest house."

My eyes widen. "That was *you*?"

He gives me a crooked smile and nudges my chin with his finger. "I wanted you to know that there was at least one person who thought she was being ridiculous."

Warmth spills inside my chest. Back then, I'd been so wrong about him.

Ras stands up, walks over to me, and squats down by my chair. His gaze pierces right through me. "Peaches, you are in no way lacking. There isn't a single thing I'd change about you. And anyone who's ever told you otherwise is either an idiot or the type of person who has to put others down in order to feel better about themselves." He lifts his knuckle to my chin. "Erase their words from your mind."

A strange emotion comes over me, something soft and vulnerable and weepy.

He pulls me into his arms. I let my head fall against his chest, my eyes growing wet. We stay like that for a while, holding each other.

We get back to our meal, and I eat until I'm thoroughly full. He smiles at me from time to time, his eyes warm and filled with a fierce happiness that suits him so damn well.

I can't believe I ever hated him. Maybe this is why he always pushed my buttons, because subconsciously I knew that he could see the real me. The flawed girl I worked so hard at hiding.

"Peaches, you are in no way lacking."

I've always been lacking in one way or another. Always.

But for the first time, I wonder if maybe I could be just enough for him.

On the morning of our fourth day in Crete, I ask Ras to let me talk to Vale.

"You mentioned yesterday we could call her," I remind him while we're having coffee out on the patio.

I get why Ras hasn't wanted me to talk to Cleo—after all, anyone of Papà's men could be monitoring her phone—but he also doesn't seem too enthused about me calling Vale, and I don't understand why.

He puts his mug on the table, and something in the way his lips twist makes a bad feeling materialize inside my gut.

"What's going on?"

373

He swipes a fallen leaf off the surface of the table. "There's something I should probably tell you."

My heart rate picks up. Did something happen to Vale? "Ras, what is it?" I ask, panic creeping into my voice.

He props his elbows on his knees and sighs. "Dem and Vale don't know we're here."

I frown. How is that even possible? "What? I thought all of this was yours and Dem's idea. Didn't you talk to him while I was with the doctor?"

"Yeah, I did. We had a slight...difference in opinion." He runs his hand over his beard.

"What does that mean?"

His gaze slides my way. "He ordered me to leave New York on my own."

Oh. *Oh.* "Are you telling me you disobeyed Damiano's orders to bring me here?"

"He wanted me to leave you behind," he says by way of an answer.

My stomach hollows out. "Ras, what happens to men who disobey their don?"

He says nothing, but his eyes give it away.

This is as good as a betrayal. He's betrayed Damiano for me. An underboss doesn't betray a don if he wants to live.

Despair dries out my throat. "You shouldn't have done that."

He looks at me from under his thick brows. "The alternative was to bring you to Rafaele. I couldn't do it, Peaches."

I stand up. "So you threw your life away on my behalf without even telling me about it? Clearly, you knew I wouldn't be happy about it since you delayed telling me for four days!"

His jaw hardens. "I didn't want *this* to happen. I didn't want you to get upset over something that's already done. I made a decision, Gemma. I knew the consequences when I made it. There is nothing for you to feel guilty about."

I shake my head in disbelief. "Damiano is your oldest friend. He's your don." I don't understand how he could have done something like this. How he can act like any of this makes any sense.

Ras stands up too. "Let me be clear about something. After I watched your father try to beat the shit out of you, there was no way, no fucking way I was going to leave you alone in that city."

My heart clenches.

He brings his hand to my face and swipes his knuckles over my bruised cheek. "I know what it cost me. And I'd pay that same damn price again and again if it means I can keep you safe."

"You had no right to keep the fine print of that decision from me," I say weakly.

"Gemma, none of it matters. Until I met you, I didn't even realize how fucking hollow my life has been. For the past decade, I've lived to serve Damiano, and I did it willingly. It gave me purpose and meaning. But it's never made me truly happy."

"And I do?"

His gaze sparks. "You make me so fucking happy that I feel like a new man."

He means it. His voice rings with certainty and conviction that I wish I felt.

Familiar doubts creep in.

Am I enough to fill in the holes he's created in his life?

How could I possibly be *all that* for him?

"Why don't you try to call Damiano? If you explain everything to him, he'll listen to you."

Ras shakes his head. "I can't risk it. I disobeyed a direct command from a don. For the Casalesi, that's an offense punishable by death."

I can feel the blood drain from my face. "Ras, he'd never do that to you."

"Maybe not, but he made it clear he didn't want me to take you away. Until I can be sure he's not going to try to track us down, I can't risk it."

"When will that be?"

"I don't know, Gemma. I'm sorry. I feel fucking terrible that you won't be able to talk to Vale for a while, but I promise you it won't be forever. I just need time to figure everything out."

My disappointment about not being able to talk to Vale seems insignificant compared to the utter tragedy I've made of Ras's life.

"You can't possibly be okay with this."

"As long as I'm with you, I'm okay." He gives me a reassuring smile, but it doesn't fool me.

There's a part of him that hurts.

He chases away the darkness by pulling me in for a kiss. My body molds to his with ease, like I was made for him.

When we're touching each other, all the problems around us disappear. They don't belong here between us. Not in this fantasy we've created.

But when we break apart, they slowly creep back in.

I wake up the next morning beside a sleeping Ras with a sense of panic lodged deep inside my gut.

Ras brought me here against Damiano's orders.

The sheets are wet with my sweat. I push them off and slip out of the bedroom to get some water.

It's early—dawn. The rising sun makes the sea look like liquid glass. I stand by the window as I drink my water and try to empty my head by focusing on the mesmerizing view.

Everything will be all right.

The mantra has no impact.

I'm not like Papà.

I don't believe the lies I tell myself.

It might take some time, but given everything I know about Ras, eventually he'll miss his friend. They have decades of history between them.

And what happens then?

He'll grow resentful.

It'll start slow, like the fuzzy white mold that appears on the surface of a peach. It's so subtle, you're not sure it's really there. But with time, the skin will soften and dull. The decay will spread, and the fruit will deteriorate until it's unrecognizable.

Until it's rotten to the core.

And then it'll be too late to fix anything.

It's day five since we left New York, and I have no idea what happened after I left. I want to talk to Cleo. She'd fill me in on everything, and maybe I'd be able to find a way out of this mess.

If I go home, Damiano might take Ras back. I can tell him that I begged Ras to do what he did, and that it's not his fault. All the blame could fall on me.

I know where Ras keeps the burners, but I'd have to get Cleo's number from my phone first because of course I don't know it off the top of my head. My phone hasn't been on since Ras turned it off back in New York. It's probably dead. I'd need to find a way to charge it.

What if the second I turn the phone on, Papà will be able to track me? I don't know how that stuff works, but maybe if I do it quickly, it'll be harmless.

I turn the idea over and over inside my head, but something nags at me.

Something horribly, awfully selfish.

I don't have to call her today, do I? I can forget what Ras told me and go back to that blissful happiness of the first few days.

If I go back home, I'll never experience this again. People spend their entire lives looking for something like what I've found with Ras. For someone who makes them feel content and wanted and *loved*.

I wrap my palm around the pendant he got me. A sailboat glides over the water in the distance.

Ras and I haven't said the words, but they're in our every action, every glance, every touch.

Yes, a few more days.

I walk back into our room and quietly enter the bathroom. The shower takes a while to warm up, so while I wait for it, I take a look at myself in the mirror. The bruise on my face is fading. The one on my ribs isn't as visible beneath the tan I've managed to acquire. Still, these marks on my skin remind me of the past I'm trying so hard to forget.

I step into the shower and lather myself up, the water running in soapy rivulets down my body.

A sound makes me turn.

It's Ras. He moves purposefully toward the shower, pulls open the door, and steps under the cascading water, backing me against the wall. There's a frisson of excitement low inside my gut at the way his hungry gaze drags over my body.

"Good morning," he says, his voice still thick with sleep. "I was wondering where you went."

"I was only gone for ten minutes," I tease him.

He's already hard, and the head of his cock brushes up against my thigh.

"I don't know what you've done to me, Peaches," he says, moving closer. "I know how fucking crazy I sound, but I swear, even a minute away from you feels too long."

My chest swells with affection so powerful that it feels like it's about to burst out.

Sometimes, when I'm lying beside him, his scent all around me and his arms wrapped around my waist, it's still not enough. I get the insane urge to burrow under his skin. To become one with him.

He presses his palm against the wall beside my head, closing me in, and leans down to kiss me. Teeth tug and bite on my lips. His tongue delves inside my mouth, and his other hand finds my breast.

I love how big he is compared to me. How when he stands like this, I can't see past his boulder-like shoulders.

He snakes his palms under my wet bare thighs and lifts me so that I can wrap my legs around his waist. My eyes follow the mesmerizing dance his muscles perform beneath his flesh. Water sluices down his hard, rippling chest and round biceps, running in rivulets between the ridges of his abs.

"Honeymoon phase. It'll fade." I gasp when his fingers drag over my slit.

He chuckles. "I fucking hope so, because the way it stands, I don't know how I'll get anything done." His fingers push deeper inside. "Right now, the only thing I want to do is you."

My head falls back as his thumb finds my clit. "God." Sparks of pleasure explode over my skin as he rubs it in slow, sure circles. I groan, loving the way he knows how to touch me just right.

He presses his lips to the side of my neck. "These sounds you make. You don't know how much I love them."

"Keep doing what you're doing, and you'll get to hear a lot more of them," I mutter, my eyes shutting against the waves of pleasure that spread over my entire body.

Ras dips his head down and catches a nipple with his mouth. When he sucks on it, shivers explode over my skin. It's like his touch is charged with electricity. The chemistry between us makes my head spin. It's always been there. We just didn't have a way to channel it in those early days.

Ras pulls back and nudges his nose against my cheek.

I blink at him lazily. "I want you inside of me."

"Fuck, I have to go get a condom," he mutters and starts to put me back down.

I stop him with a palm on his biceps.

"It's the week before my period. We don't need to use it. The risk is low."

His eyes go so dark they nearly turn black. I can feel his fingers press deeper into my thighs. "You sure?"

The tip of his cock brushes against my sensitive entrance, and I give him a nod. "Yes. I want to feel all of you."

His forehead presses to mine, and he starts inching inside of me.

I gasp at the sensation of him stretching me. "It's so damn good," I whisper against his lips.

"You like my cock stretching your tight little cunt?"

"Mm-hmm."

Ras pushes all the way in. God, he's in so deep I can practically feel him in my stomach.

"Fuck," he groans. "You're perfect."

I shiver from his praise. By now he's learned how much I like it and he heaps it onto me.

Ras kisses my shoulder and starts moving, each thrust pressing me harder against the wall. My body buzzes, my nerve endings vibrating with pleasure. Everything feels so right.

It's like my body's made for him.

His mouth latches onto mine, biting and licking at my lips. I squeeze his biceps and arch my back until the spot is just right. "Oh my God."

"There you are." His palms squeeze my ass. "Fuck, baby. Milk my cock with that tight cunt."

My muscles contract on their own at his words, and then my world shrinks to the feel of him inside of me and nothing else.

I fall over a steep edge and find oblivion.

Ras lets out a low moan and breaks apart moments after me. "Mine. You're mine."

"I'm yours," I pant, clutching onto him like he's the only tether I have left to reality.

I want to stay in this feeling. Luxuriate in it. But an intrusive thought comes right on the heels of my last words.

When the honeymoon phase ends, how long will it take for him to regret losing everything because of you?

A wave of dread crashes right through the warm haze.

Ras pulls out of me and lowers my feet to the ground. He presses a kiss to my forehead. "Let's get you cleaned up."

I let him wash my hair and lather up my body, but my mind is elsewhere.

Is this how it's going to be? Even in our best moments, will there always be an undercurrent of dread?

There's a guillotine hanging above us, and we'll remember it every time we look away from each other.

We dry off and go to have breakfast in the kitchen like everything's okay, but it doesn't take him long to notice the change in me.

He sees the look on my face and frowns. He's become so good at reading me, it's as if I'm his favorite book.

He reaches across the table and takes my hand into his. "You're tense."

I avert my eyes. "I'm fine."

"Don't lie to me," he implores, his voice low and penetrating. "Not to me."

My lip gets caught between my teeth. "I'm afraid of how this will end."

His eyes dim, like he wanted me to be honest, but maybe not *that* honest. Or maybe he's been avoiding thinking about our future because he knows there are no easy answers.

At his silence, my walls rise up. "Never mind."

"Hey." He lets go of my hand and slides off the sofa to kneel before me, putting our eyes at the same level. "This? It will never end. I know you're scared. I know. But we can figure out anything as long as we're together. You hear me? We will take it one day at a time."

Tears prick the backs of my eyes. "Don't you feel any guilt? For what happened between you and Dem? For the people that care about you wondering where you are?"

He smooths my hair back. "If guilt is the price I have to pay to be with you, I'll pay it. Gladly."

It's easy for him to say that now. But what about weeks from now? What happens when it all finally sinks in?

He sees the hesitation in my gaze and frowns. "Don't you believe me?"

I swallow down my distress and lie. "I do. Of course, I do."

CHAPTER 31

GEMMA

GUILT IS PHYSICAL. It's a parasite that grows inside your gut, getting bigger and bigger with each passing day, feeding on you.

It's day eight when I break.

If I don't fix this, the parasite will consume me entirely.

Even if Ras takes years to resent me, I'll resent myself far sooner than that.

While Ras is out at the store getting groceries, I take my old phone out of the nightstand and search the drawer in the kitchen that's filled with all kinds of cords and chargers.

When I find one that matches my phone, I take it as a sign.

I count the seconds until the screen flickers to life. I quickly write down Cleo's number, turn the phone back off, and dial her using the burner phone.

It doesn't take her long to pick up. "Hello?"

I sit down at the kitchen table, my legs wobbly at hearing her voice. "Cleo," I breathe.

There's a surprised gasp. "Gem! You came up on my caller ID as Unknown. Where are you?"

"Somewhere far. Are you okay? Tell me what's going on."

"Shit, hold on. Let me go into the bathroom to make sure no one hears. I don't even know where to start. Are you with Ras?"

"Yes."

"Okay, good," she says, sounding relieved. "Shit, Gem. No one knows where you two went. Papà's ordered all of his capos to look for you, but no one else in the clan knows you're gone. He's keeping it hush-hush and has told Rafaele he'll get you back in no time. Papà's been trying to get your location from Damiano, but Damiano says he doesn't know where you went. No one believes him."

"Do people think Ras took me away on Damiano's orders?"

"Of course. Didn't he?"

I feel a tinge of relief. Is Damiano covering for Ras? He could have made it clear that Ras acted on his own and thus deflect any blame, but he didn't. That means there's still hope they can reconcile.

I clutch the phone tighter. "So Papà's still in jail?"

"Yes. Listen, apparently the whole succession thing is now in question. Rafaele's refusing to help Papà. He said he's not doing anything until Papà delivers on his side of the bargain."

I thought that might happen. Rafaele doesn't seem like the type to hand out favors without a clear repayment plan. "And Vince? Is he back?"

"He is. I told him he's a fucking prick. Actually, I told him a lot more than that. You should have seen us when he first showed up. Ma had to practically pull me off him."

So my brother returned to New York. Now that I'm not conveniently solving all of his problems, he's had to step up.

"What's his position on all of this?" I ask.

"He's running things while Papà's in jail, but he doesn't want to be here. He says he's in love with some princess."

My eyes widen. "A princess? What does that mean?"

"She's *literally* a princess. Royalty from some European country. Not Switzerland, but maybe Sweden? I don't know. You know geography was my worst subject."

"So what does this mean?"

"It means she's the reason he doesn't want to come back. Or one of them at least."

My stomach sinks. Vince and Papà made their succession plan ages ago. Sounds like Vince was already involved with this woman back then, and yet he didn't say a word about her to me. I'm starting to get the sense I don't know my brother nearly as well as I thought I did.

"Vince had the decency to look ashamed after I went off on him," Cleo continues. "I think he regrets manipulating you with Papà, but he's not exactly embracing his responsibilities. He's working overtime trying to convince Rafaele to still go through with the deal."

I rub my forehead. It's as big of a mess as I'd expected.

"I don't think you should come back for a while," Cleo says. "When he went to see Papà he said he's going to kill Ras the next time he sees him."

Panic squeezes around my lungs. He won't. I won't let him do anything to Ras.

"Are you okay wherever you are?" Cleo asks.

"Yes, I'm safe here."

"Ras is taking care of you?"

"Yeah." But at what cost?

"How is he? How are you two getting along?"

Well, I've thoroughly fallen for him, and I think it was in the cards all along. A fuzzy memory from Ibiza surfaces—his thumb brushing over my skin, his lips forming the words, *"Who did this to you?"*

I shut my eyes and clear my throat. "We're making it work. Does Papà really not have any way of getting out without Rafaele's help?"

"I'm not sure, but it doesn't sound like it. Apparently, there were multiple rats. I don't know who, but they gave the Feds a lot of stuff on Papà."

"So unless I come back, Papà will stay in prison."

"Which is exactly where he belongs," she says harshly. "Gemma..." She exhales. "Gem, when he hit you in his office right before you left... That wasn't the first time, was it?"

"No, it wasn't."

"I'm sorry. I'm so sorry. I can't believe I didn't notice."

"I hid it from you."

"No, I've been a bitch. I've been so self-absorbed that I failed to notice what was right in front of me. I feel horrible about it. You deserve a better sister."

My eyes well up with tears. "You were going through your own stuff."

"I was rebelling just to piss Papà off, while you were getting beaten by him and being forced to marry a man you do not want. We are not the same," she says, her tone threaded with bitterness. "Thank God for Ras. When I heard the sounds coming from the office, and then when I saw you... God," she says, her voice breaking. "I've never been so scared, Gem. Not even when Rafaele killed Ludovico a foot away from me."

I take a deep breath and try to rein in my emotions. "It's okay, Cleo. I'm safe now."

"I love you so much. You know I'd do anything for you, right? I see things more clearly now, and when you come back, I promise things won't be the way they used to be."

I take a moment to compose myself, letting her words sink in. "I know. I love you too." Ras will be back soon, so I need to wrap this up. "What do you think I should do?"

"Whatever you want. You don't owe anyone anything."

Except Ras. I owe him *everything*. "If I come back, Vince can go back to Switzerland, and Rafaele will get Papà out. Everything will fall right back into place," I say, thinking out loud.

"It's not your job to fix this."

I know it's not. But I can go home and help people who don't deserve it, or I can stay here and ruin Ras's life.

The choice is obvious, but it's far from easy.

Swallowing past the ball inside my throat, I say, "Cleo, I'm going to come home. Can you tell Vince? I'll give you my location. Don't give it to him until he swears on his life that he won't send anyone after Ras and that he won't let Papà harm him either. Tell him to send a plane for me to the closest private airfield. I'll find a way to be there."

"Are you sure?"

"I am. Write it down." I give her our address in Crete.

Cleo blows out a breath. "All right, I'll take care of it. I gotta go. I think I can hear Mamma coming up. I love you, okay?"

"Love you too. Bye." I hang up.

Ras won't let me just walk out of here. He'll fight, argue, tell me whatever I want to hear to make me stay.

The only way this works is if I tell him I don't want him.

The thought of doing that makes my chest tight with pain.

I'll have to break his heart.

Can I lie to his face? Because that's what it would be—a lie.

I love him.

Which is why I have to let him go.

The sunset is particularly beautiful tonight. The sky blushes with shades of pink and orange, its reflection glimmering across the Mediterranean.

Ras and I made fresh linguine, and from my spot on one of the patio chairs, I see him carefully toss the pasta into a pot of boiling water. He feels my attention on him and shoots me a grin. "Three minutes."

He sent me out here about ten minutes ago with a glass of rosé after I kept dropping things because I'm on the verge of a breakdown. He misread my distress as clumsiness.

A big bird cuts an elegant arc through the sky just as my old phone vibrates in the pocket of my dress.

I cast a quick glance at Ras to make sure he's not looking over here and then read the message from Cleo.

Tomorrow, 10 a.m.

My palms grow sweaty. The plane is coming to pick me up and take me back to New York.

I slide the phone under the chair cushion as Ras comes out with two plates and places one on the table in front of me. The linguine is topped with homemade sugo, grated parmesan, and basil.

I pick up my fork. "It looks delicious," I say, trying to keep my tone upbeat even though I'm crumbling inside. I want to enjoy this one last dinner with him before I break the news.

He takes the seat closest to me, leaving the corner of the table between us, and places a hand on my thigh.

I take my first bite and it's *so* damn good I can't hold back a moan. He's an exceptional cook.

The sound makes him smirk. "Fuck, you're going to make me hard before we get to dessert."

I swallow my food and force a smile. "Liar. You're already hard."

His eyes spark. "Why don't you get on my lap and check?"

"I'm hungry," I say, waving my hand at my plate.

"I've got something I can feed you."

Even though I feel lower than I've ever felt before, he manages to make me laugh. "Stop it. I'm trying to enjoy this pasta."

He drags his hand up my thigh, pushes it beneath my dress, and stops at the edge of my underwear. He digs into his food, but his fingers brush back and forth over my skin, drifting closer and closer toward my center without ever quite reaching it.

Heat travels up my body in a slow wave.

He keeps his gaze on me, an amused glint in his eyes as he watches me try to pretend like I'm unaffected by his touch.

I'm wet by the time I'm done with my pasta, and my breaths come out in short pants. "Ras," I rasp.

He arches a brow. His plate is still half full.

"Eat faster," I beg as he slides the tip of his finger beneath the fabric and brushes it over my sensitive slit.

He chases his next bite with some wine and then picks up a napkin and presses it against his lip. He pulls his hand away, pushes his plate aside, and pats the surface of the table like he wants me to get on it.

Excitement runs up my spine.

I stand up.

"Take off your clothes," he commands, his voice a low rumble. Fire blazes inside his hazel eyes.

When I slip the straps of the dress off my shoulders and let it fall to the ground, Ras makes a satisfied sound. He waits until my panties fall alongside the dress and then says, "Good girl. Now, get on the table and spread those thighs open. I'm ready for my next course."

I do as he says, my clit pulsing with excitement and my nipples puckered, eager for his attention. It's easy to obey him. The thought reminds me that very soon I'll have to do the opposite... Oh God, I'll have to tell him—

He wraps his big hands over my thighs, leans forward, and buries his face inside my cunt.

His tongue momentarily chases away the thoughts pressing in on me, the ones that carve out pieces of my heart. Ras feasts on my pussy until I'm begging for him to fuck me, to get inside of me, to fill me up.

My thighs are shaking and drops of sweat are sliding between my breasts when he finally stands up and fists the hair at my nape. "So greedy," he says against my lips as he deftly undoes his belt. I taste myself on him. Smell my arousal on his beard. "I love when you're desperate for my cock." His tongue slides over my bottom teeth, and he deepens the kiss. I feel him prod against my opening. I reach between us and slide him inside of me. He groans and starts to roll his hips, his mouth still locked on mine.

It feels so, *so* good.

My heels dig into his thighs as he speeds up his thrusts. My back arches. The table jitters beneath us, the dishes and the cutlery clanking so loudly I'm afraid they'll break, but he doesn't stop, and I'm not about to ask him to. Not when I can feel my orgasm coming on, my body becoming engulfed in flames.

Mindless and all-encompassing need pulses inside of me. My nails dig into Ras's back, leaving half-moon marks and tearing at his skin.

"Fuck," he says raggedly, his cock deep inside of me, and his hot breath by my ear. "You're too good. Too fucking good. I'm going to—"

The words push me over, contractions coming on suddenly and with such force they take me aback. I gasp. There's no air inside my lungs. I've forgotten how to breathe.

I clutch onto Ras and feel him tense up as he finds his own release. He groans, his hold on me tightening until it's painful, but the pain somehow feels just right.

A tear leaks out of my eye. God, I need to pull myself together.

"I love you, Peaches," he says, tracing the words with his lips against my temple, and my blood freezes.

I love you too. When I think of you, there's this overwhelming feeling inside my chest, as if I'm coming down the peak of a roller-coaster.

I press my face against his bare chest, hiding the cascade of tears. His heart is pounding.

I can't say it back, no matter how desperately I want to. If I do, I won't be able to leave. I won't be able to break his heart, which is what I have to do.

When he pulls out of me, I'm on the verge of panic.

He's still catching his breath as he steps back, spreads my legs, and looks at where my pussy is leaking his cum all over the dinner table. Satisfaction flashes inside his eyes. He traces his fingertips over the inside of my thigh. "Seeing that makes me so fucking crazy, baby. You have no idea."

I sweep my palms over my face to wipe away the wetness and slide off the table. "I'm going to get cleaned up," I mumble, already on my way to the bathroom.

I need to numb myself. I need to separate my brain from my heart.

And then I need to tell him.

In the shower, I stay under freezing cold water until I can't stand it a second longer, and then I pad into the bedroom. Ras's lying on the bed in his boxer briefs, his arms folded behind his head, biceps bulging.

I think he might have fallen asleep, but when he hears me, his eyes spring open.

The reverent look he gives me nearly kills me.

I know with absolute certainty no one will ever look at me that way again. My conviction wavers for a moment, but I steel my spine and tighten my robe around me.

There are no other options. It has to be done.

"Ras, I have to tell you something."

"What is it?" he asks, sounding unconcerned.

"I think I made a mistake."

He gives me a kind smile. "Whatever it is, we can fix it."

"I..." My gaze drops to my feet. "I can't do this with you."

There's a long, horrible pause.

"What?" He sounds confused.

I force myself to look at him. "I'm sorry. I don't want to be here with you anymore."

He sits up. "Gemma, what are you talking about?"

"I hardly knew what was happening when you said we were leaving New York. There was no time to think. I made a mistake."

"You don't mean that. Why are you saying this shit?"

My hands are trembling. I link my fingers behind my back. "It's the truth. I can't live on the run with you for the rest of my life. I can't abandon Vale and Cleo. I don't want this."

He's shaking his head like he doesn't believe me. "You're happy here."

"They're my family," I force past my tightening throat. "I want to be able to see them."

"Just give me some time," he says. "I just need more time to figure it out."

"There is no time. I'm going back home tomorrow. I've already arranged the plane with my brother."

His face turns pale. He stands up, all of his muscled glory on display, and crosses the distance between us, stopping inches away. "You did *what?*"

I swallow.

One day, he'll wake up and realize that I wasn't worth throwing his life away. He says he loves me, but it's because he doesn't really know me. He doesn't know how pathetic I am.

I've spent my whole life chasing my parents' validation. I've allowed my father to beat me for years without standing up for myself. I'm good at shrinking myself and making myself inconsequential.

I'm not good at being brave.

And Ras? He deserves someone brave. When he finally realizes that I'm not, he'll regret all of this. He'll realize he chose a dud, a worthless, stupid thing.

I suck in a breath and say, "I'm leaving."

"Fuck, Gem!" There's astounded anger in his voice. "And what about me? What about us?"

My voice rises. "What *us*?"

He looks stricken.

"I'm going to go home, and I'm going to marry Rafaele," I say. At least then I'll do something useful. Instead of ruining one life, I'll save two.

"You don't love him."

"I don't need to love him to marry him. I didn't know what I was doing when I agreed to come here."

"And you still don't know shit," he snarls. "But I do. I know that I chose you. Despite everything stacked against us, I chose *you*. I love you. I spent a decade forgetting how to love someone, and yet a few weeks with you is all it took for me to learn it all again." His laugh is humorless. "You are the air I breathe. You are the ground that keeps me standing. Without you, I'm nothing, Gemma."

I don't answer him because I can already feel myself choking on my words. My chest feels like it's being split open.

"I'm sorry," I finally manage to whisper.

His eyes flash with desperation. "Was none of this real to you?"

"It was," I whisper. "But we don't exist in a vacuum, Ras. There's a world around us."

"Did you ever think that maybe we could mold that world to be what we want it to be if we're both willing to try?" He raises his hand like he's about to brush my hair away from my face, but I take a step back.

"I don't know how to do that. I've made up my mind. Once I'm in New York, I'll smooth things over with Rafaele, and I'll convince him not to come after you. And you can go back to Italy. You're Damiano's best friend. You're his family, and he's still covering for you. He'll take you back."

Slowly, so very slowly, his shoulders slump.

"Why are you doing this?" he rasps, all of his heartbreak stuffed inside those words.

Despair fans through me. "Because I don't love you."

He sucks in a harsh breath as if I struck him.

You've done it now. You've pushed him away. There's no coming back from this.

Inside my chest, everything fractures.

A horrible sound comes out of his mouth, a kind of broken roar. He turns and sweeps everything that's on the dresser to the ground. A vase with flowers shatters against the stone floor. He clutches the edge of the dresser, his head down and his back to me.

Tears stream down my cheeks. His name is on the tip of my tongue, so I bite on it hard enough to spill blood.

He shoves the dresser into the corner with a loud scrape and leaves the bedroom without a single glance at me.

CHAPTER 32

GEMMA

When I wake up, I'm alone.

Ras's side of the bed is cold.

A ball appears in my throat as I remember last night. I lied and said I didn't love him even though nothing could be further from the truth.

My fingers claw at the sheets, nearly tearing the fabric, and I press my face into his pillow, searching for his scent. It fills my lungs. Silent sobs wrack my chest, and my tears soak the pillowcase, but the cathartic relief is temporary. When I dry my eyes, everything is still the same.

I'm leaving the man I love today.

I pull myself together and get out of bed. I don't want Ras to see me looking like a mess, so I take my time putting on my makeup and fixing up my hair. The bruise on my cheek is gone, but the one on my heart will be there forever.

Papà's plane is supposed to come for me this morning, landing in a small private airfield a short drive from here. There isn't much to pack. I pull the linen shirt and dresses I bought at the market off their hangers and stuff them into my tote. The necklace Ras got me from the jewelry shop in town hangs off a hook in the closet. I can't bring myself to leave it, even though I know every time I'll look at it, it'll probably make me cry. I slip it around my neck, and the stone is cool against my skin.

Fifteen minutes later, I'm ready to go.

I find Ras in the kitchen, slumped on a stool by the island. He looks like he hasn't slept.

My gaze brushes over his profile, noting the dark bags under his eyes and the disheveled hair. On the counter is a half-empty bottle of whiskey. Has he been drinking through the night? There's no glass in front of him, but I spot one in the sink.

He hears me and shoots me a lifeless glance.

I don't think he's drunk.

I think he stopped drinking a while ago and spent the rest of the time thinking about what a bitch I am.

I hope that's what he did. I hope he hates me. I deserve it. God, I deserve it.

Maybe when he returns to Damiano and smooths things over with him, he'll forgive me. With time, he'll realize what a mistake it would have been to throw his life away for someone like me. He'll see me by Rafaele's side and wonder how he ever could have loved me.

No matter how much it hurts now, I'm making the right choice. After I'm home and everything is fixed, Dem will take Ras back. He'll forgive him. I'll make sure of it.

I drop my bag on the ground, pick up the burner phone and start flipping through a local newspaper for a taxi number. I should have done this yesterday, but after our fight, I was too much of a coward to face him.

"I'll take you," he says, his voice no more than a harsh rasp. He stands up and drains a glass of water.

Grief batters my insides. "I can take a taxi."

He doesn't answer, just takes the keys, picks up my bag, and brushes past me.

We get into the car. The silence is suffocating, but the alternative—speaking—would be even worse. What is there to say? Words won't make this better.

He must be thinking—*I've given up so much for her but it's still not enough to make this work. What more does she want from me? I have nothing else to give.*

He doesn't understand. When you love someone, you don't want them to lose everything because of you. You don't want to be the end. You want to be the beginning.

When we get to the edge of the airfield, my throat is in a vise. He parks the car and places his palms on his thighs, his gaze aimed forward at where the plane is waiting.

I want to kiss him, but even after the lies I've told him, I discover that my cruelty has a limit. I don't move except to curl my fingers around the pendant.

"I'll never forget this," I whisper.

His Adam's apple bobs. For a moment, it looks like he wants to say something, but then his jaw hardens, and I know he won't.

I take one final breath, savoring the way his scent is laced through the air, and then I get out of the car.

~

Vince is waiting for me in a black sedan when I come out of the airport. I'm escorted by two of Papà's guys. I'm fully aware they're watching my every move. One of them opens the car door, and I slide into the back seat beside my brother.

Vince studies me for a long moment. "You okay?" he asks finally, his tone guarded.

I give him a terse nod. "I'm fine." My anger at him pales in comparison to the other emotions swirling inside my chest. I don't have the energy for a confrontation, but I'm determined not to let him see how much I'm hurting.

His gaze lingers on the side of my face before he says to the driver, "Take us home."

A bitter feeling solidifies inside my gut. *Home.* Where we're going isn't my home. Not anymore. I don't think I'll ever be able to walk by Papà's office without remembering what happened there.

"Why did you decide to come back?" Vince asks as we start moving.

The long flight gave me a chance to put together my official story, and it hangs on my ability to mask my true feelings for Ras. I'm going to say I begged him to take me away, and that he obliged despite the grave risk to himself. I'll blame my poor decisions on my distressed state after Papà's attack. And I'll explain that when I calmed down, I realized my place is back in New York.

If anyone asks why Ras didn't escort me back, I'll say it's because Damiano summoned him back to Italy.

By now, Ras has to be on his way back home, right? What else would he do? And Damiano will take him back. He has to. I wanted to call Vale as soon as I landed so I could tell her the same story I'm about to tell Vince, but my phone was practically ripped out of my hands by the guys who came to pick me up. Something tells me it will be a while before I get it back.

"Did Cleo tell you what happened before Papà got arrested?"

Vince looks uncomfortable. "Yes."

"Then you can understand that I wasn't thinking clearly. I convinced Ras to help me get away because I didn't know what else to do. I was scared."

A jolt of surprise travels up my spine when Vince reaches over and takes my hand in his.

"Gem, I'm sorry," he says, his voice wavering. "I had no idea Papà was hurting you. Cleo told me you said it wasn't the first time either."

I bite my tongue. *You may have had an idea if you hadn't left us here to do whatever the hell you're doing in Europe.*

"It's fine."

"It's not fine. I told Papà if he ever does it again, I'll tell Rafaele to cut the five years Papà has left as don short. The only reason he's getting out of jail is because you're here now. He owes you everything."

He squeezes my limp hand, but I quickly tug it back on my lap. His words feel empty and a few years too late. I don't need his protection and love now. It's too late for that.

"When are you going back to Europe?" I ask.

"After your wedding."

"Want to make sure I don't do anything else to make your deal fall through? Don't worry. I'm going to marry Rafaele," I say dryly.

He swallows audibly. "Gem, I should have been open with you about the—"

"I don't want to hear it."

He doesn't listen and keeps going. "I didn't think you'd *mind*. You never seemed like you wished for more than this. At least not like the rest of us did."

Outrage unfurls inside my chest. How dare he? "Just because I wasn't breaking into Papà's bank account like you or doing outrageous shit like Cleo, you assumed you could take control of my life and do whatever you wanted with it? Did you really think I'd be happy being a pawn on your chessboard?"

"No, that's not—"

"Should I thank you for making all these choices for me?" I pin him with my gaze. Whatever he sees inside of it makes him pale.

"Maybe you're right," I say coldly. "What more could I *possibly* want?"

405

"I'm just saying—"

"Honestly, I don't care what you have to say at this point. I'm tired. It's been a long journey. You're getting everything you want, so maybe you can be kind enough to give me just one thing in return."

"What?" he asks.

"Silence. I don't want to talk to you."

There's remorse in his gaze, but I don't care. It does nothing to soften my feelings toward him.

"Okay," he says quietly.

I turn to the window, the backs of my eyes starting to prickle.

We pull into the driveway, and I hop out of the car as soon as it stops. Vince doesn't follow me.

Inside, the house is cold and empty. My skin still tingles with the memory of Greek sun. In a few weeks, my tan will fade. It will be like I was never there.

There are people waiting for me, house staff and a handful of made men. I barely acknowledge them. They're here to guard me. It's so obvious that there's no point in pretending that's not the case.

Mamma and Cleo aren't here. I ask about them, and I'm told they're visiting Papà and will be back soon.

I go up to my room, wash up in the bathroom, and then fold myself into the small window seat, pulling a blanket over my lap.

The stitches around my heart start to tear.

The fantasy Ras and I created was far better than reality. It was perfect.

And now it's gone forever.

Tears rise in my eyes, and before long, they're spilling down my cheeks. I move to the bed, press my face into the pillow, and cry until I pass out.

~

A sound wakes me. I sit up, my head groggy from the jet lag, and glance around the room. The door opens.

Cleo.

My chest swells at seeing my sister. She rushes over and throws herself at me, her arms looping around my waist.

I hug her back, letting the warmth of her embrace seep into my bones. It feels like it's been forever since I last saw her, even if it's only been a bit more than a week.

"You shouldn't have come back to this mess," she says, pressing her face against my chest bone.

Sighing, I run my palm over her curls. "I had to."

"Don't tell me you did it for Papà." She lets go of me and maneuvers herself to sit cross-legged by my side. "As far as I'm concerned, he's exactly where he belongs."

"No, I didn't do it for Papà," I say quietly.

Cleo frowns. "You look sad. What happened while you were gone, Gem? Tell me everything."

There's one thing I have to do first. "Do you have your phone with you? I've been trying to call Vale." I want to make sure Ras has returned safely and that Damiano isn't putting any blame on him.

Cleo shakes her head. "I don't have my phone anymore. Mamma took it from me this morning. She knows I'd give it to you if you asked, and they're keeping you under lock and key until you've got a wedding band on your finger. By the way, I have your engagement ring. You left it on the counter in the penthouse the night we stayed there."

Damn it. I won't be able to call Vale. So I just have to pray that everything worked out on that side of the world? Damiano must be in contact with Vince, though. My brother will for sure tell him what I've said about Ras.

"Gem?"

I blink, realizing Cleo's looking at me expectantly.

She nudges my knee. "What's going on?"

Can I tell her the truth? Just the thought of doing it makes an ache move down my throat. But there's no one else I can talk to about Ras, and I *do* want to talk about Ras.

It's been less than a day, and I already miss him so much.

Tears well up in my eyes. "I don't even know where to start."

My choked-up voice makes worry slip into Cleo's expression. "Are you okay?" She scans me over with her gaze. "Are you still hurt?"

"Physically, I'm fine."

"What is it then?"

I sniff. "I came back because of Ras. He took me away even though Damiano didn't want him to, and he got himself into a lot of trouble. I couldn't be responsible for ruining his life."

"Why would Ras do that?"

"Because he…" I start crying again. God, this isn't like me. I'm not usually a leaky faucet, but just thinking about what I lost sends me into despair.

Cleo moves up the bed and kneels beside me. "Something happened between the two of you."

My temple prickles in the exact place where his lips traced out the words.

"I love you, Peaches."

I'm overcome with a longing so strong that my throat closes right up.

Cleo's eyes widen. "Gemma, what did you do?" she asks quietly. "Did you fall for each other?"

All I can do is nod.

She cradles my face in her hands, her eyes turning pink at the edges. "Oh, Gem. You're so broken up over this. You should have stayed with him.

"I couldn't," I croak. "Don't you understand that if I didn't come back, Ras would have lost everything? He acted rashly in the moment because he was so upset about seeing me hurt. He disobeyed Damiano, who's his don. We would have had to live out our lives in hiding if I'd stayed."

She pulls her hands away. "And would you have minded that? I mean, you would have figured out a way to come out of hiding eventually."

I bring my knees up to my chest and wrap my arms around them. "No, I wouldn't have minded, but reality would have caught up with us sooner or later, and Ras would have regretted losing his position as the underboss of the Casalesi. How could I ask him to give up the title he's worked so hard to get? How could I ask him to turn his back on his friend, a person he so clearly loves like a brother?"

"It doesn't sound like you asked him for anything, Gem. He did it willingly. Instead of rushing to solve his problems, you should have left the choice to him."

Her words land with a sting. Why does it feel like she's attacking me right now? "I did what was right. He would have regretted it sooner or later."

"You can't possibly know that."

Frustration runs through me, and I get off the bed. "I didn't share all of this with you so you can judge my decision. This is hard enough as it is."

Cleo's expression softens as she watches me pace the room. "I know. I can see that. But you need to hear this, so I'm going to say it. I'm not going to celebrate you for sacrificing yourself anymore. I should have stopped doing it a long time ago."

"What does that mean?"

"Gem, can't you see? You've done this all your life. You make everyone else's problems your own and try to solve them no matter what it costs you. It's not your responsibility to do that."

Ras said something like that to me once. "That's just how I am."

Cleo shakes her head. "It's how our parents *forced* you to be. Their love has always been conditional, predicated on you doing things like this."

Hurt blooms inside my chest. "That's not true."

"It *is* true. I've been thinking about our childhood a lot ever since Vale ran away. Remembering things. Do you realize we were never given love by them unless we earned it? If we didn't behave the way they wanted us to, do you remember what they'd do? If we acted out at family events, they'd lock us up in empty rooms and leave us to cry on our own."

I flinch. No, that didn't happen. "I don't remember that."

"Maybe you chose to forget. What about that time at Tito's birthday when you ate a piece of chocolate cake even though Mamma said you weren't allowed. You were eight, and she was already managing your weight. When she saw chocolate smeared on your lips, she lost it. She cut off another slice, put it on a plate, and then... Don't you remember what she did?"

A fuzzy snapshot surfaces, but a moment later, it's gone. "No."

Cleo exhales a low breath. "She shoved your face into the cake in front of everyone and called you a little pig. It was cruel. You cried for hours afterward, which only made her more mad."

Horror seeps into my veins as the snapshot turns into a movie. "Oh my God."

She's right. I remember now.

That poor little girl.

I was so excited about that cake. It was the most beautiful cake I'd ever seen, with elaborate white flowers piped around it, and syrup-soaked cherries piled in the center. It sparkled. Tito was upset. He'd wanted a rainbow cake with cars on it, but they'd made a mistake at the bakery. He said this cake was too girly, but when his ma gave him a slice, he ate it anyway. That first bite made me close my eyes with pleasure. It was *so* good.

But a few minutes later, the whole day was ruined.

I sway.

Cleo jumps to the floor and leads me to sit down in a chair. "You're remembering now, aren't you?"

My eyes flood with tears. "Yes. I can't believe I forgot."

"That's just one time. There were so many others. They made you this way, Gem. They made you feel like if you aren't being perfect and doing all of these things for them, they'll reject you."

The truth in her words hits me right in the center of my chest. I fold over, my elbows on my knees and my head between my palms. More memories come flooding in.

Me at age six. Mother's Day. Mamma doesn't like the dress I picked out, even though it's my favorite—midnight blue with little sparkling stars sewn in. She tells me to change out of it because it looks cheap. I tell her I like it. She starts yelling. I start crying. She tears it off me, the buttons getting tangled and pulling out my hair, and throws it in the fire in the living room. *"You have two minutes to stop your whining or we're leaving you at home."*

Vale tries to argue with her, but she's only nine. When I come out in the dress Mamma wants me to wear, the anger leaves Mamma's expression. She smiles. *"There, Gemma. The pink dress looks so much better on you. You're a completely different girl."*

My fingers drift over my lips. It feels like a veil has been lifted, and I can see clearly for the first time.

"I can't believe I forgot."

"Maybe that's what you had to do for it not to hurt so much."

I meet Cleo's gaze. "But you didn't."

Her eyes are shining. "I stopped playing their game a long time ago. And so can you."

"I don't know how," I mumble through the tears that are now dripping down my face. "Ras told me I was enough for him, but I didn't believe him."

"Oh, Gem." She pulls me into her arms. "How could you believe him when you've been told your whole life that you're not? But he was telling you the truth. You are more than enough."

I clutch onto Cleo and squeeze my eyes shut as my emotions threaten to overwhelm me.

I don't think I've ever understood the damage our parents have done until now. They've robbed us of so much.

A happy childhood.

A loving family.

A mind that's not filled with fear and doubts.

But worst of all, they robbed me of Ras.

And I let them.

413

CHAPTER 33

RAS

It's fucking March, and New York is still a concrete refrigerator.

I pull my coat tighter around me while I wait at the crosswalk, watching a car tread through a pool of icy brown slush.

People crowd around me. I've learned in the past few days that Midtown traffic at rush hour behaves more like a liquid than a mass of discrete parts. I clench my fist when someone bumps their shoulder against mine. By the time the light turns green, I'm actually excited to get back to my shoebox apartment, if only to get a bit of personal space.

The studio apartment on 32nd Street is about the size of my closet back in Ibiza. It was the best Orrin could arrange on short notice. A week ago, I called him from Crete as I watched Gemma's plane take off and told him I needed him to get me back to New York.

He asked me why.

I told him it was none of his business.

He didn't press it further. He just sighed, told me that at this point I owed him my firstborn, and picked me up on the same cargo plane.

The truth is the location of the shoe box is convenient.

It's a block away from Gemma's Pilates studio.

I walk past my building and keep going until I see the familiar neon sign with the name *Move On*.

I drag my palm over my overgrown beard.

Touché.

I park myself by the window inside the coffee shop across the street and order a cappuccino.

Around ten fifty, the studio's traffic picks up as women and some men arrive for the eleven a.m. class, but I'm waiting for the black SUV. Gemma's always surrounded by at least two guards these days, and I know they'll stay in the car just outside the studio while she does the class. Pietra goes with her to her classes now. They've got her on a tight leash.

The car pulls up at ten fifty-five. The door opens, and Gemma emerges in a puffy coat, hair pulled back in a short ponytail, light-green leggings, and a white pair of athletic shoes.

My breath catches. I don't blink.

I only catch a flash of her face before she turns and quickly disappears inside the studio.

That's it. Fifteen seconds that are the highlight of my day. It's all downhill from here.

Since that thought is far too fucking depressing, I get myself a sandwich and decided to wait to see her leave. Drag it out a bit.

I'm like an addict searching for that next hit.

When I got back, my plan was to keep an eye on her in New Jersey, but every time I drove by her house, there were a bunch of cars there, and at least a few guys on lookout.

I couldn't risk getting caught.

I don't know what Dem told Messero or Garzolo. Gemma said he was covering for me, but at the time, I wasn't in any state to clarify what she meant by that. If Dem hasn't publicly announced that I'm no longer his underboss, and I got caught watching Gemma, he would have another problem to deal with. I don't want to do that to him.

So I do this instead. I come to this place to catch a glimpse of her.

It's nothing more than a crumb for a man who wants the whole damn cake. She comes from her house and goes straight back there after she's done.

She's been back for a week.

There are four days left till the wedding.

And I have no fucking clue what I'm doing, why I'm stalking her instead of trying to forget her.

I throw my garbage in the bin by the cafe door and start walking back to the apartment.

My phone feels like a heavy weight inside my pocket. I pull it out and check the screen. No messages.

Dem's silence is particularly loud. There were a dozen missed calls from the day Gemma and I left New York, but nothing since then. I haven't dared to contact him, not even after Gemma returned, but he must know I'm here. My phone's been on since I came back. Napoletano could track me down in minutes.

I'm embarrassed, I guess. I went against my oldest friend for a woman who left me after a week. She walked away from me, just like Sara did. I was so focused on making sure she knew she was enough for me, I never thought I might not be enough for her.

A humorless laugh leaves my lungs. The situation might be funnier if I wasn't still so damn hung up on her.

My phone buzzes.

A bubble of hope expands inside my chest for a brief moment until I see Orrin's name pop up.

"Hey. You've got plans tonight?"

I drag my fingers through my hair. It desperately needs a wash. "Yeah. It involves a bottle of scotch and a greasy pizza from the place below where I'm staying."

"Christ. I will say, your honesty is refreshing. Well, if you feel like doing something less depressing, something that might get your spirits up, I need an extra man tonight."

"What's the plan?"

"Just a few friends of mine bringing gifts from abroad. They're generous. We could use some help carrying the presents."

I read between the lines. It's some kind of a heist. Knowing what I know about Orrin, he's probably taking imported crap off a truck.

Life is just a nasty fucking cycle, isn't it? To go from underboss to a damn foot soldier...

Whatever. It's work, and I could use something to keep my thoughts off Gemma for a few hours.

Rubbing my forehead with the heel of my palm, I mutter, "All right. Tell me when and where."

Orrin and two of his guys pick me up at midnight in a cargo van and take me to an industrial area on the bank of the Hackensack River. Rows of ugly gray warehouses line the empty street, and when we get out, I press my fist to my nose.

"What the fuck is that smell?" It smells like a rotting carcass.

"Landfill." Orrin looks to the right. "About a kilometer that way. Don't worry, this won't take long."

There's a truck being unloaded ahead of us, and I have a feeling that's what we came here for. Jesus. I haven't done this kind of shit since... Well, I've never done this kind of shit. By the time I linked up with Damiano, he was already running more sophisticated schemes.

"I know the night supervisor," Orrin explains. "He'll make sure the cameras are off. Only thing we need to do is get a handle on the driver."

He turns to his guys. "Fill the van as fast as you can. I'm going to explain the situation to the driver and make sure he understands. We don't want any trouble tonight, got it?"

"Sure, boss," the one that goes by "Speedy" says.

"No problem," the other guy, Chris, adds. "Easy peasy."

Orrin nods before moving his attention to me. "Ras, you're on lookout."

"Sure."

For the first five minutes, everything goes according to plan. After a small scuffle with the driver, Orrin handcuffs him to the side of the truck and slaps some tape over his mouth. The man makes some noise for a bit before he comes to terms with the situation.

Speedy and Chris load the cargo inside our van. It's a bunch of high-end computer monitors. I'm doing the math on it in my head when the back of my neck tingles.

My eyes narrow. I've learned to trust my gut in these kinds of situations.

A black car turns into the lot, its headlights on full beam. I shield my eyes with my palm, squinting against the light, but it's hard as fuck to see anything.

"Who is it?" Orrin calls out. "We're almost done."

"Pack it up and get in the van," I yell over my shoulder. Whoever it is, they clearly knew we'd be here, and something tells me it's not the cops.

The car stops twenty feet away from the truck, and four men spill out of it.

I tighten my hold on my gun, keeping it lowered.

The newcomers block the lights with their bodies, and that's when I see him.

"Fuck," I mutter under my breath.

Nunzio breaks off from his friends and walks toward me, his steps slow and cocky. There's a gun at his side and a smirk on his face that tells me he thinks it's his lucky day.

He laughs as he stops a few steps away. "Didn't think you'd be stupid enough to come back here after what you pulled. Did you know your name was on the menu?"

I grit my teeth. Orrin had informed me of that fact when I returned. The menu is a list of names the families sign off on as being fair game. I don't know the details of how it works, but apparently, I landed on it for a while. Twenty-four hours after Gemma returned, I was off. Maybe Vince and Messero decided I wasn't worth the effort once they got what they wanted.

"Sounds like you missed your chance," I say. "It's not on it now."

Nunzio sniffs. "Don't think the boss will be too angry if someone finds your body floating in the river a few days from now. If you were smart, you'd hide in whatever hole you crawled out off."

Orrin appears at my side. *Idiot.* He should have stayed in the van. No good will come out of him associating with me.

Nunzio squints. "That you, Petraki?"

"Yeah, it's me. Want to explain what the fuck this is?"

He shrugs. "Why settle for ten percent when we can get all of it?"

"That's not how this works, and you know it," Orrin growls. "Does your capo even know you're here? Should I give him a call to inform him? This was clearly negotiated and agreed on last month."

"Last month?" Nunzio snickers. "Fuck, Petraki. That may as well have been last century with how much has happened since. Now, here's what you're going to do. Your buddies are going to get out of the van and hand us the keys. You're going to wait until we're far away from here before you start walking your ass back to Manhattan. And tomorrow, you're going to give me a call and tell me what a nice time you had tonight. Got it?"

I scan the three guys standing behind him. "You're bluffing."

Nunzio arches a brow. "How's that?"

"You don't have clearance to do this. You're just hoping to pull it off and ask for forgiveness instead of permission."

It's only because I've spent years deciphering Nunzio's emotions from the tiny movements in his face that I catch it. A small twitch in the left side of his mouth. It's always been a tell.

Orrin gives me a barely there bump with his arm, signaling he's following my lead. Four against four. I've dealt with far worse odds before.

"Yeah?" Nunzio asks, his voice low. "You sure know a lot for someone who went from Ras of the Casalesi to working for one of the most insignificant outfits in New York. How'd you end up here if you're so smart?"

I smirk. "By doing stupid, reckless shit like this."

The bullet leaves my gun before the last word leaves my mouth, but Nunzio lunges out of the way, and it only grazes his arm.

He hisses in pain and clutches his biceps. His cronies immediately draw their own weapons, but Orrin and his crew have already taken cover behind the van. I duck and roll to the left to join them as another gunshot rings out. It's followed by the sound of glass shattering, metal clanging against metal, and a muffled groan.

Orrin curses. "Fuck, they hit the truck driver."

"We need to end this quickly," I tell him, peeking around the van.

I've been in gunfights before, but this one feels different. More personal.

I can hear Nunzio barking orders to his men.

"Now," I snap.

With a nod from Orrin, Speedy and Chris emerge from behind the van, guns blazing. I follow closely behind, my own weapon steady in my grip. The sound of gunfire echoes in the empty parking lot, bouncing off the walls of the surrounding buildings.

Speedy takes a hit, toppling over, but so do Nunzio's men. They fall quickly. Nunzio himself is a different story. He's faster than I expect him to be. He dodges every bullet and manages to make it back around his car.

The air quiets.

"Leave him to me."

"Hey, don't be a hero," Orrin says. "We've got this."

"I said leave him to me." My voice is laced with steel as I step out from behind the van, gun at the ready.

Nunzio stands on the other side of their car, his own weapon pointed in my direction. He sneers at me, blood trickling down his arm.

"You really think you can take me?" he taunts.

"You're not worth anyone else's trouble."

He laughs, but it's shaky. "You've never won against me, Ras. Not once."

I don't reply, just take a deep breath and aim my gun. "Why do you think that is?"

"Because you're a fucking weak—"

My bullet pierces his skull.

Nunzio's eyes go wide as he falls to the ground.

The bastard was too arrogant to pull his trigger before he finished his sentence.

Orrin appears beside me, surveying the bodies littering the pavement. He claps me on the back. "Cleanup's going to be a bitch. I'll get the boys to drop off the goods and then come back for us with supplies."

Blood seeps out from under Nunzio's body, the pool reflecting the moon and a starless sky.

I tuck the gun inside my waistband and stare at his ruined skull. There's an unsettling emptiness inside my chest. I've fantasized about this moment for so many years, and yet I feel...nothing.

No closure, no joy, no relief.

My past has haunted me for so long, but at some point, it became irrelevant.

I scratch the side of my neck. Only one thing haunts me now, and it's Gemma's voice.

"Why are you doing this?"

"Because I don't love you."

CHAPTER 34

GEMMA

RAFAELE STARTED WORKING on getting Papà out the day I returned, and a week or so later, Papà arrives at the house.

Mamma, Cleo, and I are waiting for him in the foyer, his core crew gathered around us.

When he walks through the front door, everyone acts like he's some kind of a hero. There's cheering and clapping. Someone pops open a bottle of champagne.

Papà laughs, triumphant. Even the Feds couldn't keep Stefano Garzolo locked up. He is a legend. Weakened but undefeated. I hear the words "what doesn't kill you makes you stronger" repeated over and over again.

When he comes to me, my muscles tense up on their own accord. It must be a new automatic response I've developed to him after what happened. He takes my stiff body into his arms and presses a kiss to my cheek. Out of the corner of my eye, I notice Vince watching us, his lips a tight line.

"Gemma, my darling. I'm glad you're here," he says with a genuine smile. I guess he's elected to move on from all the trouble I've caused now that everything's fallen into place.

Has he also decided to forget the fact that the last time we saw each other, he tried to kick my ribs in? Before I muster up a response, he's being corralled away by his men into the living room where a lavish feast has been laid out.

My back straightens. I wasn't exactly expecting an apology, but this feels like a slap in the face.

I don't want to ever speak with Papà again after I'm married. I wonder if Rafaele will allow that. Probably not, but maybe he'll at least agree to never leave me alone in a room with Papà.

My shoulders slump. The fact that I'm days away from negotiating these kinds of things with Rafaele hadn't hit me until now. We're getting married in four days.

Cleo comes to stand by my side and crosses her arms over her chest. "Look at him." She jerks her chin in Papà's direction. "It's like he just came back with a gold medal from the Olympics."

The rest of our extended family arrives over the next few hours. The house starts to feel tight and loud, the level of conversation rising to deafening by the time everyone's had a few glasses of wine.

I'm not drinking. My stomach hasn't been feeling okay since this morning.

Tiredness pulls at me, but I force myself to hang around in anticipation of Rafaele's arrival. I only saw him briefly the day I returned. He came by the house to verify for himself that I was back. He asked me only one thing—if there was anything I wanted to tell him.

I said yes. Then I asked him not to blame Ras for anything. I said it was all my fault, that I was so sorry. I said I was back now and couldn't wait to get married.

He studied me for a long moment, nodded, and left. I don't know if he bought it, but according to Vince, no one in New York is concerned with Ras at this point. Word of Rafaele's succession leaked in the days after I returned, and now everyone knows it's happening. That's the only thing anyone seems to be talking about these days.

I press my back against the wall for support and try to engage in conversation with my aunts, but I can't focus on a single word.

My head hurts.

I just want to be back in Ras's arms. I'm certain that if I could do that, I'd feel better immediately. Instead, I'm surrounded by my family, but I've never felt so alone.

These pangs of longing should get better with time. At least that's what I tell myself. So far, they haven't gotten any better though. Every time one of them comes on, it feels like someone's battering their fists against my heart.

Nona comes up to me, snapping me back to the present. "*Cara mia.*" She leans in and presses a kiss to both of my cheeks. "You must have been so worried about your father. Thank goodness, he's back. You know what they say, when it rains, it pours. This family's been through so much lately."

I nod stiffly. Nona doesn't know I left. No one in the family does except for Mamma, Cleo, Vince, and a few of Papà's men, but they've been instructed to keep their mouths shut.

"I know, Nona. Hopefully, we're on the other side of it now."

"At least we have your wedding to look forward to. I can hardly believe it's happening next week."

A wave of nausea hits me.

Nona sees my expression fall and frowns. "Are you all right? You look pale."

"I'm a bit tired."

"Maybe you should go lie down. There's a nasty bug going around."

Is it possible I'm getting sick? It's the last thing I need right now. I'm barely functioning as is.

I glance around. I thought Rafaele would be here, but he's either really late or he's not coming, and I'm not even sure why I'm waiting up for him. Appearances, I guess. He's impossible to read, and I'm being careful not to do anything that might rub him the wrong way. I can't give him any reason to doubt the story I told him.

"You're right," I say, squeezing Nona's hand. "I'm going to get some rest."

She gives me a kind smile. "Go, *amore*. I'll let Pietra know."

I trudge upstairs to my room and lie down on my bed.

Where could I have picked up a virus? Maybe Pilates, since that's the only place I've been allowed to go when I want to leave the house. Even for that, I have Mamma as my escort.

There's a dull throb at the back of my head, and my stomach just won't settle. I go over everything I ate in the past twenty-four hours. Salad with canned tuna, some Greek yogurt, a veggie omelet... I doubt it could be any of those things.

Sometimes, I get a bit of a headache on the first day of my period, but this isn't the right week for it.

Hold on.

My eyes spring open. When was the last time I had my period?

I roll off the bed and hurry to check the calendar on the desk. A quick scan tells me I should have gotten my period last week, the day after I returned.

There's a sinking sensation in my gut. I'm about a week late. I'm never late. I've always been as regular as a damn clock.

There's a knock on the door. "Gem?"

It's Cleo. "Come in," I call out, my pulse loud in my ears.

She walks in, her face lined with concern. "Nona said you aren't feeling well. I wanted to check in on you."

"Close the door and sit down."

"Is everything okay?"

"No. I'm nauseous. And I just realized I'm late."

Her forehead wrinkles with confusion. "Late?" When the realization hits her, her eyes widen. "Your period? Wait, *what*? Have you—"

"Yes. With Ras." I can feel a wave of panic creeping up my spine. I climb off the bed, unable to sit still. "Cleo, the night Rafaele killed Ludovico, Ras and I..." I swallow. "We had sex. Unprotected. I took the morning-after pill. It was around the time I was ovulating."

Cleo's shaking her head. "If you took the pill, you should be fine, right?"

I should be. I mean, I took it hours after we did it and those things work well, don't they?

I blink, trying to recall the events of that morning and when I do, my stomach plummets all the way to my feet. "Oh God. Cleo, I threw up."

Right after Papà hit me. It was less than an hour after I took the pill, and that might not have been enough time for it to fully digest.

"I might be pregnant," I mutter as panic explodes inside my chest. "I need to take a test."

Shit, shit, shit. I should stay calm, at least until I know for sure what's happening, but that's easier said than done.

"How do I get one?" I ask Cleo. "I can't leave the house unescorted, especially not to a pharmacy. Mamma will just say I should tell my driver to get me what I need." I perch on the edge of the windowsill, my stomach clenching with anxiety. "I have no idea what to do."

"Okay, take a deep breath," Cleo says, squeezing my hands. "I'll get you a test."

"How?"

"Don't worry about it." She presses a kiss to my cheek and gets up. "I've got it, okay? I'll be back in five minutes."

I'm so agitated, all I can do is nod and watch as she hurries out of my room.

As soon as she's gone, the weight of my situation presses down on me. I can hardly breathe.

My throat tightens. My hands find the windowsill and curl over its edge. It's March, but winter's grip hasn't let up a single inch. Flakes of snow dance through the air in slow motion before settling on the driveway. If Ras were here, he'd no doubt be complaining about how damn cold it is.

I stare at the snow for a long time. Long enough for Cleo to return. She's wearing a hoodie over her outfit, and she takes a box out of the center pocket. "I went through the maids' cubbies. You know Melody's always having pregnancy scares, so I thought she might have one of these."

"Thank you," I say numbly as I open the box and read the instructions.

My hands shake.

It seems simple enough. Just pee on a stick and wait. What they don't say is that the three-minute wait is excruciating.

I sit on the bed biting my nails while Cleo's silent beside me. When the timer on Cleo's phone goes off, we both jump up.

"Do you want me to check it?" she asks when I don't immediately dash to the bathroom.

I swallow. "No. I'll do it."

My legs are weak as I make my way to the bathroom. My heart is pounding so loudly in my chest that it feels like it might burst. I try to take deep breaths, but they come out shaky and uneven. I close the bathroom door behind me and stare down at the stick lying by the sink.

Two lines.

Two fucking lines.

"Gem?" Cleo appears in the doorway.

I don't trust myself to speak, so I just hold up the test.

431

There's a long pause before she responds. "Shit."

I brush past her and collapse in a chair across from my bed.

Pregnant. The word echoes in my mind, refusing to be silenced. How could I have been so careless?

I know how. That day was pure chaos. I didn't even think of the morning-after pill when Ras picked me up off my father's office floor.

But now I have to think about it.

I'm fucking *pregnant*.

"This is a disaster," I say numbly. Rafaele won't marry me while I'm pregnant with another man's baby. If I tell our parents, I'm sure they'll make me get rid of it.

I feel sick just thinking of doing that. Not because of my moral beliefs, but because this is *our* baby. A part of Ras inside of me. My hand presses over my flat belly, thinking of how he'd react if he knew.

I think he'd be happy.

An ache fills my chest. I need him so badly right now. He'd know what to do.

Cleo paces the room. "Telling Mamma or Papà is out of the question. We know how they'll react."

No, we can't tell them. I'm not going to let them take this baby from me.

So I have to run, but on my own this time.

Run where?

I have to find Ras. But first I have to get to Europe, and my odds aren't good. How can I get away from Rafaele and Papà on my own? I can't just run away without a plan. But I have to do something. I can't stay here.

An aggravated groan escapes me.

"What am I going to do?" I murmur. "Rafaele and Papà need me. They'll force me to get rid of it."

"Rafaele wouldn't do that," Cleo says. "You know how traditional his family is."

"Don't be naïve. In our world, they only respect the traditions that serve them. Rafaele won't raise another man's baby."

I could pretend the baby is his. The timing wouldn't be that far off since the wedding is next week.

The moment the thought passes through my head, I know I can't do it. I can't keep Ras's child from him like that.

"I don't know what to do." My vision blurs. "I never should have left him. You're right, Cleo. I should have been brave and stayed. He loved me, and I broke his heart because I was so damn scared that one day, he'd regret sacrificing so much for me. I was so insecure and so worried about the future that I completely missed what was right in front of me. He and I could have had a family together. We would have been happy. Instead, I fucked everything up."

Cleo wraps her palm over my shoulder and peers into my eyes. "Is that what you want? Do you want to be with Ras?"

"Yes. More than anything." The lies I told him right before I left press into my brain. I'd have to beg him to forgive me and hope it's not too late.

"Are you willing to fight for it?"

433

Her words cut through the haze of my thoughts, and I nod without hesitation. I'm willing to fight for Ras, for our baby, for a life together. But how?

"I'll do whatever it takes," I say, my voice firm.

Cleo nods. "Gem, I'll take your place."

I stare at her, not understanding. "What do you mean?"

"I'll marry Rafaele."

My eyes widen. "You can't," I sputter. "You hate him. You said you'd rather die than marry him."

"I can do this. I *want* to do this for you." There's a spark of determination in her gaze. "You're pregnant with Ras's kid, for fuck's sake. I know this doesn't feel like a good thing at the moment, but it is. Just think about it, Gem. You're going to have a little baby boy or girl."

A tiny burst of excitement travels through my bloodstream.

"I'm going to be an aunt, and I'm already feeling protective," Cleo continues. "All Rafaele wants is to marry into the family to secure his succession, right? What does it matter if he marries me or you? It's a business transaction for him. As long as the outcome is the same, why would he care which daughter he's marrying?"

My mind struggles to process the enormity of what she's suggesting. It's a crazy idea. There's no way it would work. "But you're not a virgin."

"I am," she says with a small smirk.

I shake my head. "What are you talking about? Everyone knows about the pizza boy."

"Danny and I didn't have sex. I was trying to, but he just kept talking, and so I started taking off my clothes to speed things up. I don't think he'd ever seen a naked woman before, because he turned all red and told me to get under the covers. I pulled him onto the bed with me, and that's when Papà walked in. I just said we had sex to piss Papà off."

I can't believe what I'm hearing. "You *lied* about it? Cleo, they killed that boy!"

She shakes her head. "They didn't kill him. His dad's a cop. I made sure to mention that before they dragged him away."

My thoughts race with all of this new information. "Rafaele will never believe this story."

Cleo waves a dismissive hand. "He can get a doctor to check, I don't care. But he already knows."

"What?"

"When they picked me up in Ibiza, I was drunk, and I blabbed." She sits down on the bed and crosses her legs. "Rafaele was lecturing me about walking around on my own. Said it wasn't safe. I told him I wouldn't mind getting picked up by a Spanish guy—they're hot. I said maybe then I'd finally get laid. They wouldn't waste my time like Danny did. I beat myself up for days afterwards for saying that to Rafaele. You should have seen how he looked at me when he realized what I meant."

"How?" I ask, my voice a stunned whisper.

"Like I'd just delivered myself to him on a platter. I gave him my secret. I thought he'd threaten to use it against me, but he hasn't so far. He knows I'm a virgin."

"So you think he'll go for this?"

"I think it's our best bet for getting you out of this mess."

A flicker of hope appears inside my chest. What if this could really work? If Rafaele agrees to marry Cleo instead of me, I'll be off the hook.

My instinct is still to say no, because how can I ask my own sister to make a sacrifice like this for me? But I've recently learned that my instincts aren't always right. Sometimes, they're flat out wrong.

She wants to do this. I can see it in her eyes. Why not accept her help?

"Cleo..." I sit down beside her, unsure of what to do.

"Look, Papà is going to marry me off anyway," she says. "What difference does it make if it's Rafaele or someone else? It's all the same to me. At least this way, I get to help you. I wish I could have helped you all those years when you dealt with Papà's abuse on your own." Her eyes glisten. "We can't change the past, but we can influence our future."

She waits, watching me as I make this decision. The biggest decision of my life.

It's so hard to admit that I can't solve this problem on my own. It's even harder to accept that to solve it, I'll need to complicate the lives of others. It feels selfish and uncomfortable. I've gotten so good at minimizing my own needs to make everyone else's lives easier.

But I can't do that anymore, can I?

I can't keep putting myself last and pretending like my sacrifices are fulfilling enough for me.

Not if I ever want to have a chance at real happiness.

Taking a deep breath, I make up my mind.

"Okay. Let's do it."

Cleo smiles and pulls me into her arms. "It'll all work out. I promise."

I hope she's right. With Rafaele no longer a problem, all I have to worry about is Papà preventing me from going to Ras.

But can he? I'll beg Rafaele and Vince for help if I have to. I'll fight tooth and nail to get to wherever Ras is. I won't let my parents stop me, because for once, I know exactly what I want and need, and I'm not letting anyone stop me from getting it.

CHAPTER 35

GEMMA

WE HAVE a dinner planned with Rafaele's family the next day.

It's Vince, Cleo, Mamma, Papà, and I in the car, and I hold Cleo's hand the entire drive there.

Cleo and I spent hours this morning going over our plan, and now that we're about to go through with it, my mind is strangely empty.

I'm nervous, but beneath the nervousness is a breathless kind of hope. What if this works? I wrap my palm around the pendant hanging around my neck, the cool stone a visceral reminder of the man I love.

The dinner is on Rafaele's turf—an Italian restaurant he owns in Chelsea. We arrive around seven and get taken to the main dining area where a ten-person table has been set. We're the first ones here.

"Cute," Cleo comments, looking around the interior.

She's right. This place is cozy and intimate, with only about ten other smaller tables in the dining room. The décor is traditional Italian—checkered tablecloths, ornate mirrors on the walls, dark wood furniture.

Cleo walks over to study a picture frame hanging on the wall. From where I'm standing, it looks like a photo of Rafaele and his parents.

I can't help but wonder what's going through Cleo's head right about now. I've lost count of how many times I've asked her if she's sure about going through with this, and every time, she's reassured me that she is.

I know my sister well enough to know no one's going to change her mind once it's made up. Not even me.

Her sacrifice isn't something I'll ever forget.

Rafaele arrives with Nero by his side, both of them looking put together. Nero's grin is as fear inducing as always. Behind them are Rafaele's mother, his grandmother, and one of his uncles.

An anxious shiver runs down my spine as we all take our seats.

How will Rafaele react when I ask him to swap his bride a few days before the wedding? It should seem like a ridiculous proposition, if it weren't for the small things I've noticed about Rafaele over the last few weeks. I haven't said this to Cleo, because she'd tell me I'm imagining it, but there's something strange in how Rafaele behaves around my sister.

He looks at her the way he's never looked at me.

I first noticed it in Ibiza. When he dragged her out of his car, he couldn't stop glancing at her. The day of Vale's wedding, I'm convinced he chuckled at something she said. That's a big deal for a man who hardly cracks a smile.

There have been more things like that since we came back from Ibiza.

That dinner when Rafaele and Papà announced the succession plan, he was bothered that she was drinking so much. I think he was worried about her. And then the whole thing with Ludovico...

I don't know Rafaele very well, but I'm convinced of one thing. If he accepts my offer, he won't let Cleo come to any harm.

And maybe, just maybe, their match will fare better than mine and Rafaele's ever could.

The servers come out with jugs of house wine and water, and I decide there's no point in waiting to have the conversation.

I turn to Rafaele. "May I speak to you in private?"

Out of the corner of my eye, I notice Cleo stiffen. She's put on a brave face for my sake, but she must be as nervous as I am.

If Rafaele refuses our offer, I don't know what I'll do. My only hope of being set free is if Rafaele allows me to leave. Otherwise, I won't stand a chance against him and Papà. They will do whatever they want with me, and I might never see Ras again.

Rafaele glances at me and nods. "We can talk in the office."

I force myself not to spiral as I place my napkin back on the table.

Everyone looks up at us as Rafaele pulls out my chair and helps me up. Papà's eyes narrow, but I ignore it. It's incredible how little I care about what he thinks anymore.

I follow Rafaele out of the room, my palms sweaty and my pulse pounding against the side of my neck.

Be brave. You're doing the right thing.

But that doesn't mean Rafaele won't murder me on the spot for the grave insult I'm about to give him.

We walk into the wood-paneled office. It's littered with paperwork and random restaurant supplies. There's only one chair behind the desk, and I expect Rafaele to take it. Instead, he shuts the door, flicks on the overhead light, and stops a few feet away from me.

I guess we're having this conversation standing. He must think it won't take long.

"What is it?"

I have to tilt my head back to meet his eyes. They're as unreadable as ever.

"Rafael..." The light above us flickers.

Say it. You said you'd fight for Ras. For your baby. This is your chance.

I take it. "Rafaele, I can't marry you."

He doesn't react in any physical way besides sliding his palms into the pockets of his slacks. I wonder if he's doing that so he won't spontaneously break my neck.

"Why's that?" he asks.

"I'm in love with someone else."

"I don't see why that's a problem," he says coolly, like he's explaining something he assumed I knew by now. "This was never about love."

"I know. But there's something else." I bite down on the inside of my mouth. "I'm not a virgin. Actually, I'm pregnant."

The air in the room turns dense and heavy, pressing down on my lungs. Rafaele's stillness becomes absolute. Seconds tick by. It feels as if he's drilling into my brain matter with that penetrating gaze.

"Who's is it?"

There's no emotion in the question. He may as well be asking me for the time.

I shake my head.

We both know that it could only be one man. But I won't say Ras's name around him. I'm afraid of what will happen if I do.

"Look, I know this is not ideal," I say.

"Understatement of the century."

"Right. But I have a solution."

His brows furrow, and he waits to hear what I have to say.

"Cleo will marry you instead of me."

The mask he always wears falls away for one brief moment, and something vaguely hungry flashes inside his gaze.

I swallow. "She'll take my place...if you'll have her."

Rafaele drags his palm over his lips. "She offered to do this?"

"Yes."

A beat passes. "I see."

Slowly, he extracts his other hand out of his pocket. I flinch, expecting him to do something to me with that hand, but he simply holds it out like he wants me to give him something.

"The ring."

I blink. I'd thought I'd get more questions from him. What does this mean? Is this him saying he's fine with marrying Cleo?

I hesitate for a second and then slide the heavy emerald ring off my finger and place it in his palm. His fingers curl around it.

He's too calm about all of this.

Too calm about swapping his bride for a wedding that's supposed to happen in three days, one his entire family is supposed to attend.

"So does this mean you accept?" I ask carefully.

He slides the ring into his suit pocket and casts me an impartial glance. "I already fulfilled my end of the deal with your father. If this is the only way he can fulfill his, then so be it. Cleo will be my wife."

Relief fans through me. "Papà doesn't know about any of this. We'll have to tell him now."

"I gathered as much since your father didn't seem at all nervous when he arrived."

Adrenaline buzzes beneath my skin. "Once we tell everyone, I have to leave," I say. "I know you don't owe me anything, but I'm asking for a favor. If Papà tries to stop me, can you help? Just until I walk out the door."

"Where are you going to go?"

I swallow. "To him."

For a moment, Rafaele seems like he's about to say no. Why would he help me? I'm the woman who just made his life more complicated. His reputation has painted him as a ruthless monster, but I think there's far more to him than meets the eye.

Papà said he thought Rafaele had a strange moral compass. I'm not sure what that means, but while I wait for him to answer, I'm praying the arrow on that compass points in my direction.

Finally, he firms his jaw. "Fine. I'll make sure you're able to leave."

I exhale a pent-up breath.

He moves to exit the office, but there's one more thing.

"Wait!"

He pauses with his hand on the door handle. I feel like I'm tempting fate by asking so much of him, but I can't leave this last thing unsaid.

"Please take care of Cleo." My voice cracks. "I know she can be a pain in the ass sometimes, but she's clever, and funny, and insanely brave. Just look at what she's willing to do for the people she loves."

His fingers tighten on the handle. He throws me a look over his shoulder and makes the smallest of nods. "I fully intend to take care of my wife."

Before he turns away, I catch something darkly possessive swirling inside his gaze. Something that makes my breath catch.

There's no time to ruminate on that. Rafaele opens the door and motions for me to move. I brush past him, exhilaration, relief, and nerves all somehow churning in my stomach. When we reenter the private dining room, all eyes are on us.

I slide into my seat by Cleo's side. She immediately takes my hand and laces our fingers together. I squeeze twice. It's done.

Oh God. It worked. The weight on my chest slowly lifts, but a nagging thought at the back of my mind tells me that this isn't over.

Not by a long shot.

We still have to break the news to everyone. And then, I have to find Ras and convince him to take me back.

Rafaele stops by the head of the table but doesn't take his seat. "The engagement is off."

My eyes widen. Wow, he didn't waste a second.

There's a collective gasp, followed by a loud thud as my father slams his fist against the table.

I flinch before I remember to take in a deep breath. I won't let him scare me anymore.

The veins in Papà's neck pop out. "What?"

"Take a breath, Garzolo," Nero barks.

I turn my head and look at Cleo. She gives me a proud smile.

"You promised me a virgin bride," Rafaele states matter-of-factly. "And Gemma is not a virgin."

"Nonsense."

"Garzolo, she admitted to it herself," Rafaele says.

Papà's head swivels on his neck, and he pins me with his narrowed, angry eyes. "She's unwell. You know how she's been ever since she returned to us. She doesn't know what she's saying."

"I know exactly what I'm saying," I say firmly.

Nero clicks his tongue. "It seems to me like she's quite in control of her mental faculties, Garzolo."

Papà rises, his chair skidding behind him. "This is a misunderstanding. Let me talk to my daughter in private."

Does he really think I'll ever be alone in the same room as him again? That ship has sailed.

Vince and I stand up at the same time. My brother moves closer, as if to shield me if Papà tries to make a move.

"I'm done talking to you," I grind out. "It's already been decided. I won't be marrying Rafaele."

Papà tries to come closer, but Vince blocks his path. "Sit down," my brother tells him.

Papà snarls at him. "Get out of my way. Gemma, what the hell is this? How dare you—"

Enough. I don't want to hear his vitriol anymore. I'm so done with all of this. "How dare I? How dare you demand anything from me after what you've done? I spent my life trying to keep you happy, only to get beaten by you and emotionally abused by Mamma. You've never loved me. I don't think you've ever loved any of your kids. I'm through with you. My only regret is that it took me this long to get here. And by the way, I'm pregnant."

The room falls silent. Vince's eyes widen, and Mamma covers her mouth with her hands. Rafaele's family have the same pallor as a group of ghosts.

Papà looks at me with such hate that it takes everything in me not to glance away.

But I don't. I hold his gaze so that I'll never forget the kind of man he is.

He'll never touch my child. He'll never so much as lay eyes on my baby.

"Like I said, Gemma is no longer qualified to be my wife," Rafaele says, annoyance dancing at the edges of his tone. I get the sense he's eager to be done with all of this. "The stipulations in our contract were very clear. I've already delivered what I promised. I got you out of prison, and I got your charges dropped. This isn't how I do business, Garzolo."

"What do you want me to do?" Papà rasps, clearly panicking now. "I had no idea—"

"You owe me a wife." Rafaele's gaze coasts over to Cleo. "So I'm taking your other daughter."

Nero laughs, but he's the only one who seems to find the situation funny. There isn't another smile to be found in the room.

Rafaele's uncle sputters. "Everyone knows that girl is a slut."

Cleo flinches, and Rafaele sees it. His expression darkens. "I'm aware there are rumors floating around about my future wife. Good thing they're completely unfounded. From now on, anyone who speaks a word of them will lose their tongue. Have I made myself clear, Uncle?"

Cleo's eyes are wide. I don't think she expected Rafaele to stand up for her like that.

Rafaele's uncle pales. "I didn't know. I apologize."

Nero grins and claps his hands. "The matter is settled then."

I stand up, my thoughts already on how I'm going to find Ras.

"Go, Gemma," Cleo says to me, her hand still holding mine. "It's done."

She's right. We did it. I don't know how, but we did it. And now it's time for me to find the man I love.

I take a step toward the door. Then another.

"Where the fuck are you going?" Papà shouts. "Stop her!"

The driver who brought us here tries to block my path, but Rafaele's men immediately grab him and pull him out of the way.

I look back over my shoulder and meet Rafaele's gaze.

He nods, silently telling me I'm free to go.

It's an act of kindness from a supposedly unkind man.

Hope for Cleo flickers inside of me, a single match to repel the darkness.

She'll be okay with him. I know she will.

Papà starts shouting again, so I spin on my heel and flee.

I tumble out of the restaurant, my heart lodged in my throat.

I'm a tangled ball of fear, exhilaration, and anxiety. What if Papà calls his men to come after me? I have to put some distance between us. I have to disappear.

My feet move faster and faster until I'm sprinting down the sidewalk. I don't stop until I'm completely out of breath.

I pop into a corner shop, get some change, and dial Vale from a phone booth. Before we left the house, I got her number from a phonebook Mamma still keeps in the kitchen, and wrote it down on the inside of my arm.

Her phone rings and rings. Is she ignoring me because it's an unknown number?

My panic spikes. Calling her was just about the extent of my plan.

Please pick up.

Finally, there's a click on the other end of the line. "Hello?"

"Vale!"

"Gemma?" she sounds surprised. "What number are you calling me from?"

"A phone booth. Vale, I need your help."

"What happened?"

"I need to talk to Ras. Can you give me his number? I only had his US number, and actually, they took my cellphone away, so I don't have it anymore, and neither does Cleo. I don't know how to reach him. Something happened, Vale. Something I need to tell him about."

"Whoa, slow down. Where are you?"

"In Chelsea. Vale, please, I need to talk to him. Is he with Damiano? Is he—"

"Gem, Ras isn't here. Damiano hasn't heard from him since he told him to come back to Italy."

I frown. "Where is he then?"

"He's still in New York."

My stomach drops. "What?"

"Giorgio has been tracking him. He still has the same phone, and he's in New York. He came back the day after you."

My fingers squeeze the rubber cord. "He did?"

"Yes. I told Dem to get in touch with him, but he's being stubborn about their little tiff. Gem, what did you do?"

"I called off the engagement."

"You did?"

My throat tightens. "Yes. Vale, I'm in love with Ras." For a moment, I consider telling her I'm pregnant, but there's no time to explain everything, and I want Ras to know before anyone else hears, so I hold my tongue. "Look, I have to fix what happened between us. I have to see him."

There's a rustling sound. "Okay, hold on. Do you want me to give you his US number?"

"Please."

She takes a few seconds to find it, each one feeling like eternity, and I dig inside my pocket for a pen.

"Okay, here it is."

I write the damn thing on my arm right under Vale's number. "Thank you. I have to go."

"Wait, are you safe? Are you on your own?"

"I'll call you."

I hang up, my hands shaking as I dial the other number.

It rings and rings and rings.

I call ten times.

He doesn't pick up.

"Damn it!"

He's in New York. Where would he be? Who would know where he is?

My eyes widen.

Orrin.

CHAPTER 36

RAS

KNOCK, knock.

My head snaps up straight. I'm at the apartment, sitting on the ratty two-person couch, a basketball game playing on the TV.

It's late.

Orrin knows better than to show up unannounced, so it can't be him, and no one else is supposed to know I'm here. Have Garzolo's men found me?

Fuck.

Was that him calling me from an unknown number? I had a feeling it was someone trying to bait me so they could get a hit on my location, so I let the calls ring out.

I reach for my gun, check it's fully loaded, and move toward the door.

This might be my last stand.

Blood whooshes inside my ears as I turn the lock.

If I die here, at least I won't have any regrets. I did what I thought was right. I went after what I wanted.

It's too damn bad I still didn't manage to get it though.

I crack the door open.

What the... "Gemma?"

She's standing there bundled up in what looks like a man's jacket, her cheeks slightly pink from the cold, and her arms wrapped around her.

I lower the gun and frown. "What are you doing here?"

Why is she here? Something bad must have happened for her to seek me out like this.

She swallows. "Um... I... needed to talk to you."

My gaze drifts over her, hungrily committing every new detail to memory.

I've survived on a diet of short glimpses of her from a distance for over a week.

And now she's right here, right in front of me. So vivid and real.

But I don't like some of the things I see. Dark bags under her eyes. Pale skin. Has she lost some weight?

What the fuck have they been doing to her?

Tucking the gun into my waistband, I lean through the doorway and look down the hallway in both directions. "Where are your guards?"

"Not here."

Frustration spikes inside of me. She's here alone? Unprotected? "It's almost midnight. Did you lose them somewhere?"

She looks down at her hands. "I...I don't have guards anymore."

Now, I'm really fucking irritated. "What? Why would Rafaele let you wander around on your own?"

Her teeth dig into her bottom lip, and she slowly lifts her gaze to me.

It feels significant. Like whatever she's about to say might bring me to my knees.

"Because we're not engaged anymore."

I manage to keep myself standing, but the whooshing sound is back. I wrap my hand around the side of my neck, my pulse pounding against it like an off-beat drum. "Say that again. I think I heard you wrong."

"I called it off. He's... marrying Cleo instead."

I've always been quick on the uptake, but for the life of me, I can't make sense of the words coming out of her little pink mouth.

She sighs at my dumbfounded expression. "Can I come in? It's been a long night."

I step aside to let her pass.

Seeing her inside this crappy shoebox apartment only adds to my confusion. I never imagined her here.

She turns in a circle, taking it all in. "It's cozy."

I shut the door. Lock it. Take a step toward her.

That's all it takes for us to be just inches apart.

"How did you find me?"

"I went back to that coffee shop where we met Orrin. He was there." She glances down at herself. "He gave me this jacket and drove me here."

"You're telling me he brought you here but didn't think to accompany you up?" How could he have just let her go up her own?

"Ras, it's three flights of stairs," she says with a soft laugh.

"This place is dodgy," I growl.

"He tried to come, but I insisted on doing this on my own."

"Let me get this straight," I begin, sure I'm about to spew out nonsense. "You broke off the engagement."

"Yes."

"How?"

Her cheeks redden. Fuck, she's so beautiful. I'm still not convinced this isn't a mirage.

"I told Rafaele I'm not a virgin anymore."

Jesus Fucking Christ. This can't be real.

"I knew that it would disqualify me."

"And he believed you?"

She blushes again. "I think I was pretty convincing. In any case, the proof will be here in nine months."

Nine months? Suddenly, I can't breathe. "What?"

She looks at me from under her lashes. "I'm pregnant. I just found out yesterday."

My mind goes blank for a moment, trying to comprehend the news.

"The moment I found out, I knew I had to find you," she says calmly, like she has no idea the impact her words are having on me.

"Leaving you was a mistake. The worst mistake of my life. I couldn't stand the thought of you losing everything for me, but now I see that I should have trusted you to make that decision for yourself. I was scared, Ras. So scared that you'd wake up one day and realize I wasn't worth it. You told me I was enough, but I didn't believe you." She tucks a strand of espresso-colored hair behind her ear. "Cleo made me realize how my parents screwed me up. I have all of these beliefs about love and affection that are kind of messed up, and all these memories I'd forgotten and when they came back—oh I don't know what I'm saying." She drags her fingers through her hair and sighs, seemingly frustrated with herself.

I stare at her mutely.

She clenches her fists by her sides. "I'm sorry, Ras. I'm so sorry for what I said to you. For how I hurt you. I promise that if you take me back, I'll never hurt you like that again. I'll work on myself. I'm not going to let my past dictate my future." Her cheek turn pink. "I swear, I had a far better speech prepared, but I forgot it all as soon as I got here."

I put my hands on her forearms. There's something weird happening inside my chest.

"Did you say you're pregnant?"

The pink on her cheeks deepens. "Yes. I probably threw up the morning-after pill. I know this is totally unexpected. I don't expect you to be thrilled about it—"

I press my index finger against her lips. "I'm thrilled."

Her eyes soften with relief, and her lips turn up against my finger.

My heart is pounding against my ribs.

She broke off the engagement.

She's pregnant with our kid.

She must have jumped through so many hoops to come here.

And she did it anyway.

She chose me.

I engulf her in my arms. I press my nose into her hair. Her scent is the sweetest thing I've ever smelled, and now I'll have it around me forever. "*Cazzo*. I can't believe this. Do you know how badly I wished to have you back in my arms? Not an hour's gone by without me thinking about you. I feel like I'm dreaming."

"You're not mad at me?" she asks, her voice muffled against my chest.

I should be. There's a small part inside me that wants to punish her for walking out the way she did, but I push it away and focus on what's more important.

I'm going to be a father.

That's not a thought I'd expected to have today, but I am thrilled. I've always wanted to have kids, and to have them with Gemma is a gift. A privilege.

She's mine. All mine.

I press my lips to the crown of her head. "I forgive you."

Her body sags with relief.

My thoughts are still racing to make sense of everything and I pull back to look at her. "Those phone calls—"

She gives me a wry smile. "If you have just picked up, it would have made my evening a lot easier."

"Gemma." My voice cracks at the thought of her trying to reach me and not being able to.

She shakes her head. "No, not Gemma. Call me that other thing you always say to me."

I cup her cheek. "Peaches."

Her lips quirk up. There's a slight wobble in her chin. "Yeah, that. I love it when you call me that."

I slip my hands underneath her outrageous jacket, feeling the hollow of her waist and the flare of her hips. They fit perfectly beneath my palms. "You're mine now. I hope you know I'm never letting you go again."

She stands up on her toes and tips her head back, her eyes shining. "I know."

I lean down to kiss her, but she pulls back. "Wait. There's something else I need to say."

My hips press against hers. "Hurry."

"I love you," she says all in one breath.

Sparks travel across my skin. "Wait, slow down."

A wet kind of laughter bubbles up her throat. "God, you're so confusing. I. Loooooove. Yoooooou."

"Say it again."

"I lov—"

I lock my lips down on her open mouth. My tongue moves past her teeth, tasting, licking, owning every inch. She melts against me, returning the kiss with equal vigor.

A hint of cigarette smoke reaches my nostrils. That fucking jacket. I push it off her shoulders to the floor and kick it aside before burrowing my face in the crook of her neck.

There you are. Her sweet scent is strongest there.

"I still can't believe you're here," I mutter against her skin, my eyes shutting from the sheer pleasure of having her in my arms again. "I love you so fucking much."

"Why did you return to New York?" she asks, her voice coming out breathy.

"Why do you think?" I pull back to look her in the eyes. "I couldn't leave you. As soon as you got on that plane, I knew I needed to come back too. I didn't have a plan. I just had to be in the same city as you."

"If I'd known you were so close, maybe I'd have come earlier."

"You have no idea how close I got. I saw you going to Pilates. I tried to follow you whenever I could."

Her lips part in surprise. "Did you really?"

"I'm a masochist. It was torture to see you and not be able to touch you."

Unshed tears wet her eyes. "Ras..."

"I know. But that's done now. You're back where you belong —in my arms."

She stands on her toes and kisses me again, promising me everything.

～

We spend hours in bed tangled in each other until the bed frame decides to give us the middle finger and breaks beneath us with a sharp crack.

Gemma and I slide off the mattress, my cock still wet from being sheathed inside of her moments earlier. She laughs, her hair spilling over the hardwood floor. "Damn it, I was so close."

There's a wide grin on my face. It's fucking weird being this happy after being nothing but miserable for the past week. I pull her to me, throw her legs over my shoulders, and press my lips against her pussy. "I don't like leaving a job unfinished."

She moans as I lick and tease and suck on her clit until I make her break apart.

Her fingers tighten in my hair as she rides her release. "You're an animal," she says, panting from exertion. "I can't feel my legs."

I crawl up her body and give her a deep kiss. "I'm ravenous for you."

She laughs as I flip us and tuck her under my arm. "I can see that," she says, nuzzling against my chest. "I missed you too."

We lie like that for a while until Gemma insists she needs to use the bathroom. I help her up and glance down at the bed. It's a sad sight. I should at least attempt to fix it. First, I move the mattress off and then do what I can to adjust the frame. It just needs to last us the rest of the night. Tomorrow, we're getting out of this place. I'm not having the future mother of my child sleeping in this shithole.

But where do we go?

Something tells me Gemma won't be too attached to the idea of staying in New York. It's a place filled with bad memories.

I want to take her back home with me to Italy.

I want to marry her under the lemon tree in my parent's backyard at sunset and then take her to the house I bought in Casale when Dem became the don. It's an old building that needs to be restored, but we'd make it into a home. I'll build her that art studio.

I rake my fingers through my hair. Fuck, I'm getting ahead of myself.

When Gemma left me in Crete, I was so damn angry I couldn't even process her reasons for doing it. But the flight to New York gave me a lot of time to cool down and reflect on things.

She says she left because she didn't want me to sacrifice everything for her, but I wasn't the only one making sacrifices.

She loves her sisters. And what did I do? I asked her to abandon them for me. That's what spending years in hiding would have meant. I didn't even try to find a way to bring them back into her life. I was just so wrapped up in being with her in Crete.

I won't make that same mistake again.

Gemma deserves to have the people she loves in her life. And it's my job to make that happen.

I'll start with Vale. There's no reason why they should be apart, especially given how tense things are between Gemma and the rest of her family at the moment. Gemma needs Vale's support, especially now that she's pregnant.

And I... Well, I need Dem.

He's been by my side through a lot of difficult things, and he knows me better than anyone. The thought of becoming a father without him as my friend? It fucking hurts.

My emotions were running high when I told him I wasn't leaving Gemma, and while I know I did what I had to, I've made zero effort to reconcile since.

It's time I stop being a coward and have the conversation we need to have.

I release a breath and tip my head back, staring at the water-damaged ceiling.

I have to fix this.

I have to call my friend.

CHAPTER 37

RAS

"You sure you don't want me to wait downstairs while you talk to Damiano?" Gemma asks. The two of us are sitting on the broken bed. She's holding a cup of tea in her hands, still bundled up in my jacket from when we went outside. She woke up insisting she needed tea and reached for Orrin's coat, but I pulled it out of her grip and gave her my own. The only man's clothes she's wearing from now on are mine.

I liked the sight of her in them so much I barely even felt the cold when we stepped outside. Ever since she came to me last night, there's been a bonfire inside my chest keeping me warm.

I smile at her. "No, Peaches. I want you here."

She leans in and presses a kiss to my cheek. "It'll be okay. You'll see."

She's more optimistic than I am. Damiano's always been careful about who he lets into his circle, and he doesn't trust easily. It took us practically growing up together for him to trust me. He knows as well as I do that he saved my ass by bringing me onboard when he moved to Ibiza. He's given me a lot over the years.

Friendship. Respect. An opportunity to make more money than I'll ever need.

And after all of that, I refused a direct order.

In some ways, the Camorra is like the army. Disobeying your don's order is the end of your career. You're automatically discharged, and that's just the start of your problems.

In most cases, you end up dead.

But Dem hasn't tried to kill me. He hasn't even told anyone what I did, at least as far as Gemma and I can tell.

Maybe there is still hope. Can our long friendship matter more than the rules of the game we've been playing our entire lives?

I give Gemma a peck and pick up my phone.

There's no way to find out other than to face the situation head-on.

I pull up the number I've looked at a dozen times over the last few days, but this time, instead of just looking at it, I press call.

The phone rings.

Maybe I should have practiced what I'm about to say, but I don't want to sound rehearsed. Fuck, I can't remember if I've ever been so nervous to talk to Dem.

The stakes are high. I have to make him understand why I did what I did.

The line connects. "Ras."

I'm not sure if I'm reading too far into it, but I think there's a hint of relief in his voice.

"Yeah, it's me."

He clears his throat. "I presume Gemma is with you? She called Vale last night looking for you."

I glance in her direction. "She's here."

"Good. Vale will be relieved to hear it. I heard the engagement with Rafaele is off."

"It is. He's marrying Cleo instead of Gemma."

There's a wry laugh. "Fucking unbelievable."

I drag my hand over my lips and blow out a breath. "Look, we have a lot to talk about."

Gemma swipes a reassuring hand over my back.

"Yeah, you could say that." A coldness slips into Dem's tone. "I gave you a direct order, which you disobeyed, and then you disappeared off the face of the earth with my wife's sister. You're lucky I've had time to cool down. What the fuck were you thinking, Ras?"

"Dem, I did what I had to. If I'd left her here, I wouldn't have been able to live with myself. I..." I let out a long breath. "I love her. I want to be with her."

Silence.

"If it were Vale, and you were in love with her and she was engaged to another man, someone she didn't love, you'd do the same thing," I add. "You fucking know you would."

Dem huffs. "Do you remember how much shit you gave me when you thought my feelings for Vale were affecting my decisions? Now look at you."

"I know. I didn't get it then. I get it now."

"You're the only person I've ever trusted unconditionally," Dem says.

He's trying to mask it, but I hear the hurt in his tone. I look up at the ceiling. "I wish it hadn't come down to me going against your orders, but the situation was chaotic, and I had no time to think through the alternatives."

"Damn right you didn't think," he snaps. "You're so fucking stubborn. And you don't know how to ask for fucking help. That's always been your problem, even back when you were a kid. If you'd come to me and explained what the fuck was going on with you and Gemma, we could have come up with a plan in a day or two."

I shake my head. "You know that's bullshit. You were mad when you realized I'd gotten involved with her. You told me I should have known better."

There's a pause. "I may have been a bit frustrated with you."

"You kept insisting that I come back. I couldn't leave her when she was in the state she was in."

"All right, and after you left? Why didn't you call me?"

"Because I wasn't sure if you'd already sent someone for my head. I didn't want to make it easy for you to track me down and kill me."

"Seriously?" He sounds outraged. "Did you really think I'd do that to you? For fuck's sake. You're my closest friend, not to mention Vale would have had my head."

Relief fans through me. Thank fuck. We're getting somewhere. "I didn't know how you'd react to what I did. We've always been a team. Always working in sync. This was the first time we didn't. I crossed a line I've never crossed before, and I didn't know what would be on the other side of it."

There's a long pause. "*Cazzo*. All right, I'll admit I didn't leave a lot of room for discussion when you called. I didn't realize how far you'd fallen for Gemma. I thought you were just having fun with her, causing shit like always."

"I get it." That's what I'd always done before I met her.

"Every woman you've ever been with after Sara was nothing more than a fling."

"Gemma's not a fling."

"I gathered that much after you chose her over your don."

I rake my fingers through my hair. "It wasn't an easy choice. Since I left, I've had time to reflect and..." I try to put my thoughts into words that'll make sense. The reason why I never got seriously involved with anyone after Sara was because I stopped believing in love. I didn't think it was something meant for me. I couldn't put myself out there after having my heart ripped out. I couldn't be vulnerable again. But I couldn't resist it with Gemma. I knew all the possible consequences, but with her, I wanted to try anyway.

I sigh. "We've worked together for a decade, Dem. A long fucking time. And I did everything I could to help you get the things you wanted. Working for you, helping you build your empire and knocking down Sal gave me purpose. But the truth is, I never really considered what I wanted out of life. I was on autopilot. And when I met Gemma..." I look at her. She's hanging on my every word, her eyes wide. "Well, she's the first thing I've truly wanted in a long fucking time. And when I realized it, I knew I'd do anything to have her. Even if that meant failing you for the first time. I'm sorry, but I had to do it."

She wraps her arms around me and presses a kiss to my shoulder.

Damiano clears his throat. "Look, I never wanted it to be a choice between me or her. It doesn't have to be that way. I..." He blows out a breath. "Perhaps it wasn't fair of me to push you as hard as I did to come back here."

A knot inside my chest loosens.

I lean back against the broken headboard. "I should have called you earlier. I didn't know what to say until now, I guess. And when Gemma left me, I just wasn't thinking straight."

"You went back to New York to keep an eye on her?"

"Yeah. I'd never felt worse, but I think some part of me still hoped a miracle would happen."

"Sounds like it did. Vale's proud of Gemma for doing what was right for her."

"Me too. She's a warrior." I catch Gemma's eye, and she smiles at me. "There's something else you should know."

"What is it?" Dem asks.

I lie down, propping my head against Gemma's knee, and put the phone on speaker.

"Gemma's pregnant."

There's a prolonged pause. "Hold on." A beat passes, during which I'm certain he's turning on his own speaker. "Can you say that again?"

"Gemma's pregnant," I repeat.

There's a loud yelp on the other end of the line.

"Oh my God!" Now, it's Vale on the phone. "You're what?!"

Gemma and I grin at each other. "You heard it right," Gemma says. "I found out yesterday."

Vale starts yelping and offering her congratulations, and I just watch Gemma as she talks to her sister excitedly.

My chest swells. Seeing the happiness in her eyes is everything.

I let my arm fall off the bed and curl my palm around her delicate ankle. I wish I'd been there when she realized she's carrying our child. She must have been so scared during a moment that should have been filled with joy.

She'll never be in that position again.

And the next time she finds out she's pregnant—there's no way we're stopping at one—I'll be right by her side.

Dem's voice comes back on the line. "You can't stay in New York for long. We don't want to risk having Garzolo come after you. You should leave as soon as possible."

"What are you going to do about him and your deal?" I ask Dem.

"It's off. There's no fucking way we're working with him after what he did to Gemma. Vale said he's as good as dead to us."

Damn right he is. I'm still very much intent on putting him six feet under myself when things calm down here.

Dem keeps going, "But since Cleo is now marrying Rafaele, we want to maintain a relationship there. Maybe we renegotiate the deal directly with him and cut Garzolo out. If Rafaele guarantees Garzolo won't see a penny from it, there might be a path forward. It's going to be a mess to navigate." He lets out a heavy breath. "Too bad my underboss quit at the worst possible time."

My lips twitch. "What, you're saying you'd want that bastard back?"

"I had an open casting a few days ago for a replacement. No one showed up."

I snort. "An open casting... Just say you miss me, *stronzo*."

"You going to give me shit again?"

I sit up and prop my elbows on my knees. "I'll make it right, Dem. As long as you don't try to keep me away from my woman, I'll make all of this shit right."

"Your woman... Vale, he's calling Gemma's 'his woman'." There's a distant laugh on the other line, and Vale asks something I can't quite make out. "She's asking when's the wedding," Dem says.

Gemma turns bright red. I grin. It would be tomorrow if it were up to me, but something tells me Gemma might need a break from wedding talk for a little while.

Plus, I want her to have the best pregnancy possible, and I want time to show her just how fucking special she is. Her parents did a number on her. If I need to spend years showing her just how wrong they were to ever make her feel less than enough, I'll do it.

"Not sure, but you'll be the first to know," I tell Dem.

"I'll send a plane to get you out of there tomorrow."

"Sounds like a plan. Thanks, Dem."

"I'm happy for you."

A smile tugs at my lips. "I know."

I hang up.

Gemma arches a brow at me. "So, you got your job back?"

I grin at her. "Gainfully employed once again. Dem wants us back in Italy. How do you feel about that?"

She smiles back. "That's where you belong. And I belong wherever you are."

I cup her cheek. I love this woman so much. "Damn right, Peaches."

She leans into my touch and closes her eyes.

"You excited?" I whisper.

"More than words can describe."

That afternoon, we pack up our few belongings, hop into a car Orrin lets me borrow, and drive to a hotel. On our way over, Dem messages to confirm the plane is picking us up tomorrow morning.

Soon, we'll be heading to Italy, and I can't fucking wait.

"You know, I wouldn't have minded staying in the studio one more night," Gemma says, taking a sip of her tea. She seems to be on a tea kick. I wonder if it's the pregnancy hormones, and what else they'll make her crave. Hopefully, it's not some miserable American food, although if I have to, I'll send a damn plane here every week to get her whatever she needs.

"The place was awful, Peaches. And I spent some long, depressing days there. I'd much rather check you into the presidential suite and have you beneath me on one thousand thread count sheets." I want to spoil this girl in every fucking way. I don't think she realizes it yet. "Let's go somewhere nice for breakfast afterwards."

We end up making use of the presidential suite for about two hours before we remember the food, but Gemma doesn't seem to mind the delay after I make her come three times. Her cheeks are rosy, and her lips a bit swollen when we step back outside.

She gasps. "It's warm out!"

Warm is a bit of a stretch, but at least I'm not rushing to zip up my jacket as soon as the air hits my body. I look up. There aren't any clouds in the sky for what must be the first fucking time since I got here.

I lean down and press a kiss to her cheek. She looks so happy. I take out my phone and snap a photo of her.

She notices. "What's that for?"

"Need a new background picture for my phone."

Gemma grins. "God, you're such a sap. Who are you, and what happened to the mean Camorrista?"

"Mean?" I grumble. "I was never mean to you," I say as I give her ass a firm smack.

She yelps. "Forgetful too." She slides her hand into mine and squeezes.

I brush her hair out of her face, my chest swelling with a love so strong that I know I'll do anything for this woman. "Let's leave the past in the past," I tell her. "We've got a whole future to look forward to."

She smiles at me like she likes that idea as much as I do.

EPILOGUE

GEMMA

I CAN'T SLEEP.

The bed is so warm and cozy with Ras passed out right beside me, but I've been tossing and turning for the past hour, unable to get back to sleep.

Maybe it's time to accept it and embrace the new day.

I climb out from beneath the covers, careful not to make too much noise even though Ras is a deep sleeper. Sometimes, he'll pull me into his chest while he's dreaming, clutching me so tightly against his radiator chest that I start to overheat, and I have to tickle him to get him to wake up.

I glance at him, admiring his relaxed features, and the way his long hair spills over the sheets.

My lover is a beautiful man.

Yes, I've been calling him my lover in my head because boyfriend feels inadequate, and partner seems too vague. He's dropped many hints he'd like to be called "husband" sooner rather than later, and every time he does it a firework pops inside my chest.

I'd like that too. So much.

But I think we'd better wait until after we have our baby. Turns out planning for a kid is way more work than planning for a wedding.

I grab my silk robe off the hook, slip inside of it, and quietly shut the bedroom door behind me.

The nursery's a work in progress. I peek inside on my way to the kitchen. Last week, we had the wallpaper hung. Ras and I decided we wanted to keep the gender a surprise, so we went for a pattern with animals. In the corner, there's a box with the crib. Ras insisted he wanted to assemble it himself, even if the delivery included assembly. He seems to like getting hands on with things.

He's going to be a great dad.

I leave the nursery and move toward the living room.

"Good morning! Good morning!"

Churro's already wide awake in his cage in the corner of the room. I've spent some time teaching him a few new words, but it doesn't take him long to revert to old favorites. When I get closer, he squawks, *"Pretty girl! Pretty girl!"*

"Thanks, bud," I say to him as I head past him to the kitchen to make myself some tea.

While the kettle is boiling, I sit on one of the barstools by the island. My gaze catches on a big brown envelope addressed to me.

Huh. Must have arrived this morning.

Carefully, I pry it open, unsure of what's inside.

It's Cleo's wedding photos.

A weird feeling materializes inside my chest at seeing them.

Naturally, Ras and I weren't invited to attend. We were here when my sister walked down the aisle toward the man I was supposed to marry.

I thumb through the five or six pictures. Cleo looks beautiful, if not a little stiff. In most of the photos she keeps at least a few inches away from Rafaele, who's severe and handsome in his tux. They could be a royal couple given the amount of jewels Cleo is wearing. She must have been happy about that, at least.

The last photo is different. It's a candid shot, captured by the photographer while the couple is unaware, and you can practically feel the tension between these two. Cleo's got her nose upturned, looking down at Rafaele while he's sitting down at their sweetheart table, and he's looking up at her, his eyes hooded and his lips slightly quirked. He's grasping her hand in his, like he's trying to stop her from leaving.

A smile tugs at my lips. I should give Cleo a call and see how they're doing.

The kettle starts making a noise, so I leave the photos and go make myself a cup of tea.

Ras and I have settled into a routine here quicker than I expected. Since Casale di Principe is the base of the Casalesi, Ras is able to do most of his work without leaving on too many overnight trips. We've gone to Ibiza a few times to check up on things there but I always enjoy those trips, especially when Damiano and Vale join us.

Today, they're coming over for lunch.

As excited as Ras is about the baby, my sister might be the most excited of the bunch. Whatever rift I felt between us earlier has all but disappeared.

She's my confidant once again. I might be far away from the rest of the Garzolos, but between her and Ras I have plenty of support.

Ras and I have gone into Naples or Napoli as they say here on more than a few occasions. The city is full of sunshine and raw, unbridled energy. I had no idea the populace worships a soccer player as their god. Images of Diego "Dios" Maradona are graffitied on the walls, hung on banners between the narrow streets of the Spanish Quarter, and worn on T-shirts of seemingly every other Napolitani. I've even seen a few altars to his name.

And the food, oh God, *the food*. I thought I was spoiled growing up in New York, but the food in Naples has brought tears to my eyes on a few occasions. Perhaps it's the pregnancy hormones and the fact that I can eat what I want without anyone offering their criticism. My favorite is a sugar-powder covered pastry filled with ricotta cream called Fiocchi di Neve. I'm convinced it's impossible to eat just one.

My stomach growls at the memory. Maybe I'll have to get Ras to take me there again this week.

Familiar footsteps pad into the room. "Morning, Peaches," Ras says, his voice still raspy with sleep. He embraces me from behind and presses a kiss to the side of my neck, his beard scraping deliciously against my skin. "You're up early."

I lean into him. "Couldn't sleep."

His hand slides lower to my belly. "How are you feeling?"

Ras has been doting on me this entire time, checking in to make sure I'm okay at least a few times a day. I've had to tell him to chill on more than one occasion, but secretly, I love that he's so attentive.

It's so different from what I'm used to.

"Good," I tell him, sipping on my tea and turning to face him. "Do you remember Vale and Dem are coming in a few hours?"

He sighs. "Yes. Although, I'm tempted to cancel so that I can have you to myself for the entire Saturday."

"Don't you dare," I say with a smile on my lips.

He takes my mug out of my hands, places it on the counter behind me, and tugs me into a deep kiss.

I moan into his mouth. It never gets old, being kissed by him like I'm everything he could possibly ever need.

When he pulls away, his eyes are dark with lust. He pushes his fingers into my hair and presses the length of his body against mine. "They're not coming over that soon, are they?"

I roll my hips, heat spreading beneath my skin. "Not that soon."

A lazy grin unfurls on his face. "Come back to bed, then."

I do.

Vale and Damiano arrive just past noon. Vale hands me a light-blue box that smells like yeast and sugar and when I open it, I gasp. Twelve Fiocchi di Neve lined up in three neat rows.

"I was just thinking how badly I wanted these things. How did you know?"

She wraps one arm around my shoulders and presses her lips to my hair. "Sister intuition."

Damiano appears behind her. He greets me with a kiss on the cheek, and then turns to Ras and claps him on the back. "I visited the new factory this morning. It's really coming along."

"We're a few weeks away from getting the workers started," Ras says. "You might want to call Messero next week to let him know. "

Ras and Damiano cut my father out of their counterfeits deal and are now working directly with Rafaele. Ras doesn't like to talk to my ex-fiancé, so Damiano handles most of their communication.

I haven't talked to Mamma or Papà since I left, and I'm not sure when or if I ever will. Right now, I have no desire to invite them back into my life. Not after I've realized how little they truly ever cared about me.

With Vince, I've opened a line of communication. He seems genuinely remorseful about everything. He texts me every week, and from time to time we'll do a video call. We don't talk about Papà or what happened in New York, but he asks me lots of questions about my new life in Italy. He's excited about becoming an uncle, and I think he's waiting for me to invite him to visit us. I've been toying with the idea.

"No work talk," Vale chastises Damiano. "I had to stop him from calling Giorgio this morning," she says to me, giving her husband the side eye. "Him and Mari are in Venice on vacation."

"Venice? I'd love to go one day," I say.

Ras overhears and wraps his arms around my waist. "I'll take you, Peaches."

We settle around the table on the back patio and the cook brings out plates of antipasti, bruschetta, pasta with fragrant garlic sauce, and grilled fish.

The conversation flows easily. It didn't take long for Ras and Damiano to reconcile and now it's like their rift never happened. They scoot their chairs closer to each other and start discussing something in rapid-fire Italian.

Vale looks at them and sighs. "There he goes again." She shakes her head with a knowing smile. "Dem's probably telling Ras about his new obsession—a massive mozzarella factory he wants to open around here. I swear, he's always juggling at least five new business ideas in his head."

"You thinking about helping him with one of those?" I ask. Vale's mentioned she's been looking for something to do with her time. My sister's got a lot of energy, and I know she's not going to be happy with sitting around in their palatial home while Dem's busy running the clan.

"Actually, there was something I wanted to talk to you about." She puts down her glass of wine and pulls out her phone. "Take a look."

On the screen there are photos of... an empty space?

My brows pinch in confusion. "What am I looking at? A bunch of white walls?"

Vale laughs. "Okay, it's a lot more impressive in person, but it's a location in the Chiaia neighborhood in Naples that would be perfect for an art gallery." She shoots a pointed look at one of my recent paintings on the wall. "What do you think?"

My nape tingles as I try to make sense of what she's saying. "Hold on, Vale," I laugh nervously. "I just started painting. My stuff is hardly art gallery worthy."

Less than a week after we got to Casale di Principe, Ras drove me to an art supplies store and bought me half of their stock. Or at least that's what it seemed like to me. When we got back to the house, he insisted on making one of the rooms into a studio for me. I told him he was being crazy, but in truth, I've been in there nearly every day since. Painting has been therapeutic for me.

I study the watercolor on the wall. I'm proud of it, but I'm still a beginner.

Vale shrugs. "It's up to you if you want to display your work or not, but what do you think about using the space to promote local up and coming artists? We could work on it together—scout for talent, set up exhibitions, host events..."

She drifts off, watching for my reaction.

A spark of excitement appears inside my chest. I've been so busy setting up a new life here and preparing for the baby that I haven't had much time to think about what I'd do after.

But the idea of working with Vale to create an art gallery, to give a platform to artists who might not have one...

Can I do it? I'd have to learn everything from scratch about running that kind of a business. I'd probably make a bunch of mistakes at first.

I glance at Ras who's absorbed in his conversation with Damiano.

He'd tell me to do it. He'd tell me it's okay to not be perfect.

It's a lesson I'm still learning, but every day, it seeps deeper and deeper inside of me.

I give Vale a smile. "You know, I think I like that idea."

Vale whoops and hugs me, drawing the men's attention to us. "Gemma's in on the art gallery idea!" she announces.

Damiano's gaze flashes with approval. "That's great."

I'm about to explain the whole thing to Ras, but there's no surprise in his expression.

"You knew about this?" I ask.

He grins. "I was the one who first noticed the location. I asked Vale to go take a look."

Warmth unfurls inside my chest. There are times like this when he's being so damn perfect, I have to pinch myself to believe this is real.

Ras tips his head in Damiano's direction. "By the way, you've got your first customer right here. He's got lots of empty walls."

I snort a laugh. *Of course.* Art sales must be a great way to clean a portion of the Casalesi proceeds.

Vale squeezes my hand. "What do you think, Gem? You want to go into business with these two?"

I lace my fingers with hers. "Too late to be asking that question, don't you think?"

A few hours later, Vale and Damiano leave, and Ras and I lie down in the hammock he's strung up between two old oak trees on our property. The warm weather and the slow swaying of the hammock lulls me into a peaceful state. I rest my head on Ras's chest and listen to the steady beat of his heart beneath my ear.

Ras places a protective hand over my belly. I'm barely showing in my fourth month but Ras has been curiously examining my growing bump with me in the mirror nearly every morning.

The truth is, I'm nervous. I've spent very little time thinking about what it would actually be like to have a child before I got pregnant, and some small part of me is scared. I may have left New York, but like Vale, I ended up in the same dangerous world.

"What are you thinking about?" Ras asks.

I search for the right words. Unlike Cleo, I've never had the urge to run away from this life. I've always accepted it as part of me.

But now I'm bringing a baby into it as well. An innocent being who doesn't get a say.

I place my hand on top of Ras's. "He or she will be born into all of *this*."

He's silent for a long moment, and I know he understands what I mean. "We'll always keep our children safe," he says.

Children. Ras likes to speak in plural as far as our future offspring are concerned, so damn sure that we'll have more than one.

"And when they grow up?"

"We won't force them into anything," he says, smoothing his hand over my hair. "They'll make their own choices. But you have to be ready for the possibility that they choose all *this* of their own free will."

His words settle over my skin. He's right, the possibility is there. We can't control everything but we can control how we'll raise our child. We'll offer them a life filled with love, warmth, and acceptance. A life where they'll always have a family to come back to no matter what path they choose.

This world can be seductive. Its darkness has a unique allure that pulls people in.

But, even in that darkness, there's light.

Bright, and warm, and beautiful.

I snuggle up to Ras.

For me, that light is him.

THE END

BONUS SCENE

Curious about those dreams that made Gemma all hot and bothered? Read the bonus scene!

Sign up here to receive the bonus scene by email:
www.gabriellesands.com/gemmasdream

JOIN THE READER GROUP

JOIN GABRIELLE'S GALS

Talk about When She Falls with other readers and get access to exclusive content in Gabrielle's reader group!

ACKNOWLEDGMENTS

Writing this book was such a rollercoaster of emotions! I really wanted to do justice to Ras and Gemma's story which meant pushing my own emotional boundaries further than I ever have before. It was only after the final edit that I read the manuscript and finally felt like I told the story I set out to tell. I hope you, my beautiful reader, love this couple as much as I do.

My team continues to be the best team around. Huge thanks to Heidi, Maria, Lorna, Becca, and Skyler. You all contributed to this project in so many ways, supported me when I needed it, and really helped make this book the best it can be.

Thank you to my family, and in particular my incredible hubby who took such good care of me while I was hard at work on this book, making sure I was fed while I was working late nights, and being a sounding board whenever I needed it. I love you.

Finally, thank YOU, my dear reader. For picking up this book, reading my work, and hopefully, getting lost in Ras and Gemma's story. Your support truly means everything to me!

Love,

Gabrielle

Made in United States
Orlando, FL
09 November 2024

53652048R00296